SWEET EVIL

SWEET EVIL

WENDY HIGGINS

An Imprint of HarperCollinsPublishers

HarperTeen is an imprint of HarperCollins Publishers.

Library of Congress Cataloging-in-Publication Data
Higgins, Wendy.
    Sweet evil / by Wendy Higgins. — 1st ed.
        p.   cm.
    Summary: "Sweet southern girl Anna discovers at age sixteen that she is the
daughter of a guardian angel and a demon, the only one of her kind. As Anna strug-
gles to fight the dark legacy of her father, she falls for the mysterious Kaidan Rowe,
the ultimate bad boy. Forced to face her destiny, she must decide whether to embrace
her halo or her horns"— Provided by publisher.
    ISBN 978-0-06-208561-0
    [1. Angels—Fiction.   2. Demonology—Fiction.   3. Good and evil—Fiction.
4. Aura—Fiction.   5. Extrasensory perception—Fiction.   6. Love—Fiction.
7. Adoption—Fiction.]   I. Title.
PZ7.H534966Swe 2012   2011044632
[Fic]—dc23   CIP
                                                                              AC

Typography by Michelle Gengaro-Kokmen
14 15 16 CG/RRDC 10 9 8 7 6
❖
First Edition

To my mom, Nancy Parry, who always told me
I'd be a writer someday

CONTENTS

PROLOGUE *Convent of Our Mother Mary, Los Angeles*   1

CHAPTER ONE *Lies and Lust*   7

CHAPTER TWO *Good-girl Syndrome*   29

CHAPTER THREE *Sweet-sixteen Surprise*   39

CHAPTER FOUR *Lake Party*   47

CHAPTER FIVE *Likewise*   64

CHAPTER SIX *Out of the Dark Days*   74

CHAPTER SEVEN *Identity*   79

CHAPTER EIGHT *Consequences*   89

CHAPTER NINE *To Go or Not to Go*   109

CHAPTER TEN *Sense of Touch*   122

CHAPTER ELEVEN *A Healthy Fear*   142

CHAPTER TWELVE *Kaidan's Cologne*   159

CHAPTER THIRTEEN *Hiding Emotions*   171

CHAPTER FOURTEEN *Laughter*   185

CHAPTER FIFTEEN *The Great Purge*   197

CHAPTER SIXTEEN   *Mourning Heaven*   209

CHAPTER SEVENTEEN   *First Sacrifice*   232

CHAPTER EIGHTEEN   *Getting Zapped*   242

CHAPTER NINETEEN   *Unaccompanied Minor*   248

CHAPTER TWENTY   *Elephant in the Room*   257

CHAPTER TWENTY-ONE   *Tea for Twins*   267

CHAPTER TWENTY-TWO   *Envy*   284

CHAPTER TWENTY-THREE   *Seeing Demons*   305

CHAPTER TWENTY-FOUR   *Give a Little Whistle*   318

CHAPTER TWENTY-FIVE   *Back to School*   328

CHAPTER TWENTY-SIX   *Halloween*   341

CHAPTER TWENTY-SEVEN   *Holiday Cheerlessness*   349

CHAPTER TWENTY-EIGHT   *Goody Bags*   364

CHAPTER TWENTY-NINE   *New Year's*   377

CHAPTER THIRTY   *Some by Virtue Fall*   411

CHAPTER THIRTY-ONE   *Underneath*   443

Duke Names and Job Description Index   449

Acknowledgments   452

SWEET EVIL

CONVENT OF OUR MOTHER MARY, LOS ANGELES

Nearly sixteen years ago . . .

The newborn wailed as the midwife wrapped her in a receiving blanket and quickly handed her to Sister Ruth. Even stooped with age, the oldest nun at the convent exuded a regal air as she shushed the tiny bundle, attempting to shield her from the sight of her mother's last breaths.

In the corner of the sterile room a large man with a smooth, shaved head and goatee stood watching. Darkness fell over his face as the young midwife tried to resuscitate the woman on the bed.

Sweat ran down the midwife's temples as she continued chest compressions. She shook her head and spoke in a panicked murmur. "Where's the doctor? He should be here by now!"

The midwife didn't see the soft shimmer of mist rise from the patient's chest, then linger in the air above her body, but the man in the corner did.

His eyes widened as another vapor, even stronger than the first, arose from the woman's lifeless form. It took shape: a winged being of blinding purity. Sister Ruth gasped in wonder, then shifted the baby from her shoulder and cradled her upward to let her face show.

The larger spirit swooped down and covered the infant girl in a kiss as soft as a breeze. It moved next to the man in the corner, who choked out a single sob, reaching for her. A tear escaped before he reined in his emotion.

The spirit remained in front of him for one moment longer before gathering the weaker spirit into her arms and floating away as if on a wisp of wind.

"I'm sorry. I—I don't know what happened." The midwife's voice and hands shook as she pulled the sheet up over the woman's small body. She crossed herself and closed her eyes.

"You did all you could," Sister Ruth said with gentleness. "It was her time."

The silent, fearsome man looked away from the bed and fixed his hard eyes on the baby.

Sister Ruth hesitated before angling the child outward for him to see. The newborn let out a whimper and her dark eyes opened wide. For the briefest moment his features softened.

Their shared gaze was severed as the door banged open and the midwife screamed. Police rushed in, filling the small space. Sister Ruth backed against the wall and held the baby close.

"Dear God above," she whispered.

The man in the corner appeared unfazed as cops surrounded him.

"Jonathan LaGray?" asked the officer in front. "Also known as John Gray?"

"That's me," he responded in a raspy, gruff voice, lifting his frown-lined face into a wicked smile of defiance and danger.

He did not fight when they surged forward with handcuffs, reading him his rights.

"You're under arrest for trafficking illegal drugs across state and international borders. . . ."

As they pulled Jonathan LaGray from the room, citing a list of crimes, he turned again to look at the baby girl, giving her a tight, ironic grin.

"Just say no to drugs, will ya, kid?"

With that, he was yanked from sight, and the baby's wail rose again.

"Pleasure is the bait of sin."
—*Plato*

CHAPTER ONE

LIES AND LUST

I tugged the jean skirt down and tried not to fidget with the straps of the tank top as we stood in line for the show. My shoulders and arms felt naked. The outfit had been picked out for me by Jay's older sister as an early sixteenth-birthday present. And Jay got us tickets to see a few local bands play, including his latest band infatuation, Lascivious. Their name alone was a strike against them, but I wore a smile on my face for Jay's sake.

He was my best friend, after all. My only friend.

People at school assumed something was going on with Jay and me, but they were wrong. I didn't like him like that, and there was no question he didn't like me in that way either. I knew his feelings.

I could literally *see* them. And feel them if I allowed myself.

Jay was in his element now, tapping his fingers against his hips. He radiated excitement that I could see around his body as a blinding yellow-orange hue. I let myself soak in his good mood. He ran a hand over his thick, short-cropped blond hair, then pinched the square tuft of hair under his bottom lip. He was stout and short for a guy, but still a good bit taller than me.

A loud song with a thumping beat rang from Jay's pocket. He gave me a goofy grin and began to bop his head back and forth to the rhythm. Oh, no—not the crazy booty dance.

"Please don't," I begged.

Jay broke into his funky ringtone dance, shoulders bouncing and hips moving from side to side. People around us stepped away, surprised, then began to laugh and cheer him on. I pressed my fingers against my lips to hide an embarrassed smile. Just as the ringtone was about to end, he gave a little bow, straightened up, and answered the call.

"'Sup?" he said. "Dude, we're still in line; where you at?" Ah, it must have been Gregory. "Did you bring our CDs? . . . All right. Sweet. See you in there."

He shoved the phone into his pocket.

I rubbed my bare arms. It had been a gorgeous spring day in Atlanta, but the air temperature dropped when the sun disappeared behind the tall buildings. We lived an hour north in the small town of Cartersville. It was strange to be in the city, especially at night. Streetlights came to life above us, and the crowd grew louder with the arrival of dusk.

"Don't look now," Jay leaned over to whisper, "but the dude at three o'clock is checking you out."

I immediately looked and Jay grunted. How funny—the guy really was looking at me. Albeit with bloodshot eyes. He gave me a nod and I had to suppress a ridiculously girly giggle as I turned back around. I busied myself playing with a strand of my dirty-blond hair.

"You should talk to him," Jay said.

"No way."

"Why not?"

"He's . . . high," I whispered.

"You don't know that."

But I did. The colors of someone's emotions blurred when their bodies were under the influence. That guy's were fuzzy at best.

Seeing emotions as colors was an extension of my ability to sense others' feelings, their auras. I'd had the gift since infancy. The color spectrum was complicated, as were emotions, with shades of a color meaning different things. To simplify, positive feelings were always colors, ranging from bright to pastel. Negative feelings were shades of black, with a few exceptions. Envy was green. Pride was purple. And lust was red. That was a popular one.

The colors mesmerized me, the way they shifted and changed, sometimes slow, and sometimes in rapid succession. I tried not to read people constantly or to stare; it seemed like an invasion of privacy. Nobody knew what I could do, not even Jay or my adoptive mother, Patti.

The line for the club moved slowly. I adjusted my skirt again and looked down to evaluate the decency of its length. *It's fine, Anna.* At least my legs had a little muscle these days, instead of looking like a pair of toothpicks. Although I'd been pegged with nicknames like "Twiggy" and "Sticks" growing up, I didn't obsess about my figure, or lack of one. Padded bras were a helpful invention, and I was satisfied with the two small indentations in my sides that passed for a waist. Running had become my new pastime five weeks ago, after I'd read how my body is the "temple of my soul."

Healthy temple: check.

As we moved up a few more steps, Jay rubbed his palms together.

"You know," he said, "I could probably get us drinks when we get inside."

"No drinks," I immediately answered, my heart quickening its pace.

"Fine, I know. 'No drinks, no drugs.' No nothin'." He imitated me, fluttering his eyes, then nudged me with his elbow to show he was only kidding, as if he could be mean anyway. But he knew I had an abnormal aversion to substances. Even now, his comment about drugs and alcohol caused an uncomfortable, almost *physical* reaction within me; it felt like an urgent, greedy pushing and pulling. I took a deep breath to calm down.

We finally made our way to the front of the line, where a young bouncer snapped an underage wristband on me and gave me an appraising look, eyes scanning my waist-length hair before raising the velvet rope. I rushed under it with Jay on my heels.

"For real, Anna, don't let me stand in the way of all these dudes tonight." Jay laughed behind me, raising his voice as we entered the already packed room, music thumping. I knew I should have put my hair up before we came, but Jay's sister, Jana, had insisted on my keeping it down. I pulled my hair over my shoulder and wound it into a rope with my finger, looking around at the tightly packed crowd and wincing slightly at the noise and blasts of emotion.

"They only think they like me because they don't know me," I said.

Jay shook his head. "I hate when you say things like that."

"Like what? That I'm *especially special*?"

I was trying to make a joke, using the term us Southerners fondly called people who "weren't right," but anger burst gray from Jay's chest, surprising me, then fizzled away.

"Don't talk about yourself that way. You're just . . . shy."

I was weird and we both knew it. But I didn't like to upset him, and it felt ridiculous having a serious conversation at the top of our lungs.

Jay pulled his phone from his pocket and looked at the screen as it vibrated in his hand. He grinned and handed it to me. Patti.

"Hello?" I stuck a finger in my other ear so I could hear.

"I'm just checking to see if you made it safely, honey. Wow, it's really loud there!"

"Yeah, it is!" I had to shout. "Everything is fine. I'll be home by eleven."

It was my first time going to something like this. Ever. Jay had begged Patti for permission himself, and by some miracle got her to agree. But she was not happy about it. All day she'd been as nervous as a cat at the vet.

"You stay right next to Jay, and if any strangers try to talk to you—"

"I know, Patti. Don't worry, okay? Nobody's trying to talk to me." It was hard to reassure her while I was shouting and being jostled.

The deejay was announcing that Lascivious would hit the stage in five.

"I gotta go," I told her. "The band's about to come on. I'll be safe. I promise!"

"All right, honey. Maybe you can call me on your way home?" It was not a suggestion.

"Okay. Love you, bye!" I hung up before she started talking about self-defense moves or some other crazy thing. I'd barely made it out of our apartment earlier that night because of her list of warnings. Part of me thought she might be paranoid enough to follow us to the club.

"Come on." I grabbed Jay's hand and pulled him into the crowd. It was an eclectic mix—everything from punks to goths to preps. I worked us all the way to the front corner of the stage, annoying a few people with my slight pushiness, but I was careful to apologize. I figured I owed Jay a front-row seat after upsetting him.

The wooden stage was battered, like every other surface in the building. The club was small and boxy, but the ceilings were high. Cramming people inside and breaking every fire code in Georgia added to the atmosphere.

We squeezed in just as the deejay told everyone to "give it up" for Lascivious. The band was greeted by a roar of cheers, and I recognized the first song as one Jay played for us on our way to school sometimes. Despite my usual tendency to be ultrareserved, I found myself caught up in the music, jumping up and down and singing along at the top of my lungs. Jay was right there with me, doing the same. I couldn't believe it. This was *fun*. I bounced with the crowd, allowing myself to be caught up in the surrounding exhilaration.

"Dude," Jay shouted in my direction as the first song ended. "They. Are. Awesome!"

The second song started, and it was slower. I calmed down a little and looked at the band. The lead singer oozed with pride. His dark purple aura all but drowned out his tight shirt and snug jeans. His spiked hair was styled in a stiff lean to one side. He held the microphone like a lover. The tempo sped up into a frenzy of drumbeats as they hit the chorus, bringing my eyes to the drums as the wild crowd began jumping again.

I noticed several things about the drummer all at once. He was focused on the task at hand, keeping perfect rhythm. Instead of a swirl of transparent colors around his torso, there was a small, concentrated starburst of bright red at his sternum. But otherwise his aura was blank. *Huh.* That was strange. But before I could contemplate it too much, my eyes landed on his face.

Wowza.

He was smokin' hot. As in H-O-T-T *hott*. I'd never understood until that moment why girls insisted on adding an extra T. This guy was extra-T worthy.

I examined the drummer, determined to find a flaw.

Brown hair. An interesting haircut: short around the sides and back, but longer on top, hanging loose and angling across his forehead. His eyes were narrow and his eyebrows were a bit thick and . . . Oh, who was I kidding? I could pick him apart, but even the shifty slant of his eyes made him more alluring to me.

There was an intensity in the way he played, like he was unleashing his passion into the music and nothing else mattered. He was feeling it, lost in it, and he was *good*. A light sheen of sweat shone on his arms and face, dampening and darkening the hair at his temples.

Never before had I felt such instant physical attraction. The power of it was jarring. I'd noticed when guys had nice features, sure, but I was usually distracted by their emotions.

Now, with the drummer's absence of an aura, I was able to watch the muscles in his biceps and forearms flex as he slammed the drumsticks down in a whirlwind of precise movement. The beat was intoxicating, bumping each nerve ending inside of me. His whole body moved fluidly, jumping with the force of the beat, his face focused and sure.

I looked again at the red starburst on his chest. It was unlike anything I'd ever seen. I doubted he felt lustful at that moment, with his utter concentration on the music. It was weird. The song came to an end with one last crash of the cymbals; then he twirled the drumsticks in his fingers before tucking them under his arm. Jay was cheering, along with the rest of the crowd. I stood there in absolute awe.

"Are you having fun?" Jay asked.

"Yeah, definitely," I said, still watching the drummer as he swiped the straight brown locks from his eyes and looked down at two girls screaming out to him from the other end of the stage. He gave them the cutest, nonchalant half smile I'd ever seen. My heart sputtered. The girls screamed and jumped up and down, megacleavage threatening to bounce right out of their low-cut shirts. The drummer's red starburst widened a notch, and I felt an unpleasant snarling, ripping feeling in my gut—another new sensation. I wanted him to look away from them.

Jealousy? Good grief!

"It's not right, man," Jay said, following my stare. "Some guys have all the luck."

"What?" I finally broke my trance to look at Jay.

"That guy, the drummer? Get this. He's a killer musician, he gets tons of chicks, his dad's loaded, and as if that wasn't enough, he's got a friggin' English accent!"

I had to smile at Jay's mix of envy and admiration.

"What's his name?" I hollered as the third song started.

"Kaidan Rowe. Oh, and that's another thing. A cool name! Bastard."

"How do you spell it?" I asked. It sounded like *Ky-den*.

Jay spelled it for me. "It's A-I, like Thai food," he explained.

Kai, like Thai, only yummier. Gah! Who was this girl invading my brain?

The name Kaidan Rowe sounded familiar. I'd never seen him before, but I'd heard of him.

"How old are they?" I asked, nodding toward the band.

"Juniors," Jay shouted close to my ear. Okay, I was impressed. They were only a year older than us, and they had major talent. According to Jay, these guys were the next big thing. They'd recorded a small-time record that was being shopped to labels in L.A., and they'd be touring regionally this summer. Jay was such a fanboy.

An aggravated scuffle broke out behind us. I turned and saw Gregory's round face and mop of curly brown hair above a too-large Hawaiian shirt shoving through the crowd. He was Jay's musical partner in crime. They had written a few songs together, and were pretty much addicted to music. The problem was that neither of them could sing. At all.

"'Bout time, G!" Jay and Gregory did that male grab-hands-and-bang-chests-together thing in the cramped space, then Gregory and I nodded at each other. I was surprised and a little grossed out to see a flutter of red across his aura as he looked down at my legs, but it passed quickly as he turned his attention back to Jay.

"Dude, you ain't gonna believe this," Gregory said in his thick Georgian drawl. "I was just talkin' to Doug—you know, one of the bouncers—and he can get us backstage!"

My heart danced an involuntary jig all over my insides.

"No freakin' way!" said Jay. "Where're the CDs?"

Gregory held up two CDs of their compositions and lyrics. They were good songs, but I cringed at the thought of their being given to Lascivious. The band probably got that kind of thing from fans all the time. I didn't like to think of Jay and Gregory's hard work tossed aside as if they were some desperate posers. But the two of them were shrouded in such happy yellow auras that I could do nothing except be supportive.

As the current song ended, I watched Kaidan shush the cymbals with his fingers, then tuck the drumsticks under his arm and swish his damp hair from his eyes again. When he leaned down to pick up a water bottle, our eyes met. My breath stuck right where it was in my lungs, and the loud voices around me turned to static white noise. The drummer's lustful starburst throbbed for one gorgeous moment, and then his forehead creased and his gaze tightened. His eyes searched all around me before coming back to my face. He broke eye contact and took a swig of his water, tossing it back to the floor in time for the next song.

The brief encounter left me unnerved.

"I'm going to the bathroom," I told Jay, turning to go without waiting for a response. I noticed that the crowd moved much easier when one was moving away from the stage.

The air in the girls' bathroom was stagnant with smells of urine and vomit. Only one of the three stalls was unclogged, but that didn't seem to stop girls from using them anyway. I decided I could hold it. I reapplied my lip gloss at the mirror and was about to leave when I overheard two girls who had crammed themselves into one of the tiny stalls.

"I *want* Kaidan Rowe."

"I know, right? You should throw him your number. I want Michael, though. He can do to me what he does to that microphone." They squeezed out of the stall, giggling, and I recognized their voluptuous chests as the ones that had been in front of the stage. Both of their auras were faded.

I adjusted my hair clips. Jay's sister, Jana, had wrangled my mass of thin strands into well-organized disarray, which I was successfully ruining. I had let her dab a little makeup on my face, but she'd freaked out when I asked her to cover up the pesky freckle at the end of my upper lip. *Are you crazy? Don't ever cover your beauty mark!* Why did people call it that? A freckle was not beautiful. It was a small, dark attention grabber. I hated the way everyone's eyes went to it when they talked to me.

I snapped the last clip in place and scooted over so the girls could wash their hands. They shared the faucet and complained about no soap, then moved on to primping. I looked at them, so comfortable together, and wondered what it would be like to have a female friend. I was about to leave when something in their conversation stopped me.

"The bartender said Kaidan's dad is one of the head honchos at PP in New York City." My stomach lurched. PP stood for Pristine Publications: a popular, worldwide corporation that included pornographic magazines, videos, and I could only imagine what else.

"No way," her friend said.

"Yes way. Hey, we should try to get backstage!" She got excited and somehow lost her balance, stepping on my foot and grasping my shoulder. I reached out to steady her.

"Oh, sorry," she said, leaning against me.

When she seemed to have her balance, I let go of her.

Out of nowhere there was a murky tugging within me, an urge to open my mouth and say something that I knew was neither true nor nice.

"I heard that guy Kaidan has gonorrhea."

And there it was, out of my mouth. My heart pounded. I knew most people lied on some level, sometimes on a daily basis. But for whatever reason, I'd never even been prone to tiny fibs. I didn't tell people I was "fine" if I wasn't. Nobody had ever asked me whether something made their butt look big, so I suppose I'd never been truly tested. All I knew was, until that moment, I had never purposely deceived anyone. The look of shock on their faces mirrored the shock I felt at myself.

"Ew. Are you serious?" asked the girl who had called dibs on him. I couldn't respond.

"Okay, that's nasty," said the other girl.

There was an awkward pause. I didn't really know what gonorrhea was, except that it was an STD. What in the world was wrong with me? I flinched when Kaidan's girl reached out and touched my hair.

"Hey, oh my gawd. You have the softest hair. It looks like honey." Her emotional colors were so muddled from alcohol that I couldn't get a good reading, but it felt like she was sincere. Guilt soured my stomach.

"Thanks," I said, feeling terrible. I couldn't leave that ugly lie sitting out there like that.

"Um, I didn't really hear that about Kaidan." They both looked at me with confusion, and I swallowed, forcing myself to continue. "He doesn't have gonorrhea. I mean, not that I know of."

"Why would you make that up?" The friend was more sober, and she was looking at me with deserved contempt. The drunken girl still looked confused. I contemplated playing it off like I'd been joking, but that would also be a lie, and who jokes about STDs anyway?

"I don't know," I whispered. "I just . . . I'm sorry." I backed up and slipped out of there as fast as I could. It was a good thing, too, because Lascivious's last song was ending and all the girls were wobbling toward the bathroom now. It was time for the bands to switch. I wrung my hands and bit my lower lip, looking for Jay as the crowd surged around me. I wanted to go home.

"Anna!" Jay waved to me, and I had to chase him through the crowd toward a door where a gigantic man stood frowning, arms crossed over his chest in the classic bouncer pose.

I just lied! It was all I could think about. Terrible feelings slithered around in the pit of my belly.

Gregory held out a laminated card, which the bouncer glanced at before opening the door.

I grabbed Jay's arm. "Wait, Jay, maybe I should just stay out here."

He turned to me. "No way. Patti'll kill me if I leave you. It's all good. C'mon." He pulled me through the door.

We made our way around crew members who were hurriedly hauling around stage equipment. Music and raucous voices spilled from a room at the end of the hall.

"Are we really doing this?" I asked. And was my voice really all high-pitched and shaky? I needed to scream.

"Chill, Anna. It's fine. Be cool," Jay said.

A wall of cigarette smoke and alcohol fumes hit us as we entered the warm room. I put my hands on my hips and tried to be inconspicuous as I checked for sweat marks on my tank top. When I saw small dampened spots had formed I snapped my arms back to my sides.

Be cool, Jay had said. Like that could ever happen.

It took only a few seconds of scanning the room to find

him, standing in a back corner with three long-legged beauties who were obviously aware of the latest fashions. A ribbon of red aura wove around and between them. One of the girls pulled a cigarette from a pack. Like a magician, Kaidan whipped out a matchbook and flicked it open to light a match with one thumb. How did he do that?

Jay gave my hand a tug, but I pulled away.

"No, you guys go ahead. I'll wait here." I wanted to stay near the door. My stomach wasn't right.

"You sure?"

"Yeah, I'm fine. I'll be right here. Good luck, or break a leg, or something."

As Jay and Gregory turned and headed into the crowd, my traitorous eyes returned to the corner and found another pair of eyes staring darkly back.

I dropped my gaze for three full seconds, and then lifted my eyes again, hesitant. The drummer was still staring at me, oblivious to the three girls trying to win back his attention. He put up one finger at the girls and said something that looked like, "Excuse me."

Oh, my goodness. Was he . . . ? Oh, no. Yes, he was walking this way.

My nerves shot into high alert. I looked around, but nobody else was near. When I looked back up, there he was, standing right in front of me. Good gracious, he was *sexy*—a word that had not existed in my personal vocabulary until that moment. This guy was sexy like it was his job or something.

He looked straight into my eyes, which threw me off guard,

because nobody ever looked me in the eye like that. Maybe Patti and Jay, but they didn't hold my stare like he was doing now. He didn't look away, and I found that I couldn't take my gaze off those blue eyes.

"Who are you?" he asked in a blunt, almost confrontational way.

I blinked. It was the strangest greeting I'd ever received.

"I'm . . . Anna?"

"Right. Anna. How very nice." I tried to focus on his words and not his luxuriously accented voice, which made everything sound lovely. He leaned in closer. "But who *are* you?"

What did that mean? Did I need to have some sort of title or social standing to enter his presence?

"I just came with my friend Jay?" Oh, I hated when I got nervous and started talking in questions. I pointed in the general direction of the guys, but he didn't take his eyes off me. I began rambling. "They just wrote some songs. Jay and Gregory. That they wanted you to hear. Your band, I mean. They're really . . . good?"

His eyes roamed all around my body, stopping to evaluate my sad, meager chest. I crossed my arms. When his gaze landed on that stupid freckle above my lip, I was hit by the scent of oranges and limes and something earthy, like the forest floor. It was pleasant in a masculine way.

"Uh-huh." He was closer to my face now, growling in that deep voice, but looking into my eyes again. "Very cute. And where is your *angel*?"

My what? Was that some kind of British slang for boyfriend? I didn't know how to answer without continuing to sound pitiful. He lifted his dark eyebrows, waiting.

"If you mean Jay, he's over there talking to some man in a suit. But he's not my boyfriend or my angel or whatever."

My face flushed with heat and I tightened my arms over my chest. I'd never met anyone with an accent like his, and I was ashamed of the effect it had on me. He was obviously rude, and yet I wanted him to keep talking to me. It didn't make any sense.

His stance softened and he took a step back, seeming confused, although I still couldn't read his emotions. Why didn't he show any colors? He didn't seem drunk or high. And that red thing . . . what was that? It was hard not to stare at it.

He finally looked over at Jay, who was deep in conversation with the manager-type man.

"Not your boyfriend, eh?" He was smirking at me now. I looked away, refusing to answer.

"Are you certain he doesn't fancy you?" Kaidan asked. I looked at him again. His smirk was now a naughty smile.

"Yes," I assured him with confidence. "I am."

"How do you know?"

I couldn't very well tell him that the only time Jay's color had shown mild attraction to me was when I accidentally flashed him one day as I was taking off my sweatshirt, and my undershirt got pulled up too high. And even then it lasted only a few seconds before our embarrassment set in.

"I just know, okay?"

He put his hands up in mock surrender and let out an easy laugh.

"I'm terribly sorry, Anna. I've forgotten my manners. I

23

thought you were . . . someone else." He stuck out his hand. "I'm Kaidan Rowe."

I peeled one arm away from my tight self-embrace to take his hand. Every inch of my skin broke out in goose bumps, and my face suddenly burned hot. I was glad for the dimmed lighting. I wasn't one of those people who blushed pink in the cheeks; I blushed crimson in the whole face, and my neck became splotchy. Not cute. The rush of blood always made me dizzy. I should have pulled my hand away then, but he continued to hold it, and his large palm and long fingers felt so nice.

He chuckled deeply and let his hand slide away from mine until we were no longer touching. He noticed as my arms crossed over my chest again, and then he lifted his chin and sniffed the air.

"Ah, smells good. There's nothing like American hot dogs. I think I'll have one later."

Okay. Random. I sniffed.

"I don't smell anything," I said.

"Really? Lean toward the door some. Breathe a bit . . . *deeper*."

I did as he said. Nothing. Determined, I did something that was rare for me: I reached my sense of smell out farther.

There was no scent of hot dogs in the entire club. Only stale alcohol and hot bleach water for the mops. I pushed it out farther. Nothing at the restaurant next door. Farther. My nose burned and I was getting light-headed. Farther. And there it was. I smelled the nearest hot dog at a small street vendor nearly a mile away. My olfactory sense snapped quickly back and I found him watching me with expectancy. What was he playing at? He couldn't have smelled that. Why would he pretend?

I shook my head and tried to keep my face neutral.

"Hmm." He smiled. "I suppose I was mistaken, then."

Gosh, his eyes were gorgeous—the color of tropical honeymoon waters ringed in dark sapphire and enclosed by thick lashes.

What . . . ? Honeymoon waters? Get a grip!

A wispy perfumed girl walked up and stood between Kaidan and me, placing her back firmly in my face. I had to step backward.

"We're getting lonely over there." Her hands moved over his chest and up to rest on his shoulders. Red jumped out from her when she touched him, and he brought his hand up to squeeze her bony hip. I turned away, not listening to his whispered response, which appeared to appease her. She gave me an icy glance before walking back to the corner.

"Maybe I'll see you around, Anna. I'll be certain to give your boyfriend Jay's songs a listen." And with that he was gone.

"He's not my . . . ," I sputtered at his retreating back.

I'd been looking in the wrong place earlier when I searched for a flaw in Kaidan. It was not in his face; it was in his personality. Confidence was good, but overconfidence was not. I looked around, feeling stupid and alone.

Thankfully I had to stand solitary for only one long moment before Jay came back feeling over-the-moon happy. I let his emotion drench me.

"What were you and Kaidan Rowe talking 'bout?" Jay

asked me. "Man, y'all looked like you were gonna rip each other's clothes off!" I gasped and smacked his arm, but he didn't flinch.

"We did *not*." My eyes darted over to Kaidan for a fraction of a second, and though he was too far away to have heard, the wink he sent me brought another flush to my skin.

"So?" Jay said. "You gonna tell me or not? What was he sayin' to you?"

What in the world could I tell Jay that wouldn't leave him as thoroughly confused as I felt? I glanced over at Kaidan again and caught him watching me for one last second before turning his back to us.

"Nothing, really," I hedged. "It was weird. I'll tell you about it later. I need to call Patti and tell her we're on our way, then I want to hear about *you*. Who was that man you were talking to? What did he say? I guess Gregory is staying?"

The distraction tactic easily got me off the hook as we left the club. Jay always drove. After I called Patti, he gave me a breakdown of the entire conversation with Lascivious's business manager. We dissected every word for all hopeful meaning, coming to the conclusion that the band's manager was extremely impressed with the talent and ambition of Jay and Gregory, and that they would definitely obtain rock-star status by the end of the year. It was usually fun to dream big with Jay, but though I played along, tonight my mind was elsewhere.

Using my extended senses to find that stupid hot dog smell had put my thoughts in a jumble. A mile from my apartment I allowed my eyes to search, and then linger on a dark, abandoned house as we passed it. I stared at the boarded-up windows singed black, and the roof half-caved by devouring flames from long ago. If I let myself remember, I could probably still smell it and taste it like a mouthful of ash. . . .

I was awoken at two a.m. a week before my ninth birthday with the powerful smell of smoke burning my nose. Our home was on fire. I got down just as I'd been taught and crawled through the darkness to Patti's room, feeling like I might hyperventilate.

"Wake up," I said. "There's smoke!"

Patti jumped from her bed in a panic, running into the hall. And then she just stood there as I coughed and choked. She rushed through each room, and even went outside to peek at the nearby complexes.

"There's no fire in the apartments, honey. Must have been a bad dream. Climb in bed with me tonight, and I'll take care of you."

It *had* been a bad dream, but not in the way she meant. For the family a mile away whose burning home I could smell as if it were our own, it had been a real-life nightmare. It had been a long, painful night for me as well: the night my five senses began to enhance.

"Dreaming of Kaidan Rowe, huh?"

I looked up. We were parked in front of my building.

"No," I muttered. "I was *not* thinking about him."

Jay laughed and I backhanded his big arm once again.

I sighed, imagining how he would react if I told him that I had the nose of an überhound and eyes like binoculars. He was totally cool with my being eccentric, but he didn't know the extent of it.

"Thanks for taking me tonight," I said. "I had fun."

"For real? I knew you'd like it! So, I'll pick you up for school on Monday?"

"Yeah, see you then."

I climbed out and headed up the steps, feeling resentful toward that Kaidan kid for making me open my memory to things that were better off boarded up.

CHAPTER TWO

GOOD-GIRL SYNDROME

Patti was frying eggs in our small apartment when I came in from my jog on Monday morning. I leaned over the counter to watch. She used her wrist to push a strawberry blond curl from her face. When the strand fell again, I reached over and wrapped it behind her ear. A translucent, pale yellow emotion swirled around her chest, wafting warmly toward me.

She flipped the egg, *tsk*ing when the yolk broke. Watching her at the stove, I wished she were my real mother so I could have inherited some of her genetics. I'd love to share her thick curls and soft voluptuousness.

Of course she'd waited up for me to get home Saturday night, then hounded me for details, pretending to be excited for me when I could see she was overflowing with anxiety. I gave her the G-rated version, leaving out the bits about lying to people and having strange encounters with a boy. She'd bitten her lip as I spoke and searched my face, but then accepted my story and relaxed.

Patti handed me a plate and shooed me off with a wave of the spatula. I sat at our round dining table, pushing aside a pile of unpaid bills and photo proofs from her freelance photography jobs.

"What are you up to today?" I asked her.

"The *Dispatch* hired me to shoot a press conference with the governor this morning. I should be home around four."

Noticing the time, I scarfed down my breakfast and hurried to get ready.

Fifteen minutes later I kissed Patti, preparing to dash out the door, but she cupped my cheek with a gentle hand to still me.

"I love you, sweet girl." Light pink love fluttered around her body.

"Love you, too," I said. She patted my cheek and I left.

Jay always picked me up for school at exactly 7:10. He was prompt. I liked that.

"'Sup?" he said when I climbed in the car. His eyes were still puffy from his having just rolled out of bed.

"Mornin', sunshine," I said. It took two hard pulls on the creaky car door before it finally slammed shut. I twisted my wet hair and hung it over my shoulder. It would dry straight and I'd pull it back.

We usually drove to school in silence, because Jay wasn't a morning person, but we hadn't had a chance to talk since he brought me home Saturday night.

"I always wondered what your type was, but I never imagined it would be a hard-core rocker!"

Here we go. I had been hoping he'd be too sleepy for this conversation.

"He's not my type. If I had a type it would be . . . nice. Not some hotheaded, egocentric male slut."

"Did you just call him a *male slut*?" Jay laughed. "Dang, that's, like, the worst language I've ever heard you use."

I glowered at him, feeling ashamed, and he laughed even harder.

"Oh, hey, I've got a joke for you. What do you call someone who hangs out with musicians?"

He raised his eyebrows and I shrugged. "I don't know. What?"

"A drummer!" I shook my head while he cracked up at his joke for another minute before hounding me again about Kaidan. "All right, so you talked about my CDs, you had some cultural confusion with some of his lingo, then you talked about hot dogs? That can't be everything. You looked seriously intense."

"That's because he *was* intense, even though we weren't really talking about anything. He made me nervous."

"You thought he was hot, didn't you?"

I stared out of my window at the passing trees and houses. We were almost to school.

"I knew it!" He smacked the steering wheel, loving every second of my discomfort. "This is so weird. Anna Whitt has a crush."

"Fine, yes. He was hot. But it doesn't matter, because there's something about him I don't like. I can't explain it. He's . . . scary."

"He's not the boy next door, if that's what you mean. Just don't get the good-girl syndrome."

"What's that?"

"You know. When a good girl falls for a bad boy and hopes the boy will fall in love and magically want to change his ways. But the only one who ends up changing is the girl. Like Jamie Moore, remember?"

Jamie Moore! That's where I'd heard Kaidan's name before! She was a junior at our school.

We parked in our usual spot at Cass High School.

"See you at lunch," Jay said. He had his eye on a girl named Kaylah, who was climbing out of her car three spots down.

"Yeah, see you then." I walked to school while he lagged behind to say hi to her.

Jamie Moore was on my mind all day.

I sat with Jay at lunch, but my eyes kept going to Jamie, sitting with her same group of friends, but sort of an outcast now. She sat on the end, keeping to herself as the others played and flirted.

Being unsociable and fashion-backward had never been issues for Jamie Moore. She was a year older than me, beautiful, and a genuinely nice person. Her primary color used to be the sunshine yellow of happiness. At the beginning of this school year she'd been a cheerleader and president of the drama club. In the fall I heard she was dating some guy in a band from a high school in Atlanta.

Kaidan Rowe.

Her colors began to change then. Yellow to red. Red to gray. Gray to black. She was full of anger, then self-loathing, and most recently depression. Gossip flew about pictures of Jamie taken on her boyfriend's cell phone, and their eventual breakup. She was soon kicked off the cheerleading squad for failing grades. Next came stories of her partying, moving from one guy to another, but never being happy. For the first time she wasn't given the starring role in the winter play.

My heart contracted tightly as I looked at her again, sitting there at the end of the long lunch table. She still dressed trendy and took time to style her hair, which was probably why she was welcome to continue sitting with the others. But her smile and her sunshine yellow were gone, replaced by a dull gray haze.

The bell rang and I watched her shuffle out of the cafeteria.

No, I did not want to see Kaidan again. Of that I was now certain.

I made my way through the crowded halls, barely cringing anymore at the onslaught of emotion from the people surrounding me. It had been difficult adjusting to a big school after spending the first eight years in a small private school, but I was used to it now.

It was almost the end of the school year—two more weeks to go. The Georgia heat had set in, bringing with it tank tops and flip-flops, as well as shorts and skirts that kept no secrets. I shied away from showing too much skin, partly because of my own modesty, and partly because I felt kind of bad for boys. Unlike other girls, I had to see firsthand that most boys were having a hard enough time concentrating on anything besides their overpowering hormones.

Jay mussed my hair as I passed him in the hall, never pausing in his conversation with one of the guys from band class. I smiled, smoothing my hair back down.

I slipped into my Spanish class and immediately started the class work written on the board. Once finished, I peeked over at Scott McCallister, who sat next to me. He was dozing off on top of unfinished verb conjugations.

Scott was an all-state wrestler—a cutie with big brown eyes and a baby face. He'd always been courteous to me, even flirtatious at times, but I didn't take it to heart, seeing how he flirted with lots of girls.

The class finished early and we were told to work on our final project.

"Um, Senora Martinez?" I raised my hand and she nodded. "Are you going to collect the homework?"

A collective groan rose up from the students, and the guy next to Scott muttered, *"Shut up, stupid!"* I slunk down low in my seat, mortified by my own social faux pas.

"Ah, *sí*!" Senora Martinez said. *"Gracias*, Anna."

"Why you gotta be so good all the time?" Scott whispered. I lifted my eyes and caught his teasing expression. He had no assignment to pass up when the teacher came around.

My face was still warm by the time she finished collecting the worksheets. Veronica, who sat in front of me, turned and gave me a sympathetic look. She was one of the only other students who did the homework.

Nobody worked on their projects after that. Well, *I* did, of course, compulsive rule follower that I was. The class erupted into the excited chatter of free time, and Senora Martinez turned to her computer, ignoring us. Even the teachers were ready to be done with this year.

I opened my notebook.

Veronica bent to put her stuff in her bag and caught sight of my sandals.

"Cute shoes!" she said to me. "Where'd you get them?"

Oh, how I wished I felt okay about lying. I kept my eyes on my notebook when I answered, "Thanks. Um, I think they were from a yard sale or flea market or something."

"Oh." Veronica glanced at them again with less appreciation this time, and we shared a polite smile. She had short dark hair and a Grecian nose with a slight arch to it. When she caught me looking at her nose I was stunned by the wave of dark self-loathing that came off her before she turned back around to face her friends. Of course, the feature she hated most about herself was the one I thought made her naturally seductive in a way I could never dream of being.

Scott turned in his desk toward me.

"So what are you doing next Friday, shorty?"

"*Nada*," I answered.

"Huh?" His look of confusion made me smile.

"*Nada*," I said again. "You know. It means 'nothing' in Spanish?"

"Oh. Yeah. See, you must be under the impression I pay attention in here or something. Anyway, you wanna come to a party? Gene's folks have a lake house."

My stomach jumped. "Wow, that's cool. I don't know,

35

though." I leaned my elbow on the desk and pretended to study the graffiti etched into the wood.

"Jay's invited, too. Come on, we've never partied together." I probably would have felt very uncomfortable if it had been anyone other than Scott giving me that dreamy look. I glanced at his emotions. Happy. Hopeful. Slightly lustful. I couldn't help but be flattered by his invitation and apparent interest.

"I guess I can talk to Jay about it," I said, leaving out the fact that it was Patti I'd have to convince. "But you know that I don't really party, as in *party* party." I couldn't even make eye contact after saying such a lame thing, but I didn't want him having any false expectations.

"Yeah, I know," he said. "Why is that?"

How could I explain it? I didn't have any nagging judgment toward my peers for drinking and partying. I knew it was innocent rebellion and self-exploration. But there was always a promise of dangerous excitement I strongly desired. Ironically, it was that desire that repelled me.

"Are you scared?" he asked.

"Kind of," I admitted. "I don't like the fact that it might make me do something I wouldn't normally do."

"That's the fun of it. It makes you open and free."

Open and free. I wondered if that was how Danny Lawrence had felt when he passed out on the lawn of a party last year and the other drunk guys thought it would be funny to stand around peeing on him. Or the most terrible thing that happened over Christmas break, which nobody talked about at Cass—the senior girl who was high and drove off the road, killing her best friend in the passenger seat. Had she been

36

feeling bold? Every time I saw her walking the halls in a black cloud of remorse, I wanted to cry for her.

"I guess I'm just boring," I mumbled.

I was ready to close down this conversation. I looked up at the clock, thankful to see the bell was about to ring.

"Trust me, Anna." Scott leaned in. "One drink in you, or one hit of X, and you'll feel anything *but* boring."

Everything inside of me tightened. X. Ecstasy. The word bounced around in my head like a rubber ball, out of control and impossible to catch. My dark undercurrent stirred with craving and my breathing quickened. I didn't like to acknowledge that darkness. It rose at any mention of drugs and alcohol. And to be honest, it was what had drawn me to Jay last year. I saw something similar in him, though not exactly the same.

A dark strand ran under the surface of his emotions. It was always there, threatening, especially at the mention of alcohol. I didn't know what it meant, but I wanted us in it together. I thought I might be able to help him, or protect him. A funny thought, considering he was a brawny guy.

I looked at Scott, who grinned at me. Not a sinister grin, but an I-want-to-experience-something-with-you grin.

Veronica must have caught wind of our hushed conversation, because she turned and gave a conspiratorial smile to the two of us.

"Are you going to the party, Anna?" she asked.

"I don't know, maybe."

"You should come! It's gonna be crazy. Everyone will be there."

I looked down and traced the wooden grooves in the desk

with my pencil's eraser. Could I get away with changing the subject?

"So, I'm turning sixteen on Wednesday. I'm getting my license."

"I am so jealous!" Veronica said, smacking my desk. "I've been sixteen for three months already, and my dad *still* hasn't let me get mine! I'm pretty sure he hates me. Are you getting a car?"

"Uh, no." Not even close.

Everyone jumped up and grabbed their things as the bell rang, and the tension that held a viselike grip on my neck finally relaxed its vicious fingers and released me.

CHAPTER THREE

SWEET-SIXTEEN SURPRISE

I didn't feel any older when I woke up on Wednesday morning. Patti was out on our small balcony with her coffee and newspaper. She snapped to attention, and her face brightened when she saw me.

Something misty hovered beside her like a ghost. I pressed my fingers to my eyes, but when I took them away it was still there. It was about the same size as her, maybe longer, like a fuzzy white shadow. Had I developed another sight? Please, no. I'd learned to fear the acquisition of new abilities; like the choking horror of smoke from a mile away, each came with some fresh disadvantage.

"Happy birthday!" Patti said, standing and pulling me into a big hug, then cupping my face and gazing into my eyes. "You feeling okay?"

"Um . . ." My eye glided to the cloud thing, which moved around her, never changing its general appearance.

"What's wrong?" She looked down at her shoulder where my eyes were, and wiped down the length of her arm, right next to the cloud. "Please don't tell me I have dandruff." She ran a hand through her waves, pulling her hair to the side to get a look at it.

"No, you don't. Nothing's wrong. Sorry. I'm still tired, just zoning out."

She squeezed me again, kissing my head.

"I can't believe my little girl is sixteen! There's a card from Nana on the counter. Let me go make your hot chocolate." The shadow thing floated along next to her, following her into the apartment as if attached.

I sat down in a plastic chair, feeling jittery, while Patti made my cocoa. Most mornings were relaxing, sipping warm drinks on the balcony, but not today. The combination of the humid morning air and the weird vision made me feel claustrophobic.

I couldn't believe I was seeing something else. Nothing strange had happened to me for more than two years. I thought it was over. I closed my eyes and laid my forehead on the table. Would it ever end?

I sat up when Patti returned, setting my cocoa in front of me and sitting in the other plastic chair with her coffee. I sneaked another peek at the cloud when she wasn't looking.

"Are you sure you're okay?" she asked me.

Time to act normal. I cleared my throat.

"Yeah. So, there's a party next week for the end of the

school year. I was wondering if I could maybe go with Jay, if it's okay." I thought of Scott and hoped she'd say yes.

Patti sniffed and twitched her nose.

"Will this person's parents be there?" she asked in a tight tone.

Would they? "I don't know."

"Well, I'll need to talk to them first. If it's just a small get-together with parental supervision, then I'll consider it."

Sheesh. Patti made it seem like I was prone to bad behavior or something. Me! The school's Little Miss Goody-Goody. I didn't understand why she couldn't trust me. I must have been pouting, because she set the paper down and gave me a consoling pat on the arm.

"You still want to get your license after school today, hon?"

"Yes," I answered. Because that was what normal sixteen-year-olds did. And I would feign normalcy if it killed me.

"All right. And then dinner at La Tía's?"

"Yes!" I said, my mood lightening. Mexican food was our favorite. We went to the little rinky-dink restaurant for every birthday, and whenever Patti got an unexpected bonus, which wasn't very often. Newspapers and other agencies hired her sporadically, so her income had never been steady. We'd struggled during the years I attended private school, despite partial financial aid. I put my foot down after eighth grade, insisting on public school when I found a pile of late notices tucked between two cookbooks.

"Sounds good to me. I'll pick you up after school. I hate to run, but I have to get some stuff done this morning, since we'll be busy girls this afternoon!" She kissed my cheek with a loud smack. "You sure you're feeling okay?"

"Yeah, I'm sure. Love you," I said.

"Love you, too." I watched her go inside with the cloud trailing close behind.

Birds were chattering to one another in a nearby tree, and the air smelled like wet grass. I pushed my hearing out to the birds, testing my ability. I concentrated, sending it in an invisible, pencil-thin line, then bubbling it around them. The birds sounded as if they were perched on my shoulder.

The heightening of my sense of smell and taste had come together the night of the fire, leaving a deadly flavor in my mouth. It had been like being stuck in a small, closed, unvented room with a smoking barbecue grill. I had no way of knowing I could control it at first. I'd thought I was dying or going insane.

Every year or so, the nightmare would return as a new sense blossomed. My head wanted to explode when my hearing enhanced. Hundreds of voices and sounds within a mile radius shouted like blaring televisions with no volume control. I couldn't hear my own cries.

My enhanced vision, the fifth and final sense, welcomed me into my preteens. At least I could close my eyes with that one.

Mastering each sense had taken major practice, not to mention causing migraines, vomiting, and nosebleeds. Being able to hear and see and smell everything within a one-mile radius was major sensory overload. And unfortunately, perfect health did not make me immune to pain.

I'd been to the doctor only for annual checkups. Other

than the migraines, I never got sick. Cuts and scrapes and bruises healed in a matter of hours, sometimes less. It wasn't like on television, though, where a superhero's gash closed and mended itself in seconds before your very eyes. I could watch it happening over the course of a couple of hours, like a flower tilting and opening to the morning sun, but who had time for that?

I missed a lot of school during those days. The only advantage of having no friends before ninth grade was having nobody to explain myself to. At least I had Patti. She'd fostered me as an infant, adopting me as soon as the states of California and Georgia would allow. I was old enough to call her "Pat-Pat" by that point.

I couldn't hide the physical side effects of everything I went through, but Patti nurtured me through it all with no questions. She brushed my long hair with care when my sense of touch developed; it felt like each tangle would mangle my scalp forever. It hurt to move my arms because of the sensitive skin and muscle.

When a plague of migraines came and I couldn't keep food down, Patti somehow got her hands on serious prescription-strength painkillers that would supposedly knock out a grown man and have him sleeping for hours. After the first one, I felt a blessed sense of drowsy relief for about twenty minutes, then the blistering pain broke through again. Patti was horrified when she found out I'd taken six in one afternoon. The label warnings said to take no more than two per day. After she took them away, I searched the house with a blind obsession all week, but never found them.

Each physical sense got easier to rein in as I gained focus. Eventually I was able to use my normal sensory levels at all times unless I chose to strengthen them, which might have been fun if there was someone to share it with. Only there wasn't.

The hazy little clouds were everywhere, following people. Every person had one. I stared at them outright all day, which I'm sure made me seem even weirder than usual.

I watched Jay's move around him as I switched books at my locker.

"What's up, birthday girl?" he asked, glancing around himself. "Do I got a spitball on me or something?"

"No, nothing. Sorry." I forced my eyes to his face. "I'm getting my license today."

"Sweet. Good thing Patti's car is a stick shift. That means you can drive mine, too."

"Good thing," I agreed. Jay's car was a clunker. It made Patti's old sedan look mint.

I slammed my locker and we let ourselves be herded by the crowd to our classes. When Jay wasn't looking, I discreetly reached out to touch the white cloud in front of me, and my hand went through it. I turned to Jay.

"Want to go to that end-of-the-year party next Friday?" I asked him. He bumped knuckles with the president of the drama club going the opposite direction. A girl from the dance team swung her locker closed and gave Jay a flirty look as we passed. He stared over his shoulder at her before returning to our conversation.

"The one at Gene's? You really want to?"

"Yeah, I think so," I said. "If Patti will let me."

We were at my class now. Jay hitched his thumbs under the straps of the backpack on his shoulders.

"Listen." He hesitated. "Just . . . watch out for Scott, okay?"

Huh?

"Wait a sec," I said. "How can you get all excited about someone like Kaidan Rowe, but warn me about someone like Scott McCallister?"

Jay looked down and scuffed the floor with the toe of his tennis shoe, making it squeak.

"You don't hear him in the PE locker room when it's just the guys."

"Oh." I pondered this. "Does he say things about me?"

"No, not you. You think I'd let him do that?" He pulled his eyes away from me. "Look, never mind. Just forget I said anything."

I wondered whether Jay was jealous of Scott—not over me, but just in general. Scott was popular, but then again, so was Jay in a different way. I'd never sensed jealousy from Jay about anything. His color now was only a mild grayish brown of worry.

"I'll be careful," I promised. "And you'll be there, too. And I bet Kaylah will go. . . ."

"All right, all right," he said. "We'll go."

He left me, running down the hall to his class before the tardy bell. His white cloud trailed close behind him.

I slipped into my own class just in time, blinking at the roomful of floating mists around my classmates. Those were

45

going to take some getting used to. It was World History, and we were assigned group work. I had this class with Gene, so I decided to take advantage of the mild chaos of desks being moved and people shuffling places.

"Hey, Gene?" I whispered.

He looked up and gave me a nod. He was short and muscular, like Scott, from wrestling, though Gene was in a lighter weight class.

"My mother, um . . . she kind of wants to talk to your mom about the party. To make sure it's going to be supervised and all that." I tried not to cringe. His eyebrows went up for a second.

"Yeah, I hear you, girl." He tore off a corner of his paper. "Have her call this number the day before the party. Just tell her that my ma works crazy hours, so that'll be the best day to reach her. Cool?"

I felt giddy as I thanked him, slipping the paper in my pocket and heading for my group.

CHAPTER FOUR

LAKE PARTY

The next Friday was our last day of school, and it was sticky-hot. Dusk brought little relief from the muggy heat. The air conditioner in Jay's car pushed out lukewarm air even on its coldest setting. My feet were propped on his dusty dashboard on our way to Gene's lake house. I fanned us both with an old french-fry box from the floor that still smelled like grease.

I'd never been to a lake house, though I'd been to the lake plenty of times for church picnics, or afternoons with Patti. I always enjoyed the serenity of the winding drive thick with trees.

We turned down a bumpy gravel road and made our way toward the lights of other cars and a beautiful, massive log cabin. It was getting darker now as we parked and got out.

Crickets, frogs, and cicadas serenaded us from all directions in the moist, warm air.

The house was brightly lit, but our path was not, so I extended my sight to be sure I didn't trip on any rocks or fallen branches along the way. Along with being able to see far away, I could adjust my sensitivity to light. I liked to think of it as "night vision." The moon was a crescent sliver and wouldn't have been bright enough for normal eyes to see by, but it worked for me. Our feet crunched the gravel as we walked.

"Get a load of this place." Jay gawked.

"I know. It's huge." The house had three vast levels with wraparound porches and a vaulted roof. It looked like a lodge.

I pulled my sight back in as we reached the porch rimmed with lights. Voices and laughter were mingling with loud hip-hop music inside. When Gene answered the door, the change in volume hit us hard.

"No way! Look who's here, y'all! What's up, Jay?" They smacked hands in a clasp, then Gene looked at me. "Anna Whitt in the house!" He leaned in and we hugged, giving me a strong whiff of alcohol on his breath. He must have been sneaking drinks while his parents weren't looking.

We walked through, bumping shoulders with the steadily growing crowd. Jay was greeted by everyone he came across. Gene's family room had been turned into a darkened dance floor, stereo blaring. The dining room was full of kids standing and cheering, playing some kind of game. Jay and I stopped.

Girls and guys stood across the table from one another, placing their plastic cups at the edge of the table and trying repeatedly to flip the cups over one-handed. It was a race.

Kristin Miller's cup finally landed upside down and she threw her arms up in victory. The girls jumped up and down screaming while the boys moaned and shook their heads.

"That looks fun," I said to Jay as we watched from the doorway.

"It's a drinking game," he explained. "Flip Cup. You gotta drink whatever's in the cup before you can flip it. No fair being sober."

"Oh."

We moved to the gigantic kitchen, where the soaring vaulted ceiling loomed high over stainless-steel appliances and terra-cotta tiling. The entirety of the massive granite kitchen island was covered in bright-colored plastic cups, juices, sodas, beer cans, and bottles of alcohol. My stomach tightened. His parents were allowing blatant underage drinking?

A group of people stood in front of a huge window overlooking the water. Gene turned from the group and came over.

"Whatcha drinkin'?" He hitched a thumb toward the island.

"Nothing for me, thanks," I said. I sensed Jay's hesitation. *Be strong—you don't need it*, I silently urged him. He made eye contact with me and sighed before answering.

"Nah, nothing right now, man."

"You sure?" Gene eyeballed us in disbelief. "My sister just turned twenty-one, so we all put in money and told her to buy out the store and keep the change."

"Where are your parents?" I asked, glancing around.

"Bahamas."

"*Bahamas?*" I couldn't keep the shock from my voice.

"Yeah—that was my sister's cell your mom called. She can pull off the parental voice dead on. I can't believe y'all aren't drinkin'. Better get it before it runs out." The doorbell rang and he darted away, sliding on socked feet into the hall now swarming with people. I was dumbfounded.

"Patti thinks his parents are here," I muttered. Jay scratched around the stubble of hair on his head.

"Er, she does? Do you wanna leave? Is that what you're sayin'?" he asked with reluctance.

I didn't answer him. I didn't want to leave, but at the same time I felt guilty staying.

"Let's give it one hour," I compromised. "Is that okay?"

"Deal. One hour." Jay was still running his hands over his head. Then he rubbed his hands together, a nervous gray streak cutting into his yellow aura.

"I could have just one drink," he said, sounding hopeful. "You can drive us home now."

"You," I said, poking a playful finger to his chest, "are the life of the party. Other people have to drink to be how you are when you're completely sober."

He pinched his chin hair, thinking.

"I don't know what it is about you, Whitt, but I can't seem to deny you anything, no matter how bad I want it. It's really annoying."

I smiled, because I could see he was feeling a pale yellow contentment without a trace of annoyance.

Behind Jay, Kaylah's bone-straight blond hair and chic wire-rimmed glasses came into sight. She was on the dance team, and had an hourglass figure.

"I spy your crush," I whispered.

"Sweeeet," he whispered back.

"Go ahead and talk to her. I'm going out to see the view." I gave his big ole bicep a squeeze and made my way to the back door. I knew the moment Jay caught up to Kaylah, because her whole gaggle of girlfriends broke out into squeals at his loud greeting.

Nobody else was out on the deck. I walked to the edge and put my hands on the wooden rail. It was dark now. Crickets and frogs seemed to be competing for who could be noisiest. Lightning bugs flashed from every direction. There was a dimly lit walkway of stones that led down to a dock and boathouse. Distant voices and moving shadows told me there were partyers down there as well. The water glistened in the moonlight. Warm air sat heavily on my skin, but I was comfortable.

The door opened behind me, and a muddle of music and voices spilled out before it closed again.

"There you are."

I turned to the voice.

"Hey, Scott," I said. And hello, butterflies.

Ever since he'd invited me to the party he'd been on my mind. He came up and stood next to me with a red cup. It smelled doughy and sour.

"Beer," he said. "Want a sip?"

"No, thanks." I felt shy. He tipped his head back and drained it in several gulps, then turned to the side and burped. Nice.

"Excuse me," he said, setting down his cup on the ledge. "So. What are you doin' out here by yourself?"

"Just taking it all in. It's beautiful."

"Yep," he said. "Your hair looks pretty."

"Thank you." I had a strip on top pulled back with bobby pins, and the rest hung down my back.

"Remember Mr. Bunker's astrology lessons last year in Earth Science?" I asked, looking up at the sparkling sky, fascinated by the magnitude of creation.

"Uhh, *no*." Scott guffawed.

"Okay, look right there." I pointed. "It's the Big Dipper. That square box part right there is the ladle, and then those stars are the handle. See it?" Scott sidled closer as I traced the shape with an outstretched finger.

"Where? Oh, hey! I see it! Cool."

We got quiet and I realized this was a very romantic setting, if only I weren't so fidgety and unable to look in his direction.

"We should go inside," he said. "Have you seen the basement?" I shook my head. "It's awesome. I'll get you a drink and then we can check it out."

"Scott . . ." I didn't want to have to say it. Again. It would almost be easier to just have a drink so people would leave me alone about it.

"How about something nonalcoholic," he offered. "Soda? Juice?"

I *was* getting thirsty. "Sure, thanks. Anything is fine."

He took me by the hand as he led me inside. It felt strange, but nice. There were even more people now, and many of their colors were faded or gone from alcohol consumption. The clouds were still there with each person, not affected as the auras were. Even though the white shadowy things were see-through, it was still a lot to take in with so many people crammed together.

The air was heavy and hot, despite the high ceilings. As we made our way through, still holding hands, I recognized athletes from school as they called out, "What up, Scott?" and "Scottie!" They did knuckle bumps in passing, eyed me, then nodded knowingly to Scott, giving him a thumbs-up or a high-five. I pretended not to notice.

I was caught between feeling embarrassed, nervous, and, God forbid, *excited* as we came to the stairway for the basement. I wondered if this party was a "date" for us. Maybe I would get my first kiss. My legs trembled and I clasped his hand tighter.

One hour. I would give this party one hour, then I'd have to honor Patti. Okay, maybe fifteen minutes had passed since I made that deal, but I wouldn't count those. Sixty minutes starting now.

"Go ahead on down," Scott shouted close to my ear. "You can find us a seat and I'll be right down with our drinks."

My knees wobbled the whole way down the stairs. I stopped at the bottom in the entryway. The huge open-spaced recreation room was a guy's dream. A giant flat screen television was mounted on the wall, surrounded by a plush, oversize L-shaped couch. There was a pool table, a foosball table, standing arcade games, and a side area with a huge card table and bar. The walls were covered in college sports memorabilia.

As I surveyed the people in the room, two things were quickly apparent. First, the half of the room with couches was currently being used as makeout central. And second, the other half of the room was filled with older boys who I didn't recognize smoking what I instinctively knew to be marijuana, though it was my first time ever smelling the tangy-sweet smoke. The scent gripped me with a longing that nearly brought me to my knees. Panicked, I took the stairs back up two steps at a time.

At the top, I concentrated on calming my breathing as I made my way through the crowd toward the kitchen. Scott stood at the island talking to one of his friends, Kristin Miller. Something about their whispered conversation made me stop and stretch out my hearing toward them.

"She doesn't know?" Kristin asked.

"Not yet, so just keep your mouth shut," Scott said. Kristin laughed. She was a notorious gossip.

"She is going to be so mad at you."

"Nah," he said. "She'll probably thank me for it."

I stood where I was, pulling my hearing back in and wondering what they were talking about. Maybe his ex-girlfriend was here and she'd be mad to know he was talking to me? But why would he say she would thank him for it?

I caught a glimpse of Jay's fuzzy head as he bounded toward me. I was glad to see him. He gave me a bear hug, lifting me off my feet a second before setting me back down.

"You'll never believe this." He was nearly out of breath. "I just talked to this guy who was at the Lascivious show tonight, and he said the band is coming!"

Say *what?!* My heart gave a great bang in my chest. I'd almost forgotten about the drummer with the strange starburst. Or it could be that I'd blocked the encounter from my memory.

"Coming here?" I asked. "Tonight? Why?"

"Because this is the best party ever! There are people here from, like, everywhere. Everybody knows about it!"

"Still, I wouldn't get your hopes up too high." I wondered if I was saying it more for his benefit or my own.

Scott was making his way toward the basement with our two drinks held high in the air. I called out to him, jumping up and waving my arms until he noticed. His forehead creased as he glanced from me to Jay. He made his way over and handed me a cup.

"Thanks," I said. Jay and Scott nodded at each other.

"What's up, man?" Jay asked rather coolly.

"Not a whole lot. How 'bout you?"

"Chillin'. Chillin'." A heavy silence followed. I'd never noticed the feelings between Jay and Scott were about as warm and fuzzy as a bald cat. But then again, I'd never been around them both like this. Their auras brimmed with jagged gray irritation. Scott took a big drink and I looked down at my reddish-orange juice.

"So, what are you kids drinking?" Jay asked, eyeballing my cup.

"Beer for me. I just threw together some different juices for Anna. No alcohol." Scott turned to me. "You ready to go downstairs?" My heart sank.

"Oh," I said. "Um, actually I came back up here because most of the seats are taken and there were some shady guys smoking up."

His face fell.

"Jay!" We all turned toward the trilling voice of Kaylah, who was rushing at us and jumping into Jay's arms.

"Whoa, hey!" He laughed.

"I think the band you were talking about just pulled up!" she told him.

"Ha!" Jay let go of Kaylah and turned to me, doing a funny little in-your-face dance with his tongue out. "What's up now, hater?"

My heart raced and somersaulted as the two of them grabbed hands and left us. I did not want to see Kaidan Rowe again, did I? No. And besides, for the first time a boy was showing interest in me, and I was interested, too. I didn't want to worry about some disrespectful guy messing things up.

I was suddenly parched, so I took a huge gulp of my juice. Yum. Tart, but sweet . . . and something else. I took another drink. What was that? I sniffed the liquid. There was no burning smell of alcohol.

I took another long gulp, then I chugged, knowing even as I did it that there was something in that drink, but I couldn't—no, *wouldn't*—stop myself. I waited for the panic to rise, but instead I felt myself relaxing. This party wasn't half-bad after all, even if the most passive-aggressive, rudest, sexiest guy in Georgia had just shown up. I didn't have to talk to him.

"What band was he talking about?" asked Scott.

"Lascivious. They're Jay's favorite."

"Hmph. Never heard of 'em."

Kristin Miller and Veronica from Spanish class made their

way to us whispering and giggling, their cheeks flushed from drinking. They had similar haircuts, brown bobs that went up their necks and slanted downward in front to their chins. Veronica's hair was darker, though, almost black, and she had new chunky red highlights. Veronica was the drunkest, her colors blurry. She slung her arms around my neck and let out a silly, happy squeal, slurring her words.

"Girl, can I just say you are the coolest little thing ever?! I'm so glad you're here!"

Normally I would wonder whether she was making fun of me, but I was feeling very light and buoyant at the moment, so I found myself going along with it, even enjoying it.

"Thank you!" I shouted. "And I love your highlights, by the way."

Her eyes lit up. "Oh, my gawd! You are so gonna be my BFF tonight. Come on! Let's go dance!"

Kristin rolled her eyes at us.

"Wait!" said Scott. "Finish your drink so it doesn't spill on the dance floor."

Excellent idea. I finished every drop of the delicious juice and handed the empty cup to Scott.

"Come *on*! I love this song!" Veronica pulled my hand, and I let her lead me.

"Come with!" I called to Scott over my shoulder. He and Kristin followed. The four of us weaved through the people to the dance floor, where the music boomed, rattling windows with the bass.

My inhibitions dropped like bricks off of me. When Veronica hollered, "*Wooo!*" I threw my arms up and did the same. My head was so fuzzy inside. I'd lost my ability to sense other people's colors, and it was freeing. The clouds were still there, but they'd become like extensions of the people, in my mind. Nothing could bother me at that moment. I didn't care whether I saw Kaidan Rowe right then. Even he couldn't bring me down.

Veronica and I danced. It was complete and utter bliss. Everyone was being so nice, not minding when I bumped into them. The warmth of close-huddled bodies was wonderful. I could feel each brush of my own limbs against others as I let my hips move and my eyes close.

I faintly heard Kristin talking beside me.

"She can't be feeling it already?"

"Shut the hell up!" Scott's voice hissed.

Veronica lifted her cup to her mouth, but someone fell into her, knocking the cup to the ground.

"Aw, crap!" she said, and we both laughed, falling all over each other. My laughter was not right. It was smoother and lower than usual, and I was suddenly much too calm to work up a good belly laugh. I noticed how soft Veronica's shirt was. I rubbed it between my fingers.

"You're feelin' it now, girl!" she said.

"What was in my drink?" I asked, curious.

"Some crushed-up X. Don't be too mad at him. You're so lucky! I would have done it tonight, too, but my dad won't give me any money."

I wasn't mad. Just the opposite. Scott had been right. I wanted to thank him. I threw my head back, submerged in the sensation. The fact that I was high was what mattered. It was like a long-lost friend had found me and wrapped me in a cozy blanket. I wanted it to last forever.

There was a nagging feeling in the back of my mind, but I ignored it. Soon I couldn't focus on anything except the fact that my mouth felt like it had been stuffed with a sock.

"My mouth is so dry!" I yelled. "And my teeth are chattering."

"Come on. Let's go get you some water and gum. That'll help. And I need another frickin' drink, too!"

Once again Veronica pulled me through the crowd by the hand. I felt as if I were walking on a squishy cloud and everything were in slow motion. We pushed our way to the kitchen, where she spun to me and shouted, "Holy hot guy! Who the heck was that? Did you see him?"

"Who?" I looked around.

"Back in the hall. Hel-*lo*! When we passed him he was staring right at you!"

I looked in the general direction of the hall, but there were too many people.

"I don't know. I didn't see him." I shrugged. "I'm happy we're friends."

"Aww! You are so sweet. I can't believe we've never hung out before." Veronica slid a piece of gum in my mouth. I chewed like crazy, my jaw racing with a mind of its own while she made herself a drink, splashing stuff all over the counter.

Someone tapped my shoulder. My movements were sluggish as I turned, and it took a few seconds to process his face.

"Jay!" I brought my arms up to his shoulders, gazing at him and letting my head flop back.

"You okay?" he asked.

"I am so good." I tried to talk normally, but the breathy voice that came out was totally unfamiliar. I rubbed little circles on his shoulders with my palms. "You are the bestest friend, Jay. I love you."

"Are you *drunk*?!"

Uh-oh. He was upset. No, no, no. Everything was so nice. So perfect. I needed Jay to be happy, too.

"She's rollin'," Veronica said, popping some peanuts in her mouth with manicured fingers.

He looked at me with huge eyes, and then moved my arms down and took a step away from me. "What the hell, Anna?"

"Jay, please. Please don't be mad at me." I reached up to him, but he deflected my arms.

"That's a little hypocritical, don't you think?" he asked, his face tight. All I could do was stare like a fawn in a spotlight. Jay had never, ever yelled at me.

"Whatever, man, forget this." He reached between Veronica and me, grabbing a half-full bottle of clear liquor before disappearing into the movement and noise around us. I was thankful when Scott walked up and filled in the empty gap Jay left behind. I didn't want any gaps tonight.

"You just missed Jay being a total buzz kill!" Veronica said to him. "And did you know that me and Anna are totally best friends now?"

Scott looked at me hesitantly, but when I smiled he slid an arm around my waist and pulled me to him. Jay's words had already filtered through me and were gone. There was no room in paradise for anything as ugly as anger.

"Hey, you." Scott's voice was all melty and buttery in my ear. "Sorry, Veronica, but I'm going to have to steal your new best friend."

"Y'all behave yourselves, now." She winked.

I turned to her and we hugged like we'd never see each other again, and then Scott was weaving the two of us through the partygoers, up a curved wooden staircase, down the hall, and into a room.

The sudden quiet was a shock to my ears when he shut the door behind us. Scott led us to what looked like a guest bed. He sat, so I sat. He lay back on his elbows, so I did, too. When he turned his body to lean over me, I dropped my elbows and lay back, completely still.

"Are you mad at me?" he asked. I shook my head.

"Everything feels so soft." My fingers caressed the sides of my jeans. Even the normally rough feel of denim was like silk under my fingers.

"When I'm on E," he said, "I always think everyone should be naked. Just like Adam and Eve."

That made perfect sense to me at the moment, and it seemed funny. "Just completely natural and happy," I said, and we smiled at each other.

"Do you know when I first started to like you?" he asked. "Remember last year after state match, when I got the, um, cauliflower ear?"

I'd forgotten about that. He'd been so embarrassed about the grossly swollen ear that he'd gotten from the wrestling mats at the state competition. His girlfriend had even been disgusted enough to dump him.

"You were always sweet," he said. "You didn't stare at it like everyone else." He laid his arm across my belly and caressed my waist. "You know, Anna, it wouldn't take much for you to be more, I don't know, popular or whatever. I've seen you play volleyball and softball in gym. You're good. You could go out for sports and maybe wear some different clothes or something. I mean, you're pretty, but you could be, like, *hot*. You know?"

I was quiet for a second. Part of my brain contemplated being offended, but it was overruled by a heavy blanket of peacefulness in my bloodstream.

"I'm sorry, Scott, but even if I had the money, I just don't care about those things. I want people to like me for who I am. Isn't that what you want, too?"

I reached up to touch his face, but he grabbed my hand and held it.

"Have you kissed many guys?"

"I've never kissed anyone," I admitted.

"Not even Jay?"

"No way. He's like my brother." I tried to think of Jay now. What had been wrong with him earlier? It made me feel sad, but I couldn't recall why.

"How long will this last?" I asked. "This feeling?"

"About four hours. Then it takes a couple hours to come down."

Come down? That sounded awful. I wondered if I could talk Scott into giving me more.

"Anna."

"Huh?" I tried to focus on him.

"I want to be your first kiss."

"Okay," I whispered.

Before he even had a chance to lean down, the door banged open, letting in the party's earsplitting volume. We both sat up on the bed and I found myself staring into the deep blue eyes of Kaidan Rowe.

"What the—" Scott started.

"Ah, there you are, luv. Let's go, then."

Kaidan was looking at me. And waving me toward him. I sat there weighed down with shock.

"Can you walk, or will I have to carry you?" Kaidan asked.

Scott raised his voice. "What are you doing, man?"

"I need a chat with Anna." But Kaidan didn't look at Scott when he said it. His eyes stayed on me.

He remembered my name. And it sounded so lovely when he said it. Scott and I turned to each other. It never crossed my mind not to go with Kaidan. He was the most amazing part of my whole wakeful dream.

"I'll be back," I said, standing.

"I wouldn't count on it, actually," said Kaidan, coming forward to take my hand and pull me from the room. I was pondering how many people had tugged me by the arm tonight just as Scott yelled, "Dude!" and Kaidan slammed the door shut behind us.

CHAPTER FIVE

LIKEWISE

Kaidan kept a firm grip on my hand. I concentrated on where our bodies connected, marveling at my hand inside of his. I didn't recall leaving the house or walking down the dock, but when we stopped I processed the fact that we were outside the boathouse. Kaidan banged the doorway with the side of his fist.

"Everyone out," he told them with authority.

"We were here first," one of the boys inside said.

"Sod off." Kaidan's tone was scary calm.

The six figures brushed past us with weak protests and headed back to the party. When they were gone, I expected Kaidan to go into the boathouse, but instead he walked out to the end of the dock and sat. I followed, sitting on the edge with my feet hanging over, not quite reaching the water. I took in his brown T-shirt with a golden dragon stenciled down one shoulder and across the chest. It was just snug enough to accentuate his toned body underneath. When I looked at his face I was shaken to see how intensely he was looking back at me. A breeze brushed my skin like a feather.

My teeth chattered, but I didn't know if it was from the X or the cool air.

"Who *are* you?" he asked me yet again.

"I don't know how you want me to answer that."

A sudden flash throughout my body cracked my fuzzy dream state. I gasped.

"What is it?" he asked. There it was again, but longer this time. Reality was seeping back in. I was beginning to feel insecure and anxious.

"I think . . . It feels like it's starting to wear off. But he said four hours!" I couldn't sit there. I stood up, feeling panicked. I was shaking inside. Kaidan stood, too, pulling my chin up to make me look at him.

"Have you ever been sick?" he asked, holding my eyes with his.

"Sick . . . ?" I couldn't think.

"The flu. Tonsilitis. Anything?" Now he had my attention.

Another spasm pushed me further out of my dream state as I bent over with my hands on my knees.

"Maybe this little sweet will help you." He held a small white pill. *Yes!* I grabbed for it, but he was faster.

"Answer all of my questions first. Any illnesses in your lifetime?"

"No."

"How far back can you remember?"

This question stilled my trembling. We stared hard at each other. He couldn't possibly know about that. It was my ultimate secret.

He moved closer, just as he had the night we met, and lowered his voice. "Answer the question."

I stared up at his mouth, his handsome lips, and for a second I forgot about the pill. I cleared my throat.

"Fine," I whispered. "All the way back. My birth, and even before that. Happy?"

He nodded, straight-faced. I couldn't believe I'd just admitted that out loud to him, and he hadn't reacted as if it were the slightest bit strange. I looked down at his hand by his side in a tight fist, my escape from reality held within it.

"Now for the important part," he said. "Who is your father?"

"I-I don't know. I was adopted."

"Bollocks. You must have some idea." He raised his arm, and his hand hovered over the water.

"There was this one man! I remember him from the day I was born. Jonathan LaGray. I've always assumed he was my father, but I've never even talked to him. Please! I don't know anything about him. He's in prison." I stared at his hand as he lowered it to the safety of his side.

"Yes, of course," said Kaidan, eyeing me differently now. "I should have guessed from your behavior tonight."

My thoughts weren't coherent enough to care what he meant. I was shaking all over now, frantic with longing. I had

66

to stay in my escape world. I couldn't go back.

"My pill," I pleaded.

"You mean this one?" He held it up and my eyes widened. "Sorry, luv, just an aspirin." And to my horror he nonchalantly tossed it into the lake, and with a light plunk it sank.

"No!" I screamed. He stilled me by grasping my upper arms in his strong hands.

"How long ago did he give you the drug?"

"What? I don't know, maybe thirty, no, forty minutes?"

"It should be completely out of your system very soon. You'll be fine. Just sit here and try to calm yourself."

He released my arms and I sat down, resting my forehead on my knees and rocking back and forth, battling minor tremors. He was cruel for tricking me with that pill. I hadn't wanted something that badly since those pain pills years ago.

The wind blew against my skin again and I heard tiny waves splash the rocky shore. After two minutes, the thick fog in my head started to lift and I was racked with the ugliness of clarity.

I should not have come to this stupid party. I should have left the second I found out Gene's parents weren't here. I couldn't believe Scott thought it was okay to give me Ecstasy. Why had I loved it and craved more, like some kind of fiend? Ugh, I almost got my first kiss while I was high!

I looked up now and saw Kaidan sitting on the edge of the dock again, looking out at the water, and realized what his questions meant. He knew something about me. I approached him, afraid he would bolt if I pressed too hard for information.

"Why did it come and go so fast?" I asked.

"Our bodies fight anything foreign." *Our* bodies? "Germs, cancer, disease, the whole lot. Drugs and alcohol burn through quickly. Hardly worth the effort. I tried smoking. Spent days coughing up black tar."

"That's attractive," I said.

"Precisely. Can't afford to be unattractive." He laughed without any amusement.

"So . . ." I was desperate not to scare him off. "Are you like me?"

"Yes, and no, it seems."

I noticed something then. I would've seen it sooner if I hadn't been out of my mind on X.

"Why don't you have one of those cloud thingies around you?" I asked him.

He turned and looked at me in disbelief.

"'Cloud thingies'? You can't be serious."

"Do you know what I'm talking about? You do, don't you!"

He began to stand and I jumped to my feet as well. He looked up at the house, furrowing his brow.

"Are your senses back now?" he asked.

I knew he meant my special senses, and I marveled at how normal he made it sound.

"I think so," I said.

"There's a fight in the house. I think you'd better listen."

I stood up and stretched out my hearing. It was slower than normal and took more effort, but it finally broke through to the inside of the house. Yelling. Chaos. Punching and scuffling. Glass breaking, girls screaming, people shouting their names to try to break it up.

"Oh, my gosh, Scott and Jay!" I took off as fast as my legs would go down the swaying dock. I couldn't even concentrate enough to turn on my night vision, but I somehow didn't trip or fall. I threw open the back door and roughly elbowed my way through.

Three huge football players were dragging Jay out onto the front porch. He was flailing and yelling obscenities I'd never heard from him. I stopped in the doorway and looked around. The window in the front room was shattered. Girls were crying. Scott stood there in the front room, where the music and dancing had stopped and everyone was now watching. He held his nose, which was bleeding, as was his arm. His shirt was torn from the collar to the waist and was splattered with blood. He must have sobered up some, because I saw with my sixth sense how he felt now. Brittle, dark fear.

Gene stumbled his way into the open space. His shirt was off, and by the looks of his girlfriend's tangled hair they'd been occupied in makeout central.

"Aw, man, my parents are gonna *kill* me!"

"Party foul," someone whispered in the crowd.

"Gene," said Scott, sounding whiny and nasal, "Jay went crazy! He came out of nowhere and sucker punched me. He threw me into the window! I think he broke my nose."

"Damn." Gene rested his hands on top of his head and shook it back and forth.

Jay began a fresh round of thrashing outside, kicking and screaming. The three big guys tightened their grips and hollered for him to calm down and stay still. I ran through the door and down the porch steps to him.

"Jay?" He looked up at me with the eyes of a wild man I didn't know. His cheeks were flaming red. He bared his teeth and panted through them. Two guys held his arms, and one guy stood behind him, grasping him around the chest. Jay stared at me until his breathing calmed and his fierce look softened into a pitiful sob.

"He drudge you. Anna. Druvved you."

I knew what he meant. I nodded to the football players. "It's okay, guys, thank you. I'm going to take him home now." When they let go of him, he stumbled three steps backward and fell into a bush. That was going to hurt in the morning. I rushed to him.

"Here, I'll help you to the car," said the biggest guy. I think his name was Frederick, a new graduate. The other two walked back into the house. Frederick got under one of Jay's arms and lifted him, while I got under his other arm. Frederick had been a big defensive linebacker, so I didn't feel any of Jay's weight. We made our way into the darkness as music resumed inside the party.

I glanced back at the house and turned on my extra sight, looking for any sign of Kaidan Rowe. Nothing. There was so much more I wanted to ask him. Most important, why were we like this? What were we? *We.* Oh, my gosh. Just the thought of someone else being like me sent a crazed bolt of energy through my body. I had to see him again. As soon as possible.

When we got to the car, I fished Jay's keys and cell phone from his pocket, leaned the passenger seat all the way back, and stepped aside while Frederick put him in. I thanked Frederick and he went back to the party. Jay was completely passed out.

It crossed my mind that I could go back in and find Kaidan again, but what if Jay woke up? Plus, I didn't want to deal with all the drama flying around.

Instead, I pushed my hearing out to the dock and listened. It was silent. I focused my hearing around the house, scrunching up my face with the loud onslaught, and I said into the air, "I'm not finished with you, Kaidan Rowe."

From somewhere in the kitchen a solitary accented voice replied, "Likewise."

Despite the night's warmth, I got a chill.

After climbing in the car and adjusting the driver's seat, I called Jana from Jay's phone. She answered from a party of her own. She'd graduated the year before, but still lived with her family, commuting to college. When she learned of her little brother's current inability to walk himself into their home, she cursed and said she would meet us there. Maybe we could get him in without waking their parents.

What a mess.

I was nervous driving on the winding road through the pitch-dark woods, even with my night vision. I kept seeing the eyes of little animals reflected in the headlights, sometimes darting across the road and making me slam on the brakes.

It wasn't until we were out of the forest and on a main road that I finally allowed myself to think about all that happened tonight. The more I thought about what Scott had done, the more upset I got. And I was disgusted at myself for enjoying it. I would have to deal with Scott eventually. I hated confrontation, but he couldn't be allowed to get away with it. At least the school year was over and I wouldn't have to face any of those people for a couple of months.

But all of my anger toward Scott and embarrassment at my own behavior were overshadowed by the conversation with Kaidan. Just thinking about it made my heart race all over again. I couldn't believe it. He was really like me. Which was what, exactly? *He* knew, of course. I wished I could have talked with him longer. I wondered how I could get hold of him.

I supposed I could attach my phone number to a pair of my undies and throw them onstage at his next show. The thought actually made me laugh out loud. He'd probably take one look at the white cotton panties and chuck them in the trash.

Jay stirred. He tried to say something, but it came out in one big slur.

"What, Jay?" I used my soothing voice.

"Gonna be sick!"

Oh! I pulled the car over and leaned over Jay to fling open his door, which stuck, as always. I got it open just in time.

We had to stop once more after that. Poor Jay. I rubbed his back as he closed the door and leaned against it. There wasn't much else I could do. He began whimpering as we pulled into his neighborhood.

"It's okay," I said.

"No, it's not. I don't wanna be like Grampa Len." His whimper turned to a pained moan.

"Who? What do you mean?"

He didn't say anything else coherent after that. Jana stood by the curb with her arms crossed, ticked. I'd hate to be Jay tomorrow, for more reasons than one. Jana was hard-core goth and didn't take any crap.

She and I got him flopped onto his bed without waking his parents, and then Jana drove me home.

"What in the world possessed him to get so hammered?" she asked me.

"The party was a little overwhelming."

"Wait, was this the one out at the lake? Even I heard about that party tonight. Must have been insane."

"It was crazy."

We were quiet for a few minutes.

"Who's Grandpa Len?" I asked.

"Huh? Oh, he mentioned him? Yeah, that's our mom's dad. He was this raging alcoholic. To hear Mom tell it, though, he was the nicest guy sober. She was crazy about him. Everyone was. Then he would drink and it was like he had this evil twin. He hurt a lot of people. He battled his share of demons and eventually lost."

CHAPTER SIX

OUT OF THE DARK DAYS

It was already muggy and hot on our balcony at nine the next morning as I took a sip of my cocoa. There was no breeze, and the smell of cow manure wafted from a nearby pasture. Patti came out with her coffee and sniffed, crinkling her nose. She opened her paper and I opened my book. I couldn't concentrate. Too much had happened at the party last night.

I didn't like thinking about the day of my birth, partly because it was unnatural to be able to remember that far back, and partly because I couldn't make sense of it. I didn't know how it should make me feel, and I didn't want to feel the wrong thing, if that were even possible. But now that Kaidan had picked that scab, it was bleeding and needed tending.

I called the time before my birth the "dark days." Not

because they were bad, but because being in utero was *dark*. It was like being cradled in a warm hammock at night. What I remembered most was the sound of my mother's voice. She was singing the first time I was able to hear the warbled sounds. When I thought to try out my limbs, pushing out to meet the firm, smooth resistance surrounding me, she'd push back and laugh, which bounced me. Jonathan LaGray's voice had been there during my dark days, too, booming gravelly and gruff.

Being born was disorienting—too bright and too cold—but worst of all had been the feeling of having lost some sort of knowledge that had been commonplace during my dark days.

I couldn't see well with my filmy infant vision, but I remember the impact of the man's eyes as they bore down on me that day. They were filled with some of the knowledge that I now lacked.

Just say no to drugs, will ya, kid?

I never knew whether the gruff man's message to me had been serious or sarcastic. I'd never seen him again.

I could still recall the nun, a wrinkled old woman who emitted a pure lavender peace. And Patti, standing over me with her hair falling around her face the day she came to get me. She nearly exploded with love when they placed me in her outstretched hands, as if I were a fragile gift.

That was the only part of the memory I understood, and could therefore cherish freely: the moment I met Patti.

I watched her now as she turned the page of the newspaper and hummed to herself. A train passed by on the hill through a scattering of pine trees.

"I met someone who's like me," I said. The train blew its whistle.

The newspaper slipped from Patti's hands and fell to the floor in a crinkly swoosh. I was taken aback by the black storm cloud of emotion that billowed around her.

"Patti?" I whispered.

"Who was it?" The panic in her voice frightened me. She gripped the edge of the plastic table as if to steady herself.

"I-I don't really know him," I stammered, "but I talked to him last night a little."

"Stay away from him!" She pointed at me for emphasis and stared with giant eyes.

The phone rang inside the apartment as we watched each other. It rang again.

"Get the phone," she said. "I need to think."

I jumped up and ran in, answering on the third ring.

"Hello?"

"Hey," said a weak and scratchy voice.

"Jay? You sound terrible!" I sat down at the kitchen table and glanced out at Patti. She was sitting with her eyes closed, still holding the table's edge, her posture rigid.

"I feel terrible," he said. "How much do you hate me?"

"Don't be crazy, Jay. I was just worried about you. Are you sick?"

"I feel like I got hit by a Mack truck. I don't remember everything, but what I do remember makes me feel like a jackass."

"We were lucky Jana helped," I said.

"Hmph. I paid for that one. She had me up at seven o'clock making her breakfast before she had to go to work. And I'm

76

not talking about a bowl of cereal. I'm talking eggs and bacon and everything! I couldn't even stand up straight."

I held in a laugh as I imagined it.

"What do you remember?" I asked.

"I got mad at you 'cause I thought you were high, so I started chugging a bottle of gin. Ugh. I can't even think about it or I'll get sick. Then everyone was coming up to me and asking if I heard about Scott slipping you a drug, and I just lost it. I only remember pieces after that, mostly me tearing through the place trying to find him. Pretty sure I knocked a few people over. Aw, man, I can't friggin' believe I got so wasted."

"Is that all you remember?"

"Yeah. Why? What else did I do?" I looked over and saw Patti standing now, looking out at the trees with her arms across her chest. I kept my voice low.

"There was a minor occurrence involving you, Scott, and a window."

"Oh, no. Are you serious? Is everyone okay? Did the window break?"

"Yes, it broke, but everyone's okay. Scott had some cuts and his nose was possibly broken, but I think you mostly hurt his ego. Don't your knuckles hurt?"

"Everything hurts. Aw, man. There go my summer savings. I need to call Gene and get that window fixed before his folks get back. But was it even true about the drugs? You definitely weren't acting right when I saw you."

I paused. Yet another moment when I would've preferred to lie. "There was Ecstasy in my drink, and I was feeling it

77

when you saw me, but the full effects didn't stay with me, for whatever reason."

He let out a long, angry sound like a rumble.

"Listen, Jay. I want you to let it rest for now. *Please*. Thank you for sticking up for me, but I don't want you to go after him. I'll deal with it myself when the time is right. 'Kay?"

"Fine," he grumbled to placate me. It hadn't sounded believable.

"Thanks," I said anyway.

"Hey, wait a minute," he said. "What the heck was up with you and Kaidan? I was looking for you when I first heard the rumor, but someone said you left with him."

My tummy wobbled and I looked toward Patti again. She was seriously lost in thought. I whispered now.

"Nothing was up with us. We were talking on the dock. He remembered me."

"Talking about what? I can barely hear you. Is Patti next to you or something?"

"Yeah, sorry. I don't know. We talked about drugs, and our parents. Trying to have a conversation with him is really difficult."

"You two are polar opposites, but it might be good for you. You could use a little fun."

"Oh, please!" I said, forgetting to be quiet for that one second. "It's not like that. I can't explain it."

"Do you like him?" he asked.

"I'm . . . intrigued by him," I confessed.

"All right, all right." He sounded happy. "That's a start."

A start of what, I didn't know, but I wanted to find out.

CHAPTER SEVEN

IDENTITY

Patti was acting so weird that I shut myself in my bedroom with my book. I would read a few sentences, then think about last night, then read more, then wonder what was up with Patti.

She was not usually a hoverer, but for more than an hour she paced back and forth past my bedroom door.

"Are you okay?" I finally called out to her.

She came in looking sheepish, a nervous gray around her. She sat on the edge of my bed. I crossed my legs to give her room and my full attention.

"Anna." She cleared her throat. Her eyes were full of moisture and ringed in red. "The day I picked you up from the orphanage—no, let me go back further. This is all going to sound so strange."

She knew something about me! I grabbed her forearm, greedy for information.

"My whole life has been strange, Patti. If you know something, please tell me. There's nothing you can say that will scare me, or—"

She let out a huff through her nose and shook her head. "*Everything* that I'm going to tell you will scare you. Honey, I've been scared for sixteen years."

I didn't respond. I let go of her arm. The look on her face and the dark gray fear surrounding her made my heart thump harder.

"You've always been a spiritual person, Anna, but I wonder how much you actually see—how much you believe."

"You mean God? I believe—"

"I know. But what about . . . other spirits?" she asked.

"Like ghosts?"

"No. I mean angels."

My neck and scalp tingled.

"Sure," I said slowly. "I know scripture talks about angels up there—singing and trumpets and all that."

"It also talks about angels coming down here to earth. And demons, too."

"O-*kay*. I know that stuff happened back in the day, or whatever, but what does it have to do with us?"

"You know I was married," she said. I nodded, confused about where this was going. Patti stood up and paced the floor as she talked. "For three years we tried to conceive. He eventually went to the doctor and found out he wasn't the problem. That was the beginning of the end for us. I prayed my body would be fixed and we'd be blessed with a baby, but months passed and I never got pregnant. Then one night I had this dream. Actually, I told my husband it was a dream, but I knew it was real."

She stood still and stared at me. I nodded again, wishing she'd just say it, whatever it was.

"An angel came to me, Anna. He told me there was a baby waiting for me at a convent in Los Angeles."

A prickle went up my spine. She came and sat down, putting her hand on my knee as if holding me there, as if I would run from her. She spoke faster now.

"I woke up the next morning and told my husband about it, but he said I'd lost my mind. And, in a way, I had. All I knew was that I had to get to you no matter what. I bought a ticket for myself and I begged him to come with me, but he wouldn't. By the time I got home with you, he was gone. He remarried a year later. But I had you and that was all that mattered to me. Do you believe me so far?"

"Yes, of course." But even so, my brain was rapidly firing denials against the irrational ideas. I took her hands in mine, hoping to calm her.

"Before they let me take you, one of the nuns who ran the orphanage talked to me. Her name was Sister Ruth. She was the oldest person I'd ever met, at least a hundred years old at that point. She told me she'd been waiting for me and she could sense I was the right woman to raise you."

"What was that supposed to mean?" I whispered.

She paused, studying my face. "Raising you would require extra care, because you're more than human, Anna."

81

I'd always known I was different, so why did it sound like complete madness?

"Then what am I?" I asked with apprehension.

"Your parents were angels."

I let out a nervous spurt of laughter, but stopped when Patti didn't crack a smile.

"Your mother was an angel of light, and your father was . . ."

"Was what?"

"A demon."

I had to force myself to breathe.

"That's not possible," I whispered. "You don't really believe that, do you?"

"Every single thing Sister Ruth warned me about has come true. You told me when you were three years old that you remembered being born. And then all of the other things happened one by one, just like she said they would."

"You *knew* about all of that?" I was shocked. No wonder Patti never asked any questions. I'd always thought it was strange that she didn't take me to the doctor for tests when I started getting migraines from the developing senses, given her level of protectiveness over me. I thought maybe she didn't trust doctors with her *special* girl.

"I'm sorry I never told you." Patti choked up now. "It never felt like the right time."

I tried to make sense of it all in my mind. There had to be some logical explanation. But hadn't I been trying for years to come up with logical reasons for being able to do the things I did?

"Maybe she was an insane old lady with psychic powers or something," I reasoned.

"Then how do you explain the supernatural things you can do? She said when you got older you'd be able to see the guardian angels, too."

I thought about that and was struck with a blinding moment of realization.

"The white clouds!"

"You can see them?"

I sat up straight and watched Patti's cloud. It appeared to be laying its misty hand on her shoulder. I couldn't make out any features. It was just a hazy blur. Could it really be an angel? I held out my hand and watched as the cloudy hand flitted down from her shoulder and rested in my palm. I couldn't feel it, but I was overwhelmed with tremendous peace and understanding before it pulled away.

"You see, Anna?" Patti said, watching me intently. "It's all true. There's no one else on earth like you. There are others similar to you, but they're only half of what you are. This is important, Anna. Focus on me." I was still staring at her guardian angel, but I forced my eyes to hers.

"The others who are like you are all children of *demons*, Anna, demons and humans. Raised by those very demons themselves. So that means this boy you met . . ."

Where is your angel? Kaidan's words came back to me.

"He's half demon," I whispered.

It all came together, hitting me sharply in the chest and slithering through me like a flood of cold water.

"I should have told you sooner." Patti's tears came now, but

I was too shocked to cry with her. "I've been selfish. I knew once I told you, there was no going back. Things would change forever. And there are so few of these half demons on earth. What were the chances you'd meet one?"

"I'm not mad at you," I said. I couldn't focus on one particular emotion when so much was firing away inside of me. "I just don't get it. Demons and angels? *Really?* I mean, come on! This is . . . it's . . ."

She walked to my dresser and picked up my Bible. I took a tissue from my nightstand and handed it to her. Patti dabbed her eyes and sniffed, then cleared her throat. She sat down and opened the book in her lap. Passing it to me, she pointed to Genesis, chapter six, verse four. I read it out loud.

"'The Nephilim were on the earth in those days—and also afterward—when the sons of God went to the daughters of men and had children by them. They were the heroes of old, men of renown.'"

I looked up at her, hoping she might explain.

"I've done a lot of research over the years," she said. "The sons of God are the angels. The daughters of men are simply human women. A Nephilim is the child of a heavenly angel or a demon. Demons are merely fallen angels. You are a Nephilim."

The word seemed familiar.

"I thought Nephilim were giants. Like Goliath."

"It does mean giant, but you know how the Bible is." She gave a watery smile. "It's hard to tell what you should take literally and what's only metaphorical. It's easier for people to think of them as a race of actual giant people that have come and gone, or as some genetic mutation. Scripture is full of references to angels and demons, but even believers tend to think of them as fable and fantasy. It's hard to wrap our minds around so many things we can't see."

"But I don't get it. How could angels or demons have children? They're spirits, right?"

"They have to possess somebody."

Eek! Demon possessions. This was getting worse and worse.

"I asked Sister Ruth a lot of questions, and she tried to explain the angelic hierarchy. There are messenger angels, like the one who came to me. The guardian angels are the most nurturing of the souls, chosen for their obedience. They can't interfere in human lives unless they're sent divine power to do so. If it's not someone's time to die, the guardian angels can perform healing miracles or prevent disasters. Otherwise all they can do is try to soothe our pain. It's actually very beautiful to think about." Her eyes stared off wistfully, and I realized she'd spent a lot of time thinking about it over the years.

"I had so many more questions for Sister Ruth, but there just wasn't time. She gave me a message for you." Patti's hands shook as she took the Bible from me and closed it. "She said you'd need to go to her as soon as you were mature enough, which you are."

"Okay, yes. Definitely." I needed to meet this Sister Ruth. "Did she say why?"

"She wouldn't tell me. She has knowledge she'll share only with you, and it would be too dangerous to write it down. She also said you need to . . ." Here she closed her eyes and seemed to struggle. ". . . to see your father."

It took a lot to make me mad, but thinking of my "father" made me angry now.

"I don't want to see him."

"I know. I told her I was against it. The thought of you being in the presence of a demon makes me sick. But I'll tell you what she told me. She believes your parents were in love. And all angels are capable of the full range of emotion, even the fallen ones. So if he could love your mother, an angel of light, couldn't he love you, too?"

I thought of his face on the day of my birth as he watched my mother die and her spirit ascend. Yes, he'd loved her. And his eyes had shown no ill will when they looked upon me that day either. But still. All these years without a single word . . .

"How did the nun know all this?"

"She said she's one of a kind on earth, like you, only different from you and the others, though she didn't explain how. Sister Ruth was definitely special. She had a peaceful presence, like you. I'm sorry I don't have more information, Anna. It was a lot to take in that day."

"It's okay, Patti."

Part of my brain, the realistic part, didn't want to believe a word of what I was told, but the other half, the heartfelt spiritual part, knew without a doubt it was the truth. My heart usually led the way. But I was aware enough to know that when it all sank in, I would be terrified.

"Did she say anything else about, like, my nature?"

"You're not evil, if that's what you're wondering." She grabbed my hand and pulled it to her lap, holding it between both her own. "Your ability to feel other people's emotions comes from your mother. All guardian angels can see and feel human emotions. From your father you'll have a tendency toward a particular sin, but she didn't know which one."

Oh, I was pretty sure I knew. Hello, drugs and alcohol.

"But not evil," I stated, for the record.

"No, honey, not evil. An evil soul rejects the goodness and love naturally embedded in us from being made in the image of our Creator. You'll have to fight harder than the average human against temptations, but you can do it. You're basically a regular girl, but you feel everything stronger, both the good and the bad." She paused, looking down at my hand in her lap and rubbing it. "Do you forgive me, Anna?" she asked. "For not telling you sooner? I always thought it would make things harder on you if you knew, but now I don't know whether I did the right thing."

"I forgive you. I'm not mad." I leaned forward and hugged her. As we held each other, all of her actions during my entire life came into perspective: the extreme protectiveness to sustain my innocence and keep me hidden, the nurturing without question. I squeezed her tighter, realizing how much she'd given up to raise me. She pulled back now.

"This is why I always encouraged you to call me Patti instead of Mom. I know it sounds silly, but I didn't want to take that title away from your real mom when I knew she'd be looking down on you. For all intents and purposes, Anna, you are a daughter to me, and I couldn't love you more."

I wiped a falling tear from under my eye, and whispered, "I know."

"So, I have a plan." She smoothed a hand over my flyaway

hair, becoming practical once more. "I don't have any money saved right now after helping out Nana with her doctor bills, but if I start saving now, we should have enough to make a trip to California by the end of the summer. How does that sound?"

"Great. But I want to get a job, too."

"Deal. It's a date, then." I felt a wave of eagerness as we shook hands. "Now that I've told you everything I know, why don't you tell me all about these superpowers of yours." We both smiled, excited to finally be able to talk about it.

"Oh, wait. One thing, before you start. I need you to make me a promise." Her face went hard. A smoky light gray nervousness blended with the pastel green of hope in her aura.

"Okay."

"Promise me you'll stay far away from the boy you met."

I opened my mouth and hesitated. Her guardian angel, as cloudy as it appeared, seemed to stare down at me, waiting.

"Please, Anna," Patti said. "It's not safe. There are things I can't protect you from, so you've got to make smart decisions to protect yourself."

"But—"

"No." She swiftly cut me off. "I'm not sure what's up with your father, but you can be darn sure the other demons are evil. Pure, *real evil*. And this boy was raised by one of them. Understand? I need your promise."

I swallowed hard. "I promise."

CHAPTER EIGHT

CONSEQUENCES

I could not stop thinking about Kaidan Rowe.

I wondered exactly what it entailed to be the child of a demon. One without the balance of an angel side. He had been helpful and kind to me the night of the party, in his own brutish way.

Knowledge of what I was only fueled the fiery need within me to know more. I had so many questions. Patience was a virtue I'd never had a problem with until now. I needed to stay busy. Getting a job was first on my priority list.

I went to Paula's Dairy Bar just outside of our neighborhood, within walking distance, and was hired on the spot. The owner's only rules: *Smile. And don't give away my ice cream for free!* Yes, ma'am. I could manage both of those.

I worked and tried to keep my mind occupied. I jogged every day, sometimes twice, read a lot of books, and spent time researching on the internet about angels and demons. I had no idea whether anything I read was true or if it was all just folklore.

A month passed, and I now had a couple hundred dollars saved. We were getting closer. But no amount of keeping busy could make me stop thinking about *him*. He was so near. I was sure he had at least some of the answers to my questions. But I had made a promise.

Patti was being her usual cautious self, but if Kaidan intended to hurt me, he would have done it, right? She was imagining him as something terrible, but if she met him, she'd see he was just a kid, only special, like me. I sat tapping the phone with my finger, debating, then picked it up and dialed.

"Hello?" he said.

"Hi, Jay."

"Hey, princess of Popsicles! Queen of curlicue cones."

"Nice alliterations."

"Thank you very much. I try. So, what's up with you?"

"Actually, I was wondering if, um . . ."

"*Yeeees?*" he said. I bit the inside of my lip.

"Is Lascivious playing anytime soon?" I blurted.

Complete silence.

"Jay? Hello?"

"Sorry, I just passed out for a sec."

"Very funny."

"You wanna see Kaidan," he teased.

90

I exhaled into the receiver. "Yes. I do. I want to talk to him. This is going to sound really random, but I think our dads might know each other."

"Really? That *is* random. How do you figure?"

"Just some things he said when I talked to him, and some things I've found out from other people since then. Anyway, are they playing soon?"

"They've been playing venues around the state and in Alabama some. Let me hit up a few people and I'll call you back."

"Thank you."

I hung up and walked around the apartment, straightening things here and there, trying to pass the time. I didn't have any set chores. Patti and I always did whatever needed to be done at the time. I took out a duster and made my way around the house, barely noticing what I touched with it. When the phone rang, I dropped the duster on a shelf and ran.

"Hello?"

"Hey. They're not playing around here for another two weeks, but I know their practice schedule." Jay's band-stalking tendencies were coming in handy. "They practice at Kaidan's place. Greg says there's this whole sweet setup in his basement for the band. According to Greg, Kaidan always has the house to himself."

"Where's his dad?" My stomach dropped at the thought of his demonic father.

"His dad works in New York City. He commutes in his own private jet. Crazy, huh? I don't know how hard it'll be to get into the band's practice, but I can take you, just to see."

That sounded horribly awkward, but it was all I had to work with.

"Okay," I told him.

There were people pouring out of the front doors. Jay had gotten us through the Rowes' private gate by telling the man on the speaker we were friends of Kaidan's. Judging by the number of cars, a lot of people came to watch them practice. It looked like they'd had a miniconcert or a party. Jay stopped his car on the side of the circular driveway lined with vehicles. There was a fountain in the middle of the circle, directly in front of an enormous house made of gray stone, with hundreds of rose vines lining the giant arched doorway and windows. It was as close to a castle as I had ever seen, only there was no Prince Charming waiting inside.

"Want me to come in with you?" Jay asked.

"It might be better if I talk to him alone."

"That's cool. There's this instrument store out here I've been wanting to see anyway. Just call me when you're ready for me to pick you up."

"'Kay, thanks."

I got out and walked up to the door, passing people who were leaving. When I lifted my hand to knock, the door swung open. The lead singer of Lascivious, Michael, stood there in tight black jeans with a swanky girl under his arm.

"Practice is over," he said, brushing past me.

"I just need to talk to Kaidan," I said. He shrugged, walking away.

"Suit yourself," he said over his shoulder. "He's downstairs.

92

Probably busy by now."

I walked into the wide-open foyer filled with gleaming hardwoods and a grand staircase. I felt like an intruder as I followed the sound of voices through a dining room with elaborate china place settings, to an open doorway with carpeted stairs leading down. Two girls in miniskirts came up the steps, one of them stomping her feet and cussing as she went. Sounds of percussion began in the basement, following the girls upward.

"If you're here to see Kaidan," the angry one said, "don't bother." She pushed past me and continued a tirade against him as they walked away. "I am *never* calling him again."

"Whatever," her friend said. "You'll be calling him tonight."

I stopped, contemplating turning around and running from the house. The bang of each drumbeat coming up from the basement matched the deafening thud of my heart in my ears. I forced myself to move forward, and then down the steps one at a time. I stopped at the bottom and surveyed a basement that put Gene's to shame. It was bigger than my whole apartment. I stepped into the massive room and closed the door behind me.

Part of the room to the right looked like a miniature movie theater, complete with three rows of leather stadium seating and a giant screen. Right in front of me in the middle was a tiki bar area with tall tables and stools straight out of a Hawaiian scene. To the far left were two long couches in front of a stage with speakers, microphones, and drums in the center. The drums were currently being used. And used very well, I might add.

He had headphones on. The straight lines of his face were stern with concentration as his arms flexed underneath the bright red T-shirt with each jarring crash of the drumsticks. The beat he created was impeccable. I was amazed by his ability to think just far enough ahead of the sounds in order to place each stick at the exact right place at the right time, all while moving his leg up and down on the pedal in synchronization. It all happened too fast for my eyes to keep up. I was overcome by the beauty of it. I'd never felt such longing. I wanted to . . . to envelop him, wrap him up. Make him mine.

It was a frightful, shameful desire.

With a final crash, the *ting* of cymbals was the only sound. He took the headphones off and dropped them at his side, standing up and looking at me.

"Well, if it isn't little orphan Annie."

He went behind the bar and took a bottle of water from a large fridge. He drank half of it in one gulp, while I stood there unmoving, then tossed the bottle onto the bar and pulled a silver item from the pocket of his jeans. With a fast flick of his wrist, it opened into a blade. My heart stammered. He watched me watching him, twirling the open knife between his fingers. Who played with knives?

In a few easy strides, he closed the distance between us and was in front of me, very close, with his head cocked to the side. I seemed to amuse him, for some reason. But then his face went cruel, and his empty hand rested against the wall above my shoulder. Our faces were inches apart. His eyes held me frozen in place. I was very aware of the knife at his side, held in his other hand. Coming here had been a massive mistake.

"What do you want?" he growled.

"I just want to talk." I tried to keep my voice steady. "You don't have to try to scare me."

He kept a straight face, and his tone was seductively low. "There's hardly any room for fear when you're so bloody turned-on."

A flash of shock hit me at his audacity. His eyes lowered to my body, but he never moved away.

"Ah, there's anger now," he said coolly, "and a bit of embarrassment."

He was reading me—reading my colors! And I couldn't see his at all. I felt stripped bare before him, vulnerable. I concentrated on why I'd gone there to begin with.

"I know what we are now." I wished my voice weren't shaky.

"Congratulations." He stood over me for a second more, savoring his power, no doubt, and then walked away, tossing the knife in the general direction of the dartboard and hitting the bull's-eye. Never missing a beat, he swaggered to a white couch with oversize pillows. He fell back onto it, propping his big, black boots on the white cushions and lounging back with arms spread wide across the back of the sofa. He stared as if daring me to talk.

I had no idea what to say or do. I didn't know anymore why I'd come. Had I just wanted to barge in and say, *Ha, I know what we are!* and then demand information?

His face tilted upward with a jerk and his eyes lost their focus, as if listening to something far away. He jumped up from the couch and rushed toward me. I tried to step back, but he grabbed my shoulders, pressing his lips hard against my ear.

"My father is here!"

Fear paralyzed me.

A demon. A real demon was here, right now. I hadn't factored in this possibility. I'd thought he would be in New York. I wanted to run, but Kaidan pulled me toward the couch and pushed me onto the cushions. He ripped open the front of my blouse, and I sucked in a breath to scream.

Kaidan put a finger hard against my lips to shush me, then grabbed a blanket from the arm of the couch and threw it at me. He swiped his own shirt over his head and motioned for me to take mine off. I didn't know what was going on, but fear prompted me to follow his lead, wiggling out of my shirt while keeping my chest covered by the blanket.

Kaidan leaned over me. Oh, my gosh. A half-naked half demon was burying his face in my neck! His hot, smooth shoulder pressed against mine. A thrill of pleasure shot through my confusion and fear. I felt the heat of his mouth on my shoulder, and gripped the couch cushion with my hands to keep them from going where they wanted to be, which was anywhere on him.

When the basement door was flung open I let out an involuntary yelp. Kaidan pulled away a tad, but stayed in front of me, turning his head to the door.

"Father." Kaidan addressed him in a subdued, respectful tone.

I peered under Kaidan's arm at the tall man who stood there wearing a black suit with a baby blue tie that matched his eyes. His hair was darker than Kaidan's, cut shorter, and gelled back with a gentle wave. He had a red starburst three times the size of his son's. The handsome demon man smiled lightly as he took in the sight of the two of us. It even seemed as if he sidestepped to get a better look at me. I pulled up the blanket that had slipped down and revealed my bra.

"My apologies, son. I didn't realize you had company." As he moved toward me to eye me more closely I could have sworn his eyes flashed red for an instant. His voice chilled the room. "I never imagined you'd care to entertain female Nephilim."

"I don't normally." Kaidan stood now and moved away from me. "She caught me while I was bored and alone after practice."

His father sniffed and wiped his nose, as if there were an unpleasant odor in the air.

"You will come up for tea. Both of you."

He turned and went up the stairs. Kaidan closed his eyes and balled his fists at his sides. My heart was hammering. I rushed to get my shirt back on, pushing clumsy arms through the sleeves, and was horrified to see two buttons had popped off in the middle. I held it shut with trembling hands. Kaidan picked up his red T-shirt from the floor and tossed it at me. I turned away from him and switched shirts. His was gigantic on me, but it was better than exposure. I tried to ignore the fact that it smelled like a total dream: woodsy and citrusy and masculine.

I followed Kaidan up the stairs, attempting to convince myself that having tea with a demon and his knife-slinging son was nothing to be scared about.

We came to a formal living room, where Kaidan's father sat in an armchair and motioned for me to sit on the love seat nearest him. Kaidan leaned against the wall with his arms crossed over his bare chest. His father looked up at him and chuckled low.

"Look at my boy standing there," he said to me. "Such a caveman. Son, find a shirt and join us."

Kaidan walked out as a woman came in carrying a tray with a delicate tea set. She poured three cups of steaming tea, and then looked to Mr. Rowe for approval. He gave her a crooked smile, causing her aura to redden, and then he nodded her away with a pat on her bottom before returning his attention to me. Gah!

"What is your name?"

My throat was too dry to answer on my first attempt, so I swallowed and tried again. "Anna."

"Anna, my name is Pharzuph, but among humans I go by Richard Rowe. I don't think I've ever seen a badge so unusual." He stared at my chest with a bit too much interest, and I had to refrain from crossing my arms. Kaidan came back in wearing a black shirt and sat on the love seat, keeping clear distance between us.

"Do I recognize the color of Belial?" Pharzuph asked. I didn't like how he spoke, as if he were practicing his lazy, sexy drawl on me.

"I . . . I'm sorry?" I asked.

"Belial is your father's dark angel name," Kaidan explained.

"Surely she knows that," Pharzuph scoffed. But as he looked at me he got that same look of confusion Kaidan had worn the night we met.

I coughed and swallowed again, keeping my breathing

even in hopes of calming my aura. I wanted to take a drink of the tea to wet my throat, but I didn't want to spill it.

"I just found out I'm Nephilim. Kaidan explained some things to me."

My voice came out calmer than I'd expected. I was careful to say only that I'd learned from Kaidan. I didn't want to talk about Sister Ruth or Patti.

"And how did the two of you meet?"

"By coincidence," Kaidan answered for me. "She was at one of my gigs."

"I take it Belial has not taught you what it means to be of the Neph race, then?"

"No. We haven't met." I shifted, still in disbelief that I was sitting here explaining myself to a demon who looked so normal.

"I assume he doesn't know of your existence? I daresay he would not have neglected your training otherwise." Pharzuph appeared relaxed, amused even, but his tone was cold and calculating.

I didn't answer, opting for a small shrug. Playing dumb felt like the best option here.

"I can assure you that I will have him informed at once. But in the meantime, you cannot be left unattended. Kaidan will show you the ropes. First things first—you reek of innocence. Yes, that's right. I can smell it—your *virginity*." He said it like a bad word, and my face flushed hot. "Like overripened fruit. Not to mention your emotions hanging about your person for all to see. How old are you?"

"Sixteen."

He leaned forward and smacked his knee with astonished laughter at my answer. "A sixteen-year-old Neph virgin! How do you expect to be a bad influence to humans if you aren't behaving badly yourself? I assume you at least partake in substances with your peers?"

"Yes." Surely I could be given a free pass if I stretched the truth to a demon.

I tried to process all he'd said. A bad influence on humans? Oh, boy. And what had he called me? Neph? Ah, short for Nephilim.

"You must not be partaking enough or you wouldn't still have your virtue. Get my bag, Kaidan."

His bag? That sounded like creep city. Pharzuph picked up his tea and sipped it until Kaidan returned. Pharzuph pushed aside the tea tray and opened the small black bag, laying out vials of powders and liquids, baggies with various dried plants, silver pipes, syringes, and other drug paraphernalia that made my skin crawl with revulsion and need. *Please, please don't ask me to do any of these.*

"Which draws you most?" he asked me.

Steady. It was hard to choose. My hand slid toward one of the powder vials and pointed.

"Cocaine. Very nice." He leaned back and sipped his tea again, eyeing me.

I let myself breathe when Pharzuph's phone rang. He pulled it out, glancing at the screen, and pushed a button to silence it.

"I must return to work. Anna, I trust you won't mind spending time with my son?"

100

I shook my head.

"Of course you won't. Kaidan will take good care of you. He'll have you working to the best of your abilities in no time at all. Don't take too long about it, though. Learn what you need to learn, and get to work." He turned his attention to Kaidan now. "I'm expecting company this evening and you are to join us. Marissa is bringing one of her nieces."

"Yes, Father," he replied, eyes darting away from me.

Pharzuph stood and was dialing as he left the room. Kaidan packed up the little black bag.

"Have you ever been to Lookout Point?" Kaidan asked me. He made an exaggerated nod, as if I should play along. I tried to sound natural, though it felt like I'd just survived a series of small heart attacks.

"No," I said.

"Well, then, that's where we'll go."

We left together in his shiny black Hummer, which felt extremely conspicuous. It was as large as my bedroom. What boy needed a huge Hummer all to himself? As he began driving, he pointed to the odometer and held up five fingers. Five miles? Then he put a finger to his lips. Could his father hear within a whole five-mile radius? I turned enough to peek at the black bag he'd tossed into the backseat as we got in. Kaidan saw me looking.

"You'll love the view at Lookout Point."

"Great," I said, turning back to watch the road ahead. It was a notorious place for losing one's virginity. I was thankful when we passed the turnoff for Lookout Point and I could breathe a little easier.

"It's safe now," he said. "Your friend Jay brought you?"

"Yes. How did you know?"

"I was listening when you showed up, of course. I had to make everyone leave." He sounded put out. I remembered how upset the girl was who'd been kicked out.

"Oh. Sorry. Can I borrow your phone to call him?"

He handed me a high-tech gizmo that I turned in every direction before he took it back and got the touch screen to show a phone keypad. I dialed Jay's number.

"Hello?"

"Hi, Jay. I just wanted to let you know that, um, Kaidan is going to drive me home."

"Ohoho!" I couldn't bring myself to laugh with him, but I saw Kaidan grin out of the corner of my eye. "Sounds good, *chica*. Call me later."

I couldn't figure out how to hang up, so I passed the phone back to Kaidan.

"Where do you live?" he asked. "Here in Atlanta?"

"No. Cartersville. It's over thirty miles away. Is that okay?"

"Yes. He'll expect me to be gone awhile."

My stomach was still churning from the encounter with Pharzuph, not to mention Kaidan's own perplexing actions toward me. He'd been cold and confrontational when I got there. And then his father showed up and he was . . . what? Protective? It made no sense. Even now, he was driving me home instead of taking me somewhere secluded and introducing me to the dreaded black bag, among other things.

"Who's Marissa?" I asked, surprised by my own nosiness.

"Nobody," he snapped. His face went hard and his jaw

clenched. Why was he mad?

"You are the most baffling person I've ever met," I mumbled.

"*Me?!* Neph don't just show up uninvited to one another's band gigs and homes unless they're looking for trouble."

Had he felt threatened by me? The thought was so absurd that I laughed at the irony.

"I didn't even know I *was* Neph until after that party," I said.

"I realize that now."

"Only, you were right. I'm like you, but . . . I'm also not." I paused.

"I'm listening," he prompted.

I'd said too much. I was crazy for wanting to tell him about myself. There was something about him that made me want to abandon all caution. But he was in his father's back pocket, and I shouldn't risk it.

"Never mind," I said.

"No. You may as well tell me now."

"How do I know you won't run back and tell *him*?"

"I don't tell him anything if I can help it. Maybe you didn't notice, but I tried to protect you from him back there. I thought if I could distract him and make him think I was working, maybe he would leave us and not see what you were."

"I did notice." My voice softened. "Why did you do that?"

"I'm not sure." He glanced at me, but pulled his eyes away again, studying the road. "I suppose I wanted to figure you out for myself. I wasn't expecting him home until later this evening. He's usually not home during the week, but I suppose Marissa called him. You caught me off guard when you showed up. I wasn't listening, and that's not like me."

Although I couldn't see his colors, I believed him. Still, I didn't like the insecurity of not knowing for sure.

"Why can't I see your emotions?" I asked.

Kaidan let out a single laugh, as if the answer were obvious. "Because I don't want you to."

He could hide his colors on purpose?

"Is that something you can teach me?"

"I suppose. It would take time to learn, though."

More time with Kaidan wouldn't be so bad. Then I remembered—that was exactly what his father wanted.

"What will happen if I don't, you know, do all of the stuff your father told me to? Because I'm not going to."

"Oh, really?" He sounded amused. "And why not?"

"Because, well, drugs—you saw what they do to me. There would be no moderation. I just can't do it. I won't. And I'm definitely not going to push them on other people. And as far as having . . . you know . . ."

"What?" he asked.

My chest heated and it spread through my face and limbs.

"You're too embarrassed to say it? Sex. Go ahead, give it a go. Sexsexsex."

"Please just answer my question. What will happen if I don't?"

"We could both be punished. If you refuse to be 'trained,' then you'll need to lie low. Don't come to my house again, and don't do anything that might come to his attention. Neph are the least concern of the demons in our world. You'll be forgotten and overlooked within a matter of days. But if he finds out you're still a virgin, you're on your own. I'll tell him I tried and you refused. And you should know that if he does pursue you, and you continue to outright refuse to do as you're told . . ."

I nodded for him to continue, hanging on his words. "What will happen?"

"What do you think? You're dead."

My stomach dropped. Patti had known this kind of danger was out there when she made me promise to stay away from him. How could I have been so reckless? I walked into a demon's den! What if Pharzuph checked up on me and found out I was still a sober virgin?

"I don't get why it's such a problem that I'm a virgin, or why you have to be the one to . . ."

"Would you prefer another?" He spoke seriously, but there were undertones of amusement that irked me.

"No, I mean, it's not that. If it's the two of us, how is that supposed to be a bad influence on humans?"

"It would be part of your training to make you well-rounded in your sinful nature, so you can lure more humans. I don't think it's worth the risk to stay a virgin. I understand you're afraid of becoming addicted to the drugs, but what's your reasoning behind not having sex?"

Geez, could this conversation get any more personal? I squirmed a little in the seat.

"I want to wait until I'm married," I admitted, crossing my legs and uncrossing them again.

He laughed at that. Loudly. I shot him a look.

"I'm sorry. It's just that the thought of a Neph being so pure, getting married, and having a normal human life is . . ."

He stopped laughing when he looked at me. "It's not possible."

This could not be happening. In the course of an hour my life had been altered drastically. My entire future would be forever skewed and shadowed.

"Even most humans don't wait until marriage anymore." He glanced at me through choppy brown hair that hung in his eyes. "Look. It's not time to worry yet. Why don't you tell me this big secret of yours?"

I chewed the inside of my cheek. I was not entirely safe with Kaidan. I knew that. So why wasn't I scared of him? His father was a terrifying and disgusting piece of work, but Kaidan was a different story. I wanted to trust him. I wanted him to trust me.

"My mother was an angel," I blurted. "A guardian angel."

There. I prayed I wouldn't live to regret it.

He looked away from the road to study my face.

"But angels of light aren't permitted to possess humans."

"I guess she broke the rules," I said.

He ran a hand through his hair, letting it flop back down across his brows.

"That's unheard of. Definitely something you should *not* tell anyone else. Wow."

Kaidan began to chuckle then.

"What's so funny?" I asked.

"You. You're a walking contradiction. Horns and a halo. I don't believe it."

I gave a deadpan "ha, ha" at his jibe. Meeting his father had stolen my sense of humor.

"Are there a lot of other people like us?" I asked. "Nephilim?"

"Not really. More than a hundred. Used to be thousands, but that's a story for another day."

I sat there marveling at the thought of others out there who had spent their childhoods developing unusual powers, as I had.

Kaidan slowed at the exit for Cartersville and we both quieted as I pointed directions. He pulled into my neighborhood and parked outside of the apartment building. He looked up at it with skepticism and cut the engine. I wasn't ready to get out yet.

"What does it mean to be Nephilim?" I asked. "How much are we like our fathers?"

He leaned his seat back a few inches and laced his fingers behind his head.

"We feel a pull in the direction of their sinful natures. We're viewed as their property, their pawns. Nephilim work to advance the demonic cause, promoting sin among our peers."

He said it matter-of-factly, as if he had no opinion or feeling about this atrocity whatsoever.

"That is sick."

He ignored me. "The demons have specific jobs. My father is the Duke of Lust. Your father, Belial, is the Duke of Substance Abuse."

His words smacked me, leaving behind a sting. Even though I'd had a feeling about my nature, it still made me ill to hear it. And the son of Lust? He just went up a few notches on the danger scale.

"I can't believe this. It's so wrong."

He continued to ignore me, scrunching his eyes as he'd

done at his house. "Which one of these places is yours?"

I looked up at our apartment and pointed.

"Can you not hear that? Or do you never listen? There's a woman crying in there."

"Patti!" I said. I flung off my seat belt, jumped out of his car, and sprinted for the building, leaving Kaidan without a good-bye.

CHAPTER NINE

To Go or Not to Go

I rushed up the concrete stairs and into our cramped living space, not even bothering to shut the door behind me. Had the demons gotten to her? Patti was sitting on the sofa, and turned when she heard me enter. Her eyes were bloodshot. I went straight to her, crouching at her feet and putting a hand on her arm.

"What's wrong?" I asked.

"The brakes went out in the car today. I'm sorry, honey. I'll have to use all of the money I started saving for our trip." She broke into another sob, wiping at her eyes with her sleeve.

That was it? Oh, thank goodness. I let out a breath of relief and let my head fall back.

In my peripheral vision I saw movement in the corridor

and remembered I hadn't shut the door, but when I stood to close it, Kaidan was standing in the doorway, rubbing the back of his neck. Oh, crap. Crap, crap, *crap*! I didn't expect him to follow me! I moved to shut the door before Patti noticed, but it was too late. She was already looking at him. Then she looked at me.

"Anna?" Patti and I stared at each other with large eyes before she said, "That's him, isn't it?"

"Patti . . . I'm sorry."

She looked at Kaidan as if expecting him to do something threatening, but he only switched his stance from one foot to the other. He looked like he might turn and bolt. Patti stood from the couch and went to the door.

"Well, you may as well come on in," she said with attitude. He stepped in and she closed the door, then put her hands on her hips and surveyed him.

He appeared almost as nervous in front of Patti as I'd been in front of his father. It made him seem younger. What did he think she might force him to do—sing hymns with us? The absurdity of it, plus the knowledge that I was in deep trouble, made the corners of my mouth turn up, a nervous reaction. Patti narrowed her eyes at me, and I pressed my lips together. The silence stretched on and I needed to fill it.

"Patti, this is Kaidan. Kaidan, Patti."

They regarded each other with uncertainty, and then to my surprise she stuck out her hand and he shook it.

"You must be a pretty special young man if Anna is willing to break a promise to see you."

He glanced at me, and I looked down.

Patti turned her full scrutiny on me now. She wore a funny expression as she eyed me.

I remembered Kaidan's red shirt hanging on my frame and my ears got hot. I began babbling an excuse.

"Oh, this!" I said. "This is just nothing. My shirt got torn accidentally, so Kaidan loaned me one of his. I know it looks bad, but it's the truth—I promise." My heart sank as I realized my promises would never again carry the weight they once had. Patti cleared her throat and crossed her arms.

"Can I talk to you alone for a second?" I asked her.

"You can have a seat," she said to Kaidan, voice tight. "Can I get you something to drink?" Of course her Southern hospitality would kick in, even at a time like this.

"No, thank you, ma'am." Kaidan sat in the middle of the couch. He looked out of place in our living room. I glared at him as we turned toward the hall, pointing to my ear and shaking my head. He'd better not listen. Yeah, right.

We went into Patti's room, and before the door had a chance to close, my eyes were welling up.

"Patti, please, *please* forgive me. I feel awful inside. I've never been dishonest with you before, and I'm so mad at myself right now. I mean, I just . . . I knew he could answer my questions, and I knew he wouldn't hurt me. But I didn't know how to make you believe that."

I avoided looking at her guardian angel, feeling guilty enough as it was. I wanted to tell Patti she'd been right. I should never have sought him out. The information I'd learned only made me ill, and I was now in serious danger. But I couldn't tell her that. Ever. She would flip out.

111

Patti's aura shuffled back and forth between pastel pink love and light gray nervousness, landing last on pink. My tears spilled over and Patti pulled me to her. I wrapped my arms around her, needing to soak in every ounce of love and softness she offered.

"I know this is hard on you, Anna, but you can't lose your head. You can't lose who you are in here." She pulled back and tapped a finger over my heart. "Because that's what's important."

I dabbed my eyes with the sleeve of Kaidan's shirt.

"I don't want you to worry about the money, okay?" I told her. "Everything happens for a reason, right? Just fix your car. We'll make the trip as soon as we can."

She nodded and paused, thinking.

"Part of the reason I'm so upset right now is because when they shuttled me home today from the shop, the first thing I did was look up the number to the convent. I've had a bad feeling, and I hate to say it, but I was right. Sister Ruth keeps slipping in and out of consciousness. For goodness' sake, the woman has to be nearly a hundred and twenty years old by now!"

Her eyes locked with mine. "We have to find a way to get you there soon. I'll contact every paper and magazine I know and beg for extra work. If it's not this summer, then you may have to miss a little school in the fall."

"I'll see if I can get more hours at the ice-cream shop, too. We'll make it work. We'll get there in time."

And if we didn't? What would happen if Sister Ruth took the information about me to the grave?

"You know," I said, realizing something, "we could contact my father and ask for money."

"No." Patti's face went rigid for a second. "We'll find a way." She leaned her head to me and whispered, "Do you trust this boy?"

"I trust that he's probably listening to this conversation right now."

"Surely he's capable of being a gentleman and wouldn't do such a thing," she said with false sweetness. I knew she was saying it to him, not me. I wondered how Kaidan would fare against a mother's guilt trip.

"I still don't know him very well, but my gut and my heart tell me to trust him."

"That's good. Your gut and heart are very accurate. He's awfully good-looking, though. That can sometimes muddle things." She kept a straight face.

I shrugged. "He's good-looking, I guess. I know I have to be careful."

She seemed satisfied that I didn't swoon when I spoke of him. "Well, let's not leave him out there forever."

When we returned to the living room he was standing, looking at the wall of photos. I had never once in all my life had cause to feel embarrassed about the cozy place I called home. But as I looked at it then, after being in Kaidan's pristine and luxurious house, everything seemed old and quaint. Patti's artsy black-and-white pictures depicting my childhood that lined the walls were humiliating. He pointed and smirked at the photo of me at age six, where I was missing my front teeth.

I lifted my eyes skyward and sat on the couch. Patti went

into the kitchen and took down some glasses.

"Are you sure I can't get you something to drink? We have sweet tea, and . . ." She shuffled around in the fridge. "Well, that's it besides water."

"Tea would be nice, thank you," Kaidan answered.

I was pleased he'd taken her up on the offer. Patti got miffed when people turned down her hospitality.

Kaidan carefully sat down next to me on the tattered old couch. I remembered him splayed out on the fancy sofa at his house with his boots up, and I found it ironic that he would show our dingy thing more respect.

Patti gave us our drinks and he took a big swig, smiling politely.

"Thank you. I never had cold tea until I came to America."

"Really?" Patti asked. "Yes, I noticed your accent. England?"

"Mostly, yes." He took another drink. "I don't mean to pry, but I heard you mention that the car troubles are interfering with a trip you planned?"

"We are saving for a trip to California," Patti said. Her guard was up. He probably couldn't tell, but I could. She always crossed her legs and sat back when she was comfortable. At this moment she sat up straight and spoke more formally than usual.

"So I can meet my father," I added.

His eyes widened with interest.

"I love road trips. Why don't you let me take you both?"

He could not have surprised me more if he had smacked my face. Patti and I looked at each other in disbelief.

"I've made more money with the band than I know what to do with, honestly. And I have a vehicle. Or we could fly and rent a car if you prefer. My expense."

"That's a very generous offer." Patti chose her words with care. "But why would you want to do that?"

The sea green and gray swirl of emotions Patti gave off were the same ones I felt: grateful, surprised, nervous, skeptical. I wished Kaidan couldn't read us.

"I . . ."

Seeing Kaidan at a loss for words, I felt kind of bad for him. He was a smooth talker, but I knew what it was like to be under Patti's keen eye. She wasn't impressed by charm or wit. She was impressed only by genuine honesty. I hoped he could sense that.

"I don't know," he finally said, puffing out the answer as if it were the last thing in the world he wanted to admit. "I wouldn't normally offer to help someone."

"Unless there's something in it for you?" Patti's question was not laced with sarcasm or judgment, but I opened my mouth, prepared to defuse the situation. I stopped when I saw the two of them having an intense, silent conversation with their eyes.

"Yes." It was blunt honesty from Kaidan, tinged with something else. Surprise?

"I can't leave right now," said Patti. "I have the jubilee parades and the state fair to cover. If I turn down work, they won't keep offering." She stood up, walking to the sliding glass door and staring out of it with her hands on her hips. I could tell she was contemplating something by the way her toe quickly tapped the trodden carpet. "Maybe the two of you should go right away."

What? She was serious! Kaidan sat there like a portrait of innocence, but I knew how he was capable of behaving. I decided then that whatever his true motives were, it didn't matter. I trusted myself.

"I know it's a strange offer." Kaidan spoke to Patti. "I'll admit it; I'm intrigued by Anna." It was the same word I'd used to describe my feelings for him to Jay, and it warmed me all over. "I know other Nephilim, but Anna is . . . different."

"She *is* different," said Patti. "It's important for her to go as soon as possible, or I'd never consider this. She has to be kept safe. I don't want her around your father or anyone else like him."

"I don't want her around my father either." He said it with sincerity. He was really on a roll with the whole honesty thing, and Patti was eating it up.

"How old are you?" she asked him.

"I'm seventeen."

"Don't you have to be eighteen to rent hotel rooms?" After she asked it she shut her eyes, as if the thought of the two of us in a hotel room gave her a headache. Kaidan pushed forward.

"I'm emancipated as a legal adult, since my father travels so often. I have the paperwork. But we don't have to share a room."

Patti paced.

"It still doesn't feel right," she said. "And letting you pay for it—"

"I don't mind. I swear," said Kaidan. "You won't be in my debt."

"You're just kids, though. You have no way to protect yourselves."

"Well, I do have some means to protect us," Kaidan said. "Besides our senses, I mean."

She stopped and stared him down. "What do you mean? Not a gun, I hope."

"No, but I'm pretty good with a knife."

I got a chill at the memory.

Patti crossed her arms. "Really?" she challenged. "Care to demonstrate?"

Oh, boy. What in the world did she have in mind? I myself would not care for another demonstration.

Kaidan stood up and plucked a grape from the bunch on the counter. He handed the grape to Patti and then came back and sat on the other end of the couch from me.

"Just toss the grape across the room to Anna," Kaidan said, placing his hand near his pocket.

It happened so fast. The moment Patti's arm moved, Kaidan had the knife pulled out and opened. I saw the grape coming and opened my hands, but midair there was a whizzing sound and a thump. Patti and I both jumped with surprise. Then we turned our heads and stared at the wall, where the grape was impaled on the end of the silver blade.

"How did you do that?" Patti asked, impressed.

"When I focus with my senses, everything seems to slow down, while my reflexes speed up."

He stood and removed the knife from the wall, catching the sliced grape in his hand.

"I can fix this up for you," he said, brushing his fingers over the mark in the wall.

"No, no. I'll take care of it." Patti stood and took the grape from him, throwing it away.

"Don't go anywhere, okay? I need to think. Just give me a moment."

"'Kay," I said. She went back to her room and shut the door. Kaidan sat next to me again.

"Why are you really doing this?" I asked him.

"For the exact reasons I said." He sounded incredulous that I asked.

I began chewing my nails. Kaidan's offer hadn't been to take only *me*—he said he would take us *both*. That seemed significant. My mixed feelings toward him were clouding my judgment. But Patti was a good judge of character. Her decision would prove to me once and for all whether I should trust Kaidan. If she said no, I would know there was something untrustworthy about him. I sucked on the side of my pinkie finger, where I'd made myself bleed.

"You're nervous," he said.

"Mm-hm."

"You're nervous a lot," he pointed out.

"Yep. Anxiety. All my life."

"I see. Are you nervous she'll say yes or no?"

I paused. "Both."

He nodded once, as if that made perfect sense.

"What's a badge?" I asked. "Your father said mine was unusual."

Kaidan pointed to the red starburst on his chest. "Yours is not a solid color like everyone else's. It's amber, like the color of beer, but it has a swirl of white through it."

"Great," I whispered, renewing my nail chewing. I couldn't

believe I had one of those things, too. And of course mine would have to be weird. I couldn't see it in the mirror; much like aura colors, the badges didn't reflect.

Patti came back out after ten minutes and sat across from us in the recliner.

"Would you prefer to speak in private again?" Kaidan asked.

"That'd probably be best." Patti motioned him toward the balcony. "Do you mind?"

"Not at all." He stood up and let himself out the sliding glass door onto the balcony. Our eyes met and I gave him another *don't listen* glare. He grinned noncommittally and turned away.

I gave my attention to Patti.

"I'm not going to lie, honey," she began. "I'm scared to death to let you go. You haven't made the best decisions lately. I've sheltered you and protected you, and it's made you naive in so many ways—not just about demons, but humans, too. There are people who will take advantage of your sweet nature. I trust you, but you're going to be faced with a lot of hard choices. It's essential you make the right decisions. With all that being said, I don't think Kaidan is going to be one who tries to take advantage of you. I'm going to leave this up to you, Anna. If you're not comfortable, then I don't want you to go. We can go together in a couple months. It's your decision."

She sat in the wooden rocker from my infant days, and held her palms against her cheeks, watching me, encircled in a light gray aura of nervousness.

My decision. I felt woozy. Being stuck in a car with Kaidan

119

for days, being overnight with him—it was what I wanted least and most in this world. I couldn't help but think there was something decent inside him, just waiting to come out. Patti must have seen it, too.

I was intrigued. We could get to know each other. If nothing else, it was a way to see my father and Sister Ruth, sooner rather than later.

So that was it. I'd made a decision. I stood and knocked on the glass door, waving Kaidan in.

We sat back down on the couch across from Patti.

"I'm leaving it up to Anna," she explained.

As if he doesn't know. All eyes were on me.

"I'll go," I told them.

Patti turned on Kaidan then with a mother's ferocity.

"I know I'm just a human woman, but so help me, if anything happens to her while she's with you—"

"I assure you she'll be in good hands."

"Mm-hm, that's part of what I'm worried about." She pointed at his hands. "Hands *off*, mister."

His eyes widened, and so did mine.

"*Patti!*" I said.

She crossed her arms, fierce and serious. We both shrank back a fraction.

"Bring her back to me safely, *with* her virtue intact."

I closed my eyes. *Someone kill me now.*

"Yes, ma'am," Kaidan responded.

I couldn't speak or move because of my hot-faced embarrassment.

"And thank you for doing this," Patti added.

She came forward, sat down next to Kaidan, and hugged him. She *liked* him! He hesitated for a second before wrapping his own arms around her in return. It was one of the strangest sights I'd ever witnessed—an embrace between two people who didn't seem to belong in the same universe, as far as I was concerned. When Patti pulled away, her face was calm.

"So we'll leave in the morning then, yes?" Kaidan raised a lazy eyebrow at me and I shivered, breaking into a cold sweat as I nodded my agreement.

What had I done?

CHAPTER TEN

SENSE OF TOUCH

And so it came to be that at six o'clock the next morning I was flying down I-20 west in the passenger seat of Kaidan Rowe's massive SUV, headed toward California. If we drove all day for three days straight, we could make it in time for this Saturday's visiting hours at the prison.

I hadn't slept well. Patti had been restless all night, giving me the distinct feeling she wanted to call off the whole thing. And then Kaidan showed up, calming her with the reassurance that he didn't have horns and a tail.

I shifted away from the side mirror so I couldn't see the bags under my eyes. I thought about trying to sleep, but I didn't know if I'd be able to relax enough.

Instead I thought of Jay and our conversation last night.

He'd been both excited and worried at the thought of Kaidan and me going on a cross-country trip together. He went back and forth, caught between his starstruck admiration for the drummer of Lascivious and his loyalty to me as a friend. I had to shush Jay when he began singing, "Anna and Kaidan sitting in a tree."

"What are you smiling about?" Kaidan asked.

"Um, just thinking about when I talked to Jay last night."

"Your boyfriend?"

I shook my head, not letting him ruffle my feathers.

"He gave me a joke for you. How do you know if a drummer is at your door?" I didn't wait for his answer. "The knock speeds up and he doesn't know when to come in."

"Pfft. Funny guy, that one."

Kaidan's phone rang.

"I think it's your mum, er, I mean Patti." He handed me the phone.

"Hello?" I said. We were barely an hour into our trip and she was calling already. Not good.

"Oh, Anna. Thank God!" My heart gave a great pound inside my chest.

"What is it? What's wrong?"

"I think you should come back home."

"Why?" I held my breath and pressed a hand to my chest.

"This was a bad idea. Please just turn around . . ." She was starting to ramble in that nervous way of hers. I exhaled.

"Patti, you scared me to death. I thought something happened. Look, everything is—"

"No! Don't you tell me everything is *fine*!" I looked over at

Kaidan, who was biting his lip. I put a palm to my forehead. "I can't believe I let you go," Patti said. "I'm so sorry. I'm the worst mother ever. Just come back home. I'll get ahold of your father and ask for money. . . ."

When she started crying, I angled my body toward the window and leaned forward, trying to think of a way to calm her. I kept my voice moderate and mild.

"Please don't ask me to come home, Patti. You did the right thing. I need to meet Sister Ruth and my father. It's time. I'll call you every hour, if it'll make you feel better."

She was absolutely bawling now. My heart clenched to hear her pain, and my eyes burned.

"You're the best mother ever," I assured her. "Please trust me on this. We made a good decision."

She let out a deep sigh. "If anything, and I mean *anything* happens," she said, "you'd better call me right away. I don't care what I have to do to get the money, but one of us will be on an immediate flight to the other. You hear me?"

"Yes, ma'am."

When that awful conversation was over, I couldn't look at Kaidan as I passed the phone back to him. I crossed my arms over my chest and watched the miles pass through the tinted windows, hating the idea that Patti was sitting at home giving herself an ulcer.

We were coming up to a sign: WELCOME TO ALABAMA.

"Oh, yay!" I said without thinking.

"What?" He looked at me funny and my cheer deflated, chagrined.

"State border. I've never been out of Georgia."

"Never? You've been in one state your entire life?"

I nodded my head. "Well, except for the first weeks of my life."

"That's incredible."

Alabama looked a whole lot like Georgia, I thought with disappointment.

Starting at ten in the morning, Kaidan's phone chimed at least every fifteen minutes with text messages. He read each of them, propping one hand on top of the steering wheel. The messages made him smile, or laugh, or frown, but he never responded to a single one. And when his phone rang, he looked to see who was calling, but never answered. After about the tenth message and call, I wanted to throw the thing out the window.

"Would you like me to drive so you can manage your social life?" I asked. It came out much snippier than I'd intended, but he was oblivious to my tone, still looking at his newest message.

"No, no, I'm fine."

"We'd better not get in an accident because you're busy sexting and driving," I said. He burst out laughing.

"I've got my hearing senses on—the car in front of us is two and three-quarter car lengths ahead, and the one behind us is a quarter of a mile back. Next to him a compact car is passing. Engine sounds foreign, probably a Honda. He'll be passing us in about twelve seconds. He's got extra-thick treads, racing-quality tires. *Sexting . . .*"

He laughed again. Twelve seconds later a Civic zoomed past, low to the ground, with wide tires. Show-off.

He pointed out the signs to each state as we entered: first Mississippi, then Tennessee, where we read all of the signs for Elvis stuff and Kaidan did a horrible impression. He smiled when I made fun of him, a real smile that made his eyes squint in the cutest way. The sight made my heart squeeze.

We were quiet again all the way into Arkansas, where we stopped. The gas guzzler needed a refuel, which Kaidan called *petrol*. He handed me his phone so I could check in with Patti. I kept the conversation upbeat and short as I walked around the asphalt, stretching my legs. To my relief, she didn't cry again, and I hung up just as Kaidan was finishing.

"Four new states in one day," he said when we got back in. "We're covering good ground."

"Yeah," I agreed. "Let me know if you need me to drive."

"I'm good for now. You can get out some of that grub, though."

Patti had packed a cooler with all sorts of stuff: drinks, four types of sandwiches, homemade muffins and brownies, and fresh fruit in plastic containers. She'd been busy last night. We ate while we drove. Kaidan couldn't find a station he liked on the radio, so he plugged in his own music player and blasted it. The bass vibrated my seat, but I didn't mind loud music. It was nice, because I always had to keep the volume low in our apartment. Plus, with the music so loud we didn't have to worry about trying to talk. As the hours ticked by, any remnants of awkwardness between us eased.

Partway through Arkansas we hit the worst thunderstorm I'd ever experienced. The sky was black with clouds, and the rain pelted the car as hard as pebbles. Lightning lit up the air like an eerie moment of sun in a warped dream, and then thunder shook the earth as we were pressed back into darkness.

I admitted to myself I'd probably be afraid if I were with someone else, but with Kaidan I felt safe. It was a false sense of security, since even he couldn't save us from a tornado. But Kaidan used his extra senses to see and hear, while other cars had to pull over to the side of the road. The storm seemed to go on for hours.

We passed through Little Rock and the storm turned to a steady rain without thunder, and then a faint sprinkling. The weather felt spookily calm after the storm, and I half expected a twister to jump out in front of us and sweep us away. What I saw instead took my breath away.

"Look!" I pointed at the brilliant rainbow stretching all the way across the wide sky. I'd seen lots of small rainbows at home, blocked by trees, but the entire arch of this one was visible.

"Hmm," I heard him say, giving the rainbow a momentary glance.

I was way more impressed by everything on the trip than Kaidan.

"Does your father know you're on this trip with me?" I asked.

"No. We spoke for a minute before he left this morning. He knows I'm going on a trip with a particularly stubborn virgin, but that's all I told him. He commended me for my valiant efforts, although he thinks it's too much time to spend with one girl. He expects her to be good and deflowered by the end of our time together."

"Well, he'll be good and disappointed then," I mumbled, and he smirked.

I crossed my arms over my chest, wanting to say something that would knock the smirk from his face.

"Did you have fun with Marissa's niece last night?"

It worked.

"No." His tone was hard.

I left it at that, but wondered what the story there was.

By the time the drizzle completely stopped, it was dark out, and we were eating again. Kaidan had almost cleared the contents of the cooler. Patti was lucky she didn't have a teenage boy to feed; she'd never afford it.

"We should probably stop soon," he said. I nodded in agreement.

"I suppose we should get separate rooms," he offered.

My stomach lurched. I wasn't going to let anything happen with Kaidan. It seemed wasteful to make him pay for separate rooms just to satisfy my prudish modesty and Patti's overprotectiveness.

"We can share a room as long as it has two separate beds," I compromised. "And we won't mention it to Patti unless she asks."

"Fair enough."

He pulled off at the exit for Webbers Falls and found the town's only motel, the Shining Armor Inn, which was anything but shiny. Not that I cared, but Kaidan appeared apprehensive.

"Looks a bit dodgy."

"It'll be fine," I assured him, though I imagined we'd be

sharing the room with several bug families.

While he checked in, I stayed in the car and called Patti to tell her where we were. She wanted to know every detail about Kaidan. I promised her he was being kind. I told her about the rainbow, and about Kaidan's appetite, which she thought was funny. He came back to the car with a plastic key card.

"Okay, well, I'll call you tomorrow, Patti."

"All right then, sweetheart. Have a good night. I love you."

"I love you, too. Bye."

I hung up, having learned the basics about his phone, and handed it back to him. He paused in front of me.

"Do you always say that?" he asked.

"Say what?"

"That you . . . *love* each other?"

"Oh. Yeah, we always say it."

He nodded thoughtfully, and pulled our bags from the backseat. It dawned on me sadly that Kaidan might have never said those words to anyone, nor heard them from anyone in his life, except maybe girls. We walked together, looking at the room numbers as we passed them.

Inside the small room we dropped our things, kicked off our shoes, and fell onto our beds. Kaidan took the bed by the window, and I was by the wall, with the bathroom on the other side. I peeked around the room. No roaches scuttling by.

Before long we'd both turned over, lying on our sides to face each other across the space between us. I was propped on my elbow watching him play with one of his knives. I cringed as he spun it on his palm, then wove it fast between his fingers and spun it on top of his knuckles.

"It makes me nervous when you do that," I said.

"I can tell. I haven't cut myself since I was a small child, so don't worry."

"You've been playing with knives since you were a small child?"

"When I was seven I came home from school after my first fight—the brother of a girl I kissed on the playground. My father gave me a switchblade and told me to learn to protect myself, because there would be many fights to come."

"He wanted you to use a weapon in fights at school? Against other children?"

"No, no. Just preparation for defending myself when I got older, like now."

"Was he the one who taught you to use it?"

"No, I taught myself with practice. My father doesn't use a weapon. Not a physical one, anyway. He uses his influence to get himself out of situations, and he has other demon spirits who watch his back."

"Have you ever needed to use it?"

"A few times." His tone was flippant, like it was no biggie. "Only flesh wounds. No need to kill anyone. That's not my sin."

He winked at me and whipped the blade closed. Time to change the subject.

"Were you scared when your senses started getting crazy?" I asked.

He rolled to his back and rested his head in his hands, crossing his ankles.

"Scared? No, but I knew it was coming. I take it you did not."

I shook my head and he continued.

"My father was all but nonexistent my first five years, but he came home for a week before I turned six to explain 'the extraordinary changes that would set me apart from humanity.'" He mocked his father's serious tone. "He taught me how to control each sense and use them to my advantage over humans. I learned fast. I wanted to . . . please him."

"And did you?"

He grimaced up at the ceiling. "If I did, he never told me. But when I turned thirteen he began staying home more, taking an interest in my involvement in his work. I took it to mean he was proud. I felt useful."

"So, before he came back around, did you have a nanny or someone who raised you?" I imagined a Mary Poppins type singing to him and showing him gentleness.

"I had many nannies, but they were all preoccupied with thoughts of my father. He made sure of that. None of them stayed for more than a year, six months on average. When they became too overbearing, they were replaced. He bores easily."

So much for a spoonful of sugar. I felt a familiar anger at the thought of Kaidan's father: the same anger I felt toward my own father. Kaidan looked in my direction.

"You really should try to control your emotions."

I couldn't get used to the fact that someone could see my colors.

Kaidan's phone beeped again. I gave it a stare filled with

131

loathing and he grinned at my expression.

"Would you like me to turn it off?" he asked.

"Yes, please. Otherwise it'll be going off all night."

"Quite right," he said, turning it off with a chime sound and putting it on the nightstand. "Which is your favorite sense, little Ann?"

Ann. He'd called me by a nickname. That shouldn't have warmed me so, but it did.

I focused on his question. My senses hadn't been something I'd ever considered enjoyable, certainly not worthy of ranking for favoritism. It was hard to get past what a painful burden they'd been in the beginning.

"The smells can be really nice," I said. "Until you get a whiff of skunk or something. Um . . . the sight is useful, getting to read signs from so far away and stuff."

He gave me a skeptical look. "You never use them, do you?"

"Not very often," I confessed. "I like to pretend I'm normal."

"Why?"

I shrugged, intimidated by his confidence.

"You didn't mention your sense of touch," he said.

"Ugh, no. But let me guess—that's *your* favorite."

He climbed off his bed with graceful movements and came to sit next to me. I scrambled to sit up, but he put a hand on my arm.

"No, stay lying down. I want to show you something."

I eyed him with suspicion and he laughed.

"Calm down, luv."

"What are you going to do?"

132

"Nothing that will compromise your virtue and have Patti hunting me down. Now close your eyes."

I huffed a little, but I *was* curious. Maybe he could show me something useful. I set my hesitation aside, lying back and closing my eyes, but stayed ready to move if necessary.

"Now, I want you to relax and concentrate on your sense of touch. I'll be a good boy. I promise."

Just an exercise to build trust, right? Oh, what the heck?

I took a deep, calming breath and pushed out my physical sense from within me. Scalp. Neck. Shoulders. Tummy. Back. Hips. Thighs. Calves. Ankles. Toes. All tingling.

I felt the tiny grooves of thread crisscrossing in the fabric of my cotton shirt and jean shorts. The motel comforter was scratchy with thousands of polyester prickles. Stray hairs from my ponytail tickled my temples and neck. And then, oh! I sucked in a breath, but managed to keep my eyes closed as one warm fingertip pressed into the palm of my hand. I concentrated on it.

"I can sense your fingerprint!" I whispered.

He didn't answer. He lifted his finger from my palm, and a second later my foot was in his hands, throbbing with sensitivity. His fingers moved each little toe between them with the perfect amount of pressure so it wouldn't tickle, moving on to the pad of my foot, arch, and heel, all neglected muscles that sang at the divine attention. He moved up and my ankles reveled under his sculpted hands.

Sudden panic overtook me as I realized he was about to move up to my calves. I hadn't shaved!

"Wait," I said, sitting halfway up. "Not my legs. They're . . ."

I was too embarrassed to finish.

"They're lovely." His face was straight, but his eyes were smiling.

"No, please." I pulled my knees protectively up to my chest and mumbled, "I didn't have time to shave this morning." Now he laughed. It was a marvelous sound, so rich.

"All right, fine, no legs. But you're missing out. I'm not through with you. Roll onto your stomach and relax again." I obeyed, letting my arms lie limp at my sides and closing my eyes. Somehow it seemed a little safer to be on my tummy.

"Mmm." He moaned, having not even touched me yet.

"What?" I asked, muffled by the poofy pillow.

"Oh, nothing. It's just that you've got quite a nice little—"
I flipped to my side, glaring hard. He put up his hands.

"Sorry! A guy can't help but notice. Truly—best behavior—starting now."

I mentally crossed out that last thought about being safer on my stomach as I rolled onto it, taking longer to unwind this time. When he spoke, his deep voice was a smooth rumble.

"I need you to trust me and stay relaxed. I'm just going to raise your shirt a bit so that I can get to your back." I shivered at the tug of my shirt upward and the cool air brushing my bare skin. But it was nothing compared to the shiver I experienced as all ten hot fingertips found the small of my back, working in slow circles across my skin. He lifted them so they barely touched me. Every hair follicle on my body stood upright. All thoughts of protesting disappeared. And just when I didn't think I could take the teasing of his feathery touch for a second longer, his palms pressed down on my back muscles, strong thumbs circling outward from my spine to my waist. I stifled a moan of pleasure.

Okay, maybe he had a point about the sense of touch being worthy of favoritism.

With an expert movement, his stealthy hands went up the back of my shirt, past the uncomfortable bra clasp that dug into my skin, fingers tracing my shoulder blades. The tense muscles spasmed weakly, then turned to Jell-O under his touch. His hands were now on my shoulders, my shirt stretching. One of his hands came out to move my ponytail of hair to the side. And then there was the very best feeling so far: his lips on the back of my neck.

He was kissing me. On my neck. I should stop him, I thought, but the softness of his mouth was so . . . Oh. I could feel the beauty of each crease on his lips as they rested against the pores of my skin. The only sounds in the room were our beating hearts and breath. Why did he have to smell so good? Would it be so wrong to kiss him? Just one small kiss? I couldn't think straight.

I tried to gain control of my breathing as his hot mouth opened and moved under my ear. I tilted my head to give him better access. *Bad!* Each taste bud on his tongue gave its own gentle massage. Lips were now on my jaw, and I could smell him, the earth and brine and sweetness of his skin. In that moment, I fooled myself into believing I was in control—that a quick kiss would be no big deal. I turned to him, bringing my arms up over his shoulders, moving my fingers over the hair at the nape of his neck, and pulling his face up the last few inches to my waiting lips.

Kissing was far more blissful and intimate than I'd dared to let myself imagine. His cheeks and chin were rough, but our lips were soft together, careful and slow. I felt his hunger as his lips moved a bit harder, which I found that I wanted. His hand went to my waist, outlining my hip. I could have kissed him all night. It was the most wonderful feeling in the entire world. The tip of my tongue rippled against the smooth ridges on his in a playful, tantalizing sensation. I was so content with this kiss. But it was not enough for him.

His hand trailed up under my shirt, against my belly and rib cage, landing on the small curve of my bra. With one slight squeeze of his hand, the spell was broken and I was pulling my mouth from his. I reeled in my sense of touch with a tight snap.

My hands went from his hair to his chest, pushing him away and sitting all the way up. When Kaidan looked at me, lust raged in his eyes like a tumultuous island storm. He leaned in to kiss me again, but I held my arms out against his chest. His red starburst was throbbing and spinning right in front of me, as large as I'd ever seen it.

"You promised to be on your best behavior," I reminded him, breathless.

"*You* kissed *me*, Anna," he growled. His voice had gone very deep.

"Well, but you started it by kissing my neck."

"True. I hadn't planned that." His sultry voice, paired with those blazing eyes, told me I needed to get away from him. I hurried to the end of the bed, where I jumped off and began to pace back and forth, yanking out my loose hairband and pulling my hair back into a tight ponytail. I tried hard not to think about the taste of his lips. I'd had my first kiss, and I'd never be the same.

"Why did you stop?" he asked.

"Because you were moving on to other things."

He scratched his chin and cheek. "Hmm, moved too quickly. Rookie mistake."

I crossed my arms again, watching him speculate internally like a coach outlining a play that had gone wrong. Incredible. Then he sized me up in his sights again.

"But I can see you still want me."

I gave him my meanest stare, but it was hard to look at him. Gosh, he was hot! And a total player. The kiss meant nothing to him.

"Oh," he said with mock sadness, "there it goes. Mad instead? Well, sort of. You can't seem to muster a really good anger—"

"Stop it!"

"Sorry, was I saying that out loud?"

"I can read people, too, you know. Well, not *you*, but at least I have the decency to try not to notice, to give them some sort of emotional privacy!"

"Yes, how very decent of you." He hadn't moved from his languid position on my bed.

I leaned forward, grabbing a pillow and throwing it at him.

"Pillow fight?" He raised an eyebrow.

"Get off my bed. Please. I'm ready to go to sleep."

He stood up and made a grand arm gesture toward the bed. I crawled onto it, climbing under the scratchy covers and turning my back to him. I realized then that I was still wearing my clothes, but I was not about to get up. I could feel his eyes on my back.

"But I thought we might get naked, just like Adam and Eve, so natural. . . ."

I gasped. I'd forgotten all about that part of my conversation with Scott! Utter humiliation. I curled into a tighter ball.

"Oh, come on. You haven't even thanked me yet."

"For what?" I asked, still not looking.

"For saving you from snogging that plonker. You didn't really fancy him, did you?"

My cheeks burned, and I was glad to be turned away from him. I kept my mouth shut.

"So that's it, then?" he asked. I ignored him. "I always wondered what it would feel like."

That made me curious enough to turn to him.

"What *what* would feel like?" I asked.

"Rejection." He seemed in the midst of a revelation.

"What are you saying? That no girl has ever told you no?"

"Not one."

Well, that explained a lot.

"And what about you?" I asked. "Haven't you ever stopped or said no to a girl?"

He laughed as if I'd said something ridiculous. "Why would I do that?"

"Lots of reasons," I said. "Never mind, just go to sleep. We have a long day tomorrow." I turned away from him again, punching the thick pillow and laying my head down.

"I suppose I did refuse one, but she doesn't count," he said.

"Why not?"

"Because she was Neph."

Discomfort gnawed at me.

"This must be the part where I take a cold shower?" he asked.

"Good idea."

When he was in the bathroom with the water running, I jumped down and changed into my pajamas. Then I leaped back into bed and chanted to myself, *Don't think about the kiss. Don't think about the kiss.* Impossible.

I lay very still with my eyes closed when he came back in the room. A clean-scented steam passed over me. I listened as he rummaged around the room for a few minutes, then I heard the door to our room open. I sat up in bed and saw Kaidan in the doorway.

"Where are you going?" I asked, just as he was shutting the door.

He looked up. "I have to work."

Why did I feel so stunned, and a little offended, too?

"Have to? Or want to?" I challenged.

"Why should that matter, Anna?" he asked dryly. "I'm going now." He made a move to shut the door.

"Where will you go?" I called out.

"I'll go visit the girl at the front desk, just as she suggested. So unless you've changed your mind . . . ?" His eyes held a promise of seduction, and I shook my head.

I had not changed my mind. There would be nothing more going on in this room. But I wanted him to stay. I looked down at the itchy comforter.

"Didn't think so," I heard him mutter. Then he switched off the light and closed the door hard.

I lay there trying not to imagine what the girl at the front desk looked like, and how his lips would soon be on hers. I growled in frustration at my own stupidity, and flipped to my other side.

I wished I could fall asleep and put this episode behind me, but no matter what I tried I couldn't get comfortable. I considered turning on the television, but I didn't want Kaidan to know my traitorous heart was waiting up for him.

An agonizing two hours later, he came back and I lay very still, pretending to sleep. He went straight into the restroom to wash up. A few minutes later he climbed into his bed and got quiet.

"Anna?" His voice was low. Of course he knew I was awake. I didn't answer, but he was undeterred. "Did you at least enjoy your first kiss?"

I wanted to tell him to shut up, but the burst of anger tapered away.

"Just go to sleep, Kaidan."

I chewed the inside of my lip, confused. Why couldn't I stay mad at him? Thinking about what he'd just been doing filled me with a range of dreadful emotions, but anger was not one of them. I had no right to be angry. It'd been stupid to assume he wouldn't work while we were on this trip together.

I was relieved to have him back in the room. He sighed, and after a while it was clear he wasn't going to say anything else. The tension dissolved.

That night I tossed and turned, replaying my first kiss at least a thousand heavenly times.

CHAPTER ELEVEN

A Healthy Fear

Neither of us had thought to set the alarm, but the bright sunlight coming through the thin curtains worked fine. I stretched and kicked the tangled bedsheets away, turning to see whether Kaidan was awake. His eyes were blinking open, too. He yawned, causing me to yawn as well. I could have used another few hours of sleep, but this would have to do for now.

Kaidan leaned back against the headboard with his eyes closed. Each lean muscle was noticeable under his tanned skin. I got a decent tan in the summer, but nothing like him. It made me wonder about his heritage, which could have been anything from Italian to South American. He probably didn't even know himself.

While his eyes were closed I stared unabashedly. His

shoulders were rounded and his forearms tight. His entire torso was a sight to see—a toned chest angling downward to his abs with a slight ripple, but he wasn't cut in a way that might make a girl feel self-conscious of her own imperfections. His waist went down in a vee at his hips, where it met the hotel blanket.

I tore my eyes away when he stirred. From the corner of my eye I saw him throw the blankets easily aside and scoot to the edge of the bed by the window. He stood up, facing away from me, and raised his arms for a glorious stretch. When I looked again my eyes landed on his bare behind.

Dear God!

I screamed and buried my face in my pillow.

"What?!" I heard him ask. "Did you see a roach?"

"Why are you naked?!" I did not dare lift my red face.

"Huh. Is that all?" he asked. "I always sleep in the buff. I don't know how you can stand all that clothing."

"*Un*believable," I said. I pulled myself up and stomped to the bathroom.

We'd been on the road for over one hundred miles and had yet to speak. Kaidan rummaged forever through the local radio pickings. When we heard, "I'm bringing sexy back . . ." he gave a small chuckle and shake of his head before turning the station again and settling on an angsty female rocker.

I stared out the window at the edges of I-40 lined in green brush. We passed ranches and farms, some modern, some leaning and abandoned. We must have seen every breed of cattle known to man along the way.

"Hungry?" Kaidan asked. I shrugged, then nodded.

He pulled into the almost empty lot of a pancake restaurant. Inside, we seated ourselves in a booth with cracked cushions. A tired-looking waitress, not much older than us, approached. A heat of contentment rose from her womb to greet me.

"What can I get you to drink?" she asked, unfriendly.

"Coffee," said Kaidan.

She looked to me.

"Hot chocolate, please."

She walked away to get our beverages.

"She's pregnant," I whispered.

He looked at her and shook his head.

"Doesn't look like it," he said.

That didn't mean anything, though. Sometimes people didn't show until the middle of their pregnancies. A girl at school hid it from everyone until her sixth month.

"I can sense the baby, can't you?"

"No."

Maybe it was my imagination, but he seemed a little put out that I could do something he couldn't. We both watched her from behind as she filled the mugs. She herself was not content, shrouded in gray.

She brought our drinks and took our orders. I tried to smile at her, but she avoided my eyes.

Kaidan drank his coffee black. I skimmed the whipped cream off my cocoa with a spoon and ate it all before speaking. I was already dreading what I had to say.

"Kaidan . . . do you think you could try to be a gentleman,

at least while we're traveling together, and maybe wear shorts to bed?"

"Ahh . . . I see." He sat back. "The sight of my arse gave you quite a fright, did it?"

"I'm being serious," I told him.

He took a drink of coffee. "For the record, I'm not a gentleman, but I'll make an exception this once. No more sleeping nude while traveling together. Satisfied? Now you can stop with the evil eye. Look—here comes our food."

My stomach growled at the sight of my pancakes with a big scoop of butter melting on top. But it was Kaidan's meal that made my eyes bulge. Pancakes, scrambled eggs, sausage, bacon, ham, grits, and toast! It took three plates to accommodate it all. He grinned at me and dug into it.

I was famished. We ate every bite, and then leaned back in the squeaky booth, feeling dopey on food overload.

Kaidan sat up abruptly and a look of gloom passed over his face. He motioned at me to duck lower in the booth, so I slid downward. The fearful look in his eyes reminded me of when his father had come home.

"Here comes trouble," he whispered. I started to turn my head but he hissed, *"Don't look!"*

"Where?" I asked. I was looking just at him now. He tilted his head in the direction of our waitress behind the nearby counter.

"Cover your badge," he whispered. I looked around and snatched up the dessert menu, holding it in front of me.

I waited a second, then moved my eyes toward the waitress. She was pouring water into the coffeemaker. Her hand shook as she poured. Then she stopped to steady herself on the counter. Her hazy gray darkened, and her chin quivered. The thing that struck me most was that her white cloud, her guardian angel, was erratic, jumping around in agitation. I'd seen them do that before on occasion, but I didn't understand why. After a moment it calmed.

The cook behind the window asked the waitress a question about an order and she snapped a response.

"It's gone," Kaidan whispered with relief.

"What just happened?" I asked.

"The demon spirit. You couldn't see him?"

"I didn't see anything." I looked around, pressing myself smaller into the booth.

"All Neph have the ability to see them. You must not be willing."

Our waitress came to us with undisguised impatience.

"Anything else?"

"No, thank you," I told her. "Everything was good."

She smacked the check on the table and took away our dishes without another word. Kaidan dug his wallet from his back pocket and laid a twenty on top of the check.

"Do you think she's mad at us?" I asked. Although I could see emotions, I had no way of knowing their source.

"Why would she be? She's frustrated because she can't comprehend why she's feeling a surge of dark emotion out of nowhere. She'll most likely try to place the blame on something—usually another person, lack of sleep, hormones, anything—rather than dealing with the emotion. And thus begins the cycle."

"So you're saying"—I leaned toward him to whisper across the table—"that our waitress was just visited by a demon?"

He nodded, arranging the salt, pepper, sugars, and condiments in a neat row.

I thought about our bill and did the math in my head. She was getting about a five-dollar tip. Something told me her troubles began with money. I dug a ten-dollar bill from the savings I kept in my pocketbook and placed it on top of Kaidan's twenty.

"You know you can't buy happiness," he said to me. He was so devilishly handsome that I shivered and cleared my throat. I looked back at our waitress, whose guardian angel seemed to be embracing her.

"Are the guardian angels always with them?" I asked, still watching it.

"Yup. They're with their humans when they visit the loo . . . even when they're having sex."

I closed my eyes and shook my head. "You just had to go there."

"You asked. And don't worry. They're way too pure and obedient to be voyeurs."

It felt disrespectful, talking about the angels like that. I tried to think of another question.

"So the demons who visit people are in spirit form?"

"That's right. Good thing this is a long trip. I have a lot to teach you."

He stood, so I followed, just as our waitress came over. She eyed the two bills on the table.

"I'll get your change," she said.

147

"No, it's yours," Kaidan purred. He looked at her too long and her colors went from the pale green of gratitude to a rush of red.

"Yes, thank you again!" I said, louder than I'd meant to. "Have a great day!"

I nudged Kaidan's ankle with my foot and he moved. We walked out into a beautiful Shawnee, Oklahoma, morning with our feet crunching loose pebbles in the pavement.

"This is going to be a long trip if you give girls the bedroom eyes every time we stop." I tried to keep my tone light.

"Bedroom eyes?" he asked. We were climbing up into his car now. He sat in the driver's seat and turned toward me. His hair flopped over his forehead, curling up at the ends against his brows. There was no roundness to his face—it was all squared-off edges. But it was those blue eyes that did it for me.

"As if you don't know what you're doing," I said.

"I'm working."

Hmph. Well.

"That poor girl has had a bad enough day without you filling her head with ideas, too." I pulled on my seat belt with more than the necessary force and he started the car.

"I think she's perfectly capable of coming up with ideas on her own. One might think you're jealous, talking like that, but I can see you're not. It's uncanny. You're actually concerned for her?"

"Why is that so hard to believe?"

"You don't even know her," he pointed out.

"It *is* possible to feel compassion for strangers."

"She's gotten herself pregnant out of wedlock," he said.

148

"She made her own choice."

"We don't know her circumstances."

He followed the signs back onto I-40 west, and I could sense the argument was over.

"Why did you say I'm unwilling to see the demons?" I asked.

"I'd venture to say you've not opened yourself to evil. You have to be willing to really see it and accept it for what it is."

"I don't want to be open to evil. I don't even like to watch the news. I know it's out there, but the details hurt too much—feeling all of those people's suffering."

He gave me a quizzical glance. "What do you mean, 'feeling their suffering'?"

"I'm not always good at blocking their emotions, especially if it's a big group of people with a lot of dark emotion. I try to push it away, but sometimes it still seeps in, and it hurts."

"You mean you actually *feel* the emotions they emit? Not just see it?"

"Yeah," I said, "don't you?"

"No! I can only see their colors. Feeling them must be an attribute from your mother."

"Oh." I didn't know what to say to that.

"Wait," he said, the threat of a smile on his face. "Does that mean you feel lustful every time somebody near you feels it?"

"No, pervo. It's not like that—it's more like an unsatisfied longing for something. It's uncomfortable."

"Hmm. Too bad. Well, no offense," he said, "but you'll need to toughen up a bit. It would benefit you to see demons and know what they're up to."

He was right. I knew I would have to deal with it, but right now I was focused on getting information.

"What exactly do the demon spirits do?" I asked.

"They whisper not-so-sweet nothings into human ears." He drove with one hand. The other hand twirled a pen back and forth between his fingers without much attention to it.

"What do you mean?"

"You know the little voice in your head?" he asked. "The one humans like to call their 'conscience'?" I nodded. "It's actually the messages people are receiving from their guardian angels. You see, the demon spirits whisper thoughts into a person's mind, and the demon thoughts battle it out with the human's own feelings, along with the messages their guardian angels are trying to instill. The old cliché about a devil on one shoulder and an angel on the other is not far off. A demon might whisper to a girl that she's unattractive and unworthy of love. Then he's gone. His job is done. He moves on to the next victim. The girl's angel then whispers that she *is* beautiful and she *is* worthy, blah, blah, blah. Which do you think she'll choose to believe?"

It was so unfair. I pushed on with my questions.

"How often do the demons visit people?"

"It depends on the need. Once a month. Once a year. It varies from person to person."

"Why are they allowed to do this?" I couldn't help but feel betrayed on behalf of humanity. I was jolted by the bitter edge in Kaidan's response.

"Maybe because the Creator is not as good and loving as you give Him credit for."

"You're angry at Him?" I wasn't sure why it surprised me.

"He's never done me any favors. I was damned from the moment of conception, and you probably were, too, with or without your bit of angel."

"What do you mean by that?"

He ran a hand through his hair and stared hard at the road. "I mean there's no chance of redemption for the Neph. It's the first lesson we learn during training. We go to hell, just like our fathers."

Wait. What? He had to be mistaken.

"I don't see how that can be possible," I said. "Maybe your father didn't want you getting any lofty ideas about not being the prodigy lust boy."

"We'll see," he said. "Ask your own father when you meet him."

I tried to focus on the landscape and not the confused feelings inside me. I couldn't even bring myself to get excited at the Texas state line. All I could think about was the possibility of being condemned to hell. It couldn't be true. I would find out the truth, although I wished it didn't have to be from the demon who fathered me.

I leaned against the door, zoning out at the flat expanse of land in every direction, and let my eyes close.

A nudge against my arm made me crack my bleary eyes and look around. I sat up and smoothed my hair back as my vision adjusted. We were out in the middle of nowhere. Miles of flat nothingness.

"Sorry to wake you, but I have to stop for petrol."

We got gas at a small country store, along with sandwiches, apples, drinks, and rocky-road fudge made by the owner's wife.

Kaidan had been captivated by the store owner's deep Texas accent. He asked a ridiculous number of questions just to keep the man talking. He then tried to repeat the man's accent when we got in the car: "'Where are y'all young'uns headed? We got us some maps over yonder by them there h-apples.'"

I laughed out loud as he butchered the man's beautiful drawl.

"He did not say 'over yonder'!"

"I've always wanted to say that. I love Americans. You've got a nice little accent, though not nearly as wicked as his."

"I *do*?"

He nodded.

Aside from the occasional *y'all*, I didn't think I sounded Southern, but I guess it's hard to say about your own self.

"Tell me about the places you've lived." I angled in my seat toward him and unwrapped the first of his two sandwiches, winding a napkin around the bottom half and handing it to him.

"Thanks." He took a huge bite and began talking after he swallowed. "I was born in London. My mother also died in childbirth, like all mothers of Nephilim." He took another bite as I pondered this.

"I grew up back and forth between the British Isles: England, Ireland, Scotland, Wales. I spent short periods of time in France, Italy, and South Africa. This is my first time in the States. I was disappointed by Atlanta at first—I'd wanted to live in New York—but it's grown on me."

Everything about Kaidan was exciting and exotic. This was my first time traveling away from home, and he'd already seen so much. I ate my apple, glad it was crisp and not soft.

"Which was your favorite place?" I asked.

"I've never been terribly attached to any place. I guess it would have to be . . . here."

I stopped midchew and examined his face. He wouldn't look at me. He was clenching his jaw, tense. Was he serious or was he teasing me? I swallowed my bite.

"The Texas panhandle?" I asked.

"No." He seemed to choose each word with deliberate care. "I mean here in this car. With you."

Covered in goose bumps, I looked away from him and stared straight ahead at the road, letting my hand with the apple fall to my lap.

He cleared his throat and tried to explain. "I've not talked like this with anyone, not since I started working, not even to the only four people in the world who I call friends. You have Patti, and even that boyfriend of yours. So this has been a relief of sorts. Kind of . . . nice." He cleared his throat again.

Oh, my gosh. Did we just have a moment? I proceeded with caution, hoping not to ruin it.

"It's been nice for me, too," I said. "I've never told Jay anything. He has no idea. You're the only one I've talked to about it all, except Patti, but it's not the same. She learned the basics from the nun at the convent where I was born."

"You were born in a convent," he stated.

"Yes."

"Naturally."

"Anyway," I continued, "I didn't talk to Patti about any of the changes in me or the things I could do when I was growing up. So I do understand the loneliness."

"Even so," he said. "Her love for you . . ."

And there it was.

I had grown up with love, and nothing else. Kaidan had grown up with all of the knowledge of who he is, and all the material things in the world, but no love.

"What about all of the girls you've dated?" I knew I was reaching. "I'm sure there've been some who loved you, and maybe some who you could have loved, too?"

"No girl has ever loved me. You have to know someone to love them. They've all been infatuations. They wanted to own me. That's the nature of lust."

My gut wrenched with guilt as I recognized the feeling he described. And just when I was afraid he would notice, Jamie Moore's face flashed into my mind. She would have been capable of loving him, given the chance. As much as I did not want to think about her, I felt a pull in that direction.

"There's a girl at my school who you were with last year. I guess it was when you first moved here. She was really nice. Jamie Moore?"

He nodded in acknowledgment, but kept his eyes on the road. I didn't continue. I was afraid I'd pushed my luck too far, and the topic made me nervous anyway.

"Look, here's the deal," Kaidan said. "They all know up front I'm not interested in a relationship. I never lie to any of them. I don't need to. The truth hurts worse than a lie. Jamie thought she could change me. It was a foolish notion."

It seemed that he wanted me to believe he was hardened, but I didn't. I had seen cracks, glimpses of something softer hiding under it all. So I went for it.

"Do you ever feel sorry for them, or sad to see them hurting?" I rushed on before he could answer. "Please, I don't mean that as a judgment. I'm just trying to figure you out."

His grip tightened on the steering wheel, turning his knuckles white.

"What if I say no, hmm? What if I have no compassion for the ones I've hurt—no, better yet, the ones who have allowed themselves to be hurt, even sought out the pain?"

I held my hands in my lap and stared down at the half-eaten apple turning brown at the edges.

"Then I would feel bad for you," I said.

"Why?"

"Because that's a sad way to live, and . . . I care about you."

"Don't say that." His tone was edgy, almost angry. "You shouldn't say that, about *caring*. You hardly know me."

"And you hardly know me, but here we are. You offered to take me on this trip. You've answered my gazillion questions. You haven't forced me to do anything, and you haven't exposed me to your father. I'm glad to be here with you."

There. I'd said it. We searched each other's eyes for a moment before he turned back to the road and his grip on the steering wheel loosened. My pulse slowed to normal.

"Once I get a girl to be with me, it's a onetime thing," he began. "Now and then we'll hook up twice, three times max. But I try not to think of them as individuals. It's purely physical. I make no promises to call. I don't even give out my number; they get it from other people. They'll come see the band or show up at a party where I am and give me gifts—I'm sure you can imagine."

I wished I couldn't.

"But on my third time seeing Jamie, she gave me something different than anyone ever had. She made me a CD. I could see she'd put thought into it. She said each song had a killer drum solo or unique drum riff. It was an excellent collection. We saw each other for three weeks, quite often. But when she told me she loved me, I had to break it off. In the end I needed her to hate me. So I left my phone out at band practice one day with a picture she'd sent me of herself."

He gave me a quick look of defiance, and then his eyes were on the road again. I guess I had needed to hear all of that. I was knotted up inside.

"Were you falling in love with her?" I asked.

He groaned and shook his head.

"Christ, Anna." I flinched. "Right. Forgot I was riding with a saint." He sighed and ran a hand through his hair before going on. "No. I was not in love with her. I've never been *in love* with anyone. I was merely answering your question about whether or not I ever feel bad about hurting someone. The answer is yes. I felt bad about her. *God*, I can't believe I'm having this conversation with you."

I leaned back into my seat and stared out my window at the last stretch of Texas as the sun sank lower, hoping Kaidan wouldn't notice me wiping away the lone tear that slid down my face for him.

"Don't pity me, Anna, and don't think well of me for that

small revelation. Don't fool yourself into believing I haven't enjoyed the work I've done, because I have. You should know who you're dealing with."

It was time to find out more about this person I was dealing with.

"Have you ever drugged a girl or spiked her drink?" I asked, still staring out at Texas.

"No. That's for those who lack confidence."

"Have you taken advantage of a girl who was wasted or passed out?"

"No. What's the use if she can't remember?"

"Forced a girl to do something she didn't want to?"

"No. Are you training to be a psychologist?"

"I don't doubt that you've physically enjoyed yourself, Kaidan. If you want me to know who I'm dealing with, then answer me this: Do you take pleasure in hurting people?"

I watched his chest rise and sink with a silent sigh. He spoke devoid of feeling, bordering on impatience.

"I feel nothing for them. I ignore their pain. I don't let it into my thoughts. It brings me no pleasure or pain to see them hurting, with the one exception that we already spoke of. Is that touchy-feely enough for you?"

I would have to read between the lines when it came to Kaidan. To know him, I would need to know why he ignored their pain, and what would happen if he did let their suffering into his thoughts. If he took pleasure in hurting others, he would bask in their pain, not deflect it.

"Why are you trying so hard to make me think you're a bad person?" I asked.

157

"Because it would be best for you to have a healthy fear of me so you can't say you weren't warned. I'm not like boys at your school. Think of the pull you feel toward drugs. That is how I feel about sex."

Oh.

"Starting to get it now? Let me be even clearer." His voice lowered as he walked me through his work. "I can feel out someone within five minutes of conversation to know what I would have to say and do to lure her into bed. That includes you, though I admit I was off my game last night. With some people it's a matter of simple flattery and attention. With others it takes more time and energy. I do whatever it takes to get their clothes off, and then I attempt to make it so they'll never be with another person and not think of me. I know secrets of the human body most people don't even know about themselves. And when I leave, I know they're ruined when they're begging me to stay."

My heart pounded. I was afraid now. He flicked his eyes around my aura.

"It's about time," he said.

CHAPTER TWELVE

KAIDAN'S COLOGNE

We kept our thoughts to ourselves as we entered New Mexico. The abrupt change in landscape filled my mind with relief. Flat Texas plains had morphed into expanses of gently rolling hills and small mountains, patchy with shrubs. The Southwest was wide open. I was amazed how far I could see.

Kaidan slowed to exit as the sun drooped low in the sky. We parked at a fast-food place and got out to stretch our legs. The absence of moisture made the air feel thin in my lungs. I was accustomed to choking on humidity.

We ordered meals and ate them in silence, sitting in front of the glass wall that looked out at the parking lot. The setting sun caused a robe of deep pink and orange to spread itself over the landscape.

"Nice country you've got. Very diverse."

"It's gorgeous," I agreed, pushing the other half of my chicken sandwich toward him. He finished it while I nibbled the last of the fries.

"We'll go a few more hours and then stop for the night," he said. "I'll wait to fill the tank until morning."

I nodded and cleared away all of the trash to get ready to go. The thought of another night together made me nervous.

As we climbed back into the car and continued down I-40, the beauty of the Old West emboldened me. Kaidan's gaze brushed over me as I turned toward him, pulling my bare feet underneath me.

"There's someone else I need to see in L.A., besides my dad."

He nodded for me to continue. I told him the story about the angel visiting Patti, and how she came to be my foster mother. Then I told him that the nun, Sister Ruth, had requested that I come and speak to her in person.

"I just can't imagine what she needs to tell me that she couldn't tell Patti."

"Huh. I haven't heard anything about angels coming down and speaking directly to humans in recent history either."

"I'm worried she won't live much longer," I told him. "I think that's the only reason Patti let me come on this trip with you."

"We'll get there in time."

I hoped so.

"I want to know everything you know about the demons," I said.

He cleared his throat and began, matter-of-factly.

"I'm sure you've heard of the seven deadly sins: wrath, sloth, gluttony, envy, greed, lust, and pride. Pride is said to be the sin from which all others arise. So here's how their rankings work on earth: there's one demon in human form assigned to each of the seven deadly sins, except sloth and gluttony; those have been combined under one demon, since they often go hand in hand. There are six additional sins as well: lying, murder, hatred, theft, adultery, and substance abuse. That makes twelve dark angels in human bodies. They're called the Dukes, and they're the bosses of evil on earth."

"Our dads are two of the twelve Dukes?"

"That's right."

It was strange listening to Kaidan talk. His accent took on a roguish edge when he was excited or angry, but then there were times, like now, when he sounded like a refined schoolboy giving an oral report. I realized he could transform himself to suit his audience. Kaidan could play the part of a gritty bad boy or an educated gentleman as needed. But who was he really? I reached back to rub my neck, which had begun to prickle.

"So what's the difference between a Duke and the other demons, like the one in the restaurant today?"

"In spirit form they're the same, but Dukes are the only demons allowed to possess human bodies. Each Duke commands a legion of demon whisperers who haunt the earth. The whisperers are called the Legionnaires. We sometimes just refer to them as spirits. Between the Dukes and the Legionnaires, there are six hundred and sixty-six demons on earth."

A prickly chill of disbelief coursed through me.

I did the math. "So, twelve Dukes, six hundred fifty-four whisperers, or Legionnaires . . . where do the Nephilim figure in?"

"We're just a by-product. We don't count as human, but also don't qualify as being part of the demon Legionnaires. We work for our fathers and keep our mouths shut. That's it."

All I could do was nod, feeling sick as he continued.

"There used to be more Dukes. At one time there was one for each of the Ten Commandments, in addition to those that cover the seven deadly sins, but many of them became obsolete. They change as necessary. Lies and adultery are the only two of the Ten Commandments still represented. The Dukes specialize during each lifetime based on the state of society they're in at that time. My father specializes currently in pornography."

I held a bottle of water in my lap, forcing back the nausea that crept up as he spoke.

"I hear your father had a good run with alcohol last century," he continued. "But in this lifetime it's drugs. Demons feel a pull in the direction of their specialty, and their offspring get a taste of it as well. Being female, you probably have additional senses, like being able to tell when others have addictive natures, am I right?"

I nodded, thinking of how I saw it in Jay. "But what does being female have to do with it?"

"I'm not certain, but female Neph always seem to be more sensitive to things. Female intuition or whatever. My father's past daughters were able to sense virgins and fertility, as my father does, but I can't."

"That's interesting. Okay, what else?"

"Yep. Let's see. I suppose you should know that positions of Dukes are highly sought after among the demons. They all want a chance in human form. There's even been warring among the dark spirits. Lucifer himself would prefer to be on earth, but he's bound to hell, along with his right- and left-hand warriors, Beelzebub and Ammadeus."

"They can't leave?" I asked, allowing a surge of relief to surface.

"No, they can't. Lucifer lives vicariously through the Dukes and Legionnaires."

"Why are there so few demons on earth? He could send up all of them if he wanted to, right?"

"I suppose he could, but it's all run as a sort of clandestine operation, which is ironic, since everyone in heaven must know what the dark ones are up to. But Lucifer seems to want to stay under the radar, so to speak."

"He's scared," I thought out loud.

"The thing is," Kaidan said, ignoring my comment, "the Legionnaires can't *make* humans do anything. They can't take away a person's free will. They place ideas into their heads. Period. But humans are self-centered by nature. Half the time the demons are only telling them what they want to hear—encouraging their selfish instincts."

These were unpleasant things to hear. Kaidan breezed through it, giving me the straight facts as though quoting from a demon textbook.

"Do the Dukes whisper to people? I mean, what do they actually do?"

"No, they can't whisper in human form, but they have certain verbal abilities of persuasion. The Dukes weave themselves into society, landing in positions of influence over leaders and societal powerhouses."

"They don't try to become the leaders?" I asked.

"Never. Remember, the point of their jobs is to get humans to claw their way to the top and rip their own souls to shreds in the meantime."

The way he talked about humans made me sad. It was impossible not to think about the people who were being manipulated. The heartache. The fact that my own father played a heavy hand in this evil game.

Kaidan wrinkled his brow at me and said, "You've sprung a leak."

I swiped my hands across my wet cheeks. Ugh! I gave an annoyed wave of my hand. "I always cry when I'm emotional, which is pretty much all the time. Just ignore me and keep going, please."

He sighed and passed a tractor trailer, then took a swig of water before continuing.

"Okay, so the Dukes are placed strategically around the earth and they move as needed. They meet once a year to see where each demon will do the most damage, except the ones who are confined, like your father. There are three Dukes here in the United States right now: my father, your father, and Melchom, the Duke of Envy. Each Duke gets a quarterly visit from Lucifer's personal demon messenger, Azael. They give him a report of their work and the state of humanity, which is passed along to Lucifer. I hear he's satisfied with how things are going these days."

"But humans are good, too," I argued. "I'm sure plenty of people are resilient."

"I suppose, but even the devout have weaknesses. The demons have to take different measures with different cultures, because some are more accepting of sin, while others are stricter. It's all a matter of semantics and presentation. They come up with ingenious ways to promote pain and apathy, kind of like marketing schemes. Seek pleasure. Eat, drink, and be merry. *Carpe diem.*"

"Seize the day," I whispered.

The hotel outside of Albuquerque was an improvement over the first night's. Kaidan turned on his music player, placing it on the nightstand between our beds. I was starting to think of his playlist as the sound track for our trip.

I flopped down on a bed and decided to call Patti. I was surprised when I had to turn Kaidan's phone on. He must have switched it off at some point during the drive. Now that I thought about it, today had been more peaceful without the constant beeping.

Patti sounded relieved to hear my voice. I wondered what terrible things she'd imagined all day. Kaidan turned down the music and slipped out on the balcony while we talked.

"I'll be at the jubilee all day tomorrow and Saturday," she said. "How about I call you as soon as I get home these next two nights, probably around eleven o'clock—I guess that would be eight o'clock West Coast time?"

"Okay, I'll make sure to have the phone by me then."

"Anna?"

"Yes?"

"How is Kaidan? Is he still behaving himself?"

I curled up on my bed and got a tickly feeling in my belly when I thought of him.

"Yes," I answered. "Please don't worry about us. We're getting to know each other. He's teaching me a lot."

"Good," she said. "I'm glad, but still. Just be careful not to let your guard down."

Patti gave me the phone number to the convent, and we agreed I'd call when we got to California to see whether Sister Ruth was stable enough for a visitor.

We hung up after exchanging funny kissy sounds and laughing. I went to a vending machine down the hall and bought two bottles of water. Back in the room I turned the music up. I walked to the open doorway of the balcony and watched Kaidan from behind, while the waters chilled my hands.

I imagined myself putting my arms around him and leaning my cheek against the middle of his back, but he wasn't mine to touch like that. Last night's kiss had been a fluke. It already seemed like a long time ago. I couldn't afford to lose myself like that again, especially now that I'd been officially "warned."

I stepped out next to him and pressed a bottle of water against his forearm.

"Thanks," he said, taking it. We leaned against the rail, looking out at the sleepy buildings and breathing in the warm, dry air. Our arms brushed against each other and I got a light whiff of his sweet, woodsy cologne. I took a heady breath and decided to retreat back indoors. I needed to clear my head, maybe take a jog.

I went back in and grabbed my running clothes, then changed in the bathroom. I opened the door to the bathroom, stopping when I saw Kaidan's toiletry bag on the sink. I was overcome with curiosity about his cologne or aftershave, because I'd never smelled it on anyone else before. Feeling sneaky, I prodded one finger into the bag and peeked. No cologne bottle. Only a razor, shaving cream, toothbrush, toothpaste, and deodorant. I picked up the deodorant, pulled off the lid, and smelled it. Nope, that wasn't it.

The sound of Kaidan's deep chuckle close to the doorway made me scream and drop the deodorant into the sink with a clatter. I smacked one hand to my chest and grabbed the edge of the sink with the other. He laughed out loud now.

"Okay, that must have looked really bad." I spoke to his reflection in the mirror, then fumbled to pick up the deodorant. I put the lid on and dropped it in his bag. "But I was just trying to figure out what cologne you wear."

My face was on fire as Kaidan stepped into the small bathroom and leaned against the counter, crossing his arms over his chest. I stepped away. He seemed entertained by my predicament.

"I haven't been wearing any cologne."

"Oh." I cleared my throat. "Well, I didn't see any, so I thought it might be your deodorant, but that's not it either. Maybe it's your laundry detergent or something. Let's just forget about it."

"What is it you smell, exactly?" His voice took on a husky quality, and it felt like he was taking up a lot of room. I couldn't bring myself to look at him. Something strange was going on here. I stepped back, hitting the tub with my heel as I tried to put the scent into words.

"I don't know. It's like citrus and the forest or something . . . leaves and tree sap. I can't explain it."

His eyes bored into mine while he wore that trademark sexy smirk, arms still crossed.

"Citrus?" he asked. "Like lemons?"

"Oranges mostly. And a little lime, too."

He nodded and flicked his head to the side to get hair out of his eyes. Then his smile disappeared and his badge throbbed.

"What you smell are my pheromones, Anna."

A small, nervous laugh burst from my throat.

"Oh, okay, then. Well . . ." I eyed the small space that was available to pass through the door. I made an awkward move toward it, but he shifted his body and I stepped back again.

"People can't usually smell pheromones," he told me. "You must be using your extra senses without realizing it. I've heard of Neph losing control of their senses with certain emotions. Fear, surprise . . . lust."

I rubbed my hands up and down my upper arms, wanting nothing more than to veer this conversation out of the danger zone.

"Yeah, I do have a hard time reining in the scent sometimes," I babbled. "It even gets away from me while I sleep now and then. I wake up thinking Patti's making cinnamon rolls and it ends up being from someone else's apartment.

Then I'm just stuck with cereal. Anyway . . ."

"Would you like to know your own scent?" he asked me.

My heart swelled up big in my chest and squeezed small again. This whole scent thing was way too sensual to be discussed in this small space. Any second now my traitorous body would be emitting some of those pheromones and there'd be red in my aura.

"Uh, not really," I said, keeping my eyes averted. "I think I should probably go."

He made no attempt to move out of the doorway.

"You smell like pears with freesia undertones."

"Wow, okay." I cleared my throat, still refusing eye contact. I had to get out of there. "I think I'll just . . ." I pointed to the door and began to shuffle past him, doing my best not to brush up against him. He finally took a step back and put his hands up by his sides to show that he wouldn't touch me. I broke out of the confined bathroom and took a deep breath.

Shoes. I needed to get on my tennis shoes. I scrambled through my things on the floor and found them, shoving my feet in and tying the knots. Of course Kaidan Rowe would know what freesia smelled like. He probably had to take a flower course during lust training.

"Going somewhere?"

In my peripheral vision I saw him standing in the bathroom door. I wouldn't meet his eyes, afraid they'd be as stormy as they were after our kiss.

I stood and looked at the clock. It was nine. "Yeah, I'm going for a run."

"Mind if I join you?"

I huffed out a determined breath and looked at him now. "Only if you'll do something for me."

He raised his eyebrows in response.

"Teach me to hide my colors."

CHAPTER THIRTEEN

HIDING EMOTIONS

The silence between us as we ran was comfortable. It didn't take long to adjust our strides to fit each other. We passed a nearby strip mall and headed for the hills. Other than the occasional passing car, we were alone.

We came across a cluster of rocks and boulders and climbed them as high as we could go. At the top, Kaidan lay back, hands behind his neck. I stayed sitting up with my legs crossed, next to him. I stared up at the unobstructed sky, fiddling with my shoelaces.

Kaidan was so quiet and still I thought he'd fallen asleep. I peeked down and found him staring at the stars. One of his hands rested on his abdomen, and the other was at his side, close to me. It was a strong hand with long fingers, masculine knuckles, and short nails. Possessed by some basic instinct to nurture, I slipped my hand into his. For one horrible second I expected him to pull away from me, but he didn't. He continued to stare up, though his breathing seemed to slow. I slid my fingers between his. It felt nothing like when Patti and I held hands or when Scott held my hand and led me through the party. This felt intimate, yet sweet.

So much for my healthy fear.

Something scurried below us in the dirt, maybe a lizard. I liked lizards. Or it could have been a scorpion or snake. Those possibilities made me shiver.

"Cold?" he asked.

"No, just thinking about poisonous reptiles."

He chuckled. I hoped he had a knife on him, just in case. I wondered how our bodies would react to poison.

"Are you really going to teach me to hide my emotions?" I asked him.

He lifted his head up and looked at me.

"All right." As he sat up, I reluctantly untwined our fingers and was rapt with attention.

"You mentioned that you can block the emotions you feel coming from others," Kaidan said. "How do you do that?"

"I kind of ignore it when it comes at me and force myself not to think about it."

"This might be similar. Imagine each emotion as something physical in your mind, an object of your choice, and then imagine yourself physically pushing it away or throwing a blanket over it. Anything that works for you. Or as you said, flat-out ignore it, pretend it's not there. Be the boss of your mind. Let's concentrate on a positive emotion first. Think about Patti. . . . Good, I can see your love for her. Start with that."

I imagined my love for her as a physical thing, a fluffy pillow. I compacted it into a light pink dodgeball and I kicked it with my imaginary foot as hard as I could. Kaidan ran his eyes over me and his mouth pulled back in an impressed expression.

"Did it vanish?" I asked.

He nodded, and I was shocked. Maybe I could do this! It was different from blocking others' emotions, because I had to concentrate harder. Deflecting something from the outside was easier than capturing what was inside me and managing it.

"That was fast. You're good. Now for something a bit more unpleasant. Something that makes you angry or sad."

I thought of my father and the words he spoke to me on the day of my birth. I realized now that it must have been pure sarcasm. He couldn't have meant for me to stay away from drugs if that was supposed to be my job, could he? Why hadn't he tried to make me work all these years?

"Whatever you're thinking of, it's not making you angry. Try this. Think of that git who drugged you and tried to take advantage of you. Think of all the girls he was likely successful with."

"You think he's done that to other girls?"

"People who get their kicks that way are usually repeat offenders."

My stomach tightened. What if Kaidan hadn't been there that night? How far would Scott have taken things? All the way? I thought of rape victims, how they often felt guilty. I knew I would have blamed myself.

"Good," Kaidan whispered. "Now."

Anger surged inside me and I channeled it into a spiraling baseball. I swung and batted the emotion away. It was a home run. And it felt good.

The anger toward Scott still lived somewhere inside me. I wasn't making my emotions disappear. They were simply being hidden from the part of my brain that would display them.

I spent an hour practicing as Kaidan prompted me through emotions: happiness, sadness, fear, anxiousness.

"This is almost too easy for you, isn't it?" Kaidan said, leaning a little closer. "I'm very impressed." He brushed my cheek with the back of his hand, and my heart gave a rapid series of bangs.

Ignore it. Deflect it. Oh, crap, this is harder than the other feelings.

"You know, for the record, Anna, I won't think any less of you if you change your mind about doing the things my father expects."

I froze as his hand went around my ankle and up my calf, now shaved, moving upward until his fingers gave a tantalizing brush against the back of my knee. His eyes watched me as he spoke, and my breathing went quick and shallow.

"It's just you and me out here right now, Anna. I felt you come alive when we kissed, and I know you're afraid of that.

Afraid to unleash that other side of yourself. But you needn't worry. I can handle her."

A tingle shot through me. For a moment my thoughts were too distracted to grasp the feeling in my mind.

His hot hand made its way up the back of my leg and I grabbed his wrist. I forced myself to take even breaths and wrap my mental hands around this lust for him. He leaned closer. I could feel his breath against my face and I knew he could feel mine.

The look Kaidan gave me was expectant, rather than seductive. He kept stealing glances at my chest. His hand was still on the back of my thigh, a thumb caressing the sensitive skin there.

I shook my head and grabbed the oncoming lust and longing, compacting it into a red-and-black soccer ball and kicking it into the net. Goal!

"No," I told Kaidan.

He pulled his hand away and leaned back from me.

"Sorry, I had to play dirty. Some people work better under pressure. Now, if you don't mind, I should probably walk it off."

He jumped down from the boulder, landing on his feet, and I watched as he walked around the giant rocks and dirt, kicking stones and doing a series of arm and neck stretches. Five minutes later he came back to me. His voice was quiet.

"Come on," he said, reaching out for my hand.

And as I let him help me down, I knew for a fact that even though he'd only been putting on a show to test my new skill, if I had said yes, he wouldn't have hesitated to take me up on it. I was silent the entire walk to the hotel.

After our run and lesson, I sat cross-legged on the bed, flipping through local channels on the television while Kaidan showered. When he came out, his hair was darkened by the water, and he was shirtless. His baggy shorts hung low, revealing the top of boxer briefs. It was a good opportunity to practice hiding my emotions. I pushed them away and forced my ogling eyes back to the TV screen.

He leaned down and pulled a henley shirt from his bag. Once he was dressed, he ran a hand through his wet hair and cleared his throat.

"Right, then. I'll just, um, be out for a bit."

He was going out again? I hid my emotions, but I was sure the hurt was plain on my face by the way he looked away from me, shaking his head. I turned off the television and looked at him.

"Don't go." I wished I could snatch the words from the air and shove them back in my mouth.

"I have to work, Anna. Either out there or in here."

He stared at me in challenge, and I was caught inside that stormy look again.

"It wouldn't kill you to take a night off."

"Is that so?" He raised his voice now, and balled his hands into fists. "Says the little doll who's never had to work a day in her life?"

I should have just shut my mouth, but of course I couldn't.

"It's not like demons are monitoring your behavior," I said.

He closed his eyes and held an index finger up at me. "Don't push me, Anna. You don't know what you're talking about." There was a simmering undertone in his voice, as he seemed to battle down a torrent of emotion. I kept going, feeling reckless as I raised my voice.

"You can make it one night without sex! Can't you just—"

A splintering crash made me scream and jump backward on the bed. With the swipe of an angry arm, Kaidan had sent a glass lamp flying off the dresser, where it bashed against the wall. He pointed at me, eyes blazing.

"You. Don't. Understand!"

I held my breath and didn't move. I'd never seen anyone so mad, especially not at me.

"Don't wait up this time." His voice was hoarse as he strode past my bed and out of the room, slamming the door behind him.

I sat there for a few minutes, shocked by how my words had the power to touch a nerve in him. The lamp was beyond repair on the floor. I got down and picked up the smaller pieces with trembling hands, throwing them in the trash. Kaidan's temper had just bought him a really ugly broken lamp. I expected to get a knock on our door from hotel staff about the commotion, but nobody ever came. When it was all cleaned up I sat on the bed zoning out, thinking about everything for a while before I decided to get ready for bed.

The bedsheets were soft on my tired body. Sudden exhaustion hit as I took a deep breath and let it out. I didn't want to think about Kaidan working. I said a silent prayer, staring up at the ceiling.

Kaidan had to wake me the next morning. Neither of us spoke as we got ready and grabbed our bags. We went down to take advantage of the hotel's continental breakfast.

It was strange to watch Kaidan Rowe do something as ordinary as drop a bagel in a toaster. Everything seemed more significant around him. He caught me staring.

I took my plate to a table, wishing he weren't so perceptive all the time. Two girls our age whispered and nudged each other toward Kaidan at the bread station. They wore tank tops and microshorts over bathing suits.

I picked at a cheese Danish and stretched my hearing out the teensiest bit. From the corner of my eye I saw one of the girls glance toward me, then shove the other girl with her hip, causing her to bump into Kaidan.

"Oops, sorry," she said. The pushy one giggled.

"Not a problem." His voice was alluring, but he didn't break out the bedroom eyes. He focused on the cream cheese.

"Is that your girlfriend over there?"

Uh-oh, I thought. I could feel them looking toward me, and I paid close attention to the honeydew melon on my fork.

"Ah, just a friend, actually."

Hmph.

"Are you staying here at the hotel tonight?" she asked.

How very bold of her.

"No, we're leaving straightaway."

"My cousin thinks you're hot—"

"Oh, my gawd, shut up! So do you—"

Okay, back to normal hearing for me, thanks.

After a few minutes, Kaidan sat down across from me. He stared at my chest and raised his eyebrows in disapproval. Drats! I forgot about my colors. Keeping emotion hidden was hard, constant work.

"Never a dull moment," I said, after getting control. The twist in my stomach made my words sound petty. His mouth lifted as he tore off a big bite of the bagel, which was burned.

"You're cute when you're jealous." He popped the bite in his mouth.

My eyes widened and then narrowed.

"Besides," he said, "just a pair of ninnies."

I looked over at the girls now sitting with a large gathering of their family members, young and old, in complete contentment. They'd been so brazen with a complete stranger, seizing the day.

"Anna . . ." Kaidan hesitated, and I looked up at him. "Er, I'm not very good at the whole apology thing." He flicked bits of burned bread around his plate.

"Oh," I said. "Well. It's okay. Just an accident."

"No." He shook his head, dragging out the end of the word. "People don't *accidentally* lose their tempers and break things. It was a conscious decision."

"Well, I'm over it. Let's just forget about it."

He blinked at me, seeming surprised by my easy forgiveness. I gave him a small smile and took a sip of my juice. He leaned back in his chair and observed me.

"How's your orange juice, Ann? Does it have a touch of lime?"

The glass paused at my lips as I processed his innuendo, and I took a second to make sure my embarrassment stayed hidden inside. I let the drink swish over my tongue a moment before swallowing and answering.

"Actually it's a little sour," I said, and he laughed.

"That's a shame." He picked up a green pear from his plate and bit into it, licking juice that dripped down his thumb. My cheeks warmed as I set down my glass.

"Okay, now you're just being crude," I said.

He grinned with lazy satisfaction.

"I have no idea what you're talking about. I'm just enjoying my breakfast." He took another bite and I shook my head. The boy had a major effect on me, but some of the shock factor was beginning to wear off, and I found myself being less offended by his incorrigible nature.

We finished eating and Kaidan pulled up a map on his phone.

"We'll be on the road about ten hours today. The Federal Correctional Institution is just outside of L.A. Patti said visiting hours are from ten to one tomorrow."

A wave of nausea made me lean forward and rest my forehead on the table.

"No worries, luv."

His words brought me comfort, and I lifted my head.

"Do you think maybe I can drive some today?" I asked. "It might take my mind off it."

He dug the keys from his pocket and held them in front of me.

"You can have first shift."

* * *

We passed a lot of Native American reservations in New Mexico. Many of them were lit up with neon lights of casinos. As we dipped into one shallow valley, a tight-knit circular reservation came into sight. The most touristy thing about it was a brightly colored tepee in front of a little store.

"Do you mind if we stop?" I asked.

Kaidan looked up from the game he was playing on his phone. "Not at all."

I pulled into the dusty parking lot. The sun glared bright and hot as I climbed out of the car. I cupped my hand above my eyes to shield them. Dry heat made my skin feel shriveled and thirsty, like the parched, cracked earth we walked on. The outside of the store was a genuine piece of adobe architecture, pinkish brown, with rounded corners and edges. A woman with a soft yellow aura sat by the entrance, weaving on a traditional loom.

Inside, we stood in a large room that smelled of sweet earth and cedar. The walls were draped in handmade blankets woven with intricate designs and patterns. Tables around the room displayed colorful jewelry. In the corner stood an antique drink cooler that must have been fifty years old.

A couple sat at a small table to the side. An old man and woman with matching skin the rich color of the soil, both with long black-and-gray hair pulled back from their faces. They greeted us with friendly nods and smiles.

I went to their table and watched them work for a moment. She was stringing tiny beads into a bracelet by hand, creating an elaborate motif. He was carving a chunk of wood. I could make out the hind legs of a horse. Amazing. They made the art look easy in their experienced hands.

I walked around the store. Hundreds of wooden animals of all sizes stared back at us from the walls. Wolves and coyotes seemed to be the most popular. Kaidan examined an eagle with its wings spread.

"Incredible detail," he said. His appreciation made me glad, since he didn't show much admiration for humans, in general.

I ran my fingers over a coarse throw blanket as I moved around the room, and then spotted a table full of turquoise and amber jewelry. I went over and touched several of the smooth stones.

A delicate, dainty necklace caught my attention, made of silver with a turquoise charm naturally in the form of a misshapen heart. It was one of the prettiest things I'd ever seen. I looked at the price tag and balked. It would have cost me all the money I'd brought. I was sure it was worth that much, but still. I set it back down.

"See anything you like?" Kaidan asked. I hadn't heard him walk over.

"Yeah. It's all beautiful, isn't it?"

"Can I . . . get you something?"

A rush of heat flowed to my face from the surprise of his offer. I kept my eyes on the table.

"Oh. No. I don't need anything, but thank you."

He stood so close that my shoulder touched his chest and I was afraid he could hear my galloping heart.

"I guess we'd better get back on the road," I said.

"Yes."

I turned to the kind couple and thanked them. They both nodded in their quiet way. Kaidan pointed to the drink cooler as we were leaving.

"I'll get us drinks so we don't have to stop again for a while," he said, handing me the keys.

I squinted as I walked back out, cupping my hands above my eyes. I could hardly see, it was so bright. We hadn't been in the store very long, but the inside of the vehicle was already ablaze with heat. I started the engine and cranked up the AC. As I sat in the hot car with the air blasting, I watched the woman weaving outside and wondered how many demon whisperers were involved in the trampling of Native American cultures throughout history.

The stride of Kaidan's tanned legs in his baggy skater shorts shook me out of my reverie. He climbed in and put the cold drinks in the cup holders.

"New Mexico is my favorite state," I declared as we pulled onto I-40.

"I'm waiting to see it all before I decide. And by the way, your driving isn't half-bad. I expected to be terrified."

"Why?"

"I imagined a timid, overly cautious little angel, but you've got an impressive lead foot."

Whoops.

"Your car drives so quietly," I said, "I don't realize how fast I'm going. I'll set the cruise control from now on."

"Don't worry. I'll keep an ear out for cops," he told me.

"Will we be passing the Grand Canyon?" I asked. "I've always wanted to see it."

Kaidan pulled out the map and studied it.

"It's a bit out of the way, more than an hour. But how about this? We can go on the way back, since we won't have a time crunch."

I didn't know if it was the desert air or what, but I felt at ease. I still had a thousand questions for Kaidan, but I wasn't in the mood for another heavy conversation just yet. I liked talking to him. We were still guarded, and it wasn't nearly as carefree as talking with Jay, but I was beginning to imagine keeping Kaidan in my life as a friend after this trip. Time would help us forget the kiss. My crush on him would fade. If I could stop analyzing every touch and every look, then maybe it could work. I vowed to myself at that moment: No more jealousy. No more flirting. No more lustful longing for the elusive Kaidan Rowe.

CHAPTER FOURTEEN

LAUGHTER

Arizona was battling it out with New Mexico to win the title of favorite state, with more breathtaking red mountain views. At one point, the road seemed to be carved straight through a crack between two high mountains. Steep inclines surrounded us on both sides, and foreboding signs warned of rockslides, as if there were anywhere to escape. I stared out the window in awe as I drove.

There was one thing I had to do while we were in the Southwest.

"Do you like Mexican food?" I asked.

"There aren't many foods I don't like."

I should have guessed. I was confident I could find a perfect place to eat when we pulled into a town near Flagstaff that afternoon. I bypassed busy chain restaurants until I found what I was looking for: a quaint hole-in-the-wall place like the one I frequented with Patti back home.

"Interesting choice," Kaidan said.

"Trust me."

My mouth watered at the scents of chilies and fried corn inside. One wall was painted with a mural of a Latina dancing woman, a colorful skirt flowing around her. Mariachi music was twanging overhead.

A hostess led us to a private booth with high backs and a brick archway at the end. A boy brought hot tortilla chips and a bowl of salsa.

I closed my eyes for a quick blessing and opened them to find Kaidan watching me, a chip loaded with salsa in his hand.

"Do you do that at every meal?"

"Yeah." I took a chip and dunked it. "And every night before bed."

We took our bites at the same time, and a second later both reached for our ice waters, eyes bulging.

"Hot!" I said, nearly sucking down the entire glass.

Kaidan laughed and wiped his forehead with his napkin. I should have known there'd be no wimpy mild stuff out here.

A waiter approached and we gave our orders.

"I didn't see you pray either night," Kaidan said after the man left.

"I don't have to get on my knees or say it out loud. I just say it in my head while I lie there."

He was contemplative as we munched on chips.

Our food came out superfast. Kaidan's fajitas sizzled and

gave off a steamy scent of cumin and sweet onion. We didn't speak a word until we were finished, except when Kaidan said, "May I?" and skewered half of my shredded beef enchilada. When he finished, Kaidan threw his napkin down on the table in surrender.

"I promise to trust your choices from now on," he said, stretching and patting his stomach.

I handed him the keys.

We had a great view of a snowcapped mountain range in the distance as we passed Flagstaff. There were trees again now, giant pines stretching upward.

My stomach knotted at a sign for California, and I counted down the mileage until Los Angeles. Kaidan must have noticed my crazy bouncing knee, because he attempted to distract me from my thoughts.

"You haven't asked me any questions in ages," he said.

"Let's see. Okay. Basic Demonology 101. How does a demon get into a body?"

"Well, it's difficult for two healthy souls to possess a body at once. A human soul can't simply be shoved out of the way. I'm sure you've watched movies about exorcisms?"

"Heard of them, but never seen any."

"Those stories are examples of possessions gone bad, usually some dissatisfied spirit whisperer who wants to stir up trouble. The demon soul and human soul fight over the body and the body wears down. It can get gory. Most often it ends in death."

What a horrible way to go.

"Demons and angels both have free will, but rules still apply.

Demons have been forbidden to physically harm humans, and that includes possessions. You with me so far?" I nodded, and he went on. "Dukes spend a lot of their time in hospitals and emergency rooms while they're searching out a new body in their spirit form. When people are close to death and lose the will to live, the souls are just barely hanging on to their bodies, like a loose tooth. The Dukes can just pinch off the human soul and release it without protest, then enter the body before it dies and heal it with their powers. They heal much faster than us. They could share the bodies when the human souls are weak like that, but it hinders their powers within the body, so they prefer to be the only dwellers."

"How do they decide who to pick?" I asked.

"That's where it can get tricky. They seek out low-profile young or middle-aged people, preferably someone who isn't surrounded by a big, doting family. It's too much effort if there are humans who will search when the person disappears. Some Dukes want attractive bodies; some want to appear rougher. It can take a while to find a perfect match, but time doesn't matter to them. Besides, the Dukes enjoy having an opportunity to whisper to humans while they're hunting and waiting. A hospital is a perfect place to work, because emotions are already running high."

"That's disgusting," I muttered.

"As far as life span," he continued, "normal humans can live upward of one hundred and twenty years these days, but their life expectancy is lower because of health-related issues. Dukes and Neph don't have those problems, so our bodies can make it that long. We're not immune to aging, though. A body wears

188

out, no matter how healthy it is. Dukes discard their bodies before they get to that point. Then it's on to the next body and building a new false identity."

"What happens when they leave the bodies?" I envisioned zombies.

"If no other soul was inhabiting it, the body appears to die of cardiac arrest."

"Ah. I've been wondering about Nephilim souls. Are our souls half demon?"

Kaidan's mouth lifted. "The questions you ask remind me of when I was a child. I asked the very same ones of my father."

I tried to imagine young, inquisitive Kaidan looking up at the demon in his life, desperate for his attention. I wished I could hold that little boy.

"No," he answered, "our souls are neither human nor demon. We Neph have our own unique souls, but as children of dark angels our souls are marked with demonic stains."

I did not like the sound of that.

"I guess in your case you've got a bleached-out angel patch there, too," he added.

Funny.

"There's something else I'm confused about," I said. "If I had a baby someday, would the childbirth kill me?"

"Yes, it would. Why? Are you thinking of conceiving?"

I gave his arm a little shove and he grinned, but he got serious again before answering.

"I'm not certain why, but nobody survives."

I thought of my mother's singing, and her love for me inside of her. She must have known she wouldn't live to hold me, and yet she exuded pure joy.

"Were you able to sense your mother's feelings when she was pregnant with you?" I asked him.

"Yes, I suppose because we were sharing a life source. I could sense moments of affection directed at me, even brief glimpses of love, but mostly she despaired. No doubt she was suffering from obsession with my father, but he saw her only as a vessel for his use. She was chosen for her beauty, and physical characteristics in her family that complemented his. When I was very small I asked him what happened to her and he said, 'You killed her—shame, too. She was nice to look at.'"

He brought a hand up and ran his fingers through his hair, blocking my view of his face so I couldn't see any hint of emotion that might have been there. I had a violent image of kicking Kaidan's father in his prized lust parts. He cleared his throat and began again.

"My father has had one child in each life, all trained in music and manners, and highly educated."

He stated the facts without any interest.

"Are any of them still living?"

"No."

"You might have relatives out there. Maybe I do, too!"

"No, we don't. Don't get excited. There are no descendants."

"Why not?" I asked.

"The details aren't important."

"They're important to me."

"Please, Ann, not right now. I'll tell you everything later, just not right now. I'm not in the mood for your tears. It's been a nice day."

I didn't want to be protected through ignorance. I hated that he thought I would cry, and hated even more that he was probably right. Kaidan pointed out the window at a sign. We were entering California.

I took a deep breath. I would go to the prison tomorrow and meet another of Lucifer's Dukes. My own father.

What was the worst that could happen? If I prepared myself, then maybe it wouldn't hurt as badly. He could refuse to see me. He could see me, but be hateful and rude and tell me never to come back. No matter what, I would be okay. I didn't need him, I told myself. I needed information from him, yes. But I had Patti to give me love.

"Can I use your phone?" I asked.

He handed it to me, and I took out the paper with the number to the convent. A woman answered after three rings.

"Convent of Our Mother Mary, this is Sister Emily speaking."

"Hello, Sister Emily, my name is Anna Whitt—"

"Ah, yes. Sister Ruth has been waiting for you, and try as I may, she will not relay a message of any sort. She insists on seeing you."

Hope bubbled up inside me.

"That's why I'm calling. I'm in California now. I want to come see her right away."

"Unfortunately Sister Ruth has been in a comatose state for over twenty-four hours now. This isn't the first time. She's pulled herself out of it before, so we can only hope she'll do it again."

"Do you think maybe I can just come and sit with her?"

"Dear, we have someone sitting with her around the clock. Why don't you give me a number where I can contact you, and I'll let you know the moment she comes to—that is, if it's okay with you."

"Yes, please," I said. "Please call me the very second she wakes up; I don't care if it's the middle of the night."

I closed my eyes after hanging up. *Please don't let her die yet.*

"I'm curious about something," Kaidan said.

"Yes?"

"Do you even feel the full temptations of sin, or are you just extremely self-controlled? Because even when I've seen you feeling dark emotions, it's so brief."

I thought about it. "Of course I feel temptation, but I'm really aware of it, so I can sort of squash most of the urges before they have time to register. Rules are meant to protect us, so I follow them. Something might feel good at the moment, but the consequences are scary." I paused. "That sounds lame, doesn't it?"

"Just . . . fascinating, is all. Have you never outright sinned, then?"

"I disobeyed Patti when she told me to stay away from you."

"Right. I remember that one. So just once, then?"

"There was this other time. . . ." I thought about the two girls in the bathroom and stopped myself, blanching.

"Yes? Go on," he urged.

He watched the road, but excitement underscored his tone. I rubbed my dampening palms down my shorts.

"The night we met, I sort of . . . well, I flat-out told a lie. On purpose."

I thought he was trying not to smile.

"To me?" he asked.

"No. *About* you."

Now he unleashed that devastating smile of his, crinkling the corners of his eyes. My face was aflame.

"Continue. Please."

"There were these girls in the bathroom talking about you, and for some reason, I don't know why, it upset me, and I told them . . . *thatyouhadanSTD.*"

I covered my face in shame and he burst into laughter. I thought he might drive off the road.

Well, it *was* kind of funny in an ironic way, because he couldn't keep a disease anyhow, even if he had gotten one. I found myself beginning to giggle, too, mostly out of relief that he wasn't offended.

"I wondered if you were ever going to tell me!" he said through spurts of hilarity.

Duh! Of course he'd been listening! My giggles increased, and it felt so nice that we kept going until we were cracking up. It was the good kind of laughter: the soul-cleansing, ab-crunching, lose-control-of-yourself kind.

We started catching our breath again a few minutes later, only to break into another round of merriment.

"Do you forgive me, then?" I asked when we finally settled down and I wiped my eyes.

"Yes, yes. I've had worse said about me."

We passed a billboard advertising gin. It made me think of Jay.

"Hey, remember when you said the Dukes have power to persuade people?" I asked. "Do we have those powers, too?"

"We call it the influence," he said. "And no, it's only the Dukes. Why?"

"There were a few times when it seemed like I mentally persuaded Jay not to drink, but I guess not."

"No. Dukes have the ability to put an urge into a person by speaking a command out loud or even silently. But just like the whisperers, they can't force it. The influence doesn't work if the human is really strong and adamant against what the Duke tells them to do. It works best if the person is already inclined to go in that direction, but they're sort of teetering on the edge of a decision."

We watched the road now. I looked at Kaidan's hand on the steering wheel, and just for fun I said in my mind, *Tap your finger on the wheel.*

Tap, tap. Oh, my gosh! He did it! I tried it again, and this time when he tapped the wheel I tittered. He didn't even notice he was doing it.

"What's up with you?" he asked.

"Are you *sure* it's not possible for a Nephilim to have the influence?"

"I've never heard of anyone having it except a Duke, and trust me, I've tried. It doesn't work."

For twenty minutes Kaidan would periodically chuckle under his breath and shake his head. I kept grinning, too.

We were less than two hours away now.

"I know we're going to be there soon, but I really need to go to the bathroom," I said.

"Oh, all right. Loo stop." He took the next exit and we both went into a convenience store. When I came out I saw the back of Kaidan as he was walking to the exit doors. I had a sudden urge to try my power of influence again.

Spin around! I willed to his back. And to my utter disbelief, he spun midstride and then put his hand on the door handle to open it. He paused there for a moment, and then turned and looked at me with an incredulous, wide-eyed expression. I darted into the candy aisle and bent over laughing.

"Oooh, so not funny," I heard him say as the bell chimed his exit.

I couldn't stand straight as I made my way back to his car, holding my sides and cracking up, no matter how hard I tried to keep a straight face. He gave me a fake glare and shook his head when I climbed in.

"How did you do that?" he demanded.

"I don't know. Just like you said, I gave you a silent command and willed it to happen. You weren't really thinking about it, so I guess you went with it."

He continued to shake his head.

"I can't believe it. Maybe you're more powerful because you've got the double-angel parentage. That's completely unfair."

"Ha, ha," I teased.

On our way back onto the interstate we passed a long row of stores and shops, and a giant tattoo parlor.

"I had a tattoo once," said Kaidan. "Last year, just before we left England."

"What do you mean, you had one 'once'?"

"Bloody thing was gone by the morning!" His voice was indignant. "Sheets were black with ink. I put myself through all of that for hours, and my body just pushed it back out!"

And once again we were both in a fit of hysterics, sharing the world's best inside joke. We were doubled over, unable to breathe, and I accidentally snorted. Kaidan pointed at me and laughed harder, clutching his stomach.

"What was your tattoo?" I managed to push the words out.

"You had to ask. It was a deadly-looking pair of black wings on my shoulder blades."

Kaidan and I started roaring again, muscles clenching from the exertion.

We had no way of knowing it would be our last reason to laugh for a very long time.

CHAPTER FIFTEEN

THE GREAT PURGE

We made our way through the dry hills and valleys of Southern California, passing neighborhoods of homes with rounded red tiles on the roofs, and manicured lawns. By nightfall we were outside of Los Angeles. I kept checking Kaidan's phone for calls from the convent, but there was nothing.

"It's still early," Kaidan said. "Let's drive through L.A. or Hollywood. We're close enough."

"Hollywood!" I wasn't up-to-date on celebrity gossip, but it sounded exciting, and I wasn't ready to settle down yet.

We were focusing on road signs when I happened to notice writing on a small mountain.

"Oh, my gosh, Kai, look! The Hollywood sign!" I bounced

in my seat and pointed to the giant white capital letters standing on the mountainside. His head tilted to the side, peering at me.

"You called me Kai."

"Sorry," I said.

"No, it's okay. That's what my friends call me."

"Your friends?" I asked.

"As close as I have to friends, yes. Four Neph. Two I've known since childhood, although I'm not particularly close with any of them. It's more like we're all in it together."

"Will I get to meet them?"

"I don't know. I'm not going to tell them about you, because I think you need to lie low. But that doesn't mean they won't hear about you through word of mouth. The Dukes and demons are worse than a bunch of gossiping old women." That was a funny image.

"What are your friends like?"

"Well, there's Blake, the son of the Duke of Envy. He lives out here on one of the beaches. He was born in the Philippines. His job is the best, because all he has to do is get his hands on the latest material things and date the most beautiful women. I've wondered if he even feels a pull to sin. He's completely mellow. I've seen him jealous only once, and it got ugly."

"What was he jealous about?"

"A girl he liked was chatting up another bloke. Anyhow, he's a thrill seeker. Likes all the extreme sports. He travels the world to surf. He's got freakishly good balance. And then there are the twins, Marna and Ginger." His voice went a little sour as he spoke of them. "Daughters of the Duke of Adultery,

Astaroth. They're dancers. I spent a good bit of my child-hood with them, sharing tutors and whatnot. They still live in London. Marna can be a joy, but Ginger has not been pleasant for quite some time."

"Are they expected to break up marriages?" I asked.

"They just turned eighteen, so they'll be expected to now, but before they worked on other teenage couples, getting them to cheat. Neph are to steer clear of sins with adults or any spotlight while we're underage to avoid any scandal to our fathers' reputations among humans." He paused, switching lanes and swiping hair from his eyes. His face and tone were grim as he continued. "The twins' father, Astaroth, had a daughter in his last lifetime who was caught having an affair with a politician when she was only fifteen. Astaroth was dabbling in politics at the time, and there was a huge public uproar. Her actions affected his influential position, so he staged her death to look like suicide. Then he left his body and started the life he has now. Everyone thought his heart gave out from stress."

"He killed her?" I shouldn't have been surprised.

Kaidan gave a dry laugh of contempt. "Had her killed, most likely. Wouldn't want to exert his own self."

I shook my head, imagining what fear the twins must face.

"Marna and Ginger both have a special talent, like you—the female thing," Kaidan said.

"Oh, yeah? What's theirs?"

"They can sense bonds between people when the feelings are mutual. Attraction, romantic love, commitment. Their father sees the bonds, too. That's how they know who to go after."

"Wow. Girl power, only in a disturbing way. Okay, so that's

three of your friends. Who's the last one?"

"Kopano." He said this name with a slight frown and a tone akin to annoyance. "His father is Alocer, Duke of Wrath."

I shivered at the mention of Wrath. "Is he mean?" I asked.

Again with the dry laugh and strange tone. "No. He's practically a celibate monk."

"And where does he live? Kopano." I tried out his name.

"He's from Africa, but he's at college here in the States now. Kope's situation is very hush-hush. None of the demons know about this except his father, but Kopano is lucky to be alive. A few years back he turned to God and was prepared to die rather than do his father's work. But when he told Alocer, he allowed him to live."

"Why?"

"Alocer loves Kope, or respects him, at the very least. It's unheard of among our kind."

I studied Kaidan's face. There was something wistful in his voice. Jealousy?

"Kopano is a mystery," he stated. "Here's the exit."

We ended up on the Hollywood strip. I was ecstatic to see palm trees everywhere, some short and squat, some tall with skinny trunks stretching high. But my excitement faded when I caught sight of the general emotional climate of the people crowded together everywhere. There were some happy tourists, just passing through like us, but the primary sins were present in abundance, pressing in on me. I could sense the undercurrent of addiction in so many people that I found myself clutching the door handle. I gulped hard, willing the jitters to leave me.

An attractive woman passed, keeping her head down, and from a certain angle I could see that her face was not right—not natural. Her skin was tight, her lips were overly full, and her cheekbones stuck out sharply. She was dark with self-loathing. I wondered how many plastic surgeries she'd had. It was clear that underneath all of the changes, she had been a beautiful woman to begin with.

Nearly every ear had a cell phone attached to it. There were so many homeless and prostitutes. I barely saw the Chinese Theatre or the stars on the sidewalks. All I could see were the souls and emotions.

"Is it too much for you here?" Kaidan asked me.

"It's hard," I said. "But not because it's Hollywood. Even Atlanta is hard for me sometimes."

"I'll get us out of here."

We stopped at a red light. I shook my head and managed a small smile for the man who passed my window with a flyer offering tours of celebrity homes. When he walked away I met the eyes of a homeless woman sitting on some gray newspapers that matched her gray aura of despair. I opened my little wallet and pulled out two bills.

"You're wasting your money," Kaidan warned.

"Maybe. Maybe not."

She came, dragging one leg, to the window when I rolled it down and held out the money.

"God bless you," she said. Her eyes reflected the pale green swirl of gratitude around her. She was not high or drunk, nor did she have the undercurrent of addiction running through her. I wondered what awful circumstances had forced her to live in the streets.

"Wait," I called out. I snapped open my wallet and pulled out my entire savings, pressing it into her palm. Her lip trembled as she pulled it to her chest. Our eyes stayed locked until the light turned green and we drove away.

I realized too late that I would have to depend on Kaidan financially for the rest of the trip, not that he'd let me pay for anything so far anyway.

"I'm sorry," I said to him. "That was presumptuous of me. But she—"

"What on earth are you apologizing for?" His eyes were soft, taking me by surprise. I looked back down, feeling bad.

Traffic was stop-and-go on the strip. Kaidan watched the road, lost in his thoughts.

"Legionnaire," he said. My attention snapped to where he pointed. "Whispering to that man in the blue suit. If he comes this direction I'm going to ask you to hide. Be ready to move."

I nodded and slunk lower in the seat. I still couldn't see any demon, but I watched the man, walking and talking on his cell phone while his guardian angel rushed around him. He clicked the phone shut and stopped walking. He seemed to waver in indecision, looking around to see whether anyone was watching. Then he turned and, with a rush of determination, walked back to a woman standing by a light pole in a black leather dress with a faux-fur wrap. A prostitute. She dropped her cigarette and crushed it underfoot. Her colors went to a nervous light gray when he approached, changing to a soft blue relief when he passed her money in his palm. As they walked away together, a dirty cloud of guilt and apprehension spiked with yellow-orange excitement blazed around the man.

"Father would be satisfied to see the success of one of his whisperers," Kaidan said with disdain. "I shouldn't have brought you here."

I tore my eyes from the people now, and instead watched Kaidan's hand on the steering wheel, and his long legs on the pedals. This kept me busy until we were out of the city, back on the highway, where I could stare out at the city lights. Kaidan handed me his cell phone, since Patti would be calling soon.

I talked with her while he got us checked in at the hotel.

"You sound sad, honey," Patti said.

"We just drove down the Hollywood strip. There was a lot of suffering. But I don't want to think about that. Today was a good day."

I told her about the Native American reservation and the Mexican restaurant. She loved every detail. I was glad to hear the strain gone from her voice.

"Be strong tomorrow, Anna. Everything will be fine. I just know it."

"I miss you," I told her. "I wish I could have one of your hugs right now."

"I miss you, too, so much. Here's a hug." She made a *mmnnn* sound, like she was squeezing, and I giggled. "We'll talk at this same time tomorrow?"

"Yes," I said. "I love you."

"I love you, too, sweetie."

* * *

We lay on our separate beds, contemplating what to do. We weren't tired, even though we'd both changed into pajamas. I'd been surprised when Kaidan changed, but I didn't mention it.

"We could go for a swim," he suggested.

"Can't," I said. "Didn't bring a bathing suit." *On purpose.*

I sat up against the tower of pillows on my bed. I wanted to keep him talking for as long as possible, in case he planned to go out.

"Kaidan, what happened to all of the Nephilim? Why are there so few of us now?"

He came over and sat on my bed, a respectful distance away. He rubbed his face, as if weary, then began.

"All right." He sighed. "Over a hundred years ago there were thousands of Neph and their descendants on earth. The offspring down the line had full powers, just like us. It started getting difficult for the Dukes to keep track of them and control them. A few Neph were using their abilities to rise to power among humans, taking high places of leadership, starting wars, committing genocides, in general bringing too much attention to themselves. The Dukes want Neph to be like them, influencing humans to cause chaos, but not taking starring roles. So they decided on the Great Purge. All Neph were hunted down and killed, whether they'd defied the Dukes or not. Within several years they were all gone."

Kaidan's face was bleak, and I batted away depressing emotions.

"It's like the Neph are even less than humans in their eyes," I said.

"Ever since the purge, they've taken measures to make certain the Neph don't overpopulate again. The Duke of Pride, Rahab, tried to insist that the Dukes not reproduce, but he got shot down on that one. Instead they've made certain the Neph won't have children."

"You mean . . . ?" I covered my mouth, feeling very sick. "They sterilized them?" He nodded, making a snip-snip gesture with his fingers. I pointed at him, as a question.

"Yes, me, too," he said, voice soft. "All of us had the procedure."

"Except me," I said, and then I felt myself pale, imagining that my father would make me.

"The worst part is how fast the pain meds burn through our system. But it's better this way. To get someone pregnant is to kill them."

"I understand that. But it's their reasoning that makes me mad—it's the fact that everyone's choice is taken away!"

"It is what it is." I had no doubt that had been the Neph motto for thousands of years. Kaidan rested his chin on his forearms, looking down with heavy eyes.

He'd been right to think I'd cry. The thought of such cruelty. The complete lack of love and respect for life. I stood and went to look out of the window, trying to hide my tears from Kaidan.

"I knew it would only upset you," he said.

"Of course it upsets me! Doesn't it upset you?" I turned to him now, and he lifted a solemn gaze to me. Yes, it was clear

205

from the blue depths of his eyes that it upset him, too.

"There's no use wasting time thinking about things that can't be changed."

Was there nothing that could be done? Couldn't we somehow fight back? As much as I wanted to believe we could, the idea of destroying the Dukes felt monumentally hopeless.

I walked back to my bed, where Kaidan lay, and sat against the headboard with my knees pulled up to my chest. I pushed my cold feet under the covers.

Kaidan sat up on the edge of the bed and moved closer to me. Much closer. I was too busy hiding my nervousness to look up at him.

"Nervous?" he asked.

"Umm . . ."

"About tomorrow?" he specified.

"Oh." Now that he mentioned it . . . "Yeah."

"You'll do fine. I'll drop you off and come get you the moment you call."

He took my hand gently in his. My heart was beating too fast. I watched him run the pad of his thumb back and forth over my thumbnail. I knew that if I looked up now he would kiss me. I wanted him to. All I had to do was lift my face. But it felt wrong that I should keep kissing someone who wasn't my boyfriend. The thought of Kaidan as anyone's boyfriend was laughable. He probably thought *boyfriend* and *husband* were bad words.

After I'd refused to look at him for long enough, he lifted my hand to his lips and kissed my thumb. I rested my cheek on my knee and closed my eyes. The sweetness of his gesture was too much. Just as I was about to stop fighting it and turn my face up to his, he stood.

"Get some rest," he said, letting go of my hand.

I burrowed down into the covers and tried to resume normal breathing. I heard him get into his own bed and become still.

"Kaidan?"

"Yes?"

"I'm not trying to judge. I'm just curious. Um . . ." I twisted the blanket in my hands. "Are you going out tonight?"

The pause was long and weighty before he said, "I don't think I will."

Yes! I reined in any hopeful thoughts and feelings about what this might mean, but I could not deny the speed of the hummingbird zooming around inside of me.

"Ann?" he whispered.

"Yes?"

"It won't bother me if you need to, you know, properly pray, however you do it."

"Oh. Okay, thanks." He'd caught me off guard, but I felt willing to share my private moment with him.

I felt self-conscious at first as I clasped my fingers in front of me and closed my eyes, but as I began, a peace settled over me. I thought about all I'd seen that day, and what I'd be facing tomorrow. I asked for strength of heart to face my earthly father. I begged that the Nephilim could find reason to hope. And the last wish in my heart was for Kaidan to experience love in his life, both the giving and receiving.

Once finished, I reached for the lamp switch and saw his handsome face on the pillow watching me. Warmth rushed through my limbs.

"Good night," I whispered, and turned out the light.

CHAPTER SIXTEEN

MOURNING HEAVEN

I awoke at the first crack of dawn and lay listening to Kaidan's steady breathing as he slept. I was glad this day was finally here. I wanted to get it over with.

I crept to the bathroom and took a shower, then dressed in the nicest outfit I'd brought—khaki shorts and a button-down yellow shirt with a white tank top underneath. I tried to think positive, peaceful thoughts as I towel-dried my hair.

In the room, Kaidan was lying on his back with his hands resting on top of his stomach. He didn't look fully awake yet.

"I ordered us some room service for breakfast." In his sleepy state, his voice was even deeper than normal.

"Thank you," I told him.

He watched as I sat in a chair and brushed through my wet hair, snagging light tangles as I went. I was too nervous about the day to feel self-conscious. He didn't take his eyes off me the entire time I French-braided it.

Our breakfast came and I took two bites of a waffle. Nerves had shot my appetite, but I forced down half a glass of apple juice.

Kaidan stared out of the window at our grungy city view. I went and stood next to him.

"You've gotten scruffy," I said, reaching out to run a hand across the stubble on his jaw.

He grabbed my hand and pressed it against his cheek, closing his eyes for a moment. When he opened them again I was startled by the crushing, desperate look he gave me. And just as quickly, he was dropping my hand and turning back to the window, crossing his arms. I swallowed, confused. I started to turn away but then he spoke.

"I have something for you."

He pulled his hand out of his pocket, and when he opened it, sitting in his palm was the small, beautiful necklace of turquoise I'd admired in New Mexico. I stared in disbelief.

"I saw you looking at it and thought you liked it," he said.

Oh, no, not the tears. Please not the tears. I blinked the stupid things away, thinking about how much I did not want to clean mascara from my face.

"Have I upset you?" he asked.

"No! I'm not upset. I'm just surprised. I can't believe . . . I mean, I *love* it. Nobody's ever given me anything like this."

I wiped hard under my eyes and then clasped the necklace around my neck.

He cursed under his breath and roughly pushed the hair from his eyes, looking away. "This was a mistake."

"No." I grasped his arm. "It wasn't."

"Don't read into this, Anna. It would be a mistake to romanticize me."

"I'm not. It was a nice gesture. That's all." I tried to reassure him, though I wasn't certain myself.

I would deal with this torrent of emotion later. Right now I had a demon to meet.

We sat in the parking lot of the Federal Correctional Institution of Southern California. Other visitors were sitting in their cars, too, or loitering by the entrance. We hadn't spoken within five miles of the prison, in case my father was listening. I clutched at my stomach, which contracted and growled.

He gave me a soft admonishment. "You should have eaten more."

"I couldn't."

I looked at the clock; it was time.

Car doors opened and slammed shut around us. The visitor doors were unlocked.

"You're up," Kaidan said.

It took awhile to get through security. They had to look for the fax Patti had sent giving me permission to visit as a minor. She'd jumped through major hoops to make it happen. The guard who took my name became interested when I told him

I was Jonathan LaGray's daughter.

"First visitor Johnny LaGray's had in seventeen years," he stated.

Not likely, I thought, envisioning a steady stream of visiting demon spirits scoffing at the prison's security measures.

The guard gave me a rundown of the rules. Hugging and holding hands were fine in moderation, but the guards would be watching to make sure I didn't pass anything to my father. He didn't have to worry—hugs and handshakes were not on my agenda.

He explained that my father would be notified that he had a visitor, but he had the right to refuse to see me.

The other visitors and I were led into a room the size of a small cafeteria and told to sit and wait in our assigned places. Mismatched tables lined the room, surrounded by guards. I sat down in a chair as wobbly as my stomach. The room filled with murmurs of adult conversation and the high-pitched voices of children. The general atmosphere was bleak, with gray auras most prevalent.

Sounds of heavy metal doors opening and chains clanging made me panic. I worried I might get sick. Prisoners entered single file, hands cuffed in front of them, chained feet dragging, wearing orange jumpsuits. People craned their necks to see.

I recognized him at once, head shaved smooth. My heartbeat pounded in my ears. His short brown goatee from the day of my birth had grown into a long, pointed beard with a bit of gray. His badge shone a deep, dark yellow. And then I saw his eyes and remembered them from the day of my birth—small and light brown, curved downward at the corners, the same as mine.

Our matching eyes met and stayed locked as a guard marched him toward me. I saw concern and hope in his eyes, not the evil I'd feared. As he got closer, every shred of anger I'd been harboring fell from me.

He stood in front of me now, on the other side of the table, and I found myself standing, too. Both our eyes filled with moisture. Maybe it was him I needed to thank for the curse of overactive tear ducts.

The guard unlocked my father's handcuffs, keeping his ankles shackled, and we reached out for each other across the table. His hands were warm and rough. Mine were cold from nerves, but they would thaw now.

"Have a seat, LaGray," the guard said, and we sat, never looking away from each other. The guard left us.

"I can't believe you're here," he said. His voice was as scratchy and gruff as I recalled. "I wrote so many letters over the years," he continued, "but it wasn't safe to send them to you. And . . . I wanted you to have a chance at a normal life."

"There was never any chance of that," I said as gently as I could.

He nodded and sniffed. He looked like a hard man—a scary man.

"You're probably right about that. I hoped you would learn from that nun when the time was right."

"Sister Ruth?" I asked. "I haven't met her yet. She talked to my adoptive mother."

"Have they treated you well, the people who raised you?"

I was shocked by his openness with me, his obvious sensitivity.

"Yes. Just one woman. Patti. And she's as close to an angel as humans can be. I've never been without love."

He relaxed, lowering his shoulders, but his eyes still brimmed with moisture.

"That's good. That's what I hoped for. What did Sister Ruth tell her?"

"She said you and my mother were in love."

He half smiled, and for a moment his face was dreamy, a far-off look passing over it.

"I've got a lot to tell you, and that's a good place to start," he said. "Back when I was an angel in heaven. If you want to hear it."

"I want to hear everything."

We still held hands, and there was no chance either of us was letting go. His rough thumbs rubbed the soft peaks of my knuckles. We sat with our chests leaning on the table, heads inclined toward each other, keeping our conversation as hushed as possible. I listened as he began.

"Before there was earth, there were angels in heaven, billions of us. We were content. Well, most of us. Angels are genderless. So our relationships in heaven weren't clouded by the physical. It was a community of friends, which may not sound compelling to a human, but it was good. It was right."

His face softened, reverently, as he remembered. I couldn't believe I was sitting there having a civil conversation with my father. I watched him, marveling, as he continued his story.

"Even though we angels could feel the full range of

emotions, there was never any need to feel dark for more than a moment or two, and then we let it go and moved on. Everyone had a role, and we were all used to the best of our abilities. We felt secure and important.

"When I met Mariantha, our personalities clicked right off." He paused, bashful at the mention of this angel, Mariantha. His tender expression was so contradictory to his hardened outer appearance.

"Mariantha is your mother, Anna," he explained.

My heart leaped. I nodded and bit my lip, savoring each detail.

"I was drawn to her. I say 'her,' but remember—we were genderless in the heavenly sphere. Our feelings were strictly emotional. I made excuses to see her time and time again. Our souls complemented each other to the point where, eventually, we couldn't stand to be apart. During that time there was an angel in the highest hierarchy who had the kind of charisma that quickly made him like a celebrity in the heavens."

"Lucifer," I whispered.

"Yep. I'd never met anyone like him. He had the kind of personality that draws others in. I wanted to hear everything he had to say. Mariantha said he gave her a bad feeling. She didn't think that a single angel needed to stand out so brightly. It was the only thing we ever disagreed on."

His face and tone were steeped in melancholy as he looked down at our hands.

"I started going to meetings to hear Lucifer speak. He was, and is, the master of deception. He would glorify God's work and the work of the realm, and then sneak in one backhanded comment to leave us pondering. Over time, the tiny seeds of doubt started to grow, and so did the number of angels who gathered to listen. Lucifer used partial truths mixed with lies, and we fell for it. I was shocked the day I realized my feelings about everything had changed. I didn't tell Mariantha." He whispered that last line with regret. Dread filled me, knowing where the story was headed.

"Lucifer gained a huge following. He knew he'd succeeded in warping our thoughts, and was ready to go full force. He told us with total conviction that God was secretly creating a new race and a whole new realm just for these humans. Lucifer said that the Maker was obsessed like a child with a new toy. He planned to use us angels as no more than slaves to the new race: the humans. Humans would have luxuries and freedoms and experiences that angels would never be allowed. We angels would be used, and trampled, and forgotten. I was pissed— Sorry, hon. Excuse my language."

I held back a smile. How cute that this giant demon was apologizing for a light curse.

"I was such a fool." He shook his head, remembering. "I really believed God was fallible. I thought he'd lost his mind. And I wasn't alone. One-third of the angels in heaven stood behind Lucifer. An angry mob of angels. Who could have imagined?"

He let go of my hand for a brief moment to smooth down his facial hair, in thought.

"I had to tell Mariantha everything at that point. She begged me not to fight, but I knew that when it was all over and she saw the truth, she would forgive me and understand.

So I left and joined the war. You know what happened after we lost, don't you?"

I swallowed. "You were cast into the pits of hell."

He nodded, looking painfully glum. "It wasn't till I found myself down there that I realized Lucifer's deception. Others realized it, too, but most still blindly supported him. I kept to myself 'cause I knew it would be dangerous to speak out against him. My silent nature earned me respect. They thought I was broody and vengeful, but in actuality I was hating myself for what I did to Mariantha. I couldn't stop thinking about her."

He stopped to look up at the ceiling. His heart still hurt after all this time. I rubbed his hands, encouraging him to continue.

"So, time passed and we heard stories about earth and humanity's creation. Lucifer sent up spies. He became bolder and bolder, sending up rebel angels to turn humans against the Creator."

His head suddenly snapped up and he looked over my shoulder. A strange hissing whisper came from deep in my father's throat, and his eyes flashed bright red. I yanked my hands away. When he looked back at me he seemed completely normal.

"Sorry about that," he said, distracted. "They're not supposed to work in my territory."

I couldn't respond. The entire episode, lasting no more than two seconds, had been the most terrifying thing I'd ever witnessed. Was that inhuman hissing some sort of demon language? I looked around, but no one else had noticed.

"I didn't mean to scare you. This isn't exactly a conversation for their ears, you know?"

"Yeah," I said. "I just didn't understand at first, because I can't see them."

"Really?" His forehead wrinkled as his eyebrows came together in worry. "That could be a problem."

I touched my necklace, still shaken.

"I might be wrong," I said. "But it sounds to me like you actually respect God. I don't understand how that can be, though, considering your . . . line of work." I lowered my eyes, hoping he wasn't offended.

"Ironic, huh?" His mouth hitched into a satirical grin. "I deserve hell. I was led astray too easily."

His forearms were still on the table, open palms up. I slipped my hands into his again, and he squeezed them.

"I worked my way up the ladder in hell for selfish reasons. I heard each human was assigned a guardian angel, and I became obsessed with the possibility of seeing Mariantha again. Something about my dreary attitude and hard work must have impressed Lucifer, because I found myself earthbound in the 1700s, with the job of leading humans to eventual addiction."

I felt a flicker of shame at the thought of drugs, and although I was careful to keep my colors hidden, my face was harder to control.

"I'm afraid I've been too successful," he whispered. "I knew when I was made a Duke that I would have to do a good job to keep the position. It was horrible when I came to earth and saw the human souls trapped in their physical forms. They were miraculous creations, truly a work of genius and love. But they're at odds with their own bodies. My job was too easy. I focused on seeing as many guardian angels as I could across the world, hundreds of thousands of them. It was the only thing worth existing for. I'd already lost everything.

"And then, seventeen years ago, I was in a small town not too far from here called Hemet, checking on one of my dealers there. I went into his house, and I'll never forget the moment I saw her. Damn, she was a beautiful sight," he whispered, pausing as if to replay the memory. "She was leaning over a human woman who was passed out on a mattress in the corner curled up real small—I thought she was a kid at first. You're a pipsqueak like her."

His grip tightened on my hands as he studied my midsection where my aura would be.

"You feel a strong pull to drugs, don't you?" he asked.

I nodded and he shook his head, unhappy.

"I can see it. And you've got a double whammy: the pull from me, plus the addiction in your genetics. That's got to be hard."

"I'm used to it now. My body might pull, but my mind knows better."

"Good. That's what I like to hear."

"All right, back to the story," I said, gripping his fingers.

"Yep, this is where it gets good. When I saw Mariantha she was whispering to that human woman like a mother with a feverish child. Nobody in the dealer's house cared when I picked the lady up and took her. That is, except her guardian angel, my Mariantha." He chuckled. "She saw *what* I was, but didn't register *who* I was at first. She went apeshhh—um, she went crazy trying to protect her human. And then she recognized me."

He said the last sentence with such adoration that our eyes watered at the exact same time. We both laughed, wiping them dry before clasping hands again.

"Mariantha and I took the human woman to a hotel and cleaned her up. It took a whole day for her to come to, and even then she was so far gone. Her body was ruined and her soul was barely hanging on. We both knew that if the lady died, Mariantha would have to escort her soul to the afterlife. Mariantha wouldn't be allowed to come back to earth afterward. We would never see each other again. So, hoping for the best, she climbed into that body, something no angel of light had done since Old Testament times."

I squeezed his hands, hanging on to every word.

"The human soul didn't fight her; she moved easily aside. It took almost three days to detox and heal the body. It was a lot for Mariantha to deal with her first time in physical form. It was hard to watch. I had to force her to eat and drink. She fought me, but she made it through. And when her mind was clear and we were together again, it was like it'd always been, only different. For the first time we weren't just souls; we were a man and woman overcome with physical attraction and . . . well, that's how you came along."

I blushed and he looked down, shamefaced.

"I shouldn't have let it happen," he said. "Not that I'm not happy you're here. Don't get me wrong. But in all my years as a demon, I'd been careful not to father any children of my own. It didn't seem right to me."

I was thankful for that.

"She knew right away that you were with her. We couldn't

help but be happy. We knew we didn't have long together, so we cherished every single second. I left her side only once, to make my report to Azael, hell's messenger. I couldn't let them know about you two. Mariantha heard stories through the other guardian angels about one last angelic Nephilim. We didn't know where else to turn."

"Wait, what do you mean, *angelic* Nephilim?"

"That nun is a descendant of an angel of light, probably a guardian angel. I'm not sure of her exact story."

I wanted to know how she had escaped the attention of the Dukes and Legionnaires, but I didn't want to ask my father and risk exposing the source of my information about demons. I somehow didn't think he'd be pleased by my relationship with Kaidan.

"We got to the convent just in time," he said. "You came early. Do you remember that day?"

"Yes." I pressed my lips together, feeling guilty about how I'd questioned his motives all these years. He squeezed my hands and tugged them so I'd look up at him. His face was open, full of love.

"I want you to know, baby girl, after I saw Mariantha go, I never led another soul to sin."

His eyes held mine, pleading for me to believe.

"Never?" I whispered. "This whole time you've been in prison?"

"I've given false reports to Lucifer for sixteen years. I know it doesn't make up for all the damage I've done, but I had to ensure my place on earth long enough to see you and tell you. Funny thing is, now that I've met you, it makes me want to stay even longer."

When I smiled at him, he gave me a look similar to the one Patti had given me the day she broke the news about my identity. He was thankful I wasn't mad at him, and it wrenched my heart open further, letting him all the way in. I squeezed his big hands.

"Dad," I said. We both jumped at the surprising sound of the word between us. I pressed on. "Do you know what Sister Ruth needs to tell me?"

"What do you mean?"

"Sister Ruth told Patti there were things she needed to discuss, but she'll tell me only in person."

He shook his head. "No idea," he said. His hold on my hands tightened. "I need you to listen to me, Anna. This is important. Whatever the nun tells you, you can't tell anyone about it. *Anyone.* If it's something big and it gets back to Lucifer, he'll have you killed. Hell, even if it's something small he'll have you killed. Who else knows about this besides us?"

"Just Patti . . ."

"Okay. That should be okay. Is that it?"

"And Kaidan," I added. My eyes darted everywhere but his face. I was in for it.

"Who?" There was an edge to his voice.

His eyes searched mine. I didn't want to tell him a single thing about Kaidan. I knew how it would sound. I took my hands from his, pulling the braid over my shoulder to mess with it.

"He's my friend. He's the one who drove me here to see you."

"You told some human kid?"

I coughed, buying time. "He's Neph, too."

Jonathan LaGray went rigid and his ruddy cheeks paled. I squirmed as his eyes bored into mine.

"Which one's his father?" he asked through clenched teeth.

"Richard Rowe. I guess you'd know him as Pharzuph."

Oh, boy. He wasn't pale anymore.

"You came across the country—"

"Shhh!" I warned him as people looked over. He lowered his voice to a shouted whisper.

"—with the son of the Duke of *Lust*?! Son of a—"

He pounded a fist down on the table and a guard stepped toward us. I waved and nodded at the man, trying to reassure him it was fine, and my father pulled his balled hands down into his lap. After a moment the guard walked back to the wall and looked away.

"Don't worry!" I whispered. "I told you; we're just friends."

He closed his eyes and massaged his forehead with his fingers to calm his temper.

"You tell him that his father is never to know about you or whatever Sister Ruth tells you. Understand?"

"He would never tell his father anything. But, um . . ." I swallowed. "Unfortunately, Pharzuph already knows about me."

His eyes flashed red again and it nearly stopped my heart. I pressed my back into the seat, causing it to wobble.

"Aren't you worried people will see your eyes when you do that?" I asked, sure that my own eyes were gigantic at that moment.

"Humans can't see it. And don't try to change the subject. I know Pharzuph," he growled. "He's a real bastard on earth and in hell. He'd do anything to gain favor."

"Kaidan thinks he'll forget about me if I lie low."

"Maybe momentarily, while he's busy or distracted with his work, but you'll cross his mind again someday."

He fidgeted in his chair. "I need to get out of here," he said.

"Out of prison? How?"

"I've got a parole hearing coming up. I'll use my influence to make sure it goes through. I will get myself out of here, one way or another, in a matter of weeks, and I'll contact you when it's safe. Don't do anything until I'm with you. I want you to go straight home after this trip. Get there as soon as possible and stay there. Will you do that?"

"Yes. I promise."

"Stay away from the Rowe house."

"Definitely."

"Good. Good girl. We'll work this thing out together. Do you trust me?"

"Yes, sir."

We took each other's hands again. With him by my side nothing seemed impossible, and I felt happy.

"You've got a pretty smile," he said. "A natural beauty."

Nobody had ever called me a beauty except Patti. Parents didn't count as far as compliments went, but it still made me feel good. I looked at the clock and was shocked to see how much time had already passed.

"We've got an hour left, gal. What else do you want to know?"

I still wasn't ready to ask about the fate of Nephilim souls. That would have to wait until last. I thought for a second.

"Do you think Mariantha's been punished?" I asked.

"Well, she's not in hell, if that's what you mean. I would have heard about it if she were."

My stomach tightened at the mention of hell. "What's it like?" I asked hesitantly. "Down there?"

"It's another one of those things that's hard to explain." He let go of one hand and stroked his beard. "Imagine a dark, wide alleyway that goes on forever, between two skyscrapers that stretch as far up as you can see. It's hard to maintain hope. Souls burn from sheer negativity."

"You're pretty good at describing things that are hard to explain," I said, shaking off the chill from the image.

"I've had plenty of time to think about it."

"Why didn't God try to stop Lucifer from planning that rebellion?"

"He loved Lucifer. He saw that he had great power, and he allowed it. It could have gone either way. Lucifer was capable of choosing right. I think God was holding out hope that he would make the right choice. Maybe it seems cruel to test the angels and the human souls, but it's not like that. We have to face difficulties to find out what our true strengths are. How we come back from a failure is a very valuable test."

"Yes. You could have wanted revenge after the fall," I said.

"Easily. And it's all especially hard for humans, who are given the test of faith without ever seeing everything with their own eyes. That's why they're given the ability to sense the Holy Spirit."

"How does it work?"

He leaned back in his chair, rubbing his hands over his smooth head. "The Holy Spirit is like billions of cell phone signals coming from God and connecting with each soul, a direct link. People process the messages as feelings, sometimes even hearing their own voice in their mind, so it's easy to disregard."

I nodded, watching him in awe. He had an answer for everything. It was a lot to take in, yet there was so much more I still wanted to know.

"Is the fate of each person set in stone?" I asked.

"No, no, no. There is no 'fate' in that sense. Nobody was made to fail. For individual souls, there's always choice. Every time a choice is made, a new path forms. From what I understand, humans are told before going to earth that life will be difficult. They know what hardships they'll have to face. They know it's a test, and they're *eager* for it. You, too, knew before you came to earth that you'd be born into these circumstances."

A spark lit up in my mind. I gasped and sat up straighter. The lost knowledge from my dark days!

"I knew there was something more! I still can't remember it, though."

My dad chuckled at me.

"Don't beat yourself up, kid. It'll all come back once you shed that body. No soul can fathom how difficult it'll be once they're in physical form and they can't remember anymore."

I kept smiling, feeling buoyant with this new information. And then a question rose in my mind that robbed me of happiness.

"Why do mothers of Nephilim always die?"

He nodded, as if he'd expected this. Dropping his forearms to the table, he took my hands again.

"We talked about this a lot when Mariantha was pregnant. When the female body was created, it was made as a vessel to usher another human soul through the realms. You always hear people talking about the miracle of birth, and it's true. It's a miracle each time a soul makes the passage. But a Neph soul is different from a human soul. It's something *more*. The human body wasn't created to be able to expel such a complex soul into the earthly realm. It can't physically survive it."

Oh. Wow. This was huge. "And is this general knowledge among the demons?" I asked.

"Of course, but they don't go flaunting the fact that the Neph are so powerful. Don't want to put any ideas in the minds of their kids."

It was yet another way the Neph had been deceived and downtrodden. I couldn't wait to tell Kaidan the truth. I wanted to get to the bottom of everything. So many questions were bouncing around in my mind. I told him about Hollywood and how much it broke my heart to feel all of the people's suffering.

"Angels of light are extremely sensitive to the emotions of others, so you got that from your mother, which is good, Anna, but you can't be so sensitive that you're blind to the bigger picture. Didn't you ever get hurt when you were little? Fall down and skin your knee?"

"Sure."

"Does it still hurt?"

"No. I see where you're going with this," I said.

"I know it sounds trite. I would never suggest saying this to someone who's in the middle of a tragedy, but even the worst earthly pain and heartache doesn't last into the heavenly realm. And it all serves a bigger purpose."

"But what about the suffering of the Neph?" I asked, indignant. "The way they're treated . . ."

"I know. I've always believed the Nephilim are the strongest souls on earth. I think even the Dukes feel threatened by them. If anyone could overthrow the demons, it's their own children."

But the children are scared, I wanted to say. *We've been told we'll end up in hell*. I should have asked then, but I wasn't ready to hear it. I peeked at the clock. Time was going by way too fast.

"Tell me more," I said. "Tell me anything. What's the meaning of life?"

He let out a big, burly laugh.

"You thought you'd stump me with that one, didn't you? It's actually very simple. The purpose of life is to find your way back to a spiritual way of thinking and living—to be able to get past the physical stuff. That's pretty much the whole test. And every soul is given talents and strengths to help them along the way."

"That's *it*?!"

He snickered at my bug-eyed response.

"It's much harder than it sounds." He looked up at the clock now. "Ten more minutes, little one. What else you got for me?"

There was thunder in my heart. I looked at his big, weathered hands holding mine on the table. I couldn't put it off any longer.

228

"Is it true there's a stain on my soul, and I'm condemned to go to hell no matter what? That's not true, is it?"

His breathing had gone shallow as he stared at me. A tremble began to shake his chin, and he looked away. *No. Please, no.* I shook my head, pulling my hands away to cover my face. My heart ached and my eyes stung.

"Please forgive me, Anna." His voice was quiet. "This is why I never wanted children. Please look at me."

I moved my hands down from my watering eyes, pressing my fingers over my mouth.

"It might be different for you. Your mother's good might cancel out my bad. We don't know. And if it's true, then I'll be there with you. We'll stick together through the darkness."

"Why would He do that to us?" My voice rose. "To all of the Nephilim children? It's not our fault!"

He leaned across the table, grasping my hands from my face and holding them. His eyes were set on mine.

"Nothing good comes from anger," he said. "Trust me. It'll keep you from thinking clearly. I know you don't want that. Don't lose hope. Remember, hell is only a holding place. You'll get your shot at judgment. We can't know everything about the ultimate plan. It'd be like trying to teach infants quantum physics."

I rubbed my face, trying to nod and swallow the sob in my chest. I didn't want to go to hell. There was nothing more petrifying than the idea of a place absent of love.

"Two minutes!" hollered a guard by the door. "Wrap it up and say your good-byes, folks."

We both stood. I came around the table and went into his

thick, solid arms. He smelled like soap. It was surreal to be hugged by him, but so right. He kissed the top of my head.

"I love you, Dad."

"You don't know how good those words sound to me. I've loved you every day of your life. Thank you for coming to me. I'm proud of you."

He pulled away and lifted my chin to make me look at him.

"Remember everything I told you, got that?"

I nodded.

"And tell the Rowe boy to keep his paws off my little girl, 'cause I'll be out soon to take care of him if he doesn't."

"*Daaaad.*"

Embarrassing.

A whistle blew and we pulled away from each other. Everyone was standing, hugging, and walking to the doors. My stomach tightened.

"Please be careful," he urged.

"I'll see you soon?"

"You bet." He kissed my forehead and I grudgingly joined the other visitors leaving.

At the door I turned back. He was still watching me, tall and stoic. My whole life I'd fooled myself into thinking I didn't need his love, but I'd been wrong. Everyone needed their father's love.

A freshly shaved Kaidan leaned against his shiny black SUV with his arms crossed in the bright California sunshine. He stood up and took off his sunglasses when he saw me. I couldn't look at him. I walked past and opened the door, climbing in.

He didn't ask any questions. He just got in and drove, keeping his eyes on the road. When we'd driven five miles from the prison, I hid my face in my hands and let loose every tear I had in me.

CHAPTER SEVENTEEN

FIRST SACRIFICE

Across from the hotel was a tiny Laundromat with five washers and five dryers run by coin slots. I spent the afternoon doing laundry while Kaidan went to the hotel's gym. He'd given me his phone in case the convent called. I sat alone in a small chair, thinking, while the dryer ran.

I'd asked Kaidan if he'd been listening to our conversation while he waited at the prison. He admitted that when he returned that afternoon, he listened for a moment to make sure I was okay, but that was it, and I believed him.

I told him every detail of what my father said. He had been a quiet listener, not saying much. Not even *I told you so* about the final part.

The clothes were finally dry, so I stood there pulling them

out one at a time, folding them.

I jumped and let out an embarrassing squeak when two hands came around my waist.

"Just me, luv," he said, close to my ear. "Aren't you the picture of domestication? Do you cook as well?"

I put both hands on the edge of the dryer to steady myself. The machine was still hot.

"Kai," I said. I could feel his nose and mouth move over my hair. Why was he doing this to me? Telling me not to romanticize him, and then nuzzling me from behind? "You shouldn't . . ."

My knees were shaking. I was so confused. What I really wanted to do was close my eyes and lean back into him, pretending for just a moment that we were together. But I pressed on from a place inside of me that was stronger than my body. I couldn't be one of his momentary girls.

"Unless you're going to be my boyfriend, you shouldn't touch me like this."

He did not pull away, repulsed, as I had expected. Instead, he spoke into my hair.

"The Neph are not permitted to be in relationships, especially not with one another."

"Nobody has to know," I said into the air, closing my eyes. "Just us."

"It can never happen." His rejection was gentle, but firm.

Again, from the place of strength, I found myself taking his hands, untwining them from around my waist, and moving them away from me. A second later he was gone. Hot and then cold, over and over.

233

It can never happen. I had to lean on the dryer now, breathing deeply, feeling the heat. For once my eyes stayed dry.

I had known in my heart there was no chance. Of course there wasn't. He hadn't said he did not want to be with me, only that it wasn't allowed. I tried to cling to that, but I knew I shouldn't. Whatever the reason, there would never be an "us," not even in secret, certainly not exclusive, and the sooner I got my head wrapped around that fact, the better.

I piled the clothes into my arms and headed to the room.

Kaidan was watching TV on his bed. He didn't look at me. I set his clothes on the dresser and packed mine back into my bag. I saw the red T-shirt in the bottom of my bag, the one he'd loaned me at his house. I went and placed it on his pile. I thought about what to do next. My book bag sat on the floor with all my summer reading for AP English that Patti had insisted I bring. I picked it up and lugged it to my bed.

"What are you getting into?" he asked.

I guessed he was going to act like nothing happened. Well, two could play that.

"English," I said, tossing a book of American poetry and my notebook on the bed in front of me. Kaidan turned off the TV and came over, laying his long self across my bed, taking the book, and opening it.

The nerve.

And then it dawned on me painfully. Maybe he wasn't pretending it was no big deal. Maybe it really wasn't a big deal to him at all. And why would it be? Many girls, far more enticing than me, had no doubt asked him to commit, and he'd rejected each one. Why did I think I was any different? Because we shared a secret about our parents and some freaky senses?

I've heard the saying that you can't miss what you never had. Only I did. The disappointment hurt.

I found an unoccupied corner at the top of my bed and sat with my legs crossed. My head was killing me. I pulled the braid over my shoulder and tugged off the rubber band. I untwined the strands of hair and ran my nails along my sore scalp. I combed my fingers through the deep waves made by the braid to get out any tangles. Kaidan made a strange guttural sound and then coughed. When I looked over he was staring hard at the book. His eyes moved over me and went back to the book again. What was his problem?

I felt pouty, and I was glad I knew how to hide my colors now. I opened my notebook with a dramatic whoosh and yanked out the top worksheet. The first question made me grumble.

"What's the matter?" Kaidan asked.

"I can't stand these kinds of questions. 'What is the author's opinion of death, as seen in lines eighteen to twenty-one?' It's a poem, for crying out loud! The beauty of poetry is that it can mean different things to different people at different times. But you know they're expecting one specific, so-called correct answer, and any other thoughtful response will be counted off. It's wrong to dissect poetry like this!"

I threw down the paper in heated passion and felt his hand cup my cheek. I hadn't even noticed him sitting up during my tirade. My heart was already pumping hard when I turned my face to him. Kaidan's eyes were on fire, and his sweet, earthy scent slammed my senses.

"Seriously," I whispered, unable to look away. "You're doing that bedroom-eyes thing again."

We met halfway. His lips were as hot as his eyes, sending a shock wave through me. His tender mouth opened mine and I could sense the red of passion, like silk, circling us, pulling us closer. I was aware of a halfhearted battle within me, but I clambered nearer, pushing the notebook and papers to the floor.

His lips broke away from mine and moved greedily down my neck. A moan escaped me at the feel of his hot breath on my skin, and it was all the encouragement he needed. He was on top of me, and I was gripped by an unfamiliar hunger. I hushed the urgent whisper of my heart by grabbing his shirt and tugging it up until it was over his head, and his smooth brown skin was *everywhere*, emanating heat. He unbuttoned my shirt and I wiggled out of it. It was off, tossed to the floor with the notebook, and my tank top was over my head, in his hand, then soaring across the room. His lips were on mine again, our bare skin crushed together, but we still needed to be closer. He pulled his lips just far enough away to speak.

"What time will Patti be calling?"

I managed a glimpse at the clock, feeling his mouth on my collarbone.

"Not for an hour," I whispered.

"That simply is *not* going to be enough time."

In one smooth motion he flipped us so we were both sitting up, me across his lap with my legs wrapped around him. My hair brushed my skin, soft in contrast to the hardness of his hands. His perfect lips moved over my shoulders, pushing my bra straps down and nipping with just enough pressure. My head lolled back into his waiting hand. I pressed my hips against his and was rewarded when he groaned, flipping us again, so fluidly.

His mouth was on the small swell of skin peeking out from the top of my bra. My hands were in his thick hair. He kissed down my upper body to my belly button, keeping his hands under my back, concentrating on my skin. I was gasping for short breaths now, unable to control myself as his lips burned a trail down to the edge of my shorts. He flicked open the button and licked the sensitive skin there. I gasped, and he made a masculine growling sound at me before he spoke.

"Now would be the time to stop me, luv. You're about to be undressed, and trust me when I say it will be too late after that."

My body was overpowering my mind. I couldn't think. I could only smell and taste and see and hear and *feel* him.

An annoying whisper sounded from the depths of my mind again, but something else was there too: something I had managed to flatten to the bottom of my consciousness until now. The demonic doubt.

We were damned for simply being born. So why was I holding fast to rules that didn't really apply to me anyway? Why shouldn't I take from this life what I could in the time I had? This had nothing to do with what Pharzuph demanded of us, and everything to do with what Kaidan and I had become to each other.

"No, Kai," I said, arching my back under his hot fingers. "Don't stop."

His face was in front of mine again, our mouths moving in a harmonic frenzy. My hands moved from his hair, over his hard chest, down the ripple of his stomach, around his waist, and up over his firm back. I pulled him to me. I couldn't believe this was happening. Excitement and fear coursed through my blood.

And then there was . . . *confusion.*

He was murmuring something to himself that I couldn't make out, then shaking his head. I pulled him to me again, but he reached down, taking my wrists and holding them between us. I lifted my hips to him and was shocked to meet resistance. What was going on?

"We can't," he barely whispered.

"Kai?" He was pulling himself away from me, and it was such torture that I could hardly bear it.

I made one final attempt to revive the closeness, reaching for him, but he had gone to stone above me.

"Damn it, Ann, please! Don't. Move."

I lay still, breathing hard and staring into his deep blue eyes until he ripped his gaze away.

He rolled to the side of the bed and got up, moving an agonizing distance away. He groaned and grabbed his hair hard in both of his fists, then began to pace, shaking his head from side to side. His bloodred badge pumped as hard as my heart.

I sat up, mindful of my heated, exposed skin in the room's cool air. I grabbed a pillow and pressed it to my chest in a tight hug. Every inch of skin he had kissed felt like it was on fire.

Rejection swept over me, turning my heat to ice. Saying he wouldn't be my boyfriend was one thing. But this?

"You don't want me." Such a pathetic revelation would have been better left unsaid.

He groaned again, louder this time, and squatted to the floor, pushing his fists into his eyes. He was in obvious pain. I wanted to reach out to him, but I knew I couldn't.

"Don't do that." His voice was jagged. "That was the single most difficult thing I've done in my entire life."

He stood again, the sight of his body slamming into me full force.

"I don't understand, then," I whispered.

"You didn't do anything wrong, okay?" His voice edged on frantic. "And don't think for a second I don't want you—" He had to stop and growl at this, pressing his knuckles to his forehead. "It shouldn't be like this," he said.

"Like what?" I asked.

"Uncommitted. In a hotel room."

"Then commit," I said. His face tightened and he held his arms out in frustration.

"I can't!" he shouted. "And I'm *not* taking your virginity. You would regret it."

He turned away from me, leaning his forehead against the wall. He was still out of breath as he slid downward, turning and slumping in the corner of the room, elbows on his knees, face in his hands.

I let the meaning of what had just happened soak in. We'd come so close, and Kaidan denied himself. For me. He'd made his very first self-sacrifice. For me. He'd defied his demon father. For me.

A vibrant energy rushed through my body as the pieces

slammed into place. Oh, dear Lord. I was in love with him. And there wasn't a thing on earth, in heaven, or in hell that could have stopped me.

In that moment of shocking realization, he turned to me and stared. My emotional guard was down. I snapped my mind back into hiding mode, but it was too late. He'd seen it. I held my breath for his reaction. He closed his eyes and let his head drop to his chest, posture slumping. Not the response of my dreams.

I focused, finding it difficult to contain the hugeness of my emotion for him. Now that I saw it for what it was, it was all-encompassing. I closed my eyes and kept it hidden with every scrap of willpower in me.

I stood, still hugging the pillow, and walked quickly over to retrieve my shirt from the top of the television. Dropping the pillow, I pulled the tank top over my head and buttoned my shorts. I needed to leave—take a walk to clear my head and give him time to himself.

And then the phone rang. Oh, geez!

He didn't move, so I walked over to the nightstand where it lay and peeked at the caller ID. My heart leaped and my fingers fumbled to pick it up and press the green button.

"Hello?" I said.

"Miss Whitt? It's Sister Emily."

"Is she awake?"

"I'm so sorry, dear. Sister Ruth has gone to be with the Lord."

What?! My stomach plummeted and I sat hard on the bed, a profound sense of loss inundating my soul.

"No," I whispered.

"I'm afraid so. Several years ago she had a will drawn up, and she left everything to you. I've gone through her personal effects and there was only one thing besides her clothing and her Bible. A small box. Can you come to the convent?"

"Yes. I'll be right there."

CHAPTER EIGHTEEN

GETTING ZAPPED

Nestled within the big city was the small convent, quaint and hidden among a border of evergreens, overshadowed by the larger orphanage next to it. It wasn't the kind of place that would attract interest from tourists. It would go easily unnoticed by most locals, too.

Kaidan pulled the car through the open gate. Past the trees and a small lawn was a simple, two-story faded brick building, overrun on the sides by vines. We parked in a gravel area and looked at the building. I remembered it, only without as many vines.

We'd been silent the entire ride. I wished I could somehow ease the tension between us, but it had to run its course. Things had shifted tonight. In a big way.

"I'll wait here," Kaidan told me. I got out and made my way to the entrance on a cracked concrete walkway. The early evening air was still hot, but made bearable by the sweetness of honeysuckle in the air.

At the door, I read the small placard: CONVENT OF OUR MOTHER MARY. I pulled up on the heavy brass knocker and let it fall three times. A young nun answered wearing a long-sleeved flowered dress falling below her knees, with white tights and sandals. Her hair was pulled into a bun, and a crucifix hung around her neck.

The sister touched a hand to her heart. A thin stream of navy blue grief ran through the lavender peace in her aura. "You must be Anna. Thank you so much for coming."

She invited me into the foyer area and gave me a warm hug, which I needed, even from a stranger. As she left to retrieve the box, I looked around the creamy walls of the foyer and felt comforted. I could remember being there in Patti's arms as she said good-bye to Sister Ruth sixteen years ago. There was still a fountain against the wall, trickling a stream of water like a rush of nostalgia.

The young nun came down the wooden steps and handed me a small box. It was over a foot in length and sealed with layers of tape.

"Thank you for everything," I told her.

"You're welcome, dear." She clasped her hands in front of her. "I'm sorry you didn't get a chance to meet Sister Ruth. She was the most precious soul I've ever known."

"I'm sorry, too."

She dabbed at her eyes with a handkerchief, and I felt the

huge regret of loss as we hugged one last time and I turned to leave.

Sister Ruth was gone, and with her went whatever knowledge she'd held. Kaidan didn't glance at me when I climbed back in with the box on my lap. He made a fast turn and exited the lot, kicking up gravel. His mood hadn't improved.

I wanted him to say something. I ran my fingers along the taped edges of the box, sorting through a list of meaningless topics that could fill the space between us. Sister Ruth's death only deepened the void.

When we got back to the hotel, we walked to the room together. I climbed on my bed and sat with the box on my lap. I looked up at Kaidan, who was half sitting, half leaning on the table across from me with his arms crossed and his eyes far away in thought.

"May I use one of your knives?" I asked.

"Here, let me." He sat across from me and pulled out a knife, slicing around the edges. I opened the cardboard flap. Inside was a wooden box so old and smooth that the wood looked petrified. I pulled it out and set the cardboard box on the floor. A small gold clasp held the lid shut. I undid the clasp and lifted the lid. At first I couldn't process what I was seeing. It was made of silver . . . no, maybe it was gold . . . no . . . What was it? It glimmered with a range of metallic colors from bronze to platinum, as if it were alive.

"Is that a sword hilt?" I asked. Just looking at it frightened me. "What's it made of?"

Kaidan was leaning toward it and staring with rapt disbelief.

"May I?" he asked, gesturing toward it.

"Go ahead."

He gingerly picked it up and cradled it in his hand, turning it from side to side. The metal shimmered like nothing I'd ever seen.

"I don't believe it," Kaidan whispered.

"What? What is it?"

His face seemed to register the object, and he dropped it back into the wooden box, rubbing his hands together and staring down with awe-inspired terror.

I reached down to feel it myself, but when my finger touched the warm metal, a bolt of energy zapped through my finger and up my arm. I yelled and yanked my hand away. Kaidan sat up straight and stared at me, hair hanging in his rounded eyes.

"What is this thing?" I asked.

"It clearly wasn't forged on earth," he stammered. "I think . . . But it's impossible. A Sword of Righteousness?"

"What's that?"

"They were used by the angels in the war of the heavens."

Now it was my turn to gawk down at it with that same fearful respect.

"But why is she giving it to me?" My heart accelerated.

"Only the angels of light could use them. The old legends say the blade will appear only when needed if the wielder is pure of heart. Anna . . . it's the one known weapon that can take out a demon spirit."

We stared at each other, sharing a secret that could doom us.

"And why is she giving it to me?" I asked again, my heart beating as fast as it could.

I have no idea how long we continued to stare at each other, searching for meaning, before he stood up and moved away from me. He felt for his phone in his pocket and spoke to me as he was getting on his shoes and heading for the door.

"I need to clear my head. Patti called while you were in the convent and I told her about Sister Ruth. Call her on the room phone and I'll pay the charge." The door shut behind him and I sat there stunned.

Sister Ruth gave me a weapon. I didn't know what to do with a sword! Was I expected to kill demons? If only I'd come to L.A. sooner so I could speak with her.

I called Patti with the intention of telling her everything about the visit with my father and what Sister Ruth left me, and then I remembered how careful the nun had been with the information. She would tell me only in person. So I told Patti all went well and I'd give her every detail when I got home. The phone felt unsafe.

"You sound exhausted, honey," Patti said when I was finished. "Why don't you go get some rest. We can talk more tomorrow, 'kay?"

I was worn out when we hung up. As I climbed into bed I wondered what Kaidan was doing and who he might be calling, not that it was any of my business. But I was worried about him. I thought about trying to listen for him, but if he wanted privacy he would be more than a mile away by now. Kaidan didn't come back to the room until after I'd been in bed awhile, half in and half out of sleep.

I tossed and turned all night, even crying out and waking myself once with a dream I couldn't recall. Kaidan lay still all night in his own bed. I never did hear his deep-sleep breathing.

CHAPTER NINETEEN

UNACCOMPANIED MINOR

I must have finally dozed off, only to be awoken by a screeching buzz. I sat straight up. It was four thirty in the morning. Kaidan hit the alarm.

"We need to get an early start," he said, sounding wide-awake and just as forlorn as last night.

"Oh. Uh, m'kay."

It was still dark out as we sped down the interstate. Despite a hot shower, I was still sleepy. The city was calm at this early hour on a Sunday morning. There were hardly any cars on the road. We passed a sign for LAX, which bothered me, because we hadn't passed the airport on our way into the city.

"Where are we going?" I asked.

He cleared his throat and said without kindness, "You're going home today."

My jaw dropped.

"Everything's been arranged," he said. "Patti will be waiting for you when your flight arrives in Atlanta."

There it was again—rejection punching me in the stomach.

"Why?" I forced out.

His voice was soft, but still held that serious edge. "Things have gotten too complicated."

"Do you mean because of the sword, or is it me?" I asked.

"It's you." What had I done, besides care for him? This was unfair!

"Is it so unbearable to be around someone who cares for you?" I asked.

"I'd say that you're feeling a bit more than 'care' for me, Anna." He was getting snippy now, gripping the steering wheel. "I could see your emotion popping around you like pink bubble gum last night."

"So what?!" I was fully awake and working up the volume now. "I haven't tried to *say* it to you. I'm sorry that I lost focus for a second and let you see it!"

He took the airport exit, speaking to me with maddening calmness bordering on coldness. "Don't be dramatic about this."

"You don't call this dramatic? Abandoning me at the airport before daylight?"

"I'll see that you're in safe hands before I leave." His calm demeanor unnerved me.

"Don't bother," I spit. I could see now how people said hurtful things to the ones they loved out of anger. In my mind

I ran through all of the cutting things I could say to him.

He pulled up to a departure curb and put the car in park.

Just as quickly as my anger had come, it was now replaced by sadness.

"I've never even been on a plane," I said, grasping at straws.

"You will be fine."

"I want to stay with you." Desperation.

"You can't," he said in zombie mode. "Your father was right. You should get home as soon as possible. I don't trust myself with you."

"Don't trust yourself? Or don't trust me?"

He stared straight ahead as we sat there. I grabbed the fabric at his shoulder and tugged. "Answer me!"

He turned his face, and as our eyes met his calm facade cracked, unleashing his anger and fears.

"I don't trust either of us! We can't be together in *any* capacity *ever* again. It's a damn-near miracle you're still a virgin now. If that Sword of Righteousness is intended for you to use, then you should want to stay away from me, too, because I promise I could not resist if you told me to pull the car into the parking garage right now." He leaned closer. "Could you resist a drug if I repeatedly placed it on the tip of your tongue, Ann? Could you? We're playing with fire!"

He looked beyond me to the airport, breathing hard.

"So, what are you going to do now?" I asked him. "Go back to doing your father's work and pretend you never knew me?"

He sighed and his demeanor softened. "What would you have me do?"

250

What *would* I have him do? Have meaningless sex with girl after girl, or deny his father and be killed? Both thoughts shot through me like iced arrows, piercing my heart.

"You have to work," I choked out. I hated the truth of it.

The look he gave me was full of bitterness.

"Do you know what my father said when I came home the night after he met you? He said God was a fool to put you in my path. And he was right."

"No." I gritted my teeth. "Your father was wrong! And how do you know it wasn't *you* who was put in *my* path? There's a purpose for you in all of this, too."

Kaidan shook his head. I could see his jaw clenching in the indention of his temple. He looked at me hard.

"Do you want to know why my father chose to live in Atlanta, even though his job was in New York? He's got this infatuation going on with that human woman Marissa. She's the madam of an underground prostitution ring in Atlanta. International sex slavery. Young girls from starving families are sold to her. And guess who gets to introduce those girls to their new lives?"

I held my breath and froze. There were no words to comfort this kind of pain. My stomach clenched.

"Marissa calls the girls her nieces. The girl they brought me the night before our trip was the youngest ever. She couldn't have been twelve."

Dear God.

"For the first time ever I refused him, told him I couldn't. And do you know why?"

I shook my head, riveted by his eyes as the words poured

out of him fast and powerful.

"Because all I could think about was you, Anna, and how *good* you are, and what you'd think. You put thoughts into my head that Neph shouldn't have!" He paused, staring out the window. "My father let it slide for now, but he was furious. He'll be watching me now, testing me. I can't afford to have anything more to do with you."

We were quiet a long time. I didn't want to leave him yet. Not like this. I had no idea what to say.

"Kai . . . I know you're scared and freaked out. I am, too. But maybe this sword is a sign that something's going to happen. Something good for the Neph."

His head was lowered. He was staring blankly at the console between us.

"You felt power when you touched the hilt, didn't you?" he asked, lifting his blue eyes to me through strands of hair. I nodded. "Well, I didn't. I'm not worthy to help with whatever plan they have for you. So just go back to your sweet and innocent life and stay away from me."

"Please," I begged. "Don't push me away. We can be friends, and—"

He took my chin in his firm hand and looked at me.

"We can never just be friends, Anna. Get it through your head now. There can be *nothing*."

He released me and got out of the car. I sat there, hating the stinging in my eyes and throat. I watched in the side mirror as he spoke with an airline worker at the outdoor check-in. With a short extension of my senses I heard him tell the man my ticket had been purchased over the phone last night and

I was traveling as an unaccompanied minor for the very first time. The employee assured him they'd look after me.

Kaidan thanked him and walked back to the car, opening my door. I took my time stepping out. I thought about making a scene, but I couldn't bring myself to do it. He showed me a small wad of money and then pushed it into my pocket.

"You gave all yours away," he explained, then turned before I could argue and went to the check-in desk again.

In a foggy dream I was presenting my ID and receiving a boarding pass. We walked back to the car, out of the way of other passengers who were showing up. We stood facing each other. Did it have to be like this? I took a chance and leaned my forehead against his chest, expecting him to push me away, but he didn't. He let me lean against him, but he kept his own hands at his sides.

"It's time for you to go," he said.

"Wait." I looked up at him. "There's something I need to know." I was scrambling for time, and there'd been something nagging at me this whole trip, especially after last night. "Remember at the beginning of the trip, when you said you always know right away what you'd have to do to get a girl into bed . . . even me?"

He shoved his hands deep into his pockets, and I saw his forearms flex. His eyes went smoky blue in that dangerous way of his, and he gave a single nod.

"What would you have to do?" I asked. "For me?"

"Let's not go there," he said in a low voice.

"Tell me. Please."

He stared at my face, paying special attention to my freckle.

253

He wet his lips and clenched his jaw.

"Fine," he finally said. "I'd have to make you believe I loved you."

I closed my eyes. That one hurt. Mostly because I realized deep down, I *had* thought he loved me. I had a very bad case of good-girl syndrome.

Had this whole trip been a game for him, then? Was I nothing more than another silly girl who'd been foolish enough to fall for him? I shook my head. I couldn't believe that. He stared down, daring me to ask more.

"I wish, just once, that I could see your colors," I whispered.

"Well, I'm glad you can't. And I wish I'd never seen yours."

He'd been right when he said the truth could hurt far worse than any lie.

With a deep breath I turned from him, picked up my bag, and walked into the airport, not looking back.

"The mind is its own place, and in itself
Can make a heaven of hell, a hell of heaven."
—*John Milton*, Paradise Lost

CHAPTER TWENTY

ELEPHANT IN THE ROOM

If I didn't know any better, I would swear Patti could see colors and read minds. Maybe it went along with the territory of motherhood. When she picked me up from the airport, she stated halfway home, "You're in love with him."

All I could do was nod.

"You're hurting. I shouldn't have let you go," she said.

"No, I'm glad I went. I had to do it. I wouldn't take it back. Besides, unrequited love is one of those things that all teenagers have to go through, right?" I tried to smile.

"Unrequited?" She raised her eyebrows in dispute. "I'd say that boy has feelings for you, too. You're probably not the only one hurting right now."

We didn't talk anymore on the way home, but I mulled over what she'd said.

I mapped our trip backward in my mind to imagine where Kaidan might be at any given moment. I could think of nothing else. Jay didn't know I'd come home early, and I wasn't ready to talk to him yet.

My hopes rose every time the phone rang, but it was never him. I concocted stories in my mind of every possible scenario where he would come for me or call me and declare his feelings. We would run far away together, where his father could never find us.

In other words, I was delusional.

So this was what girls did after being ditched by Kaidan Rowe? Now I understood all of the messages he'd received. I wondered whether each one of them had felt as special as I had under his touch. I wondered whether it was supposed to hurt less, since he dumped me for our own good. Because it didn't.

The day I returned, I went back to work, requesting as many hours as possible.

Patti gave me a lot of space on my first day home.

The second day she tried to cheer me.

"Wanna hit up some yard sales with me?"

I shook my head.

"How about a day at the lake?"

I shook my head harder. *No way.*

"Okay, then. I know it's not officially a special occasion, but what do you say to Mexican food?" Her eyes sparkled as she waggled her eyebrows.

I burst into tears.

On the third day I was determined to get myself out of this unhealthy funk, for Patti's sake if nothing else. Self-pity was like wearing a wool jacket in the sweltering heat, and I wanted it gone. So I went for a short run first thing in the morning. It helped a little.

When I got back home, Patti saw me from where she sat on the balcony. She came into the apartment with a hint of yellow in her aura.

"Ready for your hot chocolate?" she asked.

I thought about that.

"I think I'll have coffee instead."

She eyed me, surprised, and then nodded.

We sat on the couch and she handed me a cup of hot coffee with sugar and cream. I sipped it. It was a little bitter, but bitter suited me.

"I know that you're going through a dark time right now," Patti said, rubbing my arm. "I need you to be strong. When you're hurting and afraid is when you need to dig the deepest."

I nodded, but I wasn't feeling strong. I didn't feel like the kind of person who was worthy of being entrusted with a heavenly artifact. I felt like a little girl pretending to be a coffee drinker.

She must have sensed my self-doubt, because she reached across our laps and hugged me hard enough to squeeze my head off, nearly spilling our coffees.

I ran again that afternoon. Next I read, or tried to, at least. Then I ate a ginormous bowl of rocky-road ice cream. When that was finished I listened to all the songs that used to be my favorites but somehow no longer evoked any feeling. I missed Kaidan's playlist.

Patti's constant company helped put a crack in my dark demeanor, and a tiny sliver of light now seeped in. But I needed something more. It was time to dunk myself into the ultimate cheer tank, something I'd been avoiding.

I called Jay.

"You're home! What's up, girl? How was it?"

I relaxed into the couch at the sound of his voice. "It was . . . good. I'm glad I went."

"Good? *Good?!* Okay, I can see you're gonna be difficult. I'm coming over. Stay right where you are, shorty."

Jay was in my living room in record time, full of life and a yellow-orange energy. He picked me up in a bear hug and I squealed. In the week since I'd seen him, his hair had grown into a thick fuzz, and his little chin hair was longer, too. He sprawled himself on the couch and I sat cross-legged in the recliner.

"First of all," he started, "how long did it take for you to fall for him?"

His tone was superlight, but I blanched.

"Lemme guess," he said. "Two days!"

"Four," I said softly.

Jay let out a *whoot* and smacked his knee.

"Stronger than the average girl." He gave me a proud grin. "Wait, you're not really, like, *in love* or whatever, are you?"

"I love him."

"Geez, don't sound *too* happy about it."

"Think about who we're discussing here," I reminded him.

He registered that. "Did he hurt you?"

"Not physically."

"Did you guys do it? Not that it's any of my business, but did you?"

"No." Thanks to Kaidan.

I concentrated on the unraveling upholstery on the arm of the recliner.

"You okay?" he asked.

"Not yet."

"Damn." He sat back on the couch and looked out the back door. "Well, don't take it too hard. You're way too sweet for him anyway."

I swallowed hard.

"How'd it go with your dad?" he asked.

This was more comfortable ground, although I'd have to filter almost the entire conversation.

"It was good. He's got a shaved head like a big, scary biker." I got a cozy feeling as I thought of my dad. "I'm glad I met him. I think he'll be a big part of my life now, weird as it sounds."

"That's awesome, Anna."

"Yeah." I told him all about my dad's redemption found in prison, and how he might be getting out soon. I was already looking forward to seeing him again.

Patti came home, an aura of soft blue relief blooming around her when she saw me with Jay. He hopped up to greet her with a hug.

"Good to see you, Miss Whitt."

"So good to see you, too, Jay." She rubbed his head. "And please, won't you ever just call me Patti?"

A feeling of normalcy crept back into my life with the two of them there. For those few precious moments I was happy, not thinking about anything else. Until Jay lifted his chin and looked at my neck.

"Hey, I like that necklace. I don't think I've ever seen you wear jewelry. You get that on the trip?"

I brought my hand up to the stone. "Yeah. Kai got it for me."

We all became still at the uncomfortable mention of his name. Patti and Jay exchanged a glance. I cleared my throat and shoved my hands in my pockets.

"So," Jay said, clasping his hands and rocking back on his heels. "How 'bout them Braves?"

On the fifth day I knew Kaidan would have made it home. I held my breath and called him. I listened to every charming word of his voice mail, then hung up. That evening I sat on my bed and called again. This time I left a message.

"Hi, Kai, um, Kaidan. It's me. Anna. I'm just trying to see if you made it home safely. I'm sure you probably did. Just checking. You can call me anytime. If you want. Anyway. Okay, bye."

I hung up and buried my shamed face into a pillow. Now I was leaving messages after he'd made it clear he wanted zero to do with me? Next thing I knew I'd be frequenting his shows to give him psycho stares from the back, and then doing late-night drive-bys to see what girl he was bringing home. The thought of him with another girl made me writhe in discomfort and curl up in the fetal position.

Day six was our first day of back-to-school shopping. We

still had a month before school began, but the state issued a tax-free day, so stores were having big sales. I eyed all the teensy skirts and fashionable shirts dangling on mannequins. I tried to imagine Kaidan's reaction if I came dressed like that to one of his shows, some guy other than Jay on my arm. Ugly stalker thoughts. I was full of them.

Two weeks passed, and I was still tripping over chairs to grab the phone every time it rang, like now.

This time it was Jay.

"*Duuuuude!* You're never gonna friggin' believe this!" he hollered. I distanced the phone from my ear. "I just got a call from the manager of Lascivious, and they want to buy the rights to two of our songs!"

My stomach did a flip-flop at the mention of the band.

"Wow, Jay, congratulations! That's awesome!"

I hoped I managed to sound excited, despite the churning inside me.

"You gotta come with me on Thursday, Anna. They're gonna perform one of them live!"

Big, huge flip-flop. It was a perfect excuse to see Kaidan. But it would do me no good—just the opposite. I didn't know how to break it to Jay without hurting his feelings.

"Jay," I began, sitting in a chair and resting my forehead on my palm. "I want to support you. I really do. I'd love to hear your song, but it's not a good idea for me to go. Kaidan flat-out told me he wanted me to stay away from him."

"Dude, whatever. You'll be there for me, not him. You're *my* best friend."

I was torn. It broke my heart to think of not being there for

Jay, but Kaidan had made himself clear. Still, I was the worst friend ever.

"Look, Jay, I'm going to be honest with you, even though it's embarrassing. I'm one step away from stalking him." My voice shook. "All I do is think of him. If there were no such thing as caller ID, I would call him all day just to listen to him talking on his voice mail. I'm having an extremely difficult time getting over him. If I see him again . . ."

"Sorry, man. I guess I didn't think about it that way. It's cool. I understand."

His feelings were hurt. I could tell it in his voice, and it made my eyes sting.

"I'm so sorry, Jay. Will you please call me the second you leave the show and tell me everything?" I asked. "I don't care how late it is. Promise me."

"All right. Sure."

The disappointment in his voice tore me up inside. We hung up and I got the itchy-fingered urge to call Kaidan again, this time with the excuse of talking about Jay's songs. I threw the phone away from me like a poisonous viper, into the chair across the room.

I sat on my bed with the phone on my lap at eleven thirty on Thursday night. I'd warned Patti that Jay would be calling late. When it rang I snatched it up.

"Hello?" I whispered.

"Oh, man, you just missed the best show *ever!*"

I smiled. At least he didn't sound upset with me anymore.

"How was your song? Did they do it justice?"

"Dude, I'm not even kidding. It was a million times better than I imagined it!"

I was feeling giddy for him.

"Yeah? That good, huh?"

"Definitely. I can't wait for you to hear it. Everyone was rockin' out to it! The whole place. I almost cried like a big . . . well, like *you*! Ha, ha. But I didn't." He heaved a great big sigh of contentment.

"I'm so happy for you, Jay. You deserve it." I felt very bad at that moment, regretful that I didn't go and just hide in a corner at the show or something.

"They're talking about going to L.A. to make a record in the next year."

I got quiet. Los Angeles? Would he have to move there? I lay down on my side and pulled my big pillow into a hug, keeping the phone at my ear.

"You still there?" Jay asked.

"I'm still here. Sorry. That's . . . great news."

"Yeah. Hey," he said, "there's something else, too. I don't know. Maybe I shouldn't tell you."

Uh-oh.

"Well, you have to tell me now that you brought it up."

"All right, well. Afterward, backstage, Kaidan was surrounded by all of these girls." Oh, gosh—gag reflex! "But as soon as he saw me he left 'em all hanging and came straight over. He said he liked the songs, which was cool. Then he asked where you were, and I said you were at home. And he was all, 'How is she?' And I was like, 'Well, she's been better, man.' And, I don't know, it was weird. He wasn't acting right. He bolted right after that, didn't even stay to party." He paused, quiet. "What really happened between you guys?"

I was more confused than ever when I whispered, "I don't know."

He asked about me. He didn't stay to party.

"Maybe he's just one of those players who won't let himself get too close to anybody," Jay theorized.

"Yeah," I said. "Or maybe he's got some serious daddy issues."

Jay laughed at that.

I wished I were joking.

CHAPTER TWENTY-ONE

TEA FOR TWINS

It was our last day shopping for back-to-school stuff and we'd gone to the mall. The sky was overcast, and the cramped parking garage was so dim I had to adjust my sight. I held both the shopping bags while Patti dug around in her purse for the keys. If I hadn't been using my extended vision, I might not have noticed them standing at the other end of the garage.

Four Neph: two male, two female, each with a small starburst badge. I almost dropped the bags, tightening my grip just in time. Then I casually looked around, pretending not to notice them watching me. I thought of Kaidan's words the day I'd gone to his house: *Neph don't show up unless they're looking for trouble.*

I kept my face neutral, hoping not to give away my internal

panic. I wished Patti weren't with me.

She unlocked our doors and we climbed in. I sneaked a peek and saw the four climbing into a shiny black car in the next row. They were going to follow us. I had to think.

Using a receipt from one of the bags and a pen from the glove compartment, I scribbled a note as fast as my trembling hand would allow.

We're being followed. Act normal. Don't go home.

Slow down when we go around the bend of the elementary school, and I'll jump out and run. You keep going—to the church.

I'll call your cell when it's safe.

Patti's eyes looked up and down from the road to the note that I held low between us. Her knuckles whitened and she gave a tiny frantic shake of her head. Great. She was going to be difficult.

I'll run to the ball fields!

There should be weekend games today, all sports, and lots of people. I could try to blend in and lose them. Oh—but what if they went after Patti instead of me? One way or another, this was not good. I shoved the paper in my pocket. Patti's face was pale and shiny from sweat. She gave a small nod of agreement. Now we needed to act normal. I hoped Patti would play along.

"Thanks for taking me today," I said. "I think I'm finally ready for school."

"No problem, honey. You sure you don't need another bra, though?"

I cringed and she made an apologetic face.

"Nope, I'm good," I forced out.

I glanced at the side mirror. They were four cars behind

us. I pushed out my hearing to them, but found only silence in their car.

We were coming up on the blind curve by the elementary school. They wouldn't be able to see us for about ten seconds while we rounded the slow bend. Next to the school was a patch of forest, and on the other side of those woods were soccer, baseball, and general playing fields. If I could just get there, I would have a chance.

My heart pounded as we started the turn. Patti gave my arm a squeeze. I opened the door and jumped out, closing it as quietly as I could.

I took off at a dead sprint, running faster than I ever had.

I wasn't stupid enough to think they wouldn't hear the car door close, or my footfalls as I ran. I just hoped I'd be fast enough to get somewhere I could hide. I could see the forest at the edge of the school now.

I zipped past the side of the building and ran into the mesh of trees. Branches stung my face, but I never slowed. Voices came from the nearby fields now. *Almost there.* Exhilaration flooded my senses as I flew through the woods.

I suddenly heard something coming up behind me, even louder than the voices ahead of me from the fields. It was the slamming of feet in the brush. Someone else was running. Fast.

"Stop!" It was a male's voice, strained from the effort. I pushed my legs to pump even faster, until my muscles were burning, but I knew it wasn't fast enough. I was a long-distance endurance runner. This guy behind me was a sprinter. And a defensive linebacker, it would seem, as he tackled me to the ground in one easy swipe, nearly knocking the wind out of me. I got a faceful of leaf debris and dirt.

Struggling from his grip, I rolled and flailed so he couldn't get a good hold. One of his giant arms was hooked around my hips, and he was reaching for my free arm, but I swung it sideways and busted his nose so hard I cried out from the throb of pain in my hand. The guy grunted and gave his head one hard shake, blood slinging into the dirt; then he was on top of me, using every bit of his mass to hold me down. He grabbed both of my wrists and pinned them to the ground next to my head. I panted, gasping for air.

"Be still. You are safe." His voice had a soft accent I couldn't place.

I looked at him. His nose had already stopped bleeding. His skin was dark like coffee, and his black waves of hair were cut short. He had the lightest hazel eyes I'd ever seen, and as he stared down at me I got a whiff of something cooking at the ball field concession stands: the buttery richness of hot, simmering caramel. . . . Wait. Was that his *scent*? I swallowed and pressed my head back against the dirt, trying not to breathe hard so my chest would stop pressing up against his.

Another pair of feet jogged up to us now.

"Kope!" the other guy yelled. "What the frick?! You got some cheetah blood in you or what?"

At the sound of his friend's voice, the guy on top of me lifted some of his weight.

"I will let you up now." His voice was quiet next to my ear. "Do not run."

The other guy put his hands on his knees to catch his breath. He had black hair that was bleached at the tips, and when he brushed it from his forehead, it slicked back with sweat. He was at least part Asian, with dark, almond-shaped eyes and high, pronounced cheekbones. I exhaled and closed my eyes, realizing who they were. Blake and Kopano. My relief was followed by sheer humiliation for making them chase me.

"Seriously!" insisted Blake. "How did you run so fast?"

"I am African." Without taking his eyes from mine, Kopano eased himself off me, and I sat up.

"Oh, ha, ha. A comedian," Blake said.

Kopano felt his nose as he squatted next to me.

"You're Kaidan's friends," I stated, feeling like a fool.

"Something like that," Blake said. "He's not exactly Mr. Friendly." He pulled a cell phone from his pocket and dialed, putting it to his ear.

"Hey. Come back to the school. Kope was right—she jumped and ran. It's all good, though. . . . Yeah, she's with us . . . All right, I'll tell her."

He ended the call and slid the phone into his pocket.

"Marna says to say she's sorry we scared the 'bejaysus' out of you," he said.

Kopano and I both stood and brushed ourselves off. I pulled some pine needles out of my hair. I was still shaking as I followed Blake through the trees to the empty school. I glanced back at Kopano, who walked behind me.

"Sorry about your nose," I said, shamefaced.

He kept his eyes down and nodded as if it were no big deal. I studied his smooth features and full lips for a moment before turning my head forward again. I wasn't sure what to think about the look he'd given me on the ground, or the way he'd smelled.

It felt like forever before we found the edge of the woods and made our way to the school's parking lot, empty except for the black car and two of the most beautiful girls I'd ever seen standing in front of it. I could hear their conversation.

"She's sixteen?" one asked in surprise.

"Looks more like twelve to me," the other said.

"Play nice," the first warned her.

I knew who they were at once: the identical twin daughters of Astaroth, Pharzuph's London buddy. As I looked at their summer skirts and strappy heels, I became aware of how I must look in my cutoff shorts and high, haphazard ponytail.

When Kaidan told me the twins were dancers, I'd pictured tall, lanky ballerinas. But no. Their bodies screamed salsa and tango—tiny waists nestled between amply rounded chests and hips. Any dancing they did was the booty-shaking kind. They were not much taller than me, with shiny brown hair styled into layers, and an array of perfectly fashionable accessories. Like Kaidan, they oozed sex appeal. The other two guys weren't hard on the eyes, either.

Apparently Pharzuph was not the only demon to choose an attractive body to inhabit, and an attractive mate to give him a child, which was smart. Charming, good-looking people could get away with a lot.

We were all together now, standing in a circle, surveying one another.

"Scared ya, didn't we?" Blake said, lifting an eyebrow that I just noticed was pierced. He wore a tight hemp necklace with a shell in the middle, and his badge was the poisonous green of envy.

"What are you guys doing here?" I asked, keeping my voice steady and strong.

"We heard a rumor of a Nephilim sister in these parts," said Kopano. His light eyes were striking against his dark skin.

"Rumor from who?" I asked.

Blake shrugged. "Word gets around."

"But how did you find me?"

"Marna showed her boobs to one of the spirits and he led the way—"

"Blake! Shut up." She gave him a shove. "That's not true. We got your name from Kai, and then we did a little research, because he wouldn't tell us anything else about you."

"Almost like he was hiding something," the other sister said, crossing her arms and eyeing me. The dirty look I sent her in return was ineffective. I couldn't remember the sisters' names from Kaidan's descriptions, but this girl was the snarky one.

We looked toward the entrance of the school as a car drove in. Probably a staff worker or janitor. We couldn't just stand there loitering. I made a quick decision to trust them and hoped it wouldn't turn out to be one of my naive moments.

"We can talk at my house, if you want," I offered. They looked around at one another before agreeing.

I climbed in the back with the girls while Blake took the passenger seat. Kopano drove, so I assumed it was his car. Besides my giving the occasional direction, nobody talked.

I still had the house key in my pocket, and I was surprised

it hadn't fallen out during the wrestling match with Kopano. I flushed at the memory as we parked and got out.

Kopano seemed relaxed, but the other three looked uncomfortable in the small living space of my home. The girls flipped their hair, peering around at the old furniture. I crossed my arms over my chest and tried to appear as tough as my supposedly twelve-year-old demeanor would allow.

"I need to make a call," I told them.

"To whom?" the snarky twin asked.

"The woman I was with. Patti."

I didn't feel like explaining. I ignored their stares, walked to the counter, and dialed Patti's cell. She answered on the first ring.

"It's me." I talked fast, eager to put her out of her misery of worry. "I'm fine. They're just Kaidan's friends. We're at the apartment now."

She breathed a sigh of relief.

"You can come home whenever you want," I told her.

"All right. I'll be there in about fifteen minutes. You're sure you're okay?"

"I'm sure. I'll see you soon."

I hung up.

"Doesn't your father have any money?" the mean twin asked, noting our tiny television.

"This isn't his place. I live here with my adopted mother."

"Is he still in jail?" asked the nice sister.

"Yes."

"That's what we figured. We don't like showin' up places where a *Duke* might be." She said the word *Duke* with a shudder.

We all stood there in a semicircle, sharing the awkward lull.

"What's up with your badge?" asked Blake, sounding like a valley boy.

"I'm not sure, to tell you the truth," I told him.

I looked at the girls, wishing I could tell them apart.

"So you're Ginger and Marna?"

"How do you know our names?" they asked simultaneously.

"Same way you know mine."

The mean sister narrowed her eyes at me again. What was with her?

"Word is you and Kai are *work partners*." Blake winked at me. I felt my face warm, and shrugged noncommittally. I didn't think any of them were buying my tough act.

"I haven't seen him or talked to him in a few weeks," I said.

Mean Sister pulled out her cell and scrolled through her contacts.

She dialed. "Aw, cripe, voice mail . . . Oi! Arse-face! We're at your little girl Anna's house. Ring me back straightaway." She slid it shut and glared at me. "Surprised he still has the same number," she said. "That bloke gets his number changed more than anyone I know."

I was very uncomfortable. I still didn't know what they wanted with me. Not a single one of them emitted any emotional colors, and they acted so tense.

"Why don't you all sit down and I'll get us something to drink." I'd definitely been raised by Patti Whitt.

Kopano sat at the end of the couch. Blake shrugged and sat at the other end.

"I'll just stand," Mean Sister said with a bored wave of her hand. *Suit yourself,* I thought.

I walked to the kitchen, surprised when the nicer sister followed me. She watched with interest as I filled glasses with ice and took the pitcher out of the fridge.

"What is that?" she asked.

"Sweet tea," I said. Her gray eyes widened and she smiled. She had a slender, oval face. Pretty.

"Ooh, Ginger, tea on ice! I've heard about it," she called out.

"Sounds awful," Ginger said.

"I can make you a cup of hot tea instead." I made sure to be polite, but I wasn't wasting any smiles on the mean sister, Ginger.

"Fine." She huffed and sat down between the two guys, wiggling on the springs.

I looked up at Marna as I warmed the water, wondering how wrong I was doing it, but she didn't seem interested in critiquing. I handed her a glass of iced tea and she took a sip.

"Mmm. That's different. Not bad, though. It's not bad, Ginger!"

"Good for you. Drink up. Have a ball."

It wasn't going to be so hard to tell the sisters apart after all.

"Is this your first time in America?" I asked Marna.

"Yes. We've only just turned eighteen and finished school, so we're traveling the world now."

"No, we're not, Marna. Stop telling people that. We're only visiting the United States. Then it's back to London."

"Well, it feels like it to me," she shouted, turning back to me with a sweet smile. "We met Blake and Kopano in Boston, then we drove down here together. It's a long way."

"What's in Boston?" I asked. I didn't think there were any Dukes living there.

"Kope just finished his first year at Harvard." We looked over at him, and he gave a bashful nod, then looked down.

Harvard, wow. I'd never met anyone who went to a big, famous school.

"What should I put in this?" I asked Marna about her sister's hot tea.

"Scoop of sugar. She needs it. Old sourpuss."

Musical notes filled the air and Ginger pulled out her phone. My stomach tightened as she slid it open.

"Is Pharzy home?" she asked as a greeting. *Kaidan.* "Drats. We'll stay here for now, then. . . . Don't worry. We haven't tortured the poor girl. She's the one trying to torture us with American iced tea. . . . Don't think you can weasel out of seeing us. . . . When, tonight? Hold on." She pulled the phone away from her ear and looked at me. "Do you know how to get to some club named Double Doors?"

"Um, kind of. I can find out from my friend. I'll write down directions for you."

"I don't think so," said Marna in a singsong tone. "You're coming with us."

My heart sped up. I had narrowly escaped this noose with Jay before. They watched me, and all I could think about was how Kaidan was on the other end of that phone line.

"I can't," I said with a shake of my head.

"Why not?" Ginger snapped at me.

"I'm busy." *Doing nothing.*

"Come," Kopano said. His voice seemed to reverberate around the silent room. He held my gaze, but I had to look away. His soulful eyes made me feel like he could see too much.

"Please," said Marna next to me, clasping her fingers together.

I thought about Jay and how excited he would be if I came and heard his song. I looked up into Marna's pleading eyes and over at Kopano's serious face, full of mystery.

"Okay," I whispered.

"We'll be there at seven," Ginger said, then snapped the sleek phone shut.

Oh, my goodness, I was going to see Kaidan! My whole body buzzed with excitement and dread.

I took my drink and sat down on the floor in front of the others with my legs crossed, hoping none of them was observant enough to see the slight shake of my hand.

Ginger began. "The first thing you need to know is that we can see through any and all bull. So be straight with us about everything. Understand?"

Since BSing wasn't really my thing anyway, I nodded, realizing now that sitting on the floor was a bad idea—it gave me the inferior position of having to look up at her. And I didn't like the way she was talking to me.

"First off, what's up with you and Kaidan?" she asked.

My first instinct was to say it was none of her business. Kaidan obviously hadn't told her anything or she wouldn't be hounding me for info. But there was no point being rude, and I didn't want to seem evasive. I hoped to earn their trust.

"I met him after one of his shows two months ago. I didn't

know there was anybody else like me out there. I didn't even know what I was. My father's been in prison my whole life, so I was raised by a human woman. Kaidan explained things and taught me what he thought I should know. He drove me to California to meet my dad and talk to him. And that's pretty much it."

"Belial, right?" asked Blake.

"Yes."

"Why did Kaidan take you?" Marna asked, tilting her head in interest, as though the thought of Kaidan doing something kind were peculiar.

"I don't know. Curiosity, maybe? He said at one point he wanted to figure me out, I guess to make sure I wasn't a threat. Plus, Pharzuph told him to teach me the ropes."

Blake laughed and said, "Yeah, boy." We ignored him.

"And why haven't you spoken in a while then?" Ginger asked.

I swallowed and tried to be matter-of-fact, as if it weren't really about me. As if there weren't still an open wound.

"Because we're not friends or anything. We both found out what we needed to know."

"Love 'em and leave 'em is more like it," Blake said. "I didn't think Rowe wasted his time on sister Nephs."

"It wasn't like that." It came out sounding a little too defensive.

"Wasn't it?" Ginger asked, an unkind grin on her face. "You took a holiday, just the two of you, and you're saying you didn't have a bunk-up?"

And then I remembered Kaidan's offhand remark about

the one girl he'd ever turned down being a Nephilim. Ginger's accusatory tone and bitter attitude made me pause. Could he have turned *her* down?! No way.

"We didn't . . ." I almost said, *We didn't do anything*, but that would have been a lie, so I left the thought dangling out there unsupervised.

"Right." Ginger snorted.

Marna changed the subject.

"So you've been working for Belial, even though he's not been around?"

I opened my mouth, indecisive, and then told them, "No."

They all stared at me.

"Dabbling in Daddy's goodies? Passing it out to the other kiddies?" Blake prompted me.

"I know what you mean," I said, "but I don't do drugs. They make me . . . crazy or something."

"I bet they do." Blake smiled.

"Ah, shut your cakehole." Ginger backhanded his chest and he laughed.

"Don't worry, Gin, you're the only one for me."

Ginger rolled her eyes severely high and crossed her arms and legs.

"You do not take drugs?" Kopano asked, sitting forward now. His accent was mellow, yet clipped.

"No," I said.

A hint of a smile passed Kopano's careful features, and he sat back with a different look in his eyes for me now. He was definitely the watchful, quiet type.

"How have you gotten away with that?" Marna asked.

"I guess because I wasn't raised by a Duke."

"Yes, but I can't believe he didn't leave you with someone who would teach you to do his work in his absence." Marna sounded almost in awe.

I was very nervous all of a sudden. Not for me, but for my father. If this group had heard about me, then surely others had, too, namely the Dukes. Were they all questioning the judgment of Belial—thinking he'd neglected his duties?

"This conversation can't get back to anybody." My voice shook.

Blake gave a snort of derision. "Don't worry. We don't tell our fathers jack."

I believed him.

"Belial has been in prison your whole life and you only just met?" asked Kopano.

"Yes."

"Perhaps he did not know about her," he said to the others.

I should have corrected him, but I sat silently, digesting how rebellious my father was.

"Maybe that's why there's a bit of white in your badge," Marna said. "Because you've not had to work."

"But there was no white in any of ours before we worked," Ginger pointed out.

"Maybe it has something to do with the fact that I can't see Legionnaires," I said.

Or maybe it's because my mother was an angel of light. . . .

"You can't see 'em?" Marna asked. "Lucky. Some of 'em are downright fugly. It took me a while to see them, too. Until . . ."

A silence trailed, and the four Neph shared an unpleasant

memory with one another through their gazes. Marna shifted and looked down, sullen. Ginger gave her a quick and gentle pat on the shoulder. I wondered what had happened, but I dared not ask.

"Anyway. It still doesn't make sense," Ginger said. "Even if you didn't know before, you know now. You've met your father. So why aren't you working?"

This was dangerous ground. I didn't know if I could fully trust them, friends of Kaidan or not.

"Och, let's leave her alone," Marna said.

I kept my eyes averted and the room stayed quiet.

"You'll get yourself killed if the Dukes find out, you know," Ginger stated with too much enthusiasm for my liking.

"Let her be," Kopano told her. "She does not know us. She will tell us when she is ready."

Ginger sat back. I gave Kopano a look that I hoped reflected my thankfulness.

"Where are you guys staying tonight?" I asked.

"We were going to stay at Kaidan's if Pharzuph was gone, but we'll just get a hotel," said Blake.

"I know there's not a ton of room here, but—"

"Ooh! We can have a slumber party with Anna, Gin!" Marna cut me off.

"Oooh, yes, goody," Ginger said in a deadpan tone. "The two of you can tell stories while I gag and puke."

I looked at Marna. "You can stay here if you—"

"No." Ginger cut me off. "Marna and I stay together."

Marna gave me a consoling smile. I liked her. And while Ginger's personality left much to be desired, I had to admit her loyalty to Marna was admirable. That was the only good thing I could say about her.

"How long will it take to get to this club from here?" Blake asked me.

"Maybe forty-five minutes to an hour."

"All right. We'll be back here to pick you up at six. Make sure you're ready."

"Um . . ." I felt edgy about tonight—the thought of seeing Kaidan again, the thought of hanging out with these unpredictable Neph, the thought of Jay meeting them, and the awkwardness of my two worlds colliding. "Tonight I'm going to ride down with my best friend, Jay, and you guys can follow us."

"Who's Jay?" Ginger narrowed her eyes with suspicion.

"He's just a human boy. He doesn't know anything about us. He wrote some songs, and Kaidan's band is playing one of them tonight."

"Best friends with a human," Blake stated.

"It keeps getting better and better," Ginger mumbled, standing up and holding out her cup of tea, not one sip gone. I stood and took it from her.

They walked out, Kopano giving a polite nod and Marna giving a wave with her fingers, before I closed the door behind them.

In four hours I would see Kaidan again.

Ginger's untouched tea sloshed over in my shaking hand.

CHAPTER TWENTY-TWO

ENVY

I forewarned Jay on the phone about Kaidan's four friends, but he was still struck dumb at the sight of them. I pinched his arm in the club when I caught him staring at the twins with his tongue practically hanging out. He wasn't alone. Every guy in the club was staring at them, in their tiny dresses and heeled sandals. Jay wore his Braves baseball cap backward that night.

Double Doors was a two-story club. The bar was on the second floor and it looked down over the stage and crowd. Kopano, Jay, and I wore wristbands showing we were under-age—not that it would stop the bartenders from turning a blind eye if someone slipped us a drink. The other three had fake IDs and now drinks in hand. We opted to stay on the top floor watching from the railings, rather than fight the crazy mob stagefront. Jay stood on one side of me and the Neph were on the other.

I did not look down at the drums when the band was announced. I was afraid that the others were waiting to see how I'd look at him. And I was more afraid of how Kaidan might react. Jay's song was first on the playlist. I took his hand and squeezed it when the song began.

I knew the tune well. I'd heard it played on Jay's keyboard so many times, in differing variations as he perfected it. But to hear it in its full glory with all of the instruments and a talented singer was a different experience. It wasn't just stage-worthy; it was album-worthy. I had yet to look straight at Kaidan, choosing to focus on the music, looking at Michael or the bouncing crowd, or peeking at Jay's exalted face.

At the end we broke into wild cheers, and I raised my arms to Jay for one of his giant bear hugs.

"I'm glad I came," I shouted to him. "That was too amazing! You rock."

Marna sidled up next to us and looked at Jay. "You wrote that? It *was* amazing."

Jay released me and faced Marna.

"Thanks," he said, and she twirled her hair. Their interaction made me uneasy. Marna seemed nice, but I didn't want anyone messing with Jay.

"Don't go making Jay fall in love with you, now." I said it to Marna in a teasing tone, catching her eye and holding it. "I don't want him left behind with a broken heart when you go back to London."

Jay laughed, and Marna noted my warning, giving me a small nod.

I turned back to the railing and, without meaning to, looked right down at Kaidan.

Kaidan wore the red T-shirt. The one I had borrowed from him once upon a time. I let myself imagine that he'd thought of me when he picked it out tonight. Stupid. I also wore a red shirt, but mine was baby-doll style, with sleeves that cinched together at the shoulders. It had been a spontaneous purchase on my back-to-school shopping day.

I hated myself for staring. I wanted him to notice me, but I feared what I would see in his eyes. So when his head tilted up and his eyes blasted into mine, I held my breath. Neither of us moved or reacted.

A thin arm came around my shoulder and pulled me from the rail. I ripped my eyes from Kaidan.

"Your little human is a cupcake," Marna whispered.

"Does he have a girlfriend?" Ginger asked, stepping over to us.

"No," I said.

"Then don't bother," Ginger said. "Find someone useful to work on."

"Nobody's working on Jay," I stated.

"I wasn't planning on it, honest," Marna promised me before turning on her sister. "Can't I take one flippin' night off? We're on holiday!"

Ginger's iron resolve seemed to waver as she looked at her sister's bottom lip puckered out.

"Oh, fine. Whatever. I swear, one day, Marna . . ."

Ginger leaned back against the rail with her elbows up and viewed the band over her shoulder. I watched Kaidan acknowledge her with a curt nod, and she signaled back with an unladylike hand gesture. He lifted a corner of his mouth in amusement. There had to be a story between those two. That kind of animosity didn't stem from nothing.

"Uh-oh," Marna whispered. "Cupcake might not be in such a good mood tonight after all. . . ."

Ginger and I turned to see Jay standing alone at the rail, while his guardian angel went ballistic around him. *No!* He took off his baseball hat and turned it around, pulling the bill low on his forehead. Ginger grabbed my arm when I moved toward him.

"You can't interfere!" she hissed. I pulled my arm away and watched until his angel settled.

"Is it gone?" I whispered to the girls.

"Yes, he's below us with the crowd now," Marna said.

I walked over to Jay, hoping the whisperer would not come back and take notice. Ginger cursed behind me.

His eyes were dark, partially hidden under the hat. He didn't register my hand when I put it on his forearm. Jay stared down at the band, and a noxious bright green seeped into his emotions. I looked over at Blake, who was watching me. All four of them were watching me. I took it as a sign that the whisperer was gone, and I focused on Jay.

"What are you thinking about?" I asked him.

He shook his head. His angel wrapped its cloudy wings around him. Maybe between his angel and me, we could pull him out of this.

"It just sucks that someone else has to perform *my* song." Bitterness laced each word. "I want to be able to do it myself. I'll never be in a band. I'll always be the short, fat guy behind the scenes."

"Jay!" I gasped. "First of all, you are not fat. You are healthy and handsome and strong. Second of all, any one of those guys down there would give anything to be able to create music from nothing the way you do. That song was incredible, and it's *yours*. But you can't have it all. If you could sing, but you had no creative imagination, you wouldn't be Jay. You would be shallow lead-singer Michael, with no depth at all. We can't all be performers. If there were no behind-the-scenes, there would be no music industry. How bad would that suck?"

"I hear you," he said, and the vile green slowly began to peel away in thin strips. "It'd just be nice to be the guy up front for once."

I softened my tone. "Do you think that's what every girl wants? Because it's not. Just remember it's the good guys who win in the end, Jay," I said. "Someday those girls will be fighting over which one gets to marry you."

"Sure, after they've spent years chasing after the a-holes who treat them like crap. Then we get to pick up the pieces. That ain't fair."

"No, it's not fair. You're right." I wrapped my arms around his hulky chest and squeezed him tight.

"Thanks, Anna. Sorry I'm bein' a downer." He pulled away and readjusted his hat, lifting it a little higher on his brow now. "How are you, anyway? Is it weird to be here?" He motioned in Kaidan's direction and I quickly shook my head, not wanting the others to catch his meaning.

"I'm glad I came. Everything's fine."

"We can go whenever you want. Just say the word. They've got two more songs. I'm not going backstage tonight." I noticed him glancing in Marna's direction.

"What's up with you and Kaylah these days?" I asked.

"Nah, nothin'. It's out of sight out of mind for her. She's fun to hang with, but it's not going anywhere."

"Go talk to Marna then," I said, nodding my head to the side where the twins stood. "I'll be fine by myself, promise."

He pressed his lips together, as if unsure, but I squeezed his hand and walked away. I didn't think Marna would try to hurt Jay, and if so, she and I would have serious issues.

I tried to move my eyes around and not focus solely on the drummer, but it was hard. He kept glancing up. I wondered whether he was annoyed by me, wishing I would stop watching him and go away. It hurt to imagine he might feel that way.

A warm arm grazed mine and I glanced over to find Kopano at my side.

"Hey," I said to him.

"Do you like this music?" he asked.

"Yes. Do you?"

"I have not decided." That made me giggle.

"Thanks for earlier," I whispered. He looked at his hands on the metal rail and gave a slight nod.

"When you are ready," he said, lifting his eyes to mine, "I would very much like to know your story."

I was surprised by the boldness of his statement. Once again, I found his gaze almost too personal. I felt overly aware of him there next to me, the warmth of his skin, the quiet passion in his eyes. I focused on my own hands on the rail, and then down at Kaidan, who was pausing between the songs. My eyes widened.

Kaidan stared right at me with aggression on his face. That was the reaction I'd been afraid of. My heart thumped as I severed our eye contact, tightening my hold on the railing.

Kopano looked from me to the stage.

Jay bounded up at that moment, holding a flyer. "There's an after party," he said. "You guys wanna go?"

"No, I should head home soon," I answered.

"Why?" Jay asked.

"I have to work tomorrow."

"They don't even open until eleven!"

Marna walked up and plucked the flyer from Jay's hand with her slender fingers.

"She'll be there," Marna said. "We'll all be there."

The smart, self-preserving part of me wanted to refuse, but the stupid part of me could only listen to the beat of the song starting behind me and know the person responsible for making those beats would be at the party—might even talk to me.

"I call shotgun in Jay's car," Marna said.

Jay looked at her in disbelief. "Sweet," he said. Then he lifted his hat and flipped it backward.

As promised, Ginger would not be separated from Marna, so she insisted on riding in Jay's car, too. The thought of Ginger in the tiny backseat of his car amid old fast-food bags and torn seats was hysterical to me.

"I guess I'll ride with you, if that's all right," I said to Kopano. He nodded.

We sat there in the car while the others drove off. He had a flyer of his own with directions, so I figured he was giving them a mile head start so we could talk. Something about his demeanor made me feel shy. I wouldn't look at him. I wondered for the first time how it might feel to be alone with Kopano if Kaidan weren't in the picture. He was virtually the opposite of Kaidan, but I found myself drawn to him. Maybe when it came to guys, my "type" wasn't a certain look; it was a certain intensity.

After a few minutes, he started driving. He waited until we were a mile from the club before speaking to me.

"I like you."

Okay, *that* was unexpected. I sat still, unsure how to respond.

"What I meant is," he explained, "I like you as a person. I have never witnessed one of our kind befriend a human in such a way. Even I have not allowed myself to care for them the way I should, on a personal level."

We were quiet again, and I caught myself chewing my lip, then stopped.

"Kaidan told me your story," I said. "He told me you're lucky to be alive."

"That is true. If any of the other four had defied their fathers, they would have been killed. Dukes are not meant to care for their children. My father is an exception."

"And mine," I whispered. My pulse quickened with

nervousness at my revelation. Kopano glanced my way before answering.

"I wondered if it was so. He always knew you were alive. Am I right? He let you be?"

"Yes. But please don't say anything."

"I will keep your secrets. I do not fear death."

"You don't fear . . . hell?"

"No." He spoke with calm certainty. "It will not be for eternity. Even Neph will have their day of judgment."

I was floored by his certainty. He was prepared to face whatever life and death delivered him.

"Have you said any of this to the others?" I asked him.

"In years past. But their situations are different."

"Do you think any of them believe in what they do?"

"I could not bear their presence if they did. Blake and Marna do as they are told, but minimally and with no enthusiasm. Kaidan and Ginger have been the best workers, but over time I have observed much. They have strong wills to live, and they will do what is necessary to stay alive. But they are not happy. Being controlled and being unloved is not a natural way of life."

"No, it's not. What about other Nephilim?"

"Not all Nephilim despise their lives. There are many who seem to embrace their work and believe in the cause. I suppose there is no way of truly knowing one's heart until one is put to the test."

I pondered those words as we rode in comfortable silence the rest of the way to the party.

* * *

I sat on a couch between Jay and Kopano in some stranger's old house, feeling jittery. Marna was on Jay's other side, and the two of them talked. Ginger and Blake examined pictures on the wall, many of which were autographed by musicians.

An excited throng of girls waited in the front room for the band to arrive. I should have known this would be a groupie party. I swore that the second I saw Kaidan's hands on another girl, I was out of there, even if it meant walking home. I knew he had to work, but I did not have to be a witness.

All of the guys were throwing back beers and talking animatedly about acoustics and instrumentals and the sound system that ran through the house. Local band music blared from the walls of every room.

I crossed my legs, then uncrossed them and crossed them on the other side. Kopano glanced down at my fidgeting, but did not comment.

"Oh, my gawd, they're here!" squealed one of the girls from the other room, and my abs got tight.

I had a fleeting urge to snatch the half-full beer from Marna's hand and chug it down. The door opened and people cheered. I rubbed my damp palms on the thighs of the jean skirt Jay's sister had given me for my birthday.

Jay turned to me.

"You okay?"

I nodded and forced a smile. I wasn't fooling him, of course, but he gave me that goofy half grin, and I knew he would take me home in a heartbeat if I asked him to, even if it meant cutting off his conversation with Marna.

As the band members came into the room, one by one,

the entire party converged. People huddled together, vying for attention and time to talk with them. I tried not to look at the girls surrounding Kaidan, asking him to sign their cleavage and thighs with permanent markers.

"Come," Kopano said to me, standing. I followed without question. We went into the kitchen, finding an unoccupied corner, and I checked out the beverage selection.

I reached for a Coca-Cola.

"Want some?" I asked.

"I do not drink caffeine," he said.

"Wow, you make me look like a bad girl; that's hard to do."

He cracked a big smile for the first time I'd seen, and a huge dimple appeared in his right cheek. A butterfly wing flapped in my stomach. I turned my attention back to the drinks, fumbling a little for a cup.

"Don't let me pressure you," I said. "I was only kidding. We don't need you all hyped up on caffeine. How about ginger ale instead?"

"Is that drink not only for upset stomachs?"

"Nope. It's pretty good." I poured a tiny bit into a cup and held it out. "Here, take a sip."

He took the cup and drank. "Reminds me of champagne," he said.

"You've had champagne?"

"When I was younger, before I changed my life."

I took the cup from him and filled it three-quarters full of ginger ale, then handed it back.

"What made you decide to change?"

He held his cup, speaking in serene remembrance. "When

I was fifteen, I went with my two brothers to a revival camp in a nearby town set up by missionaries from Wales. Our intentions were to make trouble and rouse their anger. When we arrived they were praying. I'd never seen anyone in prayer, and I felt . . . strange. For the first time in my life I experienced hope. I returned home and told my father I would work no more. I thought at the very least he would disown me, but he reacted with silence. He pretended not to hear what I said. In all of the years since, he has spoken only a handful of sentences to me, but never tried to make me work. When I came of age, I applied to college and left home."

My respect for him was huge. I wondered why he wasn't the one to inherit the mysterious Sword of Righteousness. If he was scared of anything, he didn't show it.

As the party grew, more people shifted into the kitchen, pushing us closer to each other. I saw Kaidan on the other side of the room, leaning against the counter while the girl next to him talked, swishing her white-platinum blond hair. My stomach tightened. I hadn't seen him come in. The girl poured a shot of something golden and handed it to Kaidan. He tipped back the shot glass and glanced my way, unsmiling, as he set it down. I put my back to him and sipped my drink.

The crowd's aura tonight was a mix of vivid, positive colors with a handful of fuzzy grays sprinkled throughout. As drinks were consumed with speed, colors began to fade and voices grew louder.

Marna and Jay squeezed through and stood with Kopano and me. Ginger and Blake were not far behind. Two minutes later Kaidan materialized through the crowd with the bottle of liquor, shot glasses, and slices of lime. He had somehow managed to rid himself of the girl.

"Tequila, anyone?" he asked our group, but his eyes were on me.

"Hell, yeah, K, break it out," Blake said.

I tried to take a step back, but I couldn't go far.

Kaidan poured the drinks, handing one to each twin and Blake.

"Jay?" he asked.

"Nah, dude. I gotta drive."

"Kope? Anna?"

We both stared at him, not answering.

"Oh, that's right, I nearly forgot," Kaidan said with smooth indifference. "The prince and princess would never stoop so low. Well, bottoms up to us peasants."

What was up with that? The group shared a round of uneasy glances. Jay's mouth was set in firm disapproval as he stared at Kaidan, who wouldn't meet Jay's eye.

The four of them raised their glasses, taking the shots and chasing them with bites of lime.

I got a strong whiff of the pungent, salty tequila and gripped the counter with one hand.

"How's your soda, princess?" Though Kaidan spoke with a calm air, there was underlying menace that pained me to hear.

"You don't need to be hateful," I whispered.

"If you ask me, I'd say the princess prefers a dark knight." Ginger smirked and took a long drink of her beer.

"She only thinks she does," Kaidan said to her.

I opened and closed my hands at my sides. After all we'd

been through, how could he stand there and have the audacity to throw temptations in my face and insult me? I wanted to say something to shut him up, but the more flustered I got, the more tongue-tied I became.

"Anna?" Jay asked. "You ready to bounce?"

There was no way Jay was ready to leave.

"No! Don't go yet," Marna begged. She yanked the front of Kaidan's shirt. "You're scaring everyone off, Kai! If you can't be nice, then don't get so pissed."

"She means *drunk*," Blake said to me in a stage whisper; then he added, "*Brits*," with a roll of his eyes.

Blake's attempt at comic relief didn't lighten the mood much.

"My apologies," Kaidan said to Marna. He slid the bottle away with the back of his hand, and Marna patted down the bit of shirt she'd crumpled. I stared at Kaidan, but he wouldn't meet my eye.

"Come on," Jay said. "It's too crowded in here. We can go out back."

The seven of us slipped onto the porch and down the deck stairs, finding lawn chairs to sit in under a giant oak tree. Kaidan leaned back in his chair, balancing it on the back two legs.

"How about a game of Truth or Dare?" Marna offered.

I was immediately apprehensive. Just as I was about to suggest something else, Kaidan spoke and my heart faltered.

"I'll go first," he said. "I dare Kope to kiss Anna."

Everything inside me flooded with fury and embarrassment. Kaidan leaned far back with his arms crossed, cocky. I stood up without thinking and hooked my foot under his

297

chair, swiftly kicking upward and causing him to topple backward. He looked up at me from the ground with a stunned expression that morphed into a grin.

The twins and Blake were in hysterics. Blake laughed so hard he fell sideways out of his own chair, which made Jay join in the laughter. I couldn't sit there with them anymore. This whole night was a disaster. I turned and walked through the yard, toward the side of the house. I heard Ginger talk between gasps of mirth.

"Maybe she's not so bad after all!"

I didn't know where I was going. I made my way between the two houses, toward the street, and I heard steps running through the grass behind me.

"Wait up!" It was Jay. "You okay?" I stopped and let him catch up.

"I knew I shouldn't have come."

"Yeah, you called it. But maybe it's not such a bad thing. He saw you flirting with that other guy, and it's got him thinking—"

"Shhh!" I said, my eyes rounding. I peered over his shoulder, but we couldn't see the others.

"What?" he asked, confused. "They can't hear us."

"I wasn't *flirting*!" I whisper-hissed.

"Well, you were standing real close and talking all serious—"

"Okay, okay! Maybe it looked bad, but we were just talking. It was crowded."

"Hey." Marna came around the corner toward us. "Don't worry about Kai. He's a nasty drunk. Come on back."

"I don't think I should," I said. I wished I could just shake it off and be cool, but he'd hurt me.

"Do I need to send him over to apologize?" she asked.

"No!"

"Kaidan!" she hollered. "Get over here!"

My pulse quickened and I crossed my arms over my chest, staring down at my feet.

I heard him approach through the long blades of grass. Marna and Jay must have walked away, because when I looked up, it was only the two of us. He stared down and nudged an old tree stump with his foot.

"Sorry," he said, concentrating on giving the stump another good thump.

Wow. An apology. I felt myself soften.

"I'm sorry, too, about the whole chair-flipping thing."

"No, I deserved it."

When we looked at each other, standing all those painful feet away, my heart constricted and it was hard to take in air. He was already sobering, but I knew the taste of tequila would still be on his lips. I had to pull my eyes down again to breathe.

"Will you come back over if I promise not to say anything else?" he asked.

I nodded, and he took a flask from his pocket, taking a long swig before he pocketed it again. Why was he drinking so much?

I followed him back to the group, where we both sat down.

"Okay, I'll go next," Marna said, seeming determined to ignore the tension in the air and play that stupid game. I was so not in the mood to participate. "Ginger, truth or dare?"

"Dare."

"Forgive me for taking the idea from Kai, but I dare you to snog Blake—" She modified the request at the insistent stare from her sister. "Oh, come on! Just the teensiest peck on the lips."

I thought she would still refuse, but apparently she wasn't one to outright turn down a dare. She turned to Blake and pointed a finger at him.

"Try to cop a feel and I'll make Anna's chair flip look angelic," she warned.

He grinned and she leaned in, both closing their eyes as she pressed her lips against his for one, two, three seconds. It appeared innocent, but they were shy when they pulled away and sat back.

"Right," Ginger said, clearing her throat. "My turn. Jay, truth or dare?"

"Truth."

"Do you fancy Marna?"

"I'm not sure what that means, but if you're asking if I like her and think she's the most beautiful girl I've ever met and I wish she would move here, then yes."

Marna and I giggled at his brazen, smitten openness.

Our attention was diverted when Kaidan threw a quick glance over his shoulder, and then stood up, moving to the hidden side of the giant oak tree and leaning against it. Right at that moment the back door creaked open and the blond girl stepped out, peering all around and staring at our group.

"Hey, is Kaidan Rowe down there?" she asked.

"Nope," lied Blake.

The girl frowned and went back in the house. Kaidan sauntered out and took his seat again.

"Dude, how did you know she was coming?" Jay asked.

"Superhuman hearing," Marna answered for him.

Jay laughed and adjusted his hat. "My turn, now?"

"No, I'm not quite finished with you," Ginger said. "Have you ever cheated on a girlfriend?"

Jay squinted at her. "No. I wouldn't."

"You would," she corrected him. "Everyone cheats."

"That's not true," Kaidan said. Everyone gawked at him and he shrugged. "Well, it's not."

"What the hell do you know about it?" Ginger asked him.

"Nothing, I suppose. I know I need another drink."

We all watched him get up and go back into the house.

"What's his problem, then?" Marna asked her sister.

"What's *not* his problem? Probably hasn't been laid in a whole hour. Gettin' snippy."

Jay was pinching his chin hair in thought. All at once our group became quiet and I heard a door slam. Kaidan stood on the deck watching me. When I looked around the other Neph were staring at me, too, or above me, around me. And then I heard a whispered voice say, *Do not be afraid.*

Who said that? I somehow knew it was spoken in my mind, not something anyone had said out loud. What was going on?

"Jay," Marna said carefully, "would you be a luv and get me another drink? A little mixed-up number?"

"Sure, be right back."

Kaidan passed him, coming down. The others stood, so I did, too.

"Whose was it?" Ginger asked.

"I couldn't tell for certain," Kaidan said.

"He looked familiar. I would swear it was Azael. But what was he doing?" Marna asked.

"Azael?" Ginger spit. "What bloody purpose would he have with her?"

"Is Azael a demon?" I asked, getting a shiver and peeking around the darkened yard behind me. The name sounded familiar. "Don't you guys see them all the time? Why are you so freaked out?"

"Not just any demon," Blake whispered. "Satan's messenger. And they don't acknowledge Neph or pay any attention to us, but he was circling you."

"*Shiza!*" Ginger hissed a foreign curse at me. "What are you not telling us?"

My stomach knotted. I locked eyes with Kaidan, who froze, listening to something. In a slow movement, he turned his head. We all followed his gaze to the darkened corner of the house, where a man stepped out. He wore jeans and steel-toed boots with a black leather jacket that sported a big amber badge dead center. His head was smooth, and the long beard was once again trimmed to a goatee. My body gave a hiccup of surprise, and joy surged up inside me, just as I was certain sheer terror surged up inside of my companions.

He ghosted his way past the deck toward us, and everyone but me took a step back.

"You're a hard one to find," he said to me in a deep, menacing grumble. "No cell phone?"

"No, sir." I wasn't at all scared; in fact, I was forcing back a smile. But sheesh, he was bad-a, all the way. He kept his eyes trained on me, not yet acknowledging the others.

"Who's the human with you?"

I didn't know how much of a charade he wanted me to put on in front of the others, so I played it safe.

"A guy from my school."

He gave another grumble. And as if on cue, Jay walked out across the deck and came down the stairs to us, drink in hand. He stopped and a series of emotions played across his face and aura as he stared at my dad, finally settling on fear.

"Jay, this is my father." Better to nip this in the bud fast. His fear fizzled enough to let in some surprise, and he managed a smile.

"Oh, wow, hi . . . sir."

"Good to meet you, Jay," my father said in a low voice. "You were just headed home. Have a good night."

Jay's eyes glazed over. My father was influencing him! I felt offended on Jay's behalf, even though he wasn't being forced to do anything harmful.

"Yeah, I mean, yes, sir. I was just leaving. Good to meet you, too. Here's your drink, Marna." He handed it to her and they gave each other bashful looks. "Well, night, everyone." Jay gave a wave and he was out of there. All eyes went back to my father. I supposed I should do a round of introductions.

"Father, this is Marna and her sister, Ginger, daughters of Astaroth." He nodded and the girls stared downward, not moving a muscle. "Kopano, son of . . . Alocer?" Kopano nodded that I was correct. "This is Blake, son of . . . I can't remember his name. I'm sorry."

"Son of Melchom, sir." He gave a small bow of his upper body, never lifting his eyes.

"And this is Kaidan—"

"Son of Pharzuph," my father cut in, his lip having gone up in a scowl as he stared at him. I had to give Kaidan a lot of credit for not peeing himself under the heat of my father's accusatory stare. He gave a respectful nod and kept his eyes averted downward, just like the others.

I wanted to put a hand on my dad's forearm to make him ease up, but I didn't need to, because he turned his stink eye away from Kaidan to me.

"You're leaving with me, girl. Time to start your training."

CHAPTER TWENTY-THREE

SEEING DEMONS

The ball was in my father's court, so I waited with impatience for him to talk. Seeing my dad behind the wheel of the basic rental car was strange. Too normal or something. I was dying to tell him what Sister Ruth had left me. After ten minutes of silence, I began to worry. When my leg started bouncing, he reached over and laid his big hand on mine.

"Know that I love you, Anna."

"I do." But there was something ominous in his voice.

"Just don't forget."

He put both hands back on the wheel and fear crept over me.

He watched the road, wearing a grave expression. "I wanted to call you when I got out, but it's not always safe. I'd rather scout out an area and talk in person. Tell me how it went with that nun at the convent."

My stomach dropped at the thought of the information we'd never know.

"We didn't make it in time. She died the night I met you. But she left me something . . . a sword hilt without a blade."

The car swerved a little. I kept talking.

"Kaidan thinks it's a Sword of Righteousness."

My father jerked the wheel hard to the side of the road and slammed on the brakes. I grabbed the door handle and braced myself against whiplash. When we stopped I looked around, but there were no cars behind us. He turned in his seat with a wild look on his face.

"Describe it to me," he demanded. I told him how it looked and what happened when both Kaidan and I touched it. He stared at me with those crazed eyes for a few long heartbeats before smacking his hands together in a loud clap and shouting, "Yeah!"

I jumped, startled. I must have missed something, because I didn't feel like cheering when I thought of the hilt. But something about his sheer excitement made me want to jump on board.

"Something's brewing. Something big. I don't know what, but the angels are gonna use you. My little soldier girl."

Soldier girl? It was hilarious in an impossible-scenario kind of way.

"What do you think I'm supposed to do?"

"Nothing yet, baby girl. There's a lot you need to learn first. I want you to be able to protect yourself when I'm not around. There might come a time when you have to do things you don't like, to stay safe. You may need to at least *appear* to be working." He ran a critical eye over me. "For starters, you've got this all-natural sweet-and-innocent thing going on. Much as I hate to say it, you probably need to do something edgier with your look. And you're gonna need to learn your drinking limits. I don't want you to end up in a situation where you don't know your boundaries."

"How am I supposed to learn?"

"You drink. Under my supervision. We'll figure out how much you can handle in a certain amount of time, and practice controlling it so you can stay coherent and not get drunk."

My heart jackhammered against my ribs.

"Are we starting tonight?" I asked.

An eerie pause passed before he cleared his throat and said, "No. We'll start tomorrow."

He pulled the car onto the road and accelerated. I noticed for the first time that we were headed toward Cartersville. He was taking me home. I had an overwhelming urge to hug him. I shot my vision along the line of trees and the road surrounding us. Nobody was in sight, so I flung my arms around his thick neck and squeezed, resting my head on his shoulder. His body shook with gruff chuckles. He kept one hand on the wheel and used the other to reach up and pat my shoulder.

"Just remember I love you," he said again, and I wondered what he thought he could ever do to make me doubt it.

That night I peered out of my bedroom window and noticed the absence of moonlight and stars. Massive gray clouds filled the winter night sky. A spooky chill was in the air, making me lock my bedroom door.

I got ready for bed, hoping not to disturb Patti, who'd had a rough day. She was having a hard time dealing with the slight shift in authority ever since I'd met my father. Patti's word was no longer the final say-so, because there was a greater, more dangerous threat that even she could not protect me from. Now all she could do was just hope that she'd raised me right.

My bed was a comfort as I sat, crossing my legs and clasping my hands together. I closed my eyes.

I don't know what You'll have me do, or where You'll have me go, but I trust You. Please show me when it's time to act. Help me to recognize the signs. Speak to my heart and let me hear.

I awoke with a start at three a.m. Rain battered the windowpane. I closed my eyes and tried to relax, pushing away the strange foreboding. Just as I began to doze again, I felt a chill of certainty that I was being watched. I wanted to scramble under the covers like a child, but I was too scared to move or open my eyes. I held my breath. Was someone in my room?

An image flitted into my mind of a young man standing in an open-air market surrounded by children and women of all ages doing their shopping. I sensed the man's anxiety and apprehension as he stood there, surveying the gathered crowd with wide eyes. He looked down at the small detonator in his hand and I realized with horror that he was strapped with bombs. He murmured something under his breath. *No, don't do it!* I shouted to him, but he didn't hear me. With a cry into the air he pressed the button, releasing a blinding flash.

I wanted to sit up, but my chest was heavy. Another scene began to play in my mind.

It was a different place now. A man in an office held a telephone—the image switched to the woman on the other end of the phone, his wife, very pregnant, setting out their dinner plates. Her face fell when he said there was a late meeting, and even as he spoke the lie, his mistress was unbuttoning his slacks. The bright red of his lust overshadowed his fog of guilt. My mind snapped into darkness.

What the heck is going on? I gasped for air and pulled the blanket to my chin.

Another image was focusing: terrified dogs, poked to agitation with sticks and then thrown together to rip at one another's flesh while the surrounding crowd of people jeered, clapped, pointed, and laughed. *Stop! It's not funny!* I was sickened by the panic in the animals' eyes and the human hunger for violence. I continued to gasp, unable to fill my lungs.

A boy now, no older than me, in some sort of basement or cellar, tying a rope to a beam and the other end around his own neck. I shook my head, trying to dispel his crushing feelings of self-doubt and loneliness that reached out to me like dark, strangling fingers. I held a hand out to him. *Let me help you*, I pleaded. *You're not alone.* But his eyes were empty and he let himself drop.

No! I yelled as he twitched and swung. He disappeared in a haze of thought.

A girl slashing the tender skin of her arm with a razor, cutting deeper, hating her life, wanting to shadow that pain with a pain of her own choosing.

A frail old woman robbed and raped, left bloody on the floor in her own house with no hope that either of her busy children would call or visit in time to find her alive.

One terrifying image was replaced by another. Emotions so heavy I thought I might suffocate on despair. I shook my head back and forth, back and forth, begging it to stop. *Someone help them!* Visions came faster now, even more vivid.

A little girl pretending to sleep as the shadow of a man loomed over her bed.

A teenage boy facedown in a pile of his own vomit.

An unarmed tribe, families with young children, hacked by dull machetes as they begged on their knees for mercy.

A mother with glazed eyes staring down at her red-faced crying infant, plunging him under the water, holding him down in the tub until his flailing stopped. Her dead eyes never looking away.

"No! No!" I clawed at my hair, which was wet with tears.

Five men were now standing over someone on the ground, filled with unfounded hatred and blind fear as they kicked him. The victim continued to change: He was black; he was white; he was Muslim; he was Jewish; he was gay. And the five men kicked and kicked, radiating hate for each victim, terrified of what they could not understand. And there was a final crunching stomp on his face that ended it all.

These were the very atrocities I'd avoided thinking about all my life, but they were out there whether I'd acknowledged them or not. I couldn't just lie there and take it any longer. I had to move.

Banging sounded on my door, and the knob rattled.

"Anna?" Patti said. "What's going on in there? Open up!"

I opened my eyes, trying to focus, and I saw them in a flickering flash of lightning.

Demons.

They took turns coming at me, whispering. The spirits were as large as men, but with grimacing gargoyle faces and slow-flapping black wings that overlapped one another, even spanning through the walls. Some had horns and fangs and claws.

Come, follow us to hell, where you belong. . . .

I screamed, scrambling backward until I banged into the headboard.

"Anna!" Patti pounded now, but I could barely hear her. "Open the door!"

Incest. Kidnapping. Molestation. A serial killer taking his time with a begging victim.

The demons surrounded me, at least ten of them, and they were cackling.

What's the matter, little girl? Scared of the bogeymen?

"Leave me alone!" I cried. "Get out of my head!"

They basked in my fear.

I stumbled from the bed, falling toward my book bag and spinning to press my back against the wall as I ripped open the zipper and pulled out the box.

Soon you'll be in your rightful home, and we can really have fun with you.

I stood, fumbling for the box's clasp and losing my grip. It fell to the floor with a crack. I went to my knees, reaching around uselessly. The spirits blurred my night vision. I rocked

311

back on my heels and squeezed my eyes shut.

Please make them leave!

Inhuman shrieks filled the room, making my eyes fly open. Demons were being sucked out through my window as if by a vacuum, until they were gone. A sudden stillness fell, and the only sound was rain crashing outside.

There was a rattling beside me, and then my door swung open and Patti switched on the light. I gasped at the sight of her guardian angel. He was clear to me now. I could make out his features and wings. He was stoic and majestic and huge, like a soldier. He peered around the room and pointed under my bed. The box was halfway underneath. He must have known what was in it. I crawled over and grabbed the box, crushing it to my chest.

"What happened, Anna?" Patti asked, near tears.

She held a flathead screwdriver that she'd used to remove the doorknob.

"I can see the demons now, and they were . . . giving me nightmares."

"That was more than a nightmare!" She squatted next to me and smoothed hair from my damp face. "You were screaming like you were being attacked."

"Just scary visions," I said, and even though it was true, it felt like so much more than that. I trembled all the way to the core of my belly. I put a finger to my lips to show her I couldn't talk about it. Someone might be listening.

We jumped at the sound of rapid, hard knocking on the front door.

I ran down the hall on weak legs, putting an eye to the

peephole. It was Kopano.

I flung open the door and he came straight in along with a cold gust of wind, looking around with those serious, somber eyes. He laid a hand on my shoulder. I grabbed his wrist and held on as I tried to catch my breath.

"Anna?" Patti had come in, staring at Kopano.

"This is my friend Kope," I told her. "He must have been listening out for me."

He went forward and they shook hands. She crossed her arms over her thin nightgown.

"I need to get my robe on." Patti headed toward her bedroom and gave us a chance to talk.

"Whisperers were here," I told Kopano. "I could see them. They showed me all these awful things. I couldn't think straight. Oh, my gosh, Kope, I think that's what hell's going to feel like."

He reached out to console me just as the front door flew open. I jumped back and screamed. Kaidan stood there with disheveled hair, his forehead creased with worry.

The neighbor's door across the hall opened, and a bent old man peered out over his oxygen tank.

"What in God's name is going on over there?" he asked in a wheezing voice.

"Nothing, Mr. Mayer, I'm so sorry."

I pulled Kaidan inside and closed the door.

"What are you doing here?!" I asked.

His eyes flickered toward our hall, where Patti now stood, holding her robe closed and taking in the scene. I turned back to Kaidan, panic building inside of me.

"They could come back any second and see us together and tell your father! Go home!"

He stood in defiance, but as he glanced at Kopano his facade cracked, revealing a desolate expression that broke my heart.

"Yes, I'll go," Kaidan said. "You've got help."

I reached for his arm as he turned, but he slipped through my fingers and walked out.

I sat on the couch, burying my face in my hands. I hadn't meant to make him think I was choosing Kopano over him. He had to know it wasn't like that. I was scared for him.

And what in the world were they both doing here, anyway? Had they been somewhere nearby listening out for me all night?

"I will go to him," Kopano said, leaving the apartment and closing the door. I pushed my hearing around to find them at the bottom of the stairs, just next to the sheet of rain falling from the roof like a waterfall. I focused hard, trying to ignore the spooky feeling that still held me.

Patti peeked around the corner and I waved her over, signaling that I was listening to something. She turned on a side lamp and sat down next to me, rubbing my chilled limbs to try to warm me.

"Let us go somewhere and talk," Kopano said to Kaidan.

"We can talk here. She never uses her senses."

Whoops. I was officially eavesdropping, but I didn't feel guilty. I was too desperate for insight into Kaidan's mind. They spoke in low tones, hard to hear with the rush of rainwater.

"Do not be upset, Kai. I feel only concern for her."

"I'll bet you do."

Kaidan's clipped, harsh response was in direct contrast to Kopano's tranquil words.

"Even you are willing to risk yourself for her, brother."

"That's because I actually know her. What's your reason? I suppose you'd like to get to know her, too?"

"You have made it very clear that she is not available in that way. Be reasonable. There is plainly more at stake here. I only wished to help."

"There's nothing you can do, Kope!"

They got quiet and I could hear Kaidan's ragged breaths through his nose.

"Please trust me, brother," Kopano said. "There is no stronger weapon for Pharzuph to use than your concern for each other. If he learns that you were here to console her, you will lose all leverage with him. Do not fool yourself into thinking he will not discard you."

"Yes, some of us have to worry about such things. Thank you for the reminder."

The sounds that came next iced my blood: heavy footfalls crashing into puddles, and the metallic zing of a switchblade. I stood up with a hand to my heart. Then there was a deep, gruff chuckle. My father's.

"Put it away, boy. Sorry to break up the testosterone party."

I jumped off the couch and ran from the apartment, down the cement stairs, until I nearly crashed into the three of them at the bottom. My father was absolutely soaked, beads of water covering his skull as he glowered at Kaidan.

"Dad!" I slapped a hand over my mouth. As he dragged his

eyes from Kaidan to me, I experienced a punch of knowledge.

"It was you," I said, heart pounding. "You sent them."

He made no attempt to deny it.

I sagged back on my heels. The demons weren't sent by someone who wanted to hurt me. It had been my father, showing some serious tough love.

A light sound of shuffling came from the landing. Patti surveyed us from the top of the steps in her robe and slippers.

"It's okay," I assured her. "I'll be in soon." She nodded, staring hard at my dad for a second before she went back up. He turned his attention back to Kopano and Kaidan, who kept their eyes trained at his feet.

"This little thing"—he made a triangle in the air, pointing between Kopano, Kaidan, and me—"isn't gonna fly. Don't worry yourselves about Anna anymore. You hear?" They both gave single nods. "Then get on out of here. And keep your heads in the game."

There was only the sound of rain now, then their cars starting and tires sloshing away too fast. Before my father could apologize or give me another sad look, I wrapped my arms around him. He let out a deep breath.

"Will you come in?" I asked, against his chest.

"I'd better not, after that look from Patti." He ran a hand down my hair. "Does she know about those two boys fighting over you?"

"They weren't fighting over me. And she cares about Kaidan."

"Hmph. Well, I'll be here at three o'clock this afternoon. Warn Patti, 'cause I'll need to come in and talk to you both first. Now go get some shut-eye. You're gonna need it. And don't worry. No more spirits will bother you tonight."

A giant bolt of lightning lit up the night sky. My father kissed the top of my head and disappeared into the rain as a roar of thunder shook the foundation under my feet.

CHAPTER TWENTY-FOUR

GIVE A LITTLE WHISTLE

My dad was going to be here any minute, and Patti was a nervous wreck. Disobedient red curls had popped out of her hair clip and now framed her sleep-deprived face. She'd spent the morning deep-cleaning the apartment with a frown, shooing me away when I tried to help.

I hadn't been able to go back to sleep right away the night before. Patti sat with me in our living room, and I realized that after I found out what I was, I had become the one withholding information to protect her. Now I finally broke down and told her everything I'd been holding back. She'd understood that the Neph were seen as property, but she hadn't known about us being forced to work, or the fact that we had "specialties." She stared heavenward and shook her head after finding out she'd sent me on a long-distance trip with the son of Lust.

But the detail that sent her over the edge was the fact that my father had me haunted by those demons. No matter how much I tried to explain that it was necessary for me to be able to see the spirits, she was livid. When three o'clock approached and her mood hadn't lightened, I started to worry.

When my dad arrived, Patti stood by the counter with her arms crossed. He appeared as large and frightening as ever. The kind of man nobody would dare to mess with.

Patti walked right up and smacked him across the face.

I jolted. He blinked. She stayed right in front of him and stabbed a finger at his chest, her other hand on her hip.

"How *dare* you do that to her? I don't care what your reasons were. Did you hear her screaming? She was terrified! Don't you ever sic those monsters on her again. Ever!"

He watched her with an even expression, allowing her to get it all out of her system. Her pointing hand went on her other hip and she stared up at him, breathing hard. She wore the steel gray of fury.

"I swear to you," my father said with care, "I will spend the rest of Anna's life trying to keep those spirits away from her."

"Then why does she have to *train* with you today? If you're going to protect her, then why is it necessary? Why can't you keep her out of danger?" Patti's voice cracked and she brought a hand up to clutch her mouth as fury turned to rolling fear. My father watched her, and when he spoke he shocked us both with what he said.

"You remind me so much of Mariantha. Not the way you look, but the way your soul feels to me. Loving, but full of that same righteous stubbornness. Yeah, Mariantha would approve, and so do I. You've done a good job. More than good. And I want to thank you."

A sob escaped through Patti's hand. He'd hit her soft spot. Not only did he compliment her mothering, but he'd compared her to an angel.

"But I failed her," Patti said, her freckled face streaked with tears. "I didn't get her to Sister Ruth in time."

"Let go of that guilt; it's all part of the plan."

"What if I messed up the plan?"

He broke into a knowing grin.

"The plan's always changing and rearranging. You can't mess it up."

She wiped her face, and the darkness of fear faded. I still hadn't moved. I was trying to wrap my mind around the fact that Patti had gone from wanting to kill him to being comforted by him.

"Would you like some sweet tea?" she asked. *Ladies and gentlemen, I give you Patti Whitt.*

"Yes, ma'am, I'd appreciate it." *And my father, the fear-provoking gentleman.*

As she went to the kitchen, he gave my shoulder a hard pat. I shook my head in wonder. We went over and sat down at the small table.

"So, where do you wanna do this thing, kiddo?" he asked.

Patti was busy with the drinks, but I knew she'd heard by the way her colors went haywire. I shrugged. I didn't want to do "this thing" in front of Patti. She brought the glasses of tea over and set them on the table.

320

"You know," she said, "I'm real tired, and I got a new book from the library yesterday, so I'll just be in my room this afternoon. Why don't y'all stay here, and I'll be nearby if you need me. I can come out and make dinner later when you're ready to take a break."

I nodded my agreement. As long as she stayed back there, I could do it. Patti leaned down to kiss my cheek, and then headed back to her room.

"Stuff's in the car." He hitched a thumb toward the door.

I went out with him to help, even though he insisted he could get it himself. My eyeballs popped when I saw the layout in the backseat. All sorts of snack foods, along with bags and bags of bottles: beer, wine, liquor, juices, sodas, condiments like cherries and limes and olives. We hefted everything up the stairs.

I can't believe I'm about to drink with my father. This was wrong on so many levels.

The drinks and ingredients that needed to be chilled were put in the fridge, and the rest were set out on the counters. I rubbed my arms, feeling jumpy inside. At least it wasn't a buffet of drugs, because I would be a harried, frantic mess by now.

"Nothing wrong with having a drink, Anna." He set out two shot glasses and I sat down in front of one while he poured something clear. I looked at the bottle. Rum. "We're never told not to drink. Just warned against drunkenness. There's a fine line between the two, and all we're doing is trying to find yours. You'll be drinking a lot of water and eating as we go. Should help you some." He pushed my shot glass forward. Mine was not as full as his.

321

"I'll need to see your colors to help me gauge your intoxication."

I assumed it would be a relief to let down my mental guard, but I felt exposed and didn't like the way my dad's eyes squinched up when he saw my colors. I'd been trying not to think about Kaidan, but that only made me think of him more. My dad pinched the bridge of his nose. I was guessing he didn't think dark pink passionate love had any business being in his little girl's wardrobe of emotions. But he didn't say anything about it—only let out a jagged sigh and began.

"Note the time. You'll need to pay close attention to the time when you drink. You got a watch?" I shook my head, and he took his off, tossing it at me. "Use this one tonight, but get yourself one right away. It's three twenty-five. Pick it up." We both lifted our tiny glasses. "Drink the whole thing at once. Don't try to sip it or take multiple swallows. And don't you dare spit it out."

Got it. No problem. I could do this. The liquid was clear, like water. A bubble of giddiness rose up inside me as I followed his lead, bringing it to my lips and tilting back my head.

Gah!

My entire face, mouth, and throat lit on fire as the gulp made its way down. I coughed and sputtered and smacked the table. My father laughed and clapped me on the back. I let out a sputtering breath and could not wipe the disgust from my face.

"Good job not spitting it out," he said.

"That was terrible! Why would anyone purposely drink that?"

And then the warmth hit. It started in my chest, went

down into my belly, and bloomed throughout my limbs.

"*Oh.*"

"Nice, huh?" he asked, but he wasn't smiling anymore. He was studying me as I ran my eyes over the bottle of rum, then up to the counter where the other bottles stood in line, waiting for me.

"By the end of the night, you won't flinch anymore. You're gonna get mad at me at some point when I tell you no more, but I need you to learn to recognize that moment in yourself when one more drink will put you over the edge. Only you can control yourself, baby girl. For tonight I'm gonna whistle when you need to slow down and rein it in. Got it?"

"Got it. But I was wondering. Um, are we going to train with drugs, too?"

"You're not gonna do drugs, Anna, ever." Deadly conviction was in his voice. "There won't be any buzz with drugs when it comes to you—you'll pass Go and head straight to the equivalent of drunkenness. Only worse. I don't plan for you to work at all, but you need to have some basic knowledge in case of some unforeseen circumstance. Now, are you ready to drink?"

I nodded my head and he frowned. It would appear I'd nodded with too much enthusiasm.

Nine hours, two pizzas, one fight, three instances of vomiting, a million whistles, tons of snacks, and countless drinks later, we learned that I could have one drink every eighteen minutes, or three in one hour. Absolutely no more. Even with my body's ability to burn the alcohol, I was what my father deemed a "lightweight" or "cheap date." If I were to drink on a regular basis my tolerance would increase, but for now we'd be conservative with our estimates.

I'd learned the recipes for the most popular cocktails. I knew I hated straight shots of anything except tequila. I was definitely a tequila girl. Wine soured my stomach. Beer was my safest bet.

There'd been another little scuffle between Patti and John Gray when she came out to make dinner. She'd been upset when he insisted we order pizza rather than making her cook. The kitchen was a disaster. But pizza was a luxury we never splurged on. When he pointed out that she was being proud, she crossed her arms and pouted, telling him to go ahead and order the "stinkin' pizza" then.

I had a good buzz going at that point, but when I started giggling at their silly spat, Patti's narrowed glare cleared my head pretty fast.

Throughout the night my dad asked a lot of questions about my life. He wanted to know every detail about Jay and the four Neph I'd met. He was especially interested in Kopano's story.

"I never would've guessed Alocer had a soft spot. Makes you wonder . . ."

"Kind of funny, huh?" I'd said in a slur. "Most people try to hide bad stuff they do, but the Dukes have to try to hide good stuff."

During my last bathroom break of the night, he brought in a purple-and-black book bag from the trunk of the rental car. It still had the tags on it.

"For you girls." He set the bag on the couch between Patti

and me. "Please take it with no arguing. And listen up. Anna, you need a watch, and you need to change your look. I expect you to get on that right away."

I nodded, barely able to keep my eyes open.

"One last thing. I don't think you gals should go to church anymore."

I'd never thought about that. There was so much about my normal, daily life that reeked of nondemon.

"We can just do our own little thing here together," Patti assured me, rubbing my back. The whole night had been an eye-opener for the two of us. We needed to make changes in order to keep up my facade and fly under the demons' radar.

"Open it." He crossed his arms and assumed the bouncer pose, nodding down to the book bag.

I unzipped it and Patti and I bonked heads trying to see what was inside. Then we stared up at each other, our faces inches apart. It was filled with stacks of cash. I knew Patti's thoughts when her aura grayed. This was drug money. Dirty money. Blood money. My father knew our thoughts, too.

"Regardless of where it came from, that money's in your possession now, and all you can do is be good stewards with what you've been given. For starters, I recommend getting a fireproof safe. You'll find a new cell phone in the side pouch. It's got my number in it. Call me if you need me. I can't guarantee I'll answer, but if I don't, and it's an emergency, just text me A-nine-one-one. It means 'Anna emergency.' Don't leave a voice message or any detailed texts."

I stood up and hugged his solid body, resting my cheek on the soft leather of his jacket. He ran his hand down my hair like he had the night before.

"When will I see you again?" I asked.

"I don't know. I'll be on the go. Do me another favor?"

I pulled away and looked up at him.

"Check out the other side pouch of your bag," he said.

I dug my hand into the small spot and pulled out a key attached to a big black key chain with buttons for locking and unlocking doors. My head jerked up to see his serious expression. Patti covered her mouth, saying nothing.

"No more boys taking you on trips, you hear?" His voice was gravelly. "You can take your own self from now on. Last thing you need is some boy distracting you and making this whole situation even more complicated. Promise me you'll stay away from that son of Pharzuph."

I opened my mouth but the words stuck in my dry throat. Hot sweat beaded up on my forehead.

"I tried that once, John," Patti warned him. "It didn't work out so well for me."

"Have you seen the way he looks at her?" He focused on Patti, but pointed at me.

"Yes, and I've seen the way she looks at him. Truthfully, I think they need each other."

"Those two need each other like a bullet needs a target. Trust me. I've seen Nephilim kids killed for falling in love and letting it get in the way of their work."

"Well, you don't have to worry, because we're not in love," I chimed in. "He doesn't like me like that."

Dad puffed out a breath of air. "Well, he must feel something, 'cause he sure doesn't want that other kid near you."

"Is there someone else you're interested in?" Patti asked.

I rolled my colors back up, tucked them inside, and yanked the barrier back into place. Then I entertained the image of Kopano's sweet dimple for a brief second before pushing it away.

"I'm not ready to think about that," I answered.

My father tilted his head up to the ceiling and pressed his giant hands to his face, muffling his speech. "I'm way too old for this."

CHAPTER TWENTY-FIVE

BACK TO SCHOOL

When school started a week later, I knew it was going to be bad. Jay warned me that there'd been a lot of speculation and gossip over the summer about what happened between Scott and me at the party. But I had expected everyone to whisper behind my back at school. Not so much.

I wasn't comfortable with the attention. It didn't help that I'd donated fourteen inches of hair to Locks of Love, gotten platinum blond highlights, and had my eyebrows waxed.

Bobby Donaldson, varsity baseball pitcher and player extraordinaire, who'd never said a word to me in my life, approached me at my locker with one heck of a lusty red aura before school started.

"Hey, girl. How you doin'?"

"Um, fine?"

"I'm Bobby. Where you from?"

Annoyed, I closed my locker, swung the purple-and-black bag over my shoulder, and attempted to stuff long bangs behind my ear.

"I'm not new. You know me. Anna Whitt?"

His eyes ran across the features of my face.

"Hot daaay-um, for real?"

I forced my eyes not to roll back, and walked past him. He ran to catch up.

"So you hooked up with Scott?" he hollered over the din of excited first-day voices.

"No, I didn't."

I sped up, dodging other hall walkers, but Bobby stayed on my heels.

"'Cause it's cool if you did. Hey, you wanna go out sometime?"

I stopped so abruptly he ran into a girl passing us.

"It's just me, Bobby. I'm the same weird, prudish girl that you've been in youth group and science class with for the past three years and never talked to. All I did was go to a party and get a haircut."

"I heard you aren't such a prude anymore."

And before I could give a lame comeback about how he'd heard wrong, he tweaked my cheek with his knuckle and headed for his own class. I swallowed down the bile in my throat and blinked back moisture building in my eyes. I was not going to cry because of Bobby. It didn't matter what he thought. I went to first period.

By lunch it was clear that I hadn't taken Jay's warnings seriously enough. The rumors were out of control. I could ignore the stares and whispers, but I couldn't pretend people weren't cornering me for information. *What happened with you and Scott? He says you're making it up about the drugs. Did you really hook up with some guy in a band? I'm having a party this weekend; wanna come?*

I told each one of them I didn't want to talk about it.

I had one class with Scott, Spanish again. He sat on the other side of the room and never looked my way. Even Veronica avoided me, maybe too embarrassed about the BFF stuff. They were the only two people in school *not* interested in talking to me.

I thought I was unsociable in years past, but for the first few weeks of this year I was a recluse. I kept my eyes down and went straight home after school. No football games. No hanging at Jay's house. And definitely no parties or clubs.

But despite how hard I tried to be invisible, all eyes were on me. Only one person was able to shake me into clarity.

Lena was a shy girl who worked hard and didn't go out of her way to impress others—traits I appreciated. She usually hid her face behind a headful of shiny black curls and kept to herself.

Lena came into the bathroom after me between classes one morning. Afterward I realized she had followed me. Lena shuffled next to me, leaning into the mirror to check out her creamy skin, catching my eye. We both messed with our hair, and then she bent down to see whether there were any feet in the stalls before speaking.

"I . . ." She bit down as if mustering courage. "I heard about what Scott McCallister did to you."

"Oh?" I continued to dig around for some pretend object, surprised she would stoop low enough to care about such gossip, and hoping she would drop it. I almost missed her next words, spoken softly.

"He did it to me, too."

I tensed and looked up at her. "He did?"

"Well, kind of." She shuffled her stance, eyeing the cracked wall tiles. "Last year at a party over Christmas break."

So Kaidan was right. It hadn't been a solitary incident. Lena's light gray nervousness darkened with apprehension when I didn't respond right away.

"I believe you, Lena."

With that reassurance, her gray worries cleared into the sky blue of relief.

"Did he—" She stopped herself, but I knew what she wanted to ask.

"No," I told her. "We were interrupted."

She continued avoiding my eyes, adjusting the book-bag strap on her shoulder. "That's good. Unfortunately we weren't. He didn't drug me. I mean, he talked me into taking it, but afterward he told me I came on too strong, and he didn't like me that way. He was just trying to be nice."

"Oh, my gosh, Lena. That's . . ." I didn't know what to say. She looked at me now.

"You're the only person I've ever told. I just wanted you to know you're not alone."

"Thank you," I said.

She nodded and rushed out the door. I stood there thinking for two minutes and received my first tardy ever.

Jay was shaking when he sat down next to me at the lunch table. Band and drama kids sat at the other end.

"Where's your lunch?" I asked.

"I'm not eating." His knee bounced as he glared around the cafeteria.

"What happened?" I pushed my tray away.

"Nothing."

I moved closer, stomach turning. "No, tell me."

"I have a feeling I'm gonna get suspended."

"Why? What did you do?" I asked.

"Nothing yet."

"Is it Scott?"

Jay nodded, mouth tightening at the mention of that name. "You should hear what he's saying."

"I don't want to," I told him. "He's not worth getting into trouble over, Jay."

"I don't know about that. It might be worth it to shut his mouth."

I followed Jay's hateful stare to where Scott stood next to a table of wrestlers, reenacting someone tripping and falling. The guys rewarded him with hearty laughs. I wondered how many girls he'd taken advantage of.

I couldn't let him get away with it, even though I loathed the idea of confrontation.

"You should tell your scary-ass dad about Scott," Jay muttered.

"He'd kill him," I said.

"Exactly."

I put a hand on his arm. "Listen to me, 'kay? I'm going to say something to Scott, but I need you to promise me you won't interfere. Just stay over here or go somewhere else."

Jay was quiet for a moment, rubbing his hands together.

"Jay."

"Fine. I'll stay here, but I'm watching."

I stood up and dumped my tray, then set it on the cart. Scott had moved on to the next table and was sitting across from Veronica and Kristin Miller. I took a deep breath and approached him on unsteady legs.

"Can I talk to you?" I asked quietly, trying not to gain everyone's attention. Blood thumped in my temples and throat. He eyeballed me up and down over his shoulder as if I'd been rolling around in a pigsty.

"Talk to me about what?" He stood and faced me, using his bulk to make me step back. "About how you're sorry you lied about me to everyone when all I did was try to be nice to you?"

I took a breath before answering. "Please, Scott, let's just go in the hall and talk alone."

"I got nothin' to hide!" He threw his arms out to the sides.

I had intended to speak with him privately, but if he wanted to make a public spectacle out of us, then so be it. I balled my fists.

"I'm not sorry, because I haven't lied about anything and you know it," I said. "I'm not the one spreading rumors."

"As if I would have needed to drug you," he said. The whole table was watching and listening now. "You were, like, desperate, hanging all over me."

I tried not to let his ugliness seep into me. I had to keep my mind sharp. I angled myself away from the spectators, but it had gone silent around us as I responded.

"I thought you were being nice by inviting me to the party, and I did wonder what a guy like you was doing giving a girl like me any attention, but now I understand. You knew that if the truth came out about what you planned to do, all these people would take your word over mine. We both know what you did. Veronica and Kristin know it, too."

Kristin gave a short laugh like I was crazy; her colors were a muddy orange of amusement at my expense. Veronica's eyes widened and she looked away, wearing a blanket of dark shame about her. As for Scott, he was cloaked in a swirl of purple pride and gray fear, a dangerous combination. For a split second I thought about willing all three of them to tell the truth. It would have brought me satisfaction, but I refused to hamper their free will.

I lowered my voice to a whisper. "And I also know I'm not the first girl you've done this to."

His eyes hardened. "You really expect anyone to believe that? You're psycho."

"Do you always ask psychos whether you can kiss them?"

Snickers rose from the table.

"Yeah, right," Scott said. "You wish."

"She's not lying." We all turned to Veronica, who'd spoken with bold confidence. But only I could see she was wrapped in the darkness of fear now.

"Shut up, you stupid lush," Scott said to her. "You and your big nose can stay the hell out of this conversation."

"You're a liar!" She jumped to her feet and ran from the cafeteria.

Scott turned his sneer on me. "Everyone knows you're just a band whore now."

My palm itched, begging to slap him. "You should be ashamed of yourself, Scott."

"Oooh!" He shook his hands in the air. "Good comeback."

"You're such a fake," I whispered, "and it's really sad. You live your life to impress a bunch of people who don't accept you for who you are. But maybe that's because *you* don't even know who you are."

A bubble of blackness rose up from his depths, hideous and raging around him. His nostrils flared and I dared to take a step forward, speaking low enough for only him to hear.

"You need to deal with that self-hatred, and stop taking it out on innocent people. It's not too late to be the person you really want to be." Surprise, guilt, and rusty hope lifted from the dark sludge of his aura. "Good luck, Scott."

I pushed past him, hurrying toward the exit to the hall. I couldn't get out of there fast enough. I found Veronica in the bathroom, brushing her hair with punishing strokes in front of the mirror. She stopped when she saw me.

"I should have called him out sooner," she said.

"It's okay."

"No, it's really not. I listened to him lie about you all summer and this whole month back at school. I kept hoping it would just blow over." She shoved her brush back into her purse and sniffed.

"Thank you for sticking up for me." I knew it wasn't easy going against the crowd.

"I know everything was messed up at Gene's party, but I had fun with you that night," Veronica said.

"Me, too."

Her feelings were only a light fog now.

"I heard about you and the drummer of that band. Is he kind of tall, with brown hair?"

I nodded and she grabbed my arm, suddenly animated again.

"Oh, my gawd, I totally think he was the guy checking you out in the hall at the party!"

"Oh, yeah, I forgot about that."

"Wanna come over and hang out sometime?" she asked. I opened myself to the pastels of her hope and gladness, letting them surge with my own.

"Sure. Maybe you can help me with my stupid hair."

I pulled at the long bangs. As she lifted layers of my hair with her fingers, checking it out and complimenting the style, I marveled about the nature of humanity, and how something as lovely as friendship could stem from something so hideous.

There was a lot to be said for having a female friend. My toes looked better than they ever had. Veronica was insistent they be painted if I was going to wear flip-flops. We had some of our best conversations sitting on the floor of her bedroom as she leaned over my feet with a bottle of polish.

"Scott hasn't talked to me at all since that day," Veronica said one late October afternoon as she applied a coat of sparkly blue polish. "That's fine by me, though."

It had been over a month since the cafeteria showdown. I'd worried that the situation would only escalate from there, but after a frenzied flurry of gossip, Scott dropped it, and talk died down. I heard he was dating a girl from another school.

I'd finally started hanging out again outside of school with Jay and Veronica, but I preferred being at one of our homes instead of going out. I was always on the lookout for whisperers when we went somewhere like the mall, paranoid about my two friends being targeted. Or me seeming too chummy with humans. Veronica swiped more polish across my toenails.

"Tell me what it was like with Kaidan," she said.

I felt excited at the initial thought of him, and then sad. Sometimes the longing was so overpowering I'd think of him for hours at a time. I told Veronica about our kisses and how he'd tease me in that flirty way. But there was too much I couldn't explain.

"You still love him, don't you?" She didn't wait for an answer. "How long has it been since you've seen him?"

"Three months or so."

"We've gotta find you a new man."

"No, I'm good. I don't want anybody."

"You still want *him*. That's the problem," she said.

I did still want him.

"What about you?" I used the same diversion tactics as I did with Jay, even though I didn't want to talk about the shady guy she'd been dating.

"I think he's starting to get impatient with me." She looked down and started painting her own toes again, which were already perfect.

"You've been together only a few weeks," I pointed out.

"I know, but it seems like it's been longer 'cause we see each other every day and talk on the phone every night, and last night he said to me, 'I don't see what the big deal is. It's not like you're a virgin.'" She mimicked his mopey boy voice.

I thought about Veronica's relationship with Mike Ramsey that had spanned our entire ninth-grade year, and I felt defensive for her.

"He shouldn't say that to you. It's still a big deal, whether you're a virgin or not. Don't do anything with him out of guilt."

"I'm not. I mean, he's not trying to be mean or anything. He told me . . . he loves me."

I'd tried telling her when they first got together that he gave me a bad feeling, but she seemed determined not to see it. And now he was telling her he loved her when he'd never shown an ounce of pink emotion in her presence. I tried to keep the upset feelings out of my voice.

"Those are just words, Roni. If he loves you he'll show it by waiting."

"Yeah, right—how long did you make Kaidan wait?"

I rubbed at a smudge of polish on the skin inside my toe.

"We never did it. We just kissed and stuff."

"Seriously?" She blinked at me and I took the polish from her, twisting the cap back on so it wouldn't spill on her ivory carpet. "So you're still a virgin, then?"

"Yes. Contrary to popular belief."

Her eyes lifted to her childhood collection of unicorn statues on a shelf.

"Sometimes I wish I still was. Not something you can take back, though."

She pushed her thick hair behind her ear. Her bob had grown down to her shoulders and was now dyed black with one purple streak in front. She cleared her throat and straightened her legs.

"You're, like, religious, right?" she asked.

"Yes."

She began giving off strong gray vibes of mixed negative feelings. I pretended to focus on my own toes still, giving her a moment to collect her thoughts.

"Do you think badly of me?" she asked. "I mean, about all that stuff last year?"

I looked at her, confused. "What stuff?"

"You know." She pulled at a strand of carpet. "The abortion."

My heart stammered. I remembered vaguely how the rumor mill had been going at the beginning of our sophomore year about someone getting an abortion, but I never poked around for details.

"I don't think badly of you, Roni."

Her relief was immediate.

"My dad made me," she said, swallowing. Veronica was a toughie, not a crier like me, but she was fighting tears.

"She would be five months old now."

"She?" I whispered.

She shrugged. "It was always a girl when I dreamed. It's

not like I wanted a baby, but . . . I don't know. My dad went ballistic. He went to Mike's parents and they all ganged up to make us stop seeing each other. Of course, Mike had a new girlfriend like that—" She snapped her fingers. "But anyway. The worst part was the day we went to the clinic. There were these people outside."

Her colors darkened again.

"Protesters?" I asked.

"Yeah. They had signs with pictures and I tried to ignore them, but this one lady spit on me when I walked past. I remember exactly what she said, too. She said, 'You're a murderer—you'll burn in hell for this.'"

I pushed Veronica's black-and-gray swirls of guilt, anger, and fear away from me because I was dealing with my own and it was too much. My chest tightened and my voice was thick.

"She shouldn't have said that to you. It was wrong. People are supposed to love and help one another, not judge. She doesn't know your heart."

Veronica let me take her hand. Our arms dangled between us, connected at the fingers. She still stared at her toes, but the darkness around her slowly receded.

CHAPTER TWENTY-SIX

HALLOWEEN

I could not believe I'd let the tag-team duo of Jay and Veronica guilt-trip me into going to this Halloween party. It was the first time I'd gone out since the night I'd met the other Neph. Four bands were headlining tonight. Lascivious was not playing, but I knew Kaidan would be there. He'd given Jay the invite. My body tensed just thinking about it.

Jay, Veronica, and I walked through a sea of cars into a giant clearing filled with hundreds of rowdy people. It was a field party with a makeshift stage for the bands. We settled ourselves on the outskirts of the crowd, near the border of the forest.

There was a crazed buzz in the air—everyone in costume. I watched a caveman throw Wonder Woman over his shoulder as she screamed in delight. A robot was helping an alien do a beer bong on one side of us, while some Pokémon characters did a keg stand on the other side. A huge crowd was jumping and moshing in front of the stage.

I wondered what kind of sexy getup Kaidan would be wearing. Maybe Adam in a loincloth? And who would be his Eve tonight? Blech.

This was a terrible idea.

I smoothed down the snug black Lycra dress I wore. At least it was long-sleeved and flowed down to my ankles. I think it was a costume of Veronica's from when she was in middle school. She swore it wasn't too tight on me. She had no qualms about lying.

My face, neck, and hands were painted green. I doctored up a fake wart with some bubble gum and put it on my nose, much to Veronica's dismay. I wore a ratty black wig and a pointy black hat.

Veronica was a seductive Minnie Mouse in red and white polka dots. Jay was a pirate with an eye patch and a freaky fake parrot sitting crookedly on his shoulder.

I stood with my arms crossed, scanning the crowd. My eyes halted on a very tall gorilla looking in our direction. He bore a red badge on his furry chest. I had no idea how long we stared at each other, unmoving, before I lifted one hand in a wave.

"Who are you waving at?" Veronica asked me.

"Um, that big monkey. I think he's staring at . . . us."

And at that moment, the gorilla lifted an arm and scratched his armpit. The silly gesture filled me with a rush of joy. But I wasn't going to him.

I faced my friends, chewing my thumbnail. *Please come over*. When I glanced again, he was walking our way. *Yes!* My pulse went erratic.

Veronica giggled when he approached, but she shut up when he took off the gorilla head and shook out his sweat-dampened hair. From the corner of my eye, I saw her white polka dots cover over in bright red. I wasn't going to lie; it annoyed me, though I could hardly blame her. I was thankful when he turned to Jay.

"Arrgh, matey," Kaidan said.

"What's up, man?" Jay reached out and they slapped palms, then grasped hands for a second.

"I've got a joke for you," Kaidan told him. Jay nodded his head, ready. "What's the difference between a drummer and a savings bond?"

"I don't know. What?" Jay beamed bright yellow.

"A savings bond matures and eventually makes money."

They did some big, barreling boy laughing, slapping hands again. While they were distracted, Veronica cocked her head toward Kaidan and raised an eyebrow at me. I shook my head and she eyed me, unbelieving. Her colors had settled down now. Kaidan looked back over at us girls.

"This is my friend Veronica," I told him. "And this is Kaidan."

"Oh, I've heard all about you." Veronica gave him a big smile.

His brow elevated, but he didn't take the bait. Instead, he stared at me funny. "Nice wart." Leaning forward without touching me, he flicked the wart from the tip of my nose.

Veronica let out a loud cackle, proving she should be the one in my costume.

"I told you it was stupid!" She gloated.

With my pointer finger, I moved the paint around my nose to fill in the blank spot. When I finished, he was still watching me.

"Your hair's grown a lot," I said to him.

"So has your bottom."

My eyes rounded and blood rushed to my face. Veronica hooted with hilarity, bending at the waist. Even Jay let out a loud snicker, the traitor.

I wished Kaidan weren't so perceptive, but it was true. The feminine curves that had always eluded me were finally making an appearance. Stupid tight dress.

"Dude, you can get away with anything," said the pirate to the straight-faced ape.

"I meant it as a compliment."

"That was awesome." Veronica grabbed Jay by the hand. "Come on. Let's go find me a drink."

She winked at me as they ambled away. I gave my attention to the dry, trampled grass and scattered cans for a moment before working up the nerve to say something.

"My dad gave me a cell phone." And a car. And a ton of money.

Kaidan set the ape head on the ground and pulled his phone from a fuzzy pocket, blowing off brown lint. Then he held his furry thumbs above the buttons and nodded at me. I started to give him my number, but his brow creased in frustration with the big, costumed hands.

"Here," I said, taking his phone. Saving my number for him gave me a thrill.

He pocketed the cell again and looked at me with curiosity. "How did things go with your father and the training?"

"It went fine. I guess." I crossed my arms. "I know my drinking limits now and all that."

He nodded, examining me. I thought I'd feel inconspicuous and hidden in the safety of a costume, but instead I wished I weren't green. My eyes scouted the crowd. I expected to see the dark shadows of whisperers at any moment, which hastened my need to be frank with Kaidan.

"I understand what you meant now about the dangers of . . . being together." I stepped closer. "I didn't get it then, Kai, but I do now."

Music started playing, and he shifted toward the stage so he wasn't quite facing me. His head moved with the beat of the song, and I wondered whether he realized he was doing it.

"I know it's risky to see each other," I went on, steady. "But we could talk on the phone when your father's not around. If you wanted."

I braced myself, waiting for his reaction. Hoping.

"That's not a good idea," he said, watching the band.

I worried I'd pushed him too far, been too open. Panic rose inside me. Any second now he would start shutting down, and this conversation would be over. I had so much I wanted to say.

Screams came from a group of people nearby. A guy dressed as Yoda was spraying beer from the keg tap at the crowd. Kaidan watched them while I took a step closer. Inches separated us now.

"I think about our trip all the time," I whispered. He continued to watch the group as they wrestled Yoda to the ground. "Do you ever think about it?"

His eyes roamed over the crowd as he responded. "Sometimes."

He was pushing me away. My alarm rose to the next level. I grabbed two handfuls of fur from his gorilla chest, wanting him to look at me, but he wouldn't.

I swallowed my emotions, not letting go. "Why did you invite Jay to this party?"

"I don't know," he said.

I gripped the fur tighter, pulling down.

"I can't keep living like this, Kai. I need to know how you feel. I need to know one way or another so I can have some sort of closure."

"I thought you'd be over it by now." When he finally cast his severe gaze down at me, I wanted to pound his chest.

"It doesn't work like that," I told him.

He held my eyes and said nothing more. So that was how it was going to be. Fine. I let go of his costume and stepped back. It was dark outside now. Two fire pits were lit, and the flames mocked me with their trippy dance. Smoke drifted our way, thick and choking.

"Don't invite Jay to any more parties, Kaidan. If there's even the slightest chance you'll be there somewhere, I'm not going. It hurts too much to see you."

"So why did you come?" he asked with little interest.

Why, indeed? The weight of the wig and hat became too much. I pulled them off and let them drop, matted hair falling across my shoulders. I couldn't think of a single thing to say.

His mouth opened as he registered my chopped, lighter hair, but he quickly shut it.

"You should go then," he said, voice low.

Stupefied, I nodded in agreement. It was over. He wouldn't open up to me, tonight or ever. It hurt to see his stubborn, hard expression of indifference. I couldn't bring myself to say good-bye as I turned away, going in no particular direction. *Don't turn back around*, I ordered myself.

I had no clue which way my friends had gone.

"Wait," Kaidan called from behind me. I squeezed my eyes shut for a second, but kept walking. Then I felt his hand around my wrist, spinning me in a half circle and pulling me to his chest. His face was so close. He reached down and cupped my face with one woolly hand, and wiped the top corner of my lip hard with his thumb. I flinched back.

"What are you doing?"

"I . . ." He appeared to have no idea himself. "I wanted to see your freckle."

A vulnerable tenderness flashed across his face, more painful to see than the coldness. It took every ounce of strength I had not to beg for one last kiss. As fast as his expression had softened, it was back to stone again.

"What do you want from me, Kai?"

"For starters?" His voice lowered to sexy, dangerous depths. "I want to introduce myself to every freckle on your body."

A powerful shiver ripped through me.

"So, just something physical, then?" I clarified. "That's all you want?"

"Tell me you hate me," he demanded. I felt the air of his words against my face.

"But I don't hate you. I couldn't."

"You could," he assured me, pulling me tighter. "And you should."

"I'm letting you go." My voice shook. "But only because I have to. I need to move on with my life, but I'll never hate you."

"The one who got away," Kaidan murmured.

"Nobody got away," I corrected him. "And so help me, if you start comparing us to an unfinished game that went into overtime—"

He released me and I stumbled back a step. I had to get away before I started clinging and begging him to admit his feelings, whatever they might have been. It was necessary to rip off this Band-Aid, and fast. So, as I'd done at the airport, I walked away from him, dragging my heart behind me. I didn't look back. Game over.

CHAPTER TWENTY-SEVEN

HOLIDAY CHEERLESSNESS

I'd seen people with depression. I'd been bowled over by the hopelessness that sank the air around them. Murky storm clouds as heavy as sandbags.

I carried around a gloomy cloud of my own after Halloween. It was far worse than when I'd returned from California. Each day I tried to rein it in, reminding myself there was always hope. Hope for the earth, hope for humanity. Just not hope for Kaidan and me.

I dealt with the pain by shutting down. The more time asleep, the better. I missed school a few times, just to lie in bed. Failed a major test. Lost weight. But I knew time would heal the ache, and everything would be okay. I could move on.

I would come back to life. Eventually. But not yet.

Patti made my favorite things on Thanksgiving: sweet potatoes with marshmallows, corn pudding, key lime pie. I knew the spectacular spread was meant to lure me out of my hole. It was just the two of us. On past Thanksgiving mornings we'd worked the food bank, and then celebrated dinner with Patti's church friends, but we couldn't be caught doing those things now.

Patti chattered away about nothing, placing a heaping plate in front of me. She tried to fake it, but she wasn't happy these days either. I watched her cut a slice of turkey and take a bite.

"Anna, please eat."

"I'm not very hungry."

"That's because your stomach's wilted away to nothing."

I busied my mouth by taking a sip of water.

"That's it." Patti threw her napkin on the table. "I'm calling Kaidan. I know this has something to do with him."

Her words poked me to life. "No!"

"Then I need you to pull yourself out of this," she said. "It's gone on long enough. For goodness' sake, Anna! If I thought medication would work for you, I'd have taken you to the doctor already. You can't give up. You have to continue putting effort into everything, especially school."

"School is . . ." I couldn't even form a coherent sentence.

"School is still important," Patti insisted. "And so are you. There's no floating through life; you have to stay alert. Your life has a purpose. Whether you're called on to fulfill that

350

purpose today or when you're a hundred, you've got to be a productive part of society between now and then! Do you think I'm going to let you lie in bed for the next however many years?"

I shook my head. She was right. I had needed the past month to mourn, but it was time to try to get back to my life.

I eyed my plate and took a small, tentative bite of sweet potatoes. Flavors and scents brought back strong memories. The rich sweetness filled me with a longing for the love and comfort of my childhood. When I looked up at Patti, tears were leaving warm trails down my face.

"I'm sorry, Patti."

"Sweet girl." She choked up and came to me. As we hugged and cried together, I let myself feel all of the things I'd been avoiding. It was more than the insecurity of never knowing how Kaidan felt. It was about the unfairness of life as a Neph.

When I was growing up, Patti and I had done this thing every Thanksgiving where we'd take turns going back and forth saying what we were thankful for. Each time it became a longer competition, neither of us wanting to be last. It came down to the silliest details, ending up in fits of laughter. As we clung to each other now, I couldn't help but be thankful for her.

I walked to the parking lot with Veronica and Jay on our last day of school before Christmas break. A cool wind blew, and I zipped up my jacket. We'd been taking turns driving to school. Today was Jay's day.

He unlocked the passenger door from the outside and yanked it open with a creak. I wrestled with the lever to lean the passenger seat forward. It finally popped and the seat flew into the dashboard. I climbed into the back. I wasn't sure when the switch had happened: me in the back and Veronica in the front.

As the line of cars crept out of the parking lot, we passed Kaylah and her group of friends. Kaylah wiggled her fingers at Jay and he lifted one hand from the steering wheel.

"You still like her or something?" Veronica asked. Green slipped out around her.

"Nah," he said.

I looked back and forth between the two of them. Huh. When had *that* started?

I'd been obtuse when it came to my friends. That made me feel bad.

I leaned forward as much as the seat belt would allow. "Hey, guys? Can we hang out over break?" I asked.

Joyful relief poured into their auras, stabbing me with guilt.

"'Bout time." Jay caught my eye in the rearview mirror.

"Yeah. Your toes are probably lookin' shabby," Veronica said.

"I'm sorry I've been so, you know, out of it."

They were both quiet, glancing at each other as if drawing mental straws to see who would get to address the issue. Veronica lost.

"What happened on Halloween?" she asked.

"Kaidan and I agreed never to see each other again."

"That kid totally messes with your head," Veronica said. "I don't like it."

"Well, it's officially over, and I'm ready to move on with my life, so yeah."

Veronica sighed. "Some things just aren't meant to be."

I lifted my feet from the cluttered floor and curled them under me, making myself smaller in the backseat.

"Everything's gonna be okay," Jay said.

I swallowed hard and nodded at him in the mirror.

Christmas had come and gone with hardly a blip on my emotional radar. I half expected my father to call, but he didn't. I wondered about him as much as I wondered about Kaidan.

A few days before the New Year I went to the mall with Veronica. Most of my winter clothes didn't fit well and I needed a dress for the New Year's party. Veronica loved shopping with me, because I let her pick out all my clothes, only now and then nixing something. But she figured out what I would and would not wear. I had cool clothes for the first time, and I liked how it made her feel good to see me dressed in outfits she'd chosen.

We went straight to her favorite store with the dimmed lighting and pop music blaring from speakers overhead. She sorted with expert speed through racks of shirts, clanging hangers as she went.

"Do you think Jay's cute?" she asked. Her eyes concentrated on the clothes as if nothing were amiss, but her colors were going haywire.

"Um . . ." I had to proceed with caution. "Yeah, I've always thought he was a cute guy, but I've never had feelings for him or anything like that. Why? Do *you* think he's cute?"

"No." She stopped sliding hangers and looked at me. "I think he's hot."

We stared at each other for a second, and then we both started laughing, relieved to have it out in the open.

Jay and Gregory met us in the food court. I nibbled on a soft pretzel while the others had pizza. Jay and Veronica were flirting so much that Gregory rolled his eyes at me. We were throwing away our trash when Jay lifted the bill of his ball cap to peer across the food court.

"I've seen that dude before," he said. "Where do I know him from?"

"Who? Where?" Veronica asked. Jay pointed him out.

Through all of the moving people there was a lone man next to the ice-cream stand, watching me. His skin was a smooth dark brown. His hair had grown into a poofy, short Afro.

"It's Kopano," I whispered, heart in my throat.

"You know him?" Veronica asked. "He's, like, a *man*."

She was right. Kope couldn't be mistaken for a boy. He must have been nineteen or twenty, just a few years older than us, but he was so serious. Manly.

What was he doing here?

"I'm gonna go talk to him," I told them. "I'll meet you guys back here in half an hour."

I stopped a few feet from Kopano, hands clasped behind my back. My pulse remained at a steady high as his eyes held me.

"Is everything okay?" I asked.

"Everything is well. I hope I have not frightened you." His gentle tone never faltered, and I wondered whether he'd ever raised his voice. How deep was his hidden wrath, and what would it take to unleash it? The thought prickled the back of my neck.

I tilted my head toward the corridor of shops. "Wanna walk with me?" I asked.

Kopano came to my side, and we moved together into the stream of shoppers who became like background noise as I concentrated on him. I was patient, hoping he would explain why he'd come.

"How have you been?" he asked.

"It was a rough semester, to be honest, but I'm doing better."

He nodded down at the polished floor in front of us.

"How about you?" I asked.

Keeping his eyes straight down, he answered, "I have thought of you often since the summer."

Heat tore through me at his blunt openness. My hands tingled. I had no idea how to respond.

We came to an open area where Santa's shop had resided a few days prior. It was now naked in its emptiness except for a fountain with a thick marble ledge around it, where we sat together. Kopano stared down at the water, full of copper and silver coins on the bottom from years' worth of wishes.

"The twins arrive tomorrow for a visit," he explained. "They fly into Atlanta, and Marna requested me to come."

"Oh," I said, realizing he hadn't come to Atlanta for the sole reason of seeing me. My initial reaction was relief that I wouldn't have to deal with a complicated situation. But disappointment followed on its heels. It wasn't fair to feel let down, since Kaidan still ruled my heart, but I did nonetheless. Maybe because I knew I could never be with Kai.

"I arrived early, hoping to see you," he continued. "I went to your home, but your mother told me you were here."

"I'm surprised she didn't call me." I pulled out my phone and rolled my eyes with embarrassment. "I guess it helps when I turn it on."

He flashed me that dimpled smile, which set my inner butterflies aflutter, as always. I peered down at my phone.

"Do you have a cell?" I asked.

He took out his phone and we exchanged numbers.

A loud group of boys were passing through the court, jeering at one another and roughhousing. When I spotted Scott among them, I moved fast, angling my body away from their group and tilting my head so my hair would shield my face.

"You know them," he stated.

"Some of them are from my school." I said no more, but tension filled the space between us.

"One of them has hurt you."

Was it that obvious, even with my colors hidden? I raised my head now that the boys' backs were to us.

"There was an incident this summer," I said.

He watched me with expectancy, so I told him a brief version of the story, keeping my head down. When I finished and looked up, my heart faltered. Kope was a display of barely contained rage as he stared in the direction Scott and his friends had gone. His nostrils flared and his mouth was taut.

"Kope?" I whispered.

No response. Sudden fright struck me as I imagined him flipping out and going after Scott. I spoke in the calm, gentle voice he always used with me.

"Kope, look at me." His chest rose and fell with rapid breaths. I reached out and laid a hand on his forearm, half-afraid he might lash out at me in his daze. He jolted at my touch, bringing his eyes to mine. For one second longer his wrath steamed below the surface, and then he closed his eyes. I didn't know whether he was counting to ten or praying, but whatever he did worked. When he opened his eyes again the fury was gone.

"I am sorry, Anna. I do not want you to fear me. I would never hurt you."

"I know," I whispered, though I was still shaken. "It's okay, Kope. And that whole situation with Scott is in the past. I dealt with him and let go of my anger. It's over."

He gave a tight nod, his gaze landing on a couple coming out of the jewelry shop, holding hands.

"What do you envision for your future, Anna?"

His abrupt question struck a nerve in me. It was the same question I'd been asking myself for months.

"I don't know," I said. "I used to know what I wanted, but not anymore."

He considered this, watching me with curiosity. "What did you want?"

I reached down and touched the water. "A family, mostly."

"And you no longer want that?"

I dried my hands on my jeans, trying not to get emotional. At one time, I wanted a loving husband and a houseful of kids more than anything in the world. But I'd let go of those dreams. I couldn't even adopt a child. What would the Dukes say if they caught me playing house?

"I can't have those things," I told him, still avoiding his stare. "And I'm tired of wanting things I can't have."

His voice was low when he responded. "Perhaps children are out of the question, but you could still have a husband, in secret."

My eyes flew up to his, and my skin sizzled as his words settled over me. I opened my mouth, but couldn't speak. His light eyes played chicken with mine, not backing down from his claim.

"It's too dangerous," I said.

"You are young." He didn't state it in a condescending way, but I still bristled. "Someday you may agree that there are dangers worth facing."

I swallowed, wishing my crazy heart would stop trying to

break out of my rib cage. Nearby footsteps sounded, coming toward us on the shiny floor.

Veronica, Jay, and Gregory approached.

"Hey, guys," I said. The three of them looked back and forth between the serious faces of Kopano and me. I couldn't spare a smile of reassurance because my heart still raced from the sound of Kope's voice and the words he'd spoken.

"Hey, man. It's Kopano, right?" Jay asked.

"Yes." Kopano stood and they shook hands.

"How you been?" Jay asked.

"Very well, and you?"

"Good, thanks." It was an awkward, but sweet exchange.

Veronica gawked the entire time. She kept giving me the big-eyed look that promised she would pester me for details afterward. I introduced Kopano to Veronica and Gregory. Unabashed, she eyed him up and down after they shook hands, wearing a bright aura of fascinated interest.

"I must be on my way," Kopano said to me.

"Will you tell the twins I said hello?"

He nodded. A silent moment ensued where we all stood there not knowing what to do next. Veronica cleared her throat and grabbed Jay's arm.

"Let's go," she told him. Jay waved good-bye to Kope and they walked away with Gregory right behind.

"Call me if you all want to hang out or anything," I told Kope.

With a hesitant movement, I stepped forward and

wrapped my arms around his waist for a quick hug. Kopano held me close like a man who'd been starved of affection. I blinked back tears and ran my palms over his back. He was big and strong, and had no interest in letting me go. So I let him hold me. I rested my face against his chest and breathed in a mild tropical smell. When I started imagining the caramel pheromones he was capable of emitting, I had to pull away, feeling too shy to meet his eye.

"Take care of yourself, Anna," he said.

"You, too," I whispered.

I spent the next day lost in thought, mulling over Kopano's comment about a husband, and also trying to figure out why the twins would fly into Atlanta instead of a city closer to Kope. Unless they wanted to see Kaidan, assuming Pharzuph was in New York. It made me jealous that the twins were allowed to call and see Kai, but I wasn't.

And then there was Kopano. His words had jarred me. For all I knew, he could have been speaking in hypotheticals, but I didn't think so. I believed he was talking about us. He was everything I wanted in a guy: gorgeous, humble, no games. If I'd met him first, there was no telling what might've happened. And as much as I knew I should let Kaidan go, I wasn't ready.

The next day, just as the sun was setting, I sat on the edge of Patti's bed while she packed her suitcase.

"I wish you would change your mind and come with me," she said.

"I already made plans with Jay and Veronica for New Year's."

One of the papers was sending Patti to cover the ball dropping in Times Square. She must have earned herself a good rep, because it was a big deal to get this kind of job. I could see it was hurting her to leave me behind.

"It's all right, Patti. I'll be fine."

"I know. But we always celebrate together. I'm going to miss you."

"I'm gonna miss you, too."

My cell phone beeped in my pocket. When I pulled it out, my pulse jumped at the sight of my dad's number. He'd never texted me before.

Meeting tonight. Your ride is on his way. Be ready.

I jumped when Patti spoke behind me.

"Everything okay, hon?" She glanced at the phone in my shaking hand.

I read her the text. Sharp, dark fear pushed through her aura as she stood in front of me rubbing my shoulders. Patti's guardian angel whispered something to her, causing her fear to lighten into a haze of nervousness.

"It's okay. It'll be fine. Your dad is there." She leaned her forehead into mine and closed her eyes. I did the same, getting a comforting whiff of her oatmeal shampoo.

My hair was in a messy bun, and I was dressed like a slob. I took a superfast shower, then put on dark jeans, a black shirt Veronica had picked out, and black boots. I ran the brush through my hair with some gel, and brushed my teeth. There

361

was no time to mess with the blow-dryer and flatiron. I managed to dab on some makeup with a shaking hand. My hair was still wet when the doorbell rang.

"I'll get it," I called out, shoving the mascara back in my makeup bag and reaching for my purple zip-up hoodie.

I heard Patti's voice as she answered the door. I darted into the living room and nearly tripped at the sight of her hugging someone. I came to a halt in the middle of the room, confused. I almost didn't recognize him.

When he stood up straight his blue eyes bore down on me with the same intensity as always. He'd had his hair cut really short all over, revealing a small cowlick that fanned out on his left temple. And he'd obviously been hitting the gym more often, because his arms and shoulders were bigger. The sight of him made me want to sit down and take a breath. He wore a black hooded sweatshirt with skulls up the side, and baggy cargo pants. He had a gray woolly cap in his hand.

"I'm sorry, Anna, but you're going to have to come with me."

"What's going on?" Patti and I asked at the same time.

"My father is having a meeting with all U.S. Dukes, and they've requested you to come. Specifically, your father requested you."

"Is there going to be trouble?" Patti asked.

"I think it's just a formality. I'm sure her father has a plan."

We stood in a triangle of worry until I broke away and grabbed my hoodie, pulling it on and hugging Patti.

"I'll call you as soon as I can," I told her. She nodded, face tight with worry. I hated leaving her there alone. Kaidan pulled the warm beanie hat over his head.

I heard Patti whispering, "Please, please, please," as I shut the door behind me.

CHAPTER TWENTY-EIGHT

GOODY BAGS

"Why did he send you instead of asking me to drive myself?" I asked as we drove out of the neighborhood.

"He told the other Dukes you had no transportation."

My dad must have wanted Kaidan to give me a heads-up.

"I'm still surprised he sent you," I admitted.

"Trust me, I think he had one of the others in mind, but my father volunteered me."

"Who else will be there?"

"My father's having a party, so there're a lot of people at the house. They've already had their official meeting. When I left, Belial and Melchom were playing cards, and my father was in the pool. I'm hoping it'll still be like that when we get there. If you can avoid going in the same room as my father, he won't be able to sense you. Go straight to your father, and then we can leave. The four other Neph you know are there, and the Dukes think we're working a party tonight. Blake's there because of his father, and the others are making a short holiday of it. The twins get away from England any chance they have. Oh, and Ginger's been a ray of sunshine today." He rolled his eyes, peeved.

There it was again: that mysterious thing between Kai and Ginger. She brought out emotions in him, even if they were negative ones.

"Okay," I said, needing a refresher course. "Remind me again—Melchom is Blake's father?"

"Yes."

I wished there were some way to hide my attention-grabbing badge. I didn't want the Dukes noticing the white swirl and wondering why I was different. Kaidan glanced at me as I bit my lip, then shook his head and looked back at the road, driving with one hand while rubbing the back of his neck.

"What?" I asked.

"Here we are, possibly in danger, and all I can think about is . . ."

"What?" Anticipatory goose bumps sprouted all over me.

"You look good," he said with reluctance. He tore off the woolly hat and scrubbed his head as if the buzzed hair were sensitive.

I pressed my lips together and did my best to appear unaffected. I didn't want to feel gratified by his words. I'd worked hard to try to push him out of my heart, and now he was slicing me wide open all over again.

"How does my dad seem tonight?" I asked, changing the subject.

"I wouldn't want to get on his bad side."

"He's intimidating, isn't he?"

"Just a bit."

I tried to imagine Kaidan's house with Dukes, Neph, and humans all together. I hoped there would be enough distractions to get us in and out fast. I was glad I'd be seeing the other Neph again. Well, mostly. Thinking of Kopano sent a fluttery jolt of nervousness through my system, and questions about the history between Ginger and Kaidan still bothered me.

"Kaidan, can I ask you something? I understand if you don't want to talk about it." He shot me an inquisitive glance, and I barreled on. "What happened between you and Ginger?"

He made an unpleasant *och* noise and rubbed the back of his neck as he thought.

"I don't know. We spent a lot of time together during childhood. We were close until I turned thirteen."

"Close?" My mouth was suddenly dry. "I always imagined you being alone."

He shook his head, face tight. "It was always Ginger and me."

"Oh." Well, that changed things. A new vision formed in my mind. I knew it was selfish, but I didn't want to think about him having a close childhood bond with her.

Kaidan began with reservation, as if words were being

siphoned from him against his will.

"It's beyond strange to even think about it. It was a different lifetime." He paused for so long I thought he was closing the conversation.

"You can tell me," I whispered.

He grumbled at my therapist voice, and then the floodgates opened, and he let it all out.

"As much as I hate to admit it, she and I are a lot alike. We both understood very early what would be expected of us, before the others did, and it made us curious. We sort of experimented together, nothing serious, just kid stuff. Her nanny caught us when I was eight and Ginger was nine. The woman told our fathers and naturally they thought it was bloody amusing. My father was sent to Italy for one year while I was twelve. The twins were turning thirteen, so that was the year they started working. When I came back to England, Ginger was changed, like a completely different person. She was hardened and critical, and viciously protective of Marna. It was a sign of things to come for me. It was never the same after that. I found it easier not to talk to her or anyone else."

He'd cut her off. He was good at that. But to have it happen as a child would have been even more traumatic.

"Maybe she thought of herself as your girlfriend," I said.

"I couldn't worry about that. Things were changing for me at that time. I couldn't think about Ginger or being a child anymore. There was no looking back. Blake started hanging with us the following year, and he was all about Ginger from the start. She's always enjoyed the attention.

One night when we were all working a party outside of London, Blake hooked up with this girl, and he was snogging her right there. Out of nowhere, Ginger started coming on to me."

"She was trying to make him jealous?"

"That's what I think. At that point I was sixteen, and I mostly hooked up with strangers who I could avoid seeing again, but it's not like I'd be able to avoid Ginger the rest of my life. Our history made things uncomfortable enough as it was. I guess she figured I hooked up casually all the time, so it wouldn't be a big deal for me. It was quite the ugly scene when I told her to go find some other bloke if she was feeling randy. It's been brutal ever since. And then there's the issue of Blake's freakout."

I leaned toward him over the armrest, captivated. "Was that the one time you said he got jealous over a girl?"

Kaidan nodded. "He'd witnessed our whole conversation. Dropped the girl he was snogging and threw a wobbler, yelling and breaking things."

I couldn't imagine Blake on an envy rampage, yelling and breaking things. There had to be so many hidden emotions under the surface of these stories.

"I think she still has feelings for you," I said.

"No. I think she's pissed off about her life and she misses being close to someone she considers her equal. Marna is more like her bear cub."

Emotions rolled through me and I pushed them down.

"You're upset I didn't tell you, aren't you?" he asked.

"Kind of." There was no use denying it.

"It was forever ago."

"But we're shaped by the things that happen to us as children. She's still hurting from it. Don't you miss her, too? As a friend, at least?"

"This is the first time I've thought about her in ages, and it's only because you asked me. Do you remember what I told you about the twins and their father, Astaroth?" he asked. "About how they can sense romantic bonds between people?"

"Yeah."

"That's why I hit the booze that night when we were all together this summer. I didn't want them to know there was anything there. I didn't want to have to explain anything or listen to their rubbish."

My pulse quickened. He was admitting there was something between us. Something mutual.

"And tonight?" I asked, playing with the zipper on my jacket. He pulled a flask out from under his seat as an answer, and my heart rate turned to a solid gallop in my chest.

"Don't worry. I'm sober right now. I'll start drinking when we pull up."

"Do I need to drink, too?"

"No. Just one of us will do the trick."

I wound a lock of hair around my finger and kept my eyes on the console in front of me, trying not to stutter when I asked, "If you didn't drink, what would they see?"

He stared at the road, clutching the wheel. It took a long time for him to answer. Too long.

"I don't know. Maybe attraction. Maybe nothing. A lot of

time has passed. Five miles is coming up now."

What did that mean, *maybe nothing*? On whose side was it possibly gone, his or mine? I shouldn't have gotten my hopes up. Of course he wouldn't want them to know he was attracted to me. But it didn't mean he felt more than that.

I scrunched down in my seat. Seeing him again was going to set me back, but there was no way I'd let myself fall into that dark place again. I closed my eyes, meditating. An image of Kopano swam into my head. He would never string me along and confuse me like this. I wished I could make myself want him the way I wanted Kai. The heart was a confusing thing.

At his house Kaidan punched a code into the security box and pulled into the driveway, which was packed with cars. I pushed my hearing into the house and moved it around until I found a gruff voice using poker lingo. I didn't recognize the other voices at the table, which meant Pharzuph wasn't there. Kaidan opened the flask and tipped it up. The sweet pungency of bourbon reached me where I sat. I could probably discern the brand if I had a sip myself. He shoved the flask into a side pocket of his pants and we got out.

We first went down to the basement, which was packed with people. Blake was showing some guy the newest high-tech thingy, causing the guy to be encased in green. Ginger and Marna were in the tiki bar area, sipping drinks and making eyes at a man across the room. He was trying to have a conversation with a woman, but he was distracted by his lust for the gorgeous twins.

Kopano sat next to Marna on a stool. Marna turned her attention to him, twisting the tips of his hair for a cool, spiky effect. He lifted his head and his gaze banged into mine. We were both very still until he gave me a nod and I returned it.

The twins assessed first Kopano and me, then Kaidan and me, moving their eyes between the two of us, and then looking at each other with knowing grins. I would have paid a chunk of my dad's money to know whether they'd seen anything.

"We'll leave for that party in a minute," Kaidan told them. He shot me a glare that screamed, *I saw that look between you and Kope.*

I raised my eyebrows, sending him a silent response of, *What's it to you?*

"Hmph," he grumbled. I followed when he went back up the stairs.

My stomach twisted as we made our way through the house full of people to the heated veranda, where men were sitting around a table, swigging top-shelf whiskey straight from the bottles and talking over one another. I saw my father and had to fight emotions from bursting out around me. I kept my head down.

His eyes were hard when he saw me.

"Come here, kid," he said with unfamiliar menace. I took small steps to stand at his side. "You got plans for New Year's?"

"Yes, sir." I cleared my throat. "A big hotel party in Atlanta." That was the truth.

"Goody bags for the party." He handed me baggies of dried green stuff and white powder. Marijuana and cocaine. *Steady, girl*, I told myself, gripping the bags to my abdomen.

"Thanks," I whispered, eyes down.

A voice next to him spoke. "Might want to consider having all of these Neph working that gig together on New Year's." I lifted my eyes to take in the sight of a handsome Japanese man, who I assumed was Melchom, the Duke of Envy. He took a fine cigar from his lips and played his hand of cards, which made the entire table groan and break into frustrated conversation about their losing hands. He smiled, putting the cigar between his lips as he gathered his winnings, and spoke from the side of his mouth. "Just saying. Could do a lot of damage if the whole group worked a big party together. I have no plans for Blake. I doubt Astaroth or Alocer will disapprove."

"All right then." My father grumbled in my direction, "You all work New Year's together."

To my relief, he made a shooing motion with his hand, dismissing me. I started to turn, then saw movement from my other side, where Pharzuph, in a robe, walked toward us from the indoor pool area.

"You still standing here?" my father snapped at me. I swiveled on my heels and headed for the door, where Kaidan stood waiting for me. From the corner of my eye I saw Pharzuph entering the veranda through the sliding doors just as we were rushing out.

"Let's go," Kaidan said out loud, to the air. By the time we made it to the front door, the four Neph had come up from the basement and were joining us, shrugging into their jackets. Kaidan tossed his keys to Blake. Their eyes were all distant, listening. I joined them, pressing my hearing toward the veranda as we left the house.

"That girl of yours leaves a stink of virtue behind her." Pharzuph spoke with quiet disdain to my father, not wanting the human men in the room to hear.

Shoot! I hadn't made it out of the room in time!

We picked up our pace, walking faster and cramming into Kaidan's car, Kai taking shotgun.

"Well, that won't last long," my dad said, sounding so believable it hurt. "She's just getting good at her job, and the rest will follow. She can drink any man here under the table, that's for damn sure."

It was all poker talk after that, but I continued to listen until we were out of range.

I chewed my thumbnail until Marna took my hand and held it in hers. As soon as Blake signaled we were out of the five-mile range of Duke hearing, Blake turned and glanced at me.

"You're a virgin?" I nodded, and he looked me over like some sort of anomaly, which I guess I was. He laughed and slapped the steering wheel. "Man, things are definitely more interesting with you around."

I wanted to crawl under the seat and hide my face. Kaidan took a drink from his flask.

"Are we really partying together on New Year's?" Marna asked.

"As if we have a choice now," Ginger stated.

We'd been ordered to go, but how would they know if we were working or not? What if one of them decided to check on us? And then it hit me: Kopano would be expected to be there working, too. I angled myself toward him.

"Maybe you can come up with an excuse or something," I offered, feeling horrible. He shook his head.

"I cannot raise suspicion against my father or any of you. I will work."

The car went ghostly silent. Nobody here had ever seen Kopano work. I closed my eyes. This was so wrong. We kept our thoughts to ourselves as the reality settled in. Marna squeezed my hand.

"So how's my little cupcake Jay doing these days?" she asked. I loved her for trying to distract me.

"Fine. Actually, I think he might have a girlfriend soon, this other girl we're friends with."

"Oh?" A look of excitement and challenge flashed in her wide eyes, and I realized my mistake. She caught herself and dropped her gaze to our hands.

"Good for him," she whispered.

The two plastic baggies were in my other hand, making me agitated. My mind kept returning to the fact that Pharzuph knew I was a virgin, and how liberating it would feel to take one bump of the powder. It was right there, far more tempting to me than alcohol. All I had to do was stick my fingernail in there and— *No!*

I had to get rid of it. I asked Kopano to switch places with me. I climbed over his lap as he scooted under, trying not to touch me. I cracked the window a few inches. No cars were behind us on the strip of road. I opened the bag of marijuana first, hands shaking, and tipped the contents out the window.

"What are you doing?" Blake asked.

"Getting rid of it," I said, feeling unusually antsy.

"That's perfectly good J!" Blake protested.

"Sorry." I dumped the last of it.

"Front-row seats at the suicide show," Ginger said. "Lovely."

I peered down at the bag of white powder in my hand. I cracked the window again and tipped the corner of the bag. I held my breath as the powder hit the rushing wind, spiraling out into a cloud behind us. I watched the cloud with a pang of yearning, and heard a funny flapping sound. Something spiraled through the air as the last of the powder poured out.

"Stop the car!" I said. "Something was in the bag!"

Blake pulled over and we all jumped out, running, using our hypervision to scan the ground.

"What was it?" Marna asked.

"I think it was paper."

"Yes, I saw it, too," Kopano affirmed.

"There!" Ginger ran toward a tree and picked up a strip of paper, holding it out to me. I tugged it open and read to myself. No, no, no. My knees buckled, but I saw Kaidan jogging over and forced myself to stand straight.

Two vehicles were coming down the road, still a good distance away. We all noticed at the same time and hurried back to the car. I handed the note over the passenger seat to Kaidan as Blake drove off, remembering the words in my mind.

They're getting suspicious of us. A lot of rumors. Legionnaire spies will be watching you on New Year's. You'll have to work. Remember your training. Ask the others how the spirits communicate.

Kaidan slammed his hand against the dashboard after he read it.

"Care to clue us in?" Ginger asked with impatience.

Kaidan turned, his anxious eyes holding mine. It was time to tell them everything.

CHAPTER TWENTY-NINE

New Year's

It took more than two hours of talking before Patti accepted my claims that I'd be okay, and decided to continue on her trip to New York. She knew the Neph and I would be expected to work on New Year's, but I'd left out the detail about demon whisperers spying on me. Spirits were a touchy subject.

The New Year's party would take place at a fancy hotel in downtown Atlanta. We talked about finding a different party where people we knew wouldn't be there, but this was supposed to be the biggest party in the area. The more people, the more distractions for the spirits. According to the Neph, demon whisperers were easily distracted. I hoped they were right, because I suffered extreme discomfort about unleashing spirits on a party where my two best friends were going to be.

Jay had recently landed a job as an assistant to the disc jockey who was doing the music for the party. That was how we got tickets to the biggest bash in town. A local radio station would be there, too. Since Jay was working part of the night, he had to get there early. I drove Veronica. The five Neph would meet us there.

It wasn't until we'd pulled into Atlanta that Veronica noticed my nerves. I hunched over the steering wheel with a stomachache. The crowded city streets hurled emotions both rainbow-colored and dark, all of which I heaved away.

"Hey, are you okay?" Veronica asked, holding her lip gloss wand in midair.

"Just nervous about the party, I guess."

The inside of the hotel was exquisite, not a detail missed. There was a waterfall fountain in the atrium, gorgeous flower arrangements on every table, and plush carpets of vivid designs stretching in all directions. Most people were in the lobby checking into their rooms. Veronica's curfew was one thirty, so we weren't staying the night. If something came up and I needed to stay, Jay could take her home. It was likely that the spies expected me to party all night.

The hotel was buzzing with excitement. Veronica clutched my arm, sporting a bright orange aura of exhilaration, as she looked around. I peered around, too. I was not excited about meeting any dark spirits again. Not at all.

I hadn't learned anything new about the demon whisperers during my one night of crash-course training from my father.

I guess he didn't think they'd be a problem for me at the time, and it was still a sensitive subject for me after being haunted. Fortunately, my Neph friends taught me the basics.

Spirits were limited in their communications because of their lack of physical mass. While their sight was keen, their hearing was dim. They could hear only up close, where the voice vibrations were strongest and they could dip into the person's mind. Parties with loud music were chaos on their hearing, which was good for us, because they wouldn't be able to listen to our conversations from a distance. They would be able to hear us only if they swooped down close, and that was also the only way we could hear them. In close proximity, we could open up our minds and speak telepathically with them, like mutual whispering.

My father assured me no Dukes would be staked out listening. Kaidan was certain his father would spend New Year's in New York City, which disturbed me, since Patti was there, but I knew she'd go right back to her hotel after the ball dropped. Still, I hated the thought of their breathing the same city air.

Veronica gripped my arm a little harder as we made our way to the hall with the ballroom.

"You sure you're okay?" she asked.

"To be honest, I don't feel so good."

She stopped walking and made me look at her. "Do you need to go home or get some medicine?"

"No. I'll be fine." I tugged us forward again until we were in the line with the other well-dressed kids, mostly college age. Those twenty-one and over were given neon orange wristbands. Those under twenty-one got huge Xs on their hands with permanent markers. Veronica frowned down at the ugly marks on her pretty hands as we walked in.

The Xs were going to put a damper on the whole drinking thing. I was sure there'd be ways around it, though I didn't know what they were. The party wasn't crowded yet, only at half capacity.

"Oh, look, there's Jay!" Veronica dashed straight to the deejay booth and bounced on the balls of her feet. "Excuse me, sir, can I request a song?"

Jay stood and looked down over the tall barrier. He pulled off his headphones.

"Wussup? You girls ready to party or what?"

I put on a closemouthed smile while Veronica let out a little, "Whoot!"

"I got you guys," said Jay, putting one side of the headphones against his ear. "This one's for you, Roni."

She hollered when her song came on, and dragged me out to the dance floor, which was too bright and empty for my comfort.

Jay had done a good thing by putting on the popular song, because more people came up to dance, and the hotel dimmed the lights in the room. Much better.

When the song ended I fanned myself with my hands and looked around. Standing at the far wall was a stunning group of people who made me drop my arms to my sides. The Neph were here, and they were staring straight through the crowd at me.

I gave myself one moment to take in the sight of Kaidan. He wore black dress slacks and a royal blue dress shirt, which made his eye color pop, even from a distance. His tie had abstract blue, black, and silver designs. His hands were shoved in his pockets, and a dangling wallet chain was his only nondressy attribute. He wouldn't avert his eyes from mine, and I flushed warm, wondering whether he'd watched me dancing.

"Is that who I think it is?" Veronica had followed my gaze, and I nodded. She wasn't too thrilled about his being there, considering the wreck I'd become after seeing him at Halloween.

"I'm gonna get a drink and go talk to Jay," Veronica said. "You want something?"

"Can you get me a water, please? I'm just going to run to the bathroom."

In the giant, luxury bathroom I tried to scrub the screaming Xs off my hands, but it wasn't happening. I angled myself at the corner sink, so as not to draw attention to myself. I felt warm bodies come up behind me and saw the twins reflected in the mirror. Ginger pulled something from her slim purse and set it on the sink.

"Use this," she said.

I squirted the gritty stuff on and used my short nails to rub the skin for several minutes. It stung like heck. When I rinsed it off there were barely shadows of the Xs remaining. It would have to be good enough, because my hands were raw. I patted them with a hand towel and noticed both twins had wristbands, even though they were only eighteen. Oh, that was right; they had fake IDs. Marna must have known what was on my mind, because she reached into her deep cleavage and pulled out another wristband, handing the warm thing to me, which I took with my fingertips.

"Er, thanks."

She laughed and took it back, deciding to put it on me herself.

"When do you think they'll get here?" I whispered. Girls were coming in and out of the bathroom, but nobody paid us any attention.

"Don't worry about that," Ginger advised me. "Just work as if they're always there."

"Anna," Marna said quietly, "do you know, when I had to start working at the age of thirteen, I still couldn't see them?"

"You don't have to talk about that," Ginger said. Marna looked at her.

"It's all right. I want to tell her." She moved closer so I could hear. "When I turned thirteen, after a year of training and everything I'd learned, I still couldn't see them. So my father sent for the sons of Thamuz to rid me of whatever innocence I had left."

"Duke of Murder." Ginger whispered the three words as if she were contemplating murder herself.

"He sent Nephilim?" I asked.

"Yes, but they're not like us. They're ruthless. I wasn't a virgin, but . . . no guy had ever hurt me like that. Every time I'd scream or cry they'd hit me. I thought they were going to kill me. And then the spirits came, whispering to me while the sons of Thamuz took turns. I think the worst part was not having my own thoughts to myself. I couldn't *not* think about what was happening."

I broke away from the sisters and hurried into the large handicapped stall, leaning my weight on the handrail. I'd almost gotten sick while Marna told her story. I yanked off some toilet paper and dabbed under my eyes. I'd sworn to myself I wouldn't be caught crying tonight. It was too dangerous.

The twins followed me into the stall. Ginger pulled the door closed and latched it. Marna stroked my hair and then my cheeks, and I allowed myself one last shudder before pulling it together.

"I only told you all that so you could be prepared," Marna said. "They're going to say things to you, and you have to ignore them. You can't let them get to you. Keep your cool and try to pretend those voices are just an annoying telly program with the volume too high. They can't hurt you unless you let them. I let them, and I don't want you to make the same mistake."

My mouth had gone dry. I took the image of sweet thirteen-year-old Marna and tucked it into the back of my mind. Right now, I could not afford to think about anything that would make me want to bawl. Marna hugged me, rubbing the silky material of my dress on my back.

"So . . . that girl you were dancing with?" Marna shifted on her heels, not continuing.

"That's Veronica," I said, swiping under my eyes one last time. "Do you see a bond with her and Jay?"

"No, but they weren't standing close enough. Come on, let's go back in."

My hands stung as we left the bathroom, a reminder of things to come. Entering the ballroom, Ginger left us to begin working, but Marna stood with me. The demons hadn't shown yet.

I was anxious to use Marna's skill to see what was up with my two friends. We spotted them at the deejay booth. Jay had the earphones around his neck, and he leaned on his forearms to watch Veronica. She was being her usual flirty self, making big hand gestures as she talked.

Marna crossed her arms, frowning.

"Uh-oh, what's wrong?"

At the sound of my question she snapped out of it, uncrossing her arms and shrugging.

"Nothing, there're just a lot more people here now. The bonds can get . . . fuddled."

"So you can't see anything?"

"They're . . . attracted." Well, darn, was that it? You didn't need superhuman bond-seeing capabilities to know they were attracted. I was hoping for something more.

"We'll have a drink together later," she said to me, and with a wink she headed back to her sister. I went to the deejay booth and stood there for a moment, not wanting to interrupt. Jay and Veronica were so absorbed in their talk they didn't notice me. Jay studied her and she seemed to blossom under his attention. Only attraction? Really?

Veronica turned, startled to see me, and laughed.

"Oh, my gosh, this boy is too much." She reached up to smack at his arm, but he grabbed her hand, and when they looked at each other . . . badda bing. Pink. A tinge of dark fuchsia swam up between their auras as they slowly pulled their hands apart. Jay and Veronica's guardian angels regarded each other with a nod, pleased.

I wanted to cheer, but instead grabbed my water from the ledge, giving myself an excuse to look away. As I sipped, I saw Marna by a table, watching. She smiled at me, but it was more forced than usual. Then the smile fell away and she stiffened.

I couldn't see them, but I knew they were there. Right behind me. The whisperers had arrived, bringing with them a feeling of spiders crawling up my back. I gathered my wits and strode away from my two friends and their sweet moment. I'd never felt more separate from them.

I knew what I had to do. I went straight to the bar.

As I walked through the crowd, I forced myself not to run, screaming, from the sensation that an ax murderer was stalking behind me. The urge to turn and gauge the danger was strong, but not as strong as my fear of what I'd actually see.

I got to the bar as a couple was walking away with their drinks. The bartender looked me over, pushing thick blond hair off his forehead. My heart still pounded with unhealthy force.

"What can I get you?" he asked, leaning on the bar top toward me.

I pondered the row of beer bottles on display and pointed to a light one. His eyes went to my wristband.

"You don't look twenty-one," he said in a friendly way, popping off the cap.

"Yeah, I know." I accepted the cold bottle he offered. Then I fished a bill out of the small black purse flung across my body, resting against my hip.

I wondered whether the whisperers were watching.

"Thanks. No change," I said, handing it over. He took it, but didn't move away from me.

I felt like I should make small talk with the bartender. He also appeared to be thinking of something to say.

"He's thinking of inviting you to his room." A deathly chill zipped jaggedly up my spine at the sound of the scratchy voice in my head. Going with my first instinct, I tipped the bottle up and took a long drink of it. Yech. I didn't like the taste of beer, but at least it didn't burn like fire. The demon laughed in my ear and it seemed to echo though my skull.

"He likes the look of your lips on that drink. Do it again."

Sick, sick, sick. I wanted to scream at it to get out of my head. I lifted my chin and drank, not stopping until the bottle was empty. The guy stared at me with a red flurry of lust surrounding him. He picked up the empty bottle and chuckled, tossing it in the wastebasket and pulling a new one from the cooler.

"That was beautiful," he said. "Here. This one's on me. I'm Trevor, by the way."

I accepted it and managed not to recoil at the disgusting chatter of the demon in my ear, telling me to keep going as it sidled away from me, over to the bartender, and circled him.

Normally, two single people flirting was not a bad thing. But this demon wanted me to make Trevor stumble, to make him focus on the physical and ultimately suffer. It wanted the bartender to burn with lust. It wanted him to screw up on his job. The whisperer made something as innocent as flirting feel wrong. I knew it was time for me to say something to Trevor, but my eyes started to sting, threatening tears. *Do not get emotional!*

"You've got pretty eyes," Trevor said. "Shiny."

The demon chortled. *"Romeo needs to work on his pickup lines. Boring."*

"Thanks, I'm Anna." I needed to flirt. I lifted the corners of my mouth and moved some hair forward with a flip of my hand. "Are you working here all night?"

"Yep, until one. Then who knows? Should be plenty to do around town after that."

"I'll bet," I said.

Now what? Should I, like, wink at him or something? Flirting with strangers might not have been my forte, but drinking definitely was, and he liked that. I took another long, cold gulp, and relaxed as the first beer hit my system and kicked things into gear. Oh, shoot, I forgot to get the time. I twisted my wrist until the silver watch was in place. Nine twenty.

A group of people came up to the bar next to me. The bartender took their orders, but he kept glancing back at me. I waved with my fingers in that coy way I'd seen girls do to Jay. I felt dumb, but he grinned and swiped his hair aside, sporting a steady stream of red in his aura.

I left the bar, wondering what the heck I was going to do now, and walked straight into the grisly shadows of two demon whisperers. Even though I couldn't feel them, I shivered with revulsion as I rushed through the vapors.

The party was coming to life now, and the deejay was on the mic, making announcements and getting everyone riled with his electric excitement. I stopped amid the moving bodies, acutely aware of being followed. Over at the deejay booth, Jay scrambled around, organizing things for his boss. I couldn't see Veronica anywhere.

I started to search for the other Neph, but caught myself. The last thing I wanted was to see Kaidan at work. I couldn't afford to be distracted. The mere thought of Kai made me empty half my drink. It was too soon to finish the second one. I was already light-headed.

"Anna! There you are! Holy . . . What is *that*?" Veronica perched a hand on her hip and pointed at my beer. "And how the heck did you get a bracelet?"

"Connections," I said, tensing as the whisperers circled the two of us, watching, trying to listen. My heart began to pound. "I needed to relax."

She blinked at me, a look of disbelief displayed on her face. I should have warned her ahead of time that I'd "changed" my attitude toward drinking. I leaned in and whispered in her ear. "Let's just be careful and have fun, 'kay?"

"Fine, okay," she shot back, still acting unsure about my out-of-character behavior. "I guess as long as you hook me up, too."

A whisperer leaned near Veronica's ear, and her guardian angel dived between them. I pretended not to see, grabbing her by the elbow and pulling her toward the deejay booth, only to stop short. Jay was leaning down, grinning, and talking with Marna. Veronica's eyes narrowed. This was about to turn into a hot mess. I changed direction, pointing us at the bar instead.

"No, hold up," she said, pulling away and watching them.

The two raunchy spirits could see the dark disappointment trickling around Veronica, swirled with green envy. The demons attacked, both whispering to her at once despite her guardian angel's efforts to stop them. My breathing went shallow as her aura darkened and the green became more vivid. Standing there, not interfering, was one of the hardest things I'd ever done.

At that moment Marna tugged Jay's arm, as if she were trying to get him to come out of the booth, and he laughed, shaking his head and pointing to his work. She went up on her tiptoes and hollered something to Jay's boss, who grinned at her and shrugged his shoulders, patting Jay on the back. Marna clapped at her success and grabbed Jay by the hand, leading him out to the dance floor. What were they thinking?

Veronica stared out at them, and the spirits, who were finished whispering, danced around her, further antagonizing her angel as Veronica struggled internally.

I whispered to her, "She's just a friend of Kai's from England. Jay met her over the summer."

"That's the English chick? He told me about her, back when we were just . . ."

"Friends," I finished for her.

Veronica never took her eyes off the two of them as they danced closer and closer, Marna's ample chest pressed up against his, their hips moving together. I felt dizzy and nauseous. I drained the rest of my beer and noted the time. Two beers in fourteen minutes. That wasn't good.

I leaned in again to tell Veronica not to worry, to tell her that the twins would be gone tomorrow, but an abrasive demon voice shot through my thoughts.

"No more whispering to the girl."

I lifted my face to the thing hovering above us. As I met its sunken, mossy eyes, my foot automatically stepped back from the malevolent stare. Even in spirit form, it appeared malnourished, with hollow cheeks and a snarling hole for a mouth. I jerked my eyes away.

"Come on, Veronica," I said to her, gripping her elbow. "Let's go get a drink."

She stood her ground, continuing to stare at Jay.

"I'm going over there." Her voice was resolute as she started forward. Then she stopped. I looked past her to the dance floor. Marna's hands were around the back of Jay's head, and they were kissing, right there for the world to see. He was caught in a whirl of red lust. Not. Good.

Veronica pushed away, running toward the exit near the bathrooms. My muscles itched to run after her. The proud spirits were air-prancing and high-fiving each other. I didn't know what to do. I couldn't comfort Veronica or say anything to Marna and Jay.

I knew I should work, so I looked around, hoping for inspiration. I worried the two demons were becoming bored with me as they bobbed up and down, assessing the crowd and swooping down to whisper to people. A rush of paranoia overcame me.

"Don't worry, they're always a bit ADHD." I turned to the quiet speaker next to me. Ginger sipped her cocktail from a small straw, watching as Jay jogged back to the deejay booth. Marna paused at the edge of the dance floor. When she saw me, she turned the other way and disappeared into the sea of bodies.

"But they won't forget about you for long," Ginger assured me. "So get back to work."

"Yeah, thanks," I said.

She strode away with major hip action. While the spirits were distracted, I left the ballroom on speedy feet. Veronica was just coming out of the bathroom with swollen red eyes. She stopped when she saw me, and her jaw trembled. I would have guessed her to be the confrontational type in a situation like this, ready to march right up and tell both of them off. The idea of her in tears tore at my heart. I went to her, checking over my shoulder and finding no spirits in sight. I fought the urge to hug her.

"I'm not going back in there," she said to me. "I want to go home."

"But . . ." Under normal circumstances I would get us out of there right away.

Behind her, a giant-winged being soared down at us, and I sucked in a short breath. It planted its gargoyle mug inches from mine. I tried not to cringe. If they'd had real bodies, their flesh and breath would no doubt smell rancid, like death. I focused through its misty form on Veronica.

"Take my car," I offered, disinterest in my voice. She sniffled and looked confused. "I need to stay and deal with some things here, but you can drive home and I'll get a ride."

The spirit, if it was possible, got even closer, and I found myself tilting my stance to lean away from it. *"Why do you show concern for this girl?"*

I did some quick thinking and mentally sent a message back to it. *"The damage has been done and I need her to think we're friends so I can keep working on her at school."*

That seemed to appease the demon, but my heart was thumping way too hard. I had to be more careful.

"I'll call you tomorrow," I told Veronica. She sniffed again and took my keys. I was glad to see her getting away from here. I just wished her heart didn't have to be broken for it to happen.

Now I had to tell Jay I might need a ride home. Back in the ballroom, it took longer to get to the deejay booth because it was a full house now. I checked behind me; one demon followed. I let out a lungful of air as I came to the ledge where Jay was working, his eyes glazed by daydreams and thoughts.

"Hey!" I hollered up at him. When he saw me he froze and looked around.

"Where's Roni?" he asked.

"She took my car and went home. I need a ride from you." His face fell and his emotions became a tangled jumble. The spirit rose up beside me to get a better look at Jay. I spun on my heels to leave.

"Anna, wait!"

"I'll talk to you later," I yelled over my shoulder, putting some distance between us.

He probably thought I was mad at him, but I didn't want that whisperer near him. He was fragile enough as it was.

Halfway to the bar I heard Jay call my name again, much closer this time, and then he grabbed my elbow. Fear for him almost made me bite his head off, but the look of anguish on his face stopped me. I crossed my arms instead.

"Why did she leave?" he asked. His expectant expression told me he knew the answer.

"She saw, Jay."

He shut his eyes, stricken. "I didn't mean for that to happen. Marna is, like, way out of my league, you know? I never expected . . . I just wasn't thinking." He rubbed his forehead.

Everyone cheated, according to Ginger. She'd even prophesied that Jay would.

"We're not even going out, officially," Jay responded to my silent thoughts. "I'm still single!"

"We'll talk later," I repeated, and nodded toward the deejay booth, signaling him to get back to work. I left him standing there. It was the coldest I'd ever been to him.

If the beginning of the night was this bad, I didn't want to see the end of it.

The spirit jumped ahead of me, knowing I was going to the bar. I stopped, struck with an idea, and the demon came back to me. I wasn't supposed to know I was being watched tonight. Maybe I could play dumb with the thing and get some information. According to the other Neph, the whisperers could be cunning and ruthless in their jobs, but they were ultimately self-serving. They followed orders from the Dukes halfheartedly and couldn't care less about what the Neph were up to. They were slippery suckers who couldn't be trusted.

I sent my thought to the spirit. *Why are you following me? I'm trying to work and you keep distracting me. Did my father send you?*

The sound of its cackle rattled my soul. *"I don't have to*

answer to you," it said in such a juvenile way that a tiny bit of my fear toward it dissipated. I realized then that the second demon spy had gone.

"*I see the other spirit abandoned you,*" I goaded. "*It's probably out doing something fun now. Without you. What will it take to make you leave me alone and let me get back to work?*"

The smile that stretched across its face was a nasty one. I expected to see maggots climbing out of that cadaverous crack.

"*Give me a show,*" the demon demanded. My heart boomed.

"*You're on.*"

I moved with purpose through the crowd, craning my neck as I searched the crowd. Raucous cheering struck me on the right, where a crowd had circled around something. I went toward it, wondering if maybe Blake was showing off some new gizmo. I got to the edge of the group and stuck my head between two guys.

Kopano was at a table with several humans, playing cards, and a sizable pile of dough sat in front of him. He'd taken off his chocolate-colored suit jacket, loosened his gold-flecked tie, and rolled his white sleeves to his elbows. So Kope was a gambling man?

"Whoa," I whispered, unable to contain it.

"This guy's incredible," the guy on my right said.

"What are they playing?" I asked.

"Blackjack. He hasn't lost yet. Must be one of those genius card readers or something. But the dude next to him's getting mad."

Kopano showed his cards with a no-nonsense face, and everyone in the crowd cheered as if watching a magician's magic trick. The spirit circled the table, seeming to grow excited as money exchanged hands and one of the guys at the table stood up, shouting about cheating. Others eagerly stepped up to argue who would play next. A tall girl in a short dress rubbed Kopano's shoulder, but when he looked up it was my eye he caught and held. My heart rate went rapid-fire and I cleared my throat, backing out of the crowd.

I'd taken only a few steps away when I heard a crunching *thunk* and shouts erupting behind me. I was shoved from behind as the swarm of people heaved. A fight had broken out at the poker table. Kopano! I stood on tiptoe, trying see him. On the other side of the frenzied crowd I spotted him walking away unscathed from the chaos with his brown dress jacket over his shoulder, head down.

I moved when hotel security flocked to the area.

My heart was still beating fast as I looked around the massive ballroom brimming with life. Jolts of apprehension zapped my belly at the sight of each short-haired boy, but I was thankful none of them was Kaidan. I shook my head, staving off wonderings of where he might be.

Another throng of people had formed around the dance floor. Curious, I grabbed a nearby chair and stood on it. Apprehension filled me about what I'd see, but it was only Blake break-dancing in the center of the open space. And that boy could *dance*. He was pulling off better moves than I'd seen on prime-time dance shows. Anyone would envy his ability. Other guys would also be envying the number of girls he'd be pulling in after this stunt. The whisperer swooped next to me, making my breath hitch.

It was time to give this demon a show.

I caught sight of the person I needed. The demon followed as I went to the laughing couple. Marna reached up and straightened the guy's tie, but her hand dropped in surprise when she saw me standing there with my evil shadow.

"Sorry," I said to the guy. I grabbed Marna's hand. "Time to do some shots."

"Wicked." She squeezed my hand and didn't spare a backward glance for her abandoned prey.

I led her straight to Trevor, nudging our way through the waiting customers and propping my elbows on the ledge. Marna squeezed in next to me. The demon poked his nosy, smoky head between us, but we didn't acknowledge him.

When Trevor saw me, I smiled at him and he bypassed the other customers.

"Finally back," he said. "Ready to pound another beer, blondie?"

I shook my head. "Two tequila shots with lime." He raised an impressed eyebrow and grabbed the bottle.

"Hey, we've been waiting over here longer," a man yelled.

"Be right with you," Trevor told him.

I glanced at my watch. Hour one was over. I could have three drinks. Trevor set two golden shots in front of us with a shaker of salt. But no limes. I looked up as he called the other bartender over and tossed him a lime wedge. The other guy grinned and nodded. What were they doing?

"If you girls want your limes, you gotta come and get 'em." Trevor and the other bartender stood side by side in front of us, balancing lime wedges perpendicularly between their teeth.

Marna laughed, licked her wrist, and shook some salt on the damp skin. No problem. I could do this. I followed suit, salting my wrist, and we both picked up our shot glasses. When we looked at each other to toast, there was a moment of understanding. An apology. An acceptance. A kindred spirit.

We clinked glasses, licked the salt from our skin, threw back the shots, and leaned over the bar. The guys leaned in as well, and I barely registered the people around us whooping over the sound of my heart pounding. I tilted my face and bit the lime from between his teeth without even touching him. But as I took possession of the fruit, he dragged his warm tongue across my bottom lip. The scent of tequila with the sensation of his tongue and the flavor of lime had me pulling away, dizzy with thoughts of Kaidan.

"That was fun." I almost leaped from my skin at the demon's sour voice. *"Now what?"*

"Another shot," I said to Trevor.

"Tequila?" he asked.

I paused, indecisive. I needed to up the stakes. I took in the faces of the people pressed to the bar around me. There were about ten of us, and many more at our backs. I had a purse full of money. I leaned to the girl next to Marna, who held an empty wine glass.

"Hey, wanna do a shot with us?" I asked her, upbeat.

"Me? Oh, no. I can't handle liquor, only wine."

"Aw, come on. It's New Year's!" I beamed at her. "I'm buying you one."

I watched her colors turn from a misty reluctance to an eager orange.

"Okay, but just one!" she said.

"You're doing a shot?" asked her friend on her other side.

"I want to get shots for everyone at the bar right now," I told Trevor. His eyebrows flew up.

"Everybody? You know how much that'll cost?"

"Yep. Don't worry, I'm good for it." I winked, my first ever wink at a guy. My skin throbbed with adrenaline.

I took a consensus vote from nearby girls as to what drink we should have. They came up with some shooter I didn't know. Trevor got busy, lining up a row of at least twenty small tumblers.

The mix of ingredients gave Trevor the opportunity to show off his skills, tossing a bottle up and catching it upside down by the neck as it poured. He did that with several bottles and jugs. Then shake, shake, shake, and pink shooters came to life. I passed them out to the crowd, being met mostly with happy thanks, and having to talk a few people into accepting. It was out of my comfort zone to be a pushy temptress, but with that demon breathing evil air down my back, I pushed those people to take the shots. I'd deal with the guilt later.

Together, twenty shots were lifted in the air as we all *whoo*ed. Marna tapped my drink and we tipped them back. It tasted like candy with a bite. The heat of two shots in a row rocked through my system, and I could feel it down to my tingling feet. My whole body begged for another. Trevor ran a hand through his hair and waited for what I'd say next. As the alcohol coursed through me, I struggled to make out his colors and the colors of others around me.

"One more, for the four of us," I said to Trevor, pointing

down the row to the other two girls who we'd befriended in our sweet, evil way. "Surprise us." He got to work without hesitation. I noted the time on my watch. This would have to be my last drink until almost midnight. I hoped it would be enough.

"Crikey," I heard Marna mumble as he set the brownish drink in front of us. I hadn't been paying attention. I expected another shot, because it was in a small tumbler glass, but this appeared to be straight liquor.

"What is it?" I asked.

"Four Horsemen." Trevor explained: "Jack, Jim, Johnny, and Jose."

Crikey about covered it.

"Oh, hell, no," said the girl next to Marna.

"What are you trying to do?" the other girl asked Trevor. "Kill us?"

The other bartender leaned in and interjected, "He's trying to get you to dance on the bar."

"This might do the trick," I said, picking up the shot glass and raising it. "Come on, girls. To New Year's and new friends."

The girl next to Marna eyed her shot glass with major trepidation before picking it up. Marna lifted hers and crinkled her nose. The four of us *tink*ed our glasses together and shot them back. I almost gagged. It was no joke. I did my father proud, setting it down without a cough or a cringe, earning high fives from all the strangers standing around us, and lastly from Trevor, who was all grins. He pushed a small, square napkin at me that said, *Room 109*, underlined twice. I folded it up and tucked it into my purse, grabbing five hundred-dollar bills while I was in there. I'd come prepared.

I handed over the money to Trevor, feeling saucy. "No change."

As the Four Horsemen hit my bloodstream, I had to wonder whether I'd just consumed more than three official drinks. Come to think of it, he'd definitely filled the glasses higher than my dad did. I felt myself listing sideways up against the boy next to me.

"Whoa, there, girl," he said, helping me right myself. I giggled.

"This is more like it," the demon purred.

"Show's not over yet," I told it. I wanted to be sure its report back to whoever left no doubt I was working.

"Time to dance," I said to Marna. I patted the bar and she nodded, on board with the idea. She leaned down to pull off her heels, and I did the same. Then we climbed up on the stool and onto the bar, helped by the hands of strangers. The place went wild. Trevor and the other bartender rushed around removing empty glasses and bottles and drying the bar top.

"You'd better get up here, too!" I told the two other girls.

Marna and I grabbed their hands and helped pull them up, laughing at our own unsteadiness. We urged other girls to join the fun, pulling people up left and right. Soon there were eight of us dancing with our hands in the air, moving our hips to the beat of the music. With the strength of the alcohol in my system, it was a wonder I stayed upright on the bar.

I looked down at Trevor, who stood right behind me, half smiling up at us, enjoying the view. He'd helped me more than he knew tonight. A rush of affection overcame me, and I squatted down, putting my hands on his face and placing a

400

light kiss on his lips. I started to pull away, but he hauled me to him and kissed me for real, invading my senses. When the kiss ended, he grinned and took my hands to help me stand back up and dance again. My legs were not cooperating one hundred percent. It must have shown, because Marna wrapped her hand around my hip.

By the end of the song, a hotel manager was signaling for us to climb down, and berating the bartenders, who put up their hands like they had no control over the crazy girls who'd taken over the bar top. As we rushed to get down, a short, thin guy held out his arms to me. I leaned down, holding his shoulders, and squealed as his hands grasped my hips and I fell into his arms. He was stronger than he looked. For a moment the room spun.

"Dance with me?" he said against my ear, and I managed to nod.

Walking proved to be difficult, as my brain seemed to have stopped sending messages to my legs that they should move forward in an orderly fashion. Luckily the guy was happy to help hold me up. He had the high-and-tight haircut and clean-shaven face of a military man.

When we got to the dance floor he lifted my arms around his neck and supported me around my waist. He held a mixed drink in one hand. It was a slow song, so I let my head flop onto his shoulder.

"What's your name?" he asked.

"Anna," I mumbled.

"I'm Ned. You thirsty? Captain and Coke?"

I lifted my heavy head to examine what he offered. I leaned

down and took a long drink from the straw. When I looked back up at him, everything was fuzzy, and I got that warm feeling of affection again, thinking about this brave soldier willing to put his life on the line. I pulled him down and gave him a sloppy kiss, though he didn't seem to mind. He chuckled, wrapping an arm around my waist.

"Girl, you're even more wasted than I thought. You'd better take it easy."

"Nah, I'm gooood." I reached for the drink in his hand, but he lifted it way up high, and I jumped for it, wobbling. His free hand still held me around the waist. His laughter was playful, but I was serious about wanting to down the rest of his drink. The fact that he wouldn't hand it over was ticking me off, and he seemed to think it was terribly cute.

I heard a familiar sound while we haggled over the drink. A whistle. It was the same intonation my dad used during training, but it wasn't his pitch. I peered around the room in what felt like slow motion.

There went the whistle again!

My slow eyes found Kope standing against the wall, sleeves still rolled up to his elbows. When he knew I saw him, he held up a glass of water.

Ned was swaying us back and forth, trying to dance.

"I have to go to the bathroom," I told him. Well, that was what I meant to say, but it was slurred, so I hoped he got the gist of it as I disengaged from his arms and stumbled in Kope's direction, bumping into people along the way. I finally got to him, and he held out the water and inclined his head to a chair. I took the water, but didn't sit. He spoke to me in that maddening calm, gentle way of his.

"Have a rest. The Legionnaire has gone."

Hallelujah. Now all I needed was another drink. I'd have to be sneaky, since Kope was trying to sober me up. Hey, come to think of it . . .

"You whistled," I said, pointing at him. He nodded but did not look at me, and I wondered whether he was ashamed of me. That thought made me clutch my stomach, saying, "I really need to go to the bathroom."

I staggered to the side, and Kope took my arm to steady me. He lifted my chin without saying a single word. I watched his hazel eyes, feeling his thumb move back and forth across my jaw, his way of saying he thought no less of me. I gathered strength from his strong gaze, knowing I wouldn't be getting another drink after all. I gave him a single nod.

When he dropped his hand from my chin, I walked away from him, dizzy, trailing a hand against the wall until I got to the nearest exit. I went to the hall with the bathroom but stopped in the entryway. Why was it so dark? Oh, wait. This wasn't right. It was some utility hall, where two people were making out.

My body locked up with the shock of recognition. Looking away would have been the smart thing to do. But my feet were weighted down by some terrible charm as I took in the sight of Kai's lean back and strong shoulders. Manicured fingernails roamed over the short hair on the back of his head as he kissed her hard. They were fully dressed, but might as well have been naked, the way his hips ground against hers. She lifted a knee, hiking her dress up to her hips and revealing red panties. She pulled his blue dress shirt out of his waistband and put her hands in, touching his back. I knew exactly how silky his skin would feel.

I finally got enough sense to back out of that hall. I rounded the corner and came nose-to-nose with Ginger, who grabbed my upper arm in a death grip. She peeked around the corner to confirm that I'd gotten an eyeful, then pulled me down the hall away from them.

"What the hell are you thinking?" she whispered through clenched teeth. "Leave him alone while he's working!"

"I was looking for the bathroom." I tried to pull my arm from her strong grasp.

"Likely," she spit.

"You don't have to talk to me like that! And freaking let me go!"

She flung my arm down, getting in my face again. I hoped Pharzuph wasn't camped out somewhere nearby listening, because Ginger obviously wasn't worried about throwing me under the bus.

"I watched you tonight, Anna. You enjoyed yourself, didn't you? You loved the attention of that bartender and the eyes of the men on you while you danced for them. Admit it. You loved it."

I wanted to deny it. All my life I'd been invisible. I'd been too good to be noteworthy. Tonight I felt accepted by the crowd, and in spite of the horrid spirit trailing me, I'd managed to have fun along the way.

"All of those guys giving you attention?" she continued. "Yeah, they wanted to get laid. That bartender? He's engaged.

I'd scouted him out before you even got here. And did you happen to notice all of the girls who were wildly envious as their boyfriends tried to get a glimpse up your dress while you danced on the bar? Because that's what was happening while you were enjoying yourself."

"Stop. That's not fair."

"Fair." She snorted, scoffing at the notion. "You're no better than the rest of us."

"I never thought I was."

As I stared into Ginger's eyes the room began to spin again. Someone was coming up behind us, talking to us. I worked hard to focus. It was Blake. He stuck out his knuckles at me, and with great effort I finally bumped his with mine.

"You know it's a good night when you lose your shoes." He laughed. We looked down at my bare feet, toenails painted sparkly red. "Who knew you'd be the kissing bandit after a few drinks, huh?"

The Four Horsemen began galloping in my belly, turning into a rodeo. I slapped a hand over my mouth and pushed past them, dropping the glass of water that Kopano had given me. Ginger screamed as it splashed up on her. I ran for the bathroom, flinging open the door and falling into the last stall just in time.

One by one I lost each drink, then I flushed the toilet and slid down the wall until I was sitting on the remarkably clean tiled floor, knees up to my chest. Someone else was getting sick at the other end of the bathroom. I leaned down and saw under the stalls that it was the two girls from the bar. The one I'd pressured was heaving and crying while her friend stood behind her. I sat back up and squeezed my eyes shut. After a few minutes they finished, leaving me alone in the restroom.

The room continued to spin, and as the image from that dark utility hall made an appearance, I closed my eyes and fought the urge to be sick again.

I heard a scuffle outside the bathroom, two people arguing, and then the door opened.

"Anna?" Oh, no. "Ann?" My heart compressed with pain at the sound of his voice.

"I'm fine, Kai." My throat was raspy.

Footsteps echoed off the high ceilings until shiny black shoes showed under my stall door.

"You're sick. Let me in."

"No. I'm fine now."

"Shall I send Marna, then?"

"No. I just want to be alone. Go away in case the spirits come back."

There was a long pause and I prayed he would hurry and leave, because the emotions I'd kept at bay all night were surfacing. I knew that when they made it to the top I was going to have an ugly, slobbering cry that needed no witnesses. *Please don't say another word. . . .*

"You did . . . well tonight." The reluctant sentiment in his voice was like a hammer busting me wide open.

"Go," I said thickly. "I want to be alone. Please just *go away!*"

There was a weird chanting sound coming from the people outside, and as I strained to listen, still unable to use my extra senses, I realized they were counting down. Cheers erupted and party horns trilled.

"Happy New Year." His feet turned to leave, and the moment the door clicked shut behind him I dropped my head to my forearms and wept.

"*Some rise by sin, and some by virtue fall.*"
—*William Shakespeare*, Measure for Measure

CHAPTER THIRTY

SOME BY VIRTUE FALL

Someone knocked on my apartment door at six thirty the next morning. Six thirty! I shuffled down the hall, unable to stand straight. My stomach was still upset, and my head pounded as I spied my dad through the peephole. I opened the door and he walked right past me, heading for the kitchen.

"Help yourself," I told him.

"Mornin' to you, too, grumpy." He poured himself a glass of tea and threw together a sandwich. I stared, bleary-eyed.

"You got sick last night."

How could he tell? Did I smell bad? He took a bite, frowning at me.

"I forgot to drink water," I mumbled.

"Or it could have been the Four Horsemen shot," he suggested.

"How did you . . . ?" I began, then figured it out. "You were nearby the whole time!" He nodded. "Well, what was I supposed to do with that spirit breathing down my neck? He said he'd leave me alone if I gave him a show. I couldn't exactly say no to the shot."

"Don't ever give a bartender free rein. Order only what you can handle."

I sighed and dropped onto the couch, pressing my temples. It was way too early.

"We'll talk about it on the plane. Get up and get ready. We're going to New York City."

Flying first class was nice. Too bad I couldn't enjoy it. My gut was wrecked and my head was splitting. I chugged water and tried to eat a croissant.

The Dukes had called an emergency summit, and all Nephilim were required to attend. Neph from all over the world had left the night before to begin the trek. My friends were flying in on Pharzuph's personal jet.

On the way to the airport I'd asked my dad why the Neph had to go. He said Neph were invited to summits only when one of them was in trouble. A strange sense of numbness had crept over me at that point. He'd sent a few of his trusted whisperers out to hunt down information, but all they learned was that a female Nephilim was not working up to par and would be dealt with as a reminder to all. We'd been silent the rest of the way to the airport, but my brain worked overtime.

It was too much of a coincidence that the Dukes would call an emergency meeting hours after I'd been tested. The unyielding tension on my dad's face told me more than he was willing to say.

"Someone whistled last night," my father said during the flight. The plane hummed with white noise from the engines. Nobody sat next to us.

"It was Kopano."

"Did you tell him about that?" he asked.

I bit my lip and shook my head.

"So he listened in on your training." He sucked air through his front teeth. "Ballsy."

"You're not mad?"

He lifted a shoulder and let it drop as if it made no difference. Then he raised the issue of the summit again, and my insides constricted.

"Sit as far away from the Dukes as you can tonight," he instructed. "Neph don't talk at summits. Don't speak out, no matter what happens. If there's a problem, I'll take care of it. And don't pull out that damn sword unless I tell you to. It's our absolute last resort. Once that cat's out of the bag there's no going back."

Together we'd rigged up a holster for the hilt around my ankle. He'd found a leather pouch to hold it so my bare skin wouldn't be zapped. I was wearing black pants that flared enough at the bottom to hide it. He hadn't thought metal detectors would be able to sense the celestial material, and he'd been right. I made it through airport security without notice.

The most terrifying thing about the summit was not

413

knowing what to expect. I needed to prepare for the worst.

Ridicule. Torture. Pain. Death. Hell.

A tremor of terror racked me at the thought of eternal damnation. At the same time the plane hit a pocket of differing air pressure and the cabin dropped, shaking. I gripped the armrest. Not eternal, I told myself. It would be only temporary; I could make it. I closed my eyes in meditation. And then another horrific thought surfaced. What if Kaidan or Kopano tried to stop the Dukes from hurting me during the summit? They'd cause themselves to be subjected to punishment, too. The idea of anyone intervening was too much. A tear trickled out.

My father reached over and wiped it away before taking my hand. I kept my head back, eyes closed.

"It might not be about you," he reassured me. *But it might.*

From the small rounded window I could see the speck of another plane passing in the distance. We would be passing Patti somewhere in the sky that morning as she returned home. I closed my eyes and pictured her face, hearing her encourage me to be strong. I couldn't think about how she would handle tonight's news. My dad had said it was too dangerous to call, so I'd left her a letter. It was not a sufficient good-bye.

A bell chimed overhead and we looked at each other. Our initial descent into New York City had begun. We had no information and no plan.

"When we get there I'll check you into a hotel. Stay in the room until it's time to go. I'll send someone to come get you."

That night, as I stepped up from the NYC subway with my five Nephilim friends, we were swallowed up by a torrent of partygoers headed toward Times Square in the freezing cold. Everyone was bundled up in thick coats, gloves, scarves, and woolly hats. I'd never seen so many people.

If it was this crazy on New Year's Day, I couldn't imagine what it'd been like the night before, when the ball dropped. Since New Year's Eve fell on a Friday this year, everyone was making a weekend of it.

I grabbed the fabric on the back of Marna's coat so I wouldn't lose her as I stared up at the massive billboards and flashing displays across buildings. I shoved my other frozen hand into my jacket pocket. Everything here was supersized: giant buildings, screens, stores, all crammed together into a barrage of images and sounds. There was no way to take it all in; you simply had to let it envelop you. Get lost in it.

I envied the cool expressions worn by the other Neph, as if nothing were amiss. Would I have been able to share in their confident swaggers if I'd been trained to reveal nothing under pressure? I concentrated on not allowing my forehead to furrow.

We were well hidden in the large, exuberant crowd. There was a mix of national and international faces, visitors who'd come from all over for the Big Apple holiday. Thousands of sheer guardian angels bobbed along with their charges. Everyone was talking and shouting their laughter. The general atmosphere was euphoric, and many auras were blurry from the influence of substances.

After walking fifteen minutes through the masses, we turned down a less busy street. It was still active, but we had more elbow room and the crowd was thinning out ahead. We were close, mere blocks away. Kaidan must have felt it, too, because he fell back next to me as he walked, continuing to look straight ahead. Being close to him made me feel better, and I reveled in the occasional brush of his arm against mine. Even through our coats I felt the electric pull between us.

A large group exited a club and filtered out, crowding the sidewalk. In a moment of boldness I caught Kaidan's pinkie with mine, knowing nobody would be able to see. I felt his hand go stiff, and then we were suddenly moving to the side. He led me by the little finger, weaving between people until we ducked down a set of narrow stairs into a dark cellar doorway, hidden by shadows. Euphoria exploded inside me at our nearness.

His mouth found mine in the dark, fiery and rough. I gave a tiny whimper before melting into him and pulling his face down to mine even harder. In that kiss we spoke all of the things we couldn't say. He kissed me with an urgency born of some strong, unstable emotion: fury. I tried to imagine the nature of that feeling. Was he angry because of how I made him feel? Angry that he was powerless to change tonight's outcome? I didn't know, but I welcomed it.

I needed this kiss. I needed this last moment of feeling alive. My body pushed against his, thanking him, memorizing him. His hands roamed roughly down my back and over my hips, yanking me even closer, tighter.

We were breathless when we broke the kiss and he rested his forehead on mine. My hands slid from the back of his neck to his face. I ran my thumbs across his eyebrows and over his cheekbones. He watched me in the dimmed light, searching me. Our heated breath turned to fog in the cold air. Then I stretched up to place a sweet, soft kiss on his lips. He closed his eyes and we lingered there with our lips barely touching.

If I could take all my earthly memories into the cold afterlife with me, this would be the one I'd replay to keep me warm and sane until the final day of judgment.

"Ahem!"

I jumped away from Kaidan at the sound of someone clearing her throat from the entrance of the stairwell.

Ginger stood there with both hands on her hips, a city goddess in her knee-high boots and sleek black coat. Marna stood at her side, nervously peering around. Ginger shook her head at us in exasperation. She stomped off in the direction we needed to go, with her sister close behind.

Kaidan gave me one last crushing stare and I saw him swallow. I wanted nothing more than to stay there with him, but we'd already pushed the limits of our luck. Staying near each other, we climbed the stairs and blended back into the crowd. Up ahead, Kopano turned his head enough to meet my eye. I felt Kaidan stiffen next to me, noting our interaction, but I couldn't look away from Kope's soulful, sad eyes. I stared back, at a loss, knowing he'd heard Kaidan and me take that dangerous moment for ourselves. He gave me a small nod of acknowledgment, and his gaze slid to the ground before he faced forward again.

We were almost there. One block to go. I had to scold my feet into moving forward. My body revolted against this entire thing, screaming, *Remind us again why we're walking straight into certain death?* It was unnatural.

The streetlights above began to flicker. None of the humans seemed to notice. The lights flickered again.

"Legionnaires," Kai whispered, signaling to the sky with an upward jut of his chin.

Hundreds of demon spirits swarmed the air above us, coming in from all directions and blotting out light like fast-moving gray clouds. The street was under attack as demons darted down at random, whispering in unsuspecting ears. The atmosphere on the street immediately changed, and I felt a painful rush of negative emotion rumble through the people.

A fight broke out between two men right in front of us. Kopano had to jump out of the way, and the rest of us swung wide to get around them, while other people were cramming in closer to get a better view. The volume of the crowd increased. Laughter became more raucous, and a woman behind us screamed. I couldn't tell what had happened. Chaos was taking over. Spirits flipped above us, completely in their element, dive-bombing into the mass of people with evil glee.

"Ready for your first summit, little drinker?" I flinched at the voice in my head and looked up at the grisly face of one of the whisperers from last night's party. I kept walking.

Something flew through the air and landed right on Blake's shoulder. Ginger gave an insulted scoff and swatted it off. We stepped over the offending black lace bra.

Blake half grinned and said, "Nice," before we were jostled and forced to keep moving.

Up ahead we passed the shirtless lady, who was now

arguing with a guy. He shoved a shirt at her, attempting to cover her, and she kept pushing it away, opting to throw her head back and spin around instead. The man glowered as onlookers cheered and catcalled.

Kaidan pulled a flask out of his back pocket and guzzled it down. A strong whiff of bourbon wafted over, making me queasy.

The twins veered to the side and stopped in front of a glass door that had been painted black. We were here. This was it. The small sign above the door said SIR LAUGHS-A-LOT and showed a jolly knight. The Dukes had rented an underground comedy club to hold their summit. The irony of it made me despise them even more than I already did.

As Ginger reached for the door handle I battled a surge of terror. I couldn't go in there. I took a step back, then another, my breath becoming shallower until I knew I was on the verge of a panic attack. I spun around, prepared to run, only to face a dapper, frowning gentleman in a fine gray suit. He had salt-and-pepper hair and a long, oval face. But his most compelling feature was the giant purple badge in the middle of his chest, like a pulsating, vile eggplant of pride. Rahab, the Duke of Pride.

I spun back around, trying to play it off like I'd not just been planning to run like heck. I stumbled forward a little in my attempt to walk with Mr. Evil Incarnate at my back. The other Neph were already inside. Kaidan stood holding the door open with an expressionless face, eyes averted downward.

"After you, Duke Rahab," he said. I stepped out of the way

and let Rahab pass me with a frigid breeze. Then my eyes met Kaidan's and we stood there.

"Get in and close the damn door!" an Australian male voice hollered from inside. "You're lettin' in a draft."

There was a tense second when I knew Kaidan thought I might run, and if I did, he would run with me. But I couldn't do that to him. So I slipped inside and felt him enter the club behind me, closing the door.

I had to adjust my pupils in the dim entryway. The place was dingy and smelled like years of stale smoke and mildew hiding under drab old carpets, but it was warm. Walls were plastered with advertisements for comedians and shows, past and present. The thin hall was empty except for a host podium by the door. Everybody else had already gone in.

"Son of Pharzuph," said a redheaded male Neph. He was short and lean, but had the body and stance of a fighter. His fiery red hair was buzzed so short it was barely fuzz. In his hand he wielded a metal-detecting wand.

Kaidan returned the greeting with a nod, saying, "Son of Mammon." So this was the Duke of Greed's son.

"Arms up, mate. You know the drill." He spoke with a heavy Aussie accent. Kaidan lifted his arms and widened his feet. I got nervous when the wand passed his pockets, but it didn't beep. It did beep when it got to his shoes, though.

"Take 'em off," he told Kaidan, who sighed and bent down to untie his black boots. I wondered whether they had steel in them. I glanced up when I felt the Neph's eyes on me. He brazenly stared me up and down before giving me a wide-mouthed smile.

"Who're you?"

"Anna. Belial's daughter." I still felt stupid saying, "Daughter of Belial," like a *Beowulf* character. The guy stared at my badge.

Kaidan stood up and cleared his throat, making the other Neph return his attention to the boots. He did a halfhearted scan of them before nodding that they were fine and turning his attention back to me.

"Name's Flynn Frazer," he said, stepping close.

I took a step outward and raised my arms to the side. He stood a little closer than necessary as he waved the wand over me. And, yeah, he totally patted me down, paying close attention to my hips and bottom, which made Kaidan cross his arms and scowl.

My heart began a fierce pounding as the wand neared my ankle, but it passed over without a sound, and he didn't touch it. I let out a frayed breath when Flynn stood back up, swiping his tongue over his bottom lip.

"Still waitin' on a few more. See ya down there." He nodded toward a doorway at the end of the hall. Kaidan took another long drink from a second flask as we walked down the narrow black corridor. I wondered how many flasks he had packed away on himself tonight. I kind of wished right then that I had one myself. But I needed my wits about me.

At the end of the walkway I put my hand on the glass door's handle and took a deep, calming breath. I felt Kaidan's warm presence close behind me. Eight months of memories tumbled into my heart right then. Just eight short months ago I didn't know who or what I was. I'd never been passionately kissed. If someone had told me then that I would soon be dying at the hands of demons posing as gentlemen, I would have laughed and questioned their sanity. How quickly life could change.

I pulled the door open and music bounded up the dark stairs. The Dukes listened to techno? That seemed so weird that I almost burst into an inappropriate moment of nervous laughter. But I caught myself and choked it back. Time to move. One foot in front of the other.

As I descended into the den of pulsating music and awaiting evils, I silently chanted something I'd read countless times. I'd always thought the words were beautiful, but never once considered that I might need the power of their beauty for myself someday: *Though I walk through the valley of the shadow of death, I will fear no evil: for Thou art with me.*

I let the meaning of those words reverberate deep in my soul as I stepped into the darkened area, surveying the scene. The room was rectangular and flat, like a recreation hall, with about thirty tables that each seated four. A small stage was in the middle, about a foot and a half high. The short ceiling made me feel hemmed in, as if it might collapse on us at any moment.

I don't know what I expected when I got down there, but there was no fanfare as I entered the room. A few Neph glanced up, but the Dukes did not seem to notice or care. I exhaled.

Nephilim were spread out around the room, sitting and standing alone or in small groups, silent and still. There were over a hundred, young and old. I felt a kinship and commonality as I glanced around at the strangers. How many of them felt the way my friends and I did about doing our fathers' work?

The Dukes made themselves at home, lounging at the prime tables surrounding the stage. My eyes darted over them. Pharzuph sat at a table full of rowdy Dukes, leaning back in his gray suit and laughing. His shiny black dress shoes were propped up on the table.

It was eerie how handsome they all were. Even the rough-edged, rugged ones maintained fit bodies and confident postures that held appeal. I marveled at their respectable-businessmen appearances, their fine Italian suits, and ornate, traditional garb from around the world. If it weren't for the multicolored badges of sin crested on their chests, they would seem like nothing more than powerful, self-assured humans. One woman sat among them. I'd been told of her—Jezebet. She was a picture of sophisticated Russian fashion, with short auburn hair that winged elegantly around her sharp, angular face and ears.

And then there was my father, sitting at the table next to Pharzuph's with three other subdued Dukes. My dad stared at me. I swallowed the rush of overwhelming emotion that he caused me to feel. Knowing there was one power player on my side gave me a sliver of hope that I didn't dare put stock in. He looked away from me, rubbing his thumb and finger down his goatee.

Kaidan poked me in the side. I spotted my group of Neph friends at the other end of the elongated room, farthest away, and headed toward them. I kept close to the wall with my head down, hoping Pharzuph would not catch my scent if I kept this distance.

Blake and Kopano sat together, and the twins sat at the table next to them. Kaidan went to the guys and I sat with the girls. We moved our chairs around so we'd all be facing the stage, with our backs to the wall. Nobody was behind us.

As I sat there I could feel my blood pulsing fast, buzzing under my skin. I kept my head down with my hair framing my face. I was able to see what was going on in the room, while feigning indifference.

Marna gave my leg a quick pat when it bounced. It took great effort to sit still. How much longer?

At the next table Kaidan continued to drink. The stress made my body crave drugs worse than ever. The glorious escape. A deep, dark, yearning pull made me want to scream and rail.

My head snapped up as the door to the comedy club opened a fraction. The redheaded guy, Flynn, entered, closing the door behind him and then standing guard in front of it. He gave a nod to the Dukes and the music cut off.

The desires of my sinful nature cracked and fell away like brittle glass, replaced by thick fear as Pharzuph stood and took the stage. He nodded his elegant head as he surveyed the room. His black hair was especially shiny tonight.

"Welcome, all. I trust that everyone had enjoyable travels to this wonderful city of New York. I regret we had to rush, but a certain problem has been put off too long. With all of the visitors to the city this weekend, we thought this would be the perfect opportunity to wreak havoc. The Dukes, Legionnaires, and Nephilim will reach many souls this night. So without further ado, let us complete our business at hand so we can move on to the greater joys of our life's work. Shall we?"

Pharzuph gave a dazzling smile, and cheers of agreement ensued from the Dukes.

"Let us first call forth the messenger Azael so our lord Lucifer may be informed of these proceedings."

Azael! He was the one who'd whispered to me at that party. My father trusted him.

In unison the Dukes emitted low hisses from the backs of their throats—a long hiss followed by two short ones, and repeated a second time. This was not a human sound. It had to come from deep in their souls, the stuff of horror films. Every Neph in the room went stock-still. I was covered in goose bumps and was starting to sweat, despite a triple layer of antiperspirant. I wanted to wipe my forehead, but I didn't dare move and draw attention to myself.

Azael appeared as if coming up through the ground. He flitted grandly, with widespread wings, and then folded them in, a gray ghost hovering over the stage floor next to Pharzuph. Azael's face appeared less frightening than those of the demons who had haunted me and stalked me the previous night. This one had catlike features, reminding me of a lion.

"Welcome, Azael. I trust our lord Lucifer is well?"

Azael inclined his head and Pharzuph continued.

"Well, then. Thank you for joining this summit. I hope you can return to him soon with news that will gladden him." He turned to the Dukes. "And now we summon our Legionnaires."

There was a great, loud slurring of hisses as each Duke sent out a personal message to his Legionnaires. The eeriness never lessened. It took all of my willpower not to cover my ears.

They came in from every direction, packing in on top of one another like smoky sheets of paper. The demon spirits blocked all ceiling lights, like an immense dreary fog hanging over our heads. Candlelight from the tabletops lit the room with a low, wavering glow. I kicked on my night vision. There was only one exit in the room. To say I was trapped would be a vast understatement.

"Welcome, loyal Legionnaires," Pharzuph cooed at the blackness, with his arms open wide to them. They gave him space around the stage, but I still had to slump down a little in my chair to see.

Pharzuph focused on the Dukes now.

"You have done well since last we gathered. Humanity spoils and rots like never before in history. Soon, very soon, we will be fully prepared to take back what is rightfully ours, and nobody will keep us from the realms of our choosing!"

There was great uproar of applause from the Dukes, who bellowed their approval. Wonderful. Pharzuph was a demon cheerleader. His smile was broad as he motioned Rahab to join him onstage. This was it.

Please give me strength. Please make it fast. Please give me peace.

A ripple of peace went through me, fluid and cool, shaking off the panic that clung. I closed my eyes for a moment and envisioned Patti's loving face.

Rahab greeted everyone with a heavy French inflection. Unlike Pharzuph, he did not smile or attempt to rile them.

His tone was sobering and cold.

"Many years have passed since there was a need to address the Nephilim." He spit the word with disgust. "And yet, just as the stupid humans do not learn from errors of the past, neither does your lesser race. It is very simple. Your life is not your own. You were bred to serve us. You work for us, or you lose the privilege of being on earth. There is one among you who has been warned, and yet still chooses poorly. Sin is a beautiful thing, but even we must not allow our sins to control us. Because when it does, we cannot properly influence humans. Simple enough, wouldn't you say?"

Where was he going with this?

Rahab's beady dark eyes scanned the room and I held my breath. His eyes passed over our group and stopped on a table in the middle of the room. He clasped his hands behind his back and paced back and forth on the stage. Pharzuph watched him from the side with a zealous look of worship. Rahab stopped and stared at that table in the middle again. I dared not move my body, but my eyesight stretched and zoomed, as I tried to figure out who he kept looking at. There were at least a dozen different Neph clustered at those tables in the middle.

"Gerlinda." The way Rahab said her name felt like a slither in my ear. "Daughter of Kobal."

Kobal? Ah, the Duke of Gluttony. What in the world was going on?

Rahab pointed, hatred and contempt blazing in his eyes. A high-pitched, pained yelp sounded from the middle of the room, like someone kicked a puppy. Suddenly chairs were scraping the old tiles, pushing back from the tables that surrounded Gerlinda. The Nephilim around her fled, leaving her in the middle alone.

Gerlinda was a tall woman in her thirties. Her straw-colored short hair was smoothed down around her face. She appeared tidy, but one thing worried me: The Dukes and Neph were always so careful to be in shape. I wasn't good at guessing weight, but Gerlinda was likely over three hundred pounds.

She held a hand over her mouth, which had apparently emitted the yelp without her permission. Panic shone in her eyes.

"Can you manage to make it up here, Gerlinda, daughter of Kobal?" Rahab asked her in that slithery, scaly, antagonizing voice. "Or do you need an incentive?" He pulled a candy bar from his pocket and waved it in a taunt.

Gerlinda gaped with her eyes, frozen to her seat as the Dukes let out an uproar of laughter.

"Go on, salad dodger!" yelled a Fabio-looking Duke with an English accent. That had to be Astaroth, the twins' father. How gross.

The next few minutes were filled with lewd comments and shrill laughter from the rowdier Dukes.

"Perhaps we need to roll her onto the stage."

"I've got something in my pocket for you, all right."

On and on it went.

I ran through a series of emotions during those moments. Pure joy that I was saved. Revulsion at the treatment of this girl. Dread that I would have to sit through whatever they had planned for her.

One of the Dukes threw something at Gerlinda, and suddenly there was a shower of junk food raining down. Baked goods, candies, cheese puffs. They had planned for this. I looked at my father's table. He sat with Jezebet, Melchom, and Alocer, the fathers of Blake and Kope. The four of them watched with boredom, as if they were too cool to partake in the spectacle, but the vicious Dukes around them didn't care.

Food continued to hit Gerlinda, and tears slid down her rosy cheeks. She didn't try to move or shield herself from it. My heart broke for her. I wondered if this poor woman was the sole reason for tonight's summit, or if she was just a prelude to the main show.

A tall, thin man with icy eyes and light hair stood up, pointing to the woman and shouting in German, "Gerlinda! *Erhalten Sie auf der Bühne jetzt!*" He pointed to the stage. It had to be her father, Kobal. His cheeks were red with anger. Gerlinda shook her head, and when she didn't move he shoved his chair back, knocking it over, and made a beeline toward her. He grabbed her hard by the arm, and she screamed out as he pulled her to her feet, pushing and shoving her toward the stage. The Dukes cheered him on.

I couldn't watch. My stomach was in a tight, hard ball and everything good inside me cried out against the injustice. How many times in history had innocent people been brutalized while bystanders stood by and did nothing? Could I be one of those bystanders? I wanted to slam my eyes shut and cover my ears, but even if I couldn't see or hear, I would know a terrible atrocity was being done.

I doubted Gerlinda had a single person in her life who

loved and encouraged her. Unlike drugs, food couldn't be avoided. We all had to eat. Would I have done as well with my self-control if my sin were gluttony? I couldn't imagine doing small amounts of drugs and not going overboard. It was all or nothing.

When Kobal got his daughter on the stage, he stomped back to his table, receiving slaps on the backs from his "brothers" for his manhandling abilities.

Gerlinda stood next to Rahab on the stage, slumping with silent sobs.

Rahab sneered at her. "Enough with this sniveling. Your father was good enough to warn you years ago. He even went so far as to seek medical attention for you. Did you not undergo a surgical procedure?"

Gerlinda nodded and let out a heart-wrenching cry, as if she were trying her best to hold it in but no longer had the strength. I clamped my teeth together and swallowed several times, blinking away the burn in my eyes.

"So what is the problem then?" Rahab's French drawl became harder to decipher as he shouted, and drops of spittle flew from his lips. "You allow your appetite to make you disloyal to our cause. Overindulgence is for humans. Not for Neph. Your kind need not seek enjoyment and comfort. You are nothing!"

Rahab inclined his head to Pharzuph, who picked up a small round table sitting next to the stage. There were three plates on it, each with a different food item: chocolate cake, a hamburger, and a slice of lemon meringue pie. Pharzuph set the table in front of Gerlinda, and stepped down from the stage, joining the disorderly table of Dukes.

"Since you have spent your life shoving food into your face, we are doing you the kindness of letting you eat your way out of this life. You get a choice, Neph girl. Aren't you so lucky? Two of these delicacies contain poisons that will bring your death. One poison kills quickly. The other promises you will struggle, vomiting and bleeding until your guts are eaten away." Rahab paused, allowing his malicious information to set in. "The third plate contains no poison at all. If you choose the food with no poison, you will be given one more year to prove yourself to us."

No. They couldn't do this. My father and the other three at his table watched with polite disinterest, not sharing in the mirthful murmurs and occasional laughter. I wanted my dad to stop this; he must have felt my eyes, because he tilted his head to meet my stare. A vicious warning was issued to me in those brown eyes. He didn't want me saying a word.

My jaw quivered and I bit my bottom lip. My father went back to watching the show.

"Which will it be, big Gerlinda?" Rahab waved a hand over the three plates. "Will your death be fast, or will you writhe in pain as the poison eats away your stomach lining?" He grinned at the cake. "Death by chocolate. I bet you never dreamed it would be so good."

"Take the chocolate!" one of the Dukes yelled. And then that whole rowdy table was calling out their choices, as if it were a game show.

Feeling severely queasy, I scooted to the end of my chair, entranced. There was hope—she could choose the one without poison. I wanted to look at my friends but couldn't take my eyes away from the stage. My father angled himself in the chair, scratching the side of his face with two fingers. He shot me a fast, stealthy glance and continued to move those two fingers up and down his face in an unnatural manner. Two. *Two.* A signal. His eyes darted to me again, and then to the table with the food.

The second dish wasn't poisoned! My father knew I had an ability that set me apart from other Neph. I was capable of mind influence, but none of the other Dukes knew it. They wouldn't suspect me. I hoped I was close enough to the stage.

"It is time to choose," Rahab purred. Dukes were chanting their own choices, and the spirits above us bounced with anticipation, in constant movement. "Which one will you choose, Gerlinda? What will be the last flavor on your lips before you meet our revered leader?"

She broke down now, shaking her head back and forth, crying, "*Nein, nein, nein.*"

The second one, Gerlinda! I willed to her. *Choose the hamburger!*

"Choose now, or I will choose for you," Rahab said as her wails became incoherent. "And you can only imagine what I will pick."

She managed to lift the fork, shaking violently, and cut into the slice of lemon meringue pie. *No!* Several Dukes cheered when she chose the one they'd been vying for, and others booed.

"Go ahead then, *chérie.*" Rahab smiled. "Enjoy it. I know we will."

Not the pie, Gerlinda! No! The burger has no poison! I leaned so hard against the table that it moved, and I almost fell forward. Gerlinda dropped the fork with a clatter and crammed her fingers into her temples, shutting her eyes.

Good girl! I told her. *It's the second plate. That's the one.*

Panting, she picked up the burger, and Rahab frowned. The pie Dukes hollered angrily at the change, and the burger Dukes raised a triumphant cheer. She held it in front of her face and grimaced as if it were a live rodent. And then, with a deep breath, she stopped crying and steeled herself. She took the bite.

The room went silent. She chewed and chewed, bending over and dropping the rest of the burger on the plate, covering her mouth to keep from spitting it out. She swallowed the bite and placed both hands palms down on the table, gasping to catch her breath. Finally, after what felt like forever, she stood up straight, not looking at any of the Dukes. She lifted her chin and stared straight ahead. She had survived.

When it became apparent she wasn't going to give them a show, the Dukes went ballistic, standing and shaking their heads, shouting over one another. I slid back into my seat, biting back a smile. We did it!

Rahab raised a hand to silence his fellow Dukes. They settled down and watched as he made a slow circle around Gerlinda, hands clasped behind his back.

"Do you think you are a clever girl? Or merely a lucky one? Hm?" She did not respond, only continued to look dead ahead. Rahab sidled up next to her.

"You were promised one year, yes?" She was silent. "It's too

433

bad for you that honesty is not our strong point."

He reached behind his back and pulled out a gun with a silencer, which he placed to her temple. The room went quiet, but the glee from the Dukes and spirits was palpable. Gerlinda closed her eyes, and Rahab's hand tightened as he tensed to shoot.

"No!"

I was as surprised by my outburst as everyone else in the room. I pressed the fingertips of both hands against my lips. Every head in the room faced our group. My friends stared straight ahead like statues. I dropped my hands, knowing it was too late. I'd condemned myself.

"Which one of you dares to speak out at this sacred summit?" Rahab demanded.

Grabbing the table edge, I stood up, praying my friends would keep silent, unlike I had.

"She's mine." My father also stood, wearing a dark expression of stress and annoyance. "She's still in training. I should have warned her. She's not used to our ways."

"That may be so, brother Belial," Rahab said. "But the girl must be taught a lesson for her interference and insubordination."

"I agree. And I'll take care of it. Let's finish this meeting and get down to our real business out there." He pointed upward toward the city, then turned and glared at me. "Now sit down, girl, and keep your mouth shut."

I sat.

"That is not the proper protocol, brother." Rahab's tone was as irritated as that of a spoiled child who hadn't gotten his way. "A breach such as hers should be dealt with immediately."

"With all due respect, Rahab," said a mellow female voice. Everyone turned to Jezebet. "That may have been the case when there were thousands of Nephilim at our disposal. With their small ranks now, I personally believe punishments should be dealt at each Duke's discretion. Kobal wanted his daughter's to be public. Bravo to him. Belial wants his private. I say we allow it. I trust her suffering will be adequate. A little leverage for Belial, hm? It *is* his first offspring, after all."

Rahab snarled at her. "We will put it to a vote! All in favor of immediate punishment for this girl, raise your hand."

All but the four Dukes at my father's table raised their hands. Eight to four. We lost. Fear coiled within me. My father stared around at the Dukes, cracking his neck, then his knuckles while working his jaw side to side. I regretted that my actions were putting him through this.

For a moment during the summit, I'd let myself believe I would make it through the night after all. But there was something to be said about refusing to be a bystander. My heart was tender and vulnerable, but even now I refused to see that as a weakness.

"Daughter of Belial, come forward. Now." Rahab's eyes bored into me, daring me to challenge him again—something that had probably never been done at a summit.

I couldn't feel my legs as I stood and began to walk. I wondered vaguely whether I looked as funny as I felt. There was a barrage of scratchy noises in my brain as the legion of demons whispered above me: hundreds of voices compounding like the sound of rushing wind through dry trees.

I came up to the stage on my father's side of his table, steering as clear as I could of Pharzuph, but it wasn't far enough. As I stepped onto the stage next to Gerlinda I heard a cough and a theatrical gagging sound. Pharzuph waved a hand in front of his face. Drama king.

"Good Hades, Belial! She's *still* a virgin!" The Dukes all gasped.

My father stood, leaning down on the table with fists like rocks and a face even harder, and told Pharzuph to mind his own business. He threw in some colorful words, and I got a clear image of the life he'd led with hardened criminals.

"You think I don't know she's a virgin? She's a virgin because I've damn well told her to stay one. It's the leverage we're using on a boy who's proven to be a hard sell. She's on the cusp of breaking him down, and her virginity will be gone by the time it's over. It's all been included in my reports to the boss, so shut your trap."

"Her odor is offensive," Pharzuph said.

"Deal with it."

"This virginity is not even necessary to lure men," Pharzuph argued. "Women have been successfully fooling men into believing they're virgins since the dawn of time."

"Enough!" scolded Rahab.

He shoved Gerlinda backward, hollering for her to get out of my way. Before I could turn away he punched the side of my head and I staggered to the side, bending and catching myself with my hands on the floor. My ear rang and my head throbbed, but with slow movements I got to my feet. I kept my eyes down, scared to see the bloodlust in his eyes.

I saw his arm lift and I braced myself. He hit the other side of my face. I didn't fall this time, but I did let out a small cry from the sharp pain in my ear. Taking shallow breaths, I straightened again and balled my hands at my sides.

I thought about the hilt. My dad said he would give me a sign if it was necessary to use it. At the moment his face was murderous. He kept still, so I did the same.

Rahab moved beside me, setting the gun on the table.

"Pick it up," he told me. Was he serious? One look at his feral eyes told me he was. With a trembling hand I picked it up. It was heavier than it appeared. I held it in front of me.

"To make amends for disrupting our session, you will complete it for us."

I swallowed and it got stuck in my dry throat. Rahab stepped back and pointed at Gerlinda.

"You will kill her yourself."

My body's immediate response was to shake my head back and forth. No. No. No.

"Rahab . . ." My father's voice came out even deeper than normal. But Rahab only grinned, knowing he'd chosen the perfect punishment. The fact that it bothered my father only sweetened the deal.

"Either you kill her and live, or you both die." He emitted a singular chuckle. Several Dukes joined him. Together their laughter rose until my scalp tingled.

"You will obey me now, daughter of Belial. Raise the gun."

Gerlinda and I looked at each other for the first time since I'd gotten onstage. Her eyes held no hope. She believed I would kill her to save myself.

"Brother Rahab," one of the Dukes called to him, and tossed up another gun, which Rahab caught. He pointed it at my forehead. I held my breath. This was it. I was going to die, and my poor father and friends would have to watch.

There was only one who could save me now. *Please help me.*

"Last chance." Rahab gloated, cocking the gun with a click.

Scraping noises, like chairs pushing back, came from the side of the room where my friends sat. Before anyone had a chance to look, somebody shone a flashlight—no, a *spotlight* in the back of the room. Every head turned at once toward the blinding light.

As confused and curious as I was, my mind wandered back to the noise I'd heard. I tore my eyes from the growing light to find Kopano and Kaidan standing. A knife gleamed in Kaidan's hand.

Sit down! I willed to them, panicked. They both wavered, and Kopano sat. Kaidan's eyes locked on mine. I pleaded with him as he stood there, obstinate. The light was further brightening the room, distracting anyone who might have noticed our interaction.

Dukes shielded their eyes, even my father, and Rahab's gun arm dropped to his side.

Please sit, I willed to Kaidan once more, begging. And this time he did.

A sudden peace rolled over me, ironing out the creases of anxiety and fear in my soul.

The light was now a gaping, bright hole in the back wall, blinding, and from it walked an angel, then another, and another, until their ranks filled every open space in the room.

These were not the sweet-natured type of angels that guarded humans. These were warrior angels, brimming with justice. They wore armor that shimmered like the hilt. Each had flowing hair of differing lengths and enormous white wings. Everything about these angels was fierce and ethereal, stoic and gallant. I could barely breathe.

The Dukes stumbled, pressing back toward the stage. Gone were their cheers and jeers. The demon spirits above us flattened themselves to the ceiling, hissing like cornered alley cats.

"Wh-wha—" Rahab caught himself stuttering and stood up straighter. "How dare you come here!"

"We go where we are sent," answered the angel in the center.

"Yes, yes, of course you do," Rahab spit. "No minds of your own. What do you want?"

"You will not kill the daughter of Belial." The room went ghostly quiet. My heart soared.

"The Nephilim have never been your concern. They are *ours*!"

"Nothing on earth is yours, dark one."

Rahab turned beet red, droplets of foam forming at the corners of his mouth. "Your kind is not supposed to interfere in our work! We've been granted the right to test humanity and deal with our own ranks."

"It is not her time." The angel regarded me. "She will serve as a test to many souls."

There was a dense pause. And then Rahab smiled.

"Fine. It is not her time now." He waved the gun at me.

"But it is *hers*." Before anyone could stop him, he pointed the gun at Gerlinda's forehead and fired. I screamed at the sickening crack and spray of blood. She fell back, hitting the wall and sliding down, dead. Her spirit wrenched itself from the body and was captured by two Legionnaire spirits who swept her from our sight.

The gun I held clattered to the floor and I crouched down. I was so certain Rahab would go against the angel's orders and try to kill me, too, that I felt for the hilt at my ankle. My hand found the leather cover and fumbled to open it.

The ranks of angels moved toward the stage in unison, filled with righteous anger. None of the Dukes dared move. Rahab stumbled back as several angels surrounded me in a circle of protection.

A long-haired angel noticed what I was doing and swooped down, shielded from view by his brethren.

"You are not to reveal the Sword of Righteousness this night, child," the angel whispered to me.

Its voice was a balm to my soul, and I uncurled my fingers from the hilt, no longer burdened with the fearful instinct to protect myself. I stood, shaken but strangely at peace.

Every one of the angels stared at Rahab, stricken and offended by the loss of life they'd just witnessed. The leader in the center seemed to fight a battle within, wanting nothing more than to disobey orders so he could take care of Rahab then and there.

"Someday," the angel promised him. He and Rahab glared at each other as the angels moved backward toward the light, one by one disappearing into it. When the last angel entered the light, darkness descended on the room once again.

A palpable tension filled the room in their absence.

"Someday we will take back what is ours," Rahab whispered, seething. He turned on my father. "You will punish her within an inch of her death! Now get your filthy offspring out of our sight. All of you! Go!"

There was pandemonium as I jumped off the stage and ran to grab my coat. Nephilim were scrambling, falling over chairs and one another to grab their things and get out of there. My friends stared at me in disbelief. Their faces showed that they'd been through hell that night just as surely as I had. Even Ginger looked worn. But it was Kaidan's glassy, blank stare that killed me.

During those split seconds I watched him until his sight focused. Seeing me up there had broken something inside him.

Someone grabbed me by the elbow: my father.

"Get out," he growled, shoving me toward the exodus of Nephilim. Ginger grabbed Marna's hand and they ran, with Blake close behind. My father pushed me forward and we crushed into the crowd.

I turned, looking for Kaidan. I had to say good-bye. My dad shook his head. In the madness I made eye contact with Kopano, whose worried eyes tore at me.

My father continued to shove me from behind, up the narrow stairs and down the darkened hall, shoulder-to-shoulder with other Neph. I kept turning, trying to peer around my dad's solid body, frantic for a glimpse of Kai.

And there he was, also attempting to push through the people. I reached my arm back, feeling my dad's hands firm around my waist. Kaidan's warm fingers locked around mine, and our gazes held. In those blue eyes was a shattered look that made my soul ache.

"Enough!" my father scolded gruffly, pulling me and breaking my connection to Kai. I screamed out. We burst into the frozen night, where my father hailed a waiting cab, opening the door and flinging me inside. He gave directions to the cabdriver.

"Straight to the hotel," my dad said to me, throwing cash on my lap. "I'll deal with you later."

He slammed the door shut.

"What's going on at that club?" the cabbie asked as he laid on the gas pedal. "There a fire in there or something?"

I couldn't answer. I spun around in the seat, staring at Kaidan on the edge of the sidewalk, hands on his head, air condensing like smoke from his lips, watching me leave.

CHAPTER THIRTY-ONE

UNDERNEATH

Going back to school after that weekend was surreal. I tried to focus on Jay and Roni, who were both hurting. They weren't talking at the moment, despite Jay's efforts to apologize. The depth of their sadness only gave me more hope for their possible future. It was clear how much they cared for each other.

I kept thinking about how the angel said I would be a test for many souls. Maybe he was bluffing Rahab. Could angels bluff? No matter what he said, there was no way I'd do the work of my father. I would rather die.

Marna had come to me bearing bad news the day after the summit. Kaidan was moving to L.A. right away, and the band would soon follow. I'd been given instructions not to call. He'd left without saying good-bye. Knowing he lived so close had been my security blanket, and now he was gone.

Marna revealed another piece of information about the night of the summit. Kaidan had hidden a knife in the sole of his boot, which would explain the one he held when he'd stood, ready to fight for me. Fortunately nobody had noticed, because the light had been the room's focus.

It was better this way, I told myself. Safer. I repeated it to myself like a mantra.

I checked the mail and took it up to the apartment when I got home from school. Patti wasn't home from work yet.

I almost threw the small postcard away with the rest of the junk mail, but the Arizona postmark caught my attention.

It was hard to say how long I stared at that postcard, overwhelmed, before I grabbed my keys. I ran out of the apartment, in a hurry to drive and get my bearings. It didn't matter where. I just needed to be on the open road.

Halfway to Atlanta I ended up at the top of Lookout Point. Since it was the middle of the day, I was the only one up there. I felt the rush of being somewhere otherwise forbidden, and staring out at the great expanse, I understood why I'd been drawn to that particular place.

I cut the car off and sat there looking at the postcard in my lap. On the front was a picture of the Grand Canyon. Though it was a beautiful scene, I knew the picture could not do it justice. I flipped the postcard over and read the tiny, boxy scratch of male handwriting next to my name and address.

I'm sorry.

That was all it said. But those two words spoke many things to me. Sorrow and regret. Heartache and lost opportunity. And ultimately, sacrifice.

I tried to imagine Kaidan driving a moving van with all his stuff, making a detour and standing at the edge of the enormous abyss. How small he must have felt. Did he realize, as I did now, that it was all so much bigger than us?

I climbed out of the car, clutching the postcard in my hand and bracing myself against the chilly wind of the higher altitude. Walking to the roped edge, I looked out at the vastness of the divide. Our own canyon, though not so grand. The valley before me dipped low, and every inch of plant life was covered in a leafy vine, like a rain forest jungle. Kudzu: the vine that ate the South. I'd always thought it was beautiful, in a wild sort of way, but not today. Today I felt bad for the trees that suffocated underneath.

I pulled out my cell phone, scrolled down, and dialed before I had time to change my mind. I didn't know what I'd say or what I wanted to hear him say. I didn't even care if we said nothing, and simply shared silent airtime. Maybe I could bask in the sound of his voice mail one last time. . . .

"The number you dialed has been disconnected. . . ."

Or not. I hung up, shoving the phone in my pocket and letting my head fall back as the wind picked up.

It was over. Truly over. My eyes fluttered closed and I heard the patter of rain moments before I felt it against my skin. The fresh drops from heaven were soft on my face. In that moment I was embraced by the elements, comforted just as if Patti held me in her arms. In the safety of that feeling, I let the pain tumble out of my heart with cries I'd held in. I grieved with my face in my hands until there was nothing left to cry. I lifted my face to the sky once again, letting the rain wash away the salty tears.

Now I understood what Kai tried to get me to see: There was nothing healthy about desperately wanting something you couldn't have. I would never have a husband and children. He would never have the freedom to let himself be loved. And each time we saw each other was a painful reminder of those facts.

Patti told me that to truly love someone, you must hold them in an open hand. That was how I needed to love Kai. It was necessary to uncurl my fingers and let him go.

As if pleased with my revelation, the rain stopped and another wind blew through. Clouds shifted until a ray of winter sun poured across the valley and onto the peak of Lookout Point, warming my face, encouraging me. I nodded and took a deep breath, managing a small smile. I might have inherited a legacy of sin from my father, but I was also given a heritage of hope from my mother, and that was the one I needed to embrace.

I didn't know if I would ever see Kaidan again, or when, but I knew I would love him all my life. We would always have our memories: the sound of each other's laughter and the feel of each other's lips. I'd always know he'd been willing to die for me. Nobody could take those things away.

Like humans, I had no idea what was in store for me or

how my life might be used in the scheme of things. But I didn't doubt I would, indeed, be used. If life was a game, like everyone said, then I wanted to win. I held up my hands to the heavens.

Deal me in.

DUKE NAMES AND JOB DESCRIPTIONS INDEX

Duke Name: Job Description: Their Children
(Neph who appear in *Sweet Evil*)

Alocer (Al-ō-sehr): *Wrath*: spurning love, opting for destruction; quick to anger; unforgiving: Kopano (Kō-pah-nō)

Astaroth (As-tə-roth): *Adultery*: breaking marriage vows; cheating on one's spouse: Ginger and Marna

Belial (Beh-leel): *Substance abuse*: physical addictions; primarily drugs and alcohol: Anna

Jezebet (Je-zə-bet): *Lies*: being dishonest or deceptive

Kobal (Kō-bal): *Gluttony*: consumption of more than one's body needs or requires: also *Sloth*: avoidance of physical or spiritual work; laziness; apathy: Gerlinda

Mammon (Ma-mun): *Greed*: desire for earthly material gain; avarice; selfish ambition: Flynn

Melchom (Mel-kom): *Envy*: desire for others' traits, status, abilities, or situations; jealousy; coveting: Blake

Pharzuph (Far-zuf): *Lust*: craving for carnal pleasures of the body; sexual desire outside of marriage: Kaidan (Ky-den)

Rahab (Rā-hab): *Pride*: excessive belief in one's own abilities; vanity; sin from which other sins arise

Shax (Shaks): *Theft*: stealing

Sonellion (Sō-nee-lee-un): *Hatred*: promotes prejudices; ill will toward others; hostility

Thamuz (Thā-muz): *Murder*: taking the life of another person

Acknowledgments

I'd like to thank my agent, Neil Salkind; my editor, Alyson Day; and the staff of HarperCollins for taking a chance on this little ole Inkpopper.

Much appreciation goes out to my first reader and gorgeous friend Courtney Fetchko. Thank you for falling in love with Kaidan during those *horrid* early drafts. Your enthusiasm fueled me more than you'll ever know. And to my other three cheerleaders and earth angels, Ann Kulakowski, Janelle Harris, and Joanne Hazlett, thanks for always reminding me who's in control. Oh, and thanks to Janelle's husband, Jimmy, for the drummer jokes.

I must thank a few others who read along the way: Meredith Crowley and three of my Dugout Girls: Holly Andrzejewski,

Hilary Mahalchick, and especially the keen-eyed Carol Moore. LYLAS!

My heart is filled with gratitude for more than five hundred people on Inkpop.com who gave feedback and support to this story when it was *Angel Prophecy*, especially the handful who critiqued the entire rewrite. I wish I could name everyone, but I have to give credit to Kelley Vitollo, Carolee Noury, Bobbi Doyle, Lia Sunny, Evelyn Burdette (Evie J—smile! You're on *Candid Camera*), Morgan Shamy, Leigh Fallon (my big sis in publishing), and her real-life little sis, Jen Conroy, for dialect help. It's amazing the friendships that can be formed via the Internet.

I don't know how anyone can write a book and go through the process of publication without a supportive family. To my precious Autumn and Cayden, *muah, muah*—Mommy owes you lots of snuggles. To my wonderful parents, my siblings (Frank, Dan, Jeff, and Lucy), and my in-laws—you guys rock. Thank you.

Lastly, I'm blessed with a husband who doesn't make me feel like too much of a freak for all of my writing quirks, the burned dinners, and my insane bouts of impatience with the entire process. Nathan, thank you for believing I could achieve this dream even when I didn't believe it myself.